Patricia Scanlan was born in Dublin, where she still lives. She is the bestselling author of *Divided Loyalties; Double Wedding; Two for Joy; Francesca's Party; Finishing Touches; Promises, Promises; Mirror, Mirror; City Girl; City Woman; City Lives; Apartment 3B* and *Foreign Affairs*. She is also the author of *Winter Blessings*, a collection of quotes, blessings, poems and reminiscences. She is the series editor and a contributing author to the *Open Door* series. She also teaches creative writing to second-level students and is involved in Adult Literacy.

Also by Patricia Scanlan

Foreign Affairs
Finishing Touches
Promises, Promises
Apartment 3B
Mirror, Mirror
City Girl
City Woman
City Lives
Francesca's Party
Two for Joy
Double Wedding
Winter Blessings
Divided Loyalties

PATRICIA SCANLAN

FORGIVE AND FORGET

TRANSWORLD IRELAND

TRANSWORLD IRELAND
an imprint of The Random House Group Limited
20 Vauxhall Bridge Road, London SW1V 2SA

www.rbooks.co.uk

First published in 2008 by Transworld Ireland

A CIP catalogue record for this book
is available from the British Library.

ISBNs 9781848270008 (tpb)
9781848270169 (cased)

Addresses for Random House Group Ltd companies outside the UK
can be found at: www.randomhouse.co.uk
The Random House Group Ltd Reg. No. 954009

The Random House Group Limited supports The Forest Stewardship
Council (FSC), the leading international forest-certification organization. All our
titles that are printed on Greenpeace-approved FSC-certified paper carry the FSC logo.
Our paper procurement policy can be found at
www.rbooks.co.uk/environment

Typeset in 11/14pt Palatino by
Falcon Oast Graphic Art Ltd.

Printed and bound in Great Britain by
Clays Ltd, Bungay, Suffolk

2 4 6 8 10 9 7 5 3

Mixed Sources
Product group from well-managed
forests and other controlled sources
www.fsc.org   Cert no. TT-COC-2139
© 1996 Forest Stewardship Council
FSC

In memory of my beloved mother who was, is,
and always will be my role model in how to
live an exemplary life

'In the Kingdom of Hope There Is No Winter'

PROLOGUE

'I'm engaged!'

How often in the last few years had Debbie Adams heard these words and been ashamed of the stabbing envy that had assailed her? As she'd congratulated the lucky brides-to-be, who'd held out their hands for her to admire the sparkler on the third finger of the left hand, she'd tried to be as sincere and congratulatory as possible, all the time wondering, *When will it be me?*

And now, finally, she was the one wearing the ring; she was the one holding out her hand for people to admire her diamond solitaire. She'd seen the flashes of yearning and jealousy in the eyes of the unbetrothed and unattached. Her boss, Judith Baxter, had barely managed a clipped, 'very nice, congratulations,' while her married friends had been genuinely delighted for her.

Debbie sighed as she studied her precious ring, holding it this way and that to let the prisms of sunlight glisten and sparkle on the beautiful diamond. She'd been so looking forward to coming into work this morning to tell her friends and colleagues her great news. And it *had* been satisfying and exciting for a little while before everyone had drifted back to their desks and things had returned to normal.

Somehow or other, she'd thought she'd feel more exhilarated, more secure and content. Debbie chewed the inside of her lip as she logged on to her work computer. She knew *exactly* what was taking the edge off her excitement and happiness. Getting engaged meant getting married, eventually, and that was where the problem lay. One thing Debbie was absolutely certain of . . . she emphatically did not want her father, stepmother or stepsister next or near her on the happiest day of her life. Her father, Barry, would not be best pleased, but tough. She scowled. He could throw a strop as much as he liked. He'd forfeited his right to walk her up the aisle a long time ago.

But what was her mother, Connie, going to have to say about *that*? Knowing her as she did, Debbie knew the eventual trip up the aisle would be far from smooth.

THE ENGAGEMENT

CHAPTER ONE

'God, I feel so hot! I'm baked alive. I must have a temperature,' Connie Adams complained, wiping the perspiration off her upper lip. She delved into the depths of her handbag and pulled out a thermometer.

'Sometimes it's good to be a nurse,' she grimaced as she stuck the cone into her ear, frowning as she heard a steady *ping*. 'Normal. Tsk. I don't understand it.' She stared at the result. 'I wonder have I glandular fever or something?' She prodded the glands on either side of her neck.

'You're a hoot,' snorted her sister-in-law, Karen. 'What age are you?'

'You know as well as I do, that's a sore subject. It's very insensitive of you to bring it up. *Still* late forties!' Connie scowled.

'*Exactly!*' Karen retorted. 'And you call yourself a nurse? You're probably having a hot flush, you idiot.'

Connie's jaw dropped in absolute horror. 'Oh cripes! The friggin' menopause! *That's* all I need.' She looked at the other woman in dismay. 'That's why my boobs feel as if they're going to explode and my brain's turned into mush lately. I never even thought of it. I put it down to the stress of the wedding. Oh, Karen,' she wailed, 'I feel I haven't even hit my prime yet and now I'm going to turn into a dried-up old crone. It's . . . it's just not fair!' She couldn't hide her consternation.

'It's not so bad,' her sister-in-law assured her. 'Maybe you're only peri-menopausal. At least yours had the decency to wait until you were forty-eight. I started mine at forty-five, remember, so I've a good two years of it over me and I'm still here to tell the tale. But now you'll understand what I've been moaning about. It comes to us all, dearie.' She grinned at Connie.

Connie laughed in spite of herself. Karen was irrepressible and she loved her dearly. Her sister-in-law was one of the good things to have come out of her marriage, she mused as she took a sip of her cappuccino and bit into a tuna bap. Technically, Connie supposed she was her ex-sister-in-law but she never thought of her as such. When she and Barry split up twenty years ago after five years of marriage, Karen had resolutely refused to take sides. She had supported both of them in their mutual decision to separate, despite the fierce opposition of both their families. It had been a horrendously difficult time, and Connie's mother had accused both Barry and Connie of being completely selfish and ignoring the needs of their daughter, Debbie.

Connie sighed deeply. Maybe they *had* been selfish. Debbie had been devastated, despite her parents' constant assurances that their break-up was nothing to do with her and that they both adored her.

'That sigh came from the toes,' Karen observed, arching an eyebrow at her.

Connie made a face. 'I was just remembering how angry my mother was when Barry and I separated. She told us we were thoroughly selfish and ignoring Debbie's needs. I still feel guilty sometimes, even after all this time,' she confessed.

'Well, don't be, you both did what you had to do. You both did what you felt was right, and I think you made the right decision, for what it's worth. Neither of you was happy, so what was the point in struggling for another ten or more years?'

'I guess if either of us had been having an affair Ma would have felt there was some excuse . . . some valid reason. But just to split because we were unhappy and not in love with each other any more was not sufficient,' said Connie wryly, licking some mayonnaise off her fingers.

'Is it because of the wedding all this is bothering you again?' Karen queried astutely.

'I suppose.' Connie sighed again. 'When your only child is getting married to a bloke you're not mad keen about, it does bring up stuff. I just wish she'd never met Bryan. I can't take to him. I much preferred Cezar, he was a lovely fella. Pity he had to go back to Poland when his father got sick. Debbie should have given it a chance instead of rushing things with Bryan.'

'It's a tough one, all right. I don't know what I'd do if Jenna brought home a chap I didn't like and announced that she was engaged to him.' Karen reached across the table and squeezed her friend's hand. 'Do you want me to say anything? Do the old godmother speech? It might not sound so bad coming from me. She wouldn't feel as resentful hearing a few home truths from me as opposed to you?'

'What are you going to say . . . that he's a spoilt, lazy lump who needs a good hair cut and a kick up the ass to get out there and do a bit more than he does, instead of spending all his time looking at himself in the mirror?' Connie asked morosely.

'Something like that,' laughed Karen.

'I mean, Karen, he's thirty; up until he and Debbie bought the house he shared an apartment with his sister and her friend and they spoilt him rotten. His mother did his washing for him. He drives one of those flashy soft-tops so that the wind can muss his hair, just so, on his way to the races. Did you ever see him? He's always running his fingers through it. He really thinks he's God's gift. He thinks he knows everything. What does she see in him?' she burst out.

'Well, he's very . . . very . . . personable and good-humoured, not to talk about good-looking, I suppose.' Karen shrugged. 'I'd give anything for his eyelashes.'

'Good-looking! Huh! In a pretty-boy way maybe, with his perfectly styled hair and manicured nails. He wears moisturizer. I've seen it in their bathroom! He's got those eyebrows that are too close, I never trust a man with eyebrows like his. I dated a guy who did the dirt on me. He had eyebrows like Bryan's.' Connie knew she was being irrational but she was on a roll.

'Never trust a man with funny eyebrows,' teased Karen, laughing.

'You may laugh, but it's true and give me a *real* man any day. Bryan's a little consequence who does damn all while his women dance attendance on him.' Connie drained her cappuccino and brushed the crumbs of her bap on to the ground for the little sparrows that twittered around on the footpath. A Dart rumbled into Dun Laoghaire station and she frowned.

'I guess I'd better be making a move,' she said reluctantly. 'Barry's coming over to talk about the wedding later. We've to do the table placings with Debbie. *That* will be jolly,' she added dryly, wishing she could stay drinking cappuccinos with Karen and watch the gulls wheel and circle between the masts of the yachts in the marina. A balmy breeze blew in off the glittering, azure sea, cooling her down and blowing her coppery hair away from her face. 'She really doesn't want Aimee and Melissa there, but Barry wants his wife and child at the wedding and I can't say no, especially when he's paying so much towards it. She said she's not having a top table as such because it's a barbecue, so I might have to put them with you and John. Is that OK?' She looked doubtfully at her sister-in-law.

'Yeah, I can cope with Aimee for an hour or two,' Karen said cheerfully.

'Thanks, Karen, I appreciate it. She won't really know anyone there, and I don't want to put her at Mam's table—'

'Absolutely not,' grinned Karen. 'Arctic conditions would prevail and you'd never hear the end of it.'

'Oh God!' Connie buried her face in her hands. 'I wish I could run away.'

'I don't envy you,' Karen. said with feeling. 'But, look, it might not be as bad as you think. Try and look on the bright side.'

'What bright side?' Connie snorted. 'Right now it seems I'm a peri-menopausal woman who can't stand her future son-in-law and who has to do place settings with her ex-husband when their daughter is vehemently opposed to him, his second wife and their daughter coming to the wedding. What bright side *exactly* would you be talking about?'

'Well, just think, in a few years' time, with luck, you'll be a grandmother. Granny Adams – now isn't that something to look forward to?' Karen's brown eyes twinkled and she burst out laughing.

'You're a wagon but I love you.' Connie guffawed. Laughing heartily, the pair gathered their belongings and crossed over to the Dart station to take the train to Greystones, where they both lived.

'Tell you what, when the wedding and the whole palaver is all over, why don't we head off to our apartment in Spain for a girls' week and just flop completely?' Karen suggested as they sat on a bench waiting for their train.

'That sounds bliss. You're on. A week away from everyone is just what I need.'

'See! That's called looking on the bright side. Here's our train.' Karen jumped up as the sun reflected silver and gold metallic glints on the green Dart in the distance.

Connie smiled as she followed her sister-in-law further along the platform. Whatever happened in the next few weeks, she knew Karen would be there to offer support, stalwart and reliable as always. She was a great friend, and a week away with her would be just the tonic she needed to get over the wedding. Her mobile rang and Debbie's name came up on the screen.

'Mam, hi, I can't make it tonight. Bryan wants us to go to an art exhibition one of his friends is having—'

'Look, Debbie, we made this arrangement ages ago. Your father is coming over to have a chat about the wedding. The least you can do is be there. He *is* paying for half of it, after all.'

'Big deal,' Debbie said sulkily. 'Bryan wants me to come with him. He *is* my fiancé, after all, not the man who deserted me when I was a child and then went off and married someone else and had another child, who gets everything she wants, no matter what the cost.'

'Debbie, that's very unfair. You know as well as I do that's not the way it was, and your father has *always* looked after you financially. Grow up!' Connie said tetchily as someone getting off the train jostled into her.

'Yeah, sure, Mam. I'm not going to argue with you about it. You deal with him and work out your seating stuff and I'll sort it with you tomorrow. And don't forget: one of the reasons we decided to have a barbecue was so there wouldn't *be* hassle about where people sit. We don't want a stuffy, formal wedding. It's you and Dad that want to organize seating, so do it, I don't have to be there. Bye.'

Connie's lips tightened as the phone went dead. Her daughter was being totally unhelpful and seemed to have regressed to teenhood. She was acting more like a fifteen-year-old than a twenty-five-year-old. Barry would be hurt, and she'd have to listen to him moaning about Debbie's insensitive, wounding behaviour. It wasn't just the seating that they needed to organize – they had to arrange readings and lifts. Connie knew that Barry had been going to ask Debbie to reconsider her decision not to let him walk her up the aisle.

It was all just so fraught and she was fed up with it. It was a pain being stuck in the middle and trying to keep the peace between them.

Bryan knew about tonight's arrangements. He hadn't made things easier by asking Debbie to accompany him to the art exhibition. He just expected to get his own way, as usual, but of course Debbie couldn't see that. It annoyed Connie that her daughter could be such a doormat sometimes, allowing Bryan to walk all over her. He really was such a spoilt brat, Connie thought resentfully as she trudged through the carriage and plonked herself down in a seat beside Karen.

'Debbie's just phoned to say she can't make it tonight. She's off to an art exhibition with Adonis.'

Karen gave a snort of laughter. 'Stop it, someday you're going to call him that – or I will – and Debbs would be really hurt.'

'Don't talk about hurt. Her father's not going to be at all impressed at being stood up. It's bad enough that she won't let him give her away; she might at least make an effort to be civil to him about the wedding. He's being very decent about it. He told her if she wanted a wedding planner, he'd pay for one, when friggin' Adonis suggested it. I had to put my foot down there. It was far from bloody wedding planners we were reared. I'd say Aimee would have had a fit if she knew. I think she's whingeing about the cost as it is. She was a bit miffed when Debbie refused her offer of a marquee – she can get one at cost price, because she's in the catering business. I think Barry was just as glad though; if anything went wrong it wouldn't be landed at his door.' Connie frowned.

'Just as well you've only got one child getting married,' Karen declared. 'I said that to Aimee one day and she gave me one of her frosty glares and said Barry would never shirk his responsibilities even if he had a dozen.'

'She can do frosty very well, but so can I,' Connie said firmly. 'It will be interesting to see what sort of a wedding Melissa will have in years to come. I suppose Aimee will be wearing a designer outfit to our little bash.'

'She wears clothes very well, doesn't she? She's reed-thin.' Karen eyed her own generous curves regretfully.

'And tall – that helps,' Connie mused. 'Anyway, the sooner it's all over the better. Miss Debbie can ring her father herself and tell him she's not coming. I'm not blinkin' Kofi Annan,' she informed her amused sister-in-law as she dialled her daughter's number.

She got voicemail.

'Ring your dad yourself and tell him you're not coming tonight. Do your own dirty work, Debbie,' she ordered crossly, and then sent it in a text for good measure, just so her daughter couldn't say she hadn't got the message.

It would be good enough for the lot of them if she just took off to Karen's apartment in Spain and let them all get on with this bloody wedding without her, she thought as the train slowed into Killiney.

Chapter Two

Debbie Adams frowned as she switched off her mobile and slid it back into her shoulder bag. She didn't want to risk getting a call back, which could start a row. Her mother was annoyed, but tough. It was Connie who'd insisted that her father's second wife and their daughter be invited to her wedding. It was bad enough having Barry there, without the step-family muscling in too. The thought of having to be nice to Madam Aimee and sulky Melissa when she truly did not want them anywhere next or near her was annoying in the extreme. So much for her 'Big Day'.

Sometimes her mother really got on her nerves. Connie was falling over backwards to accommodate her father, even inviting relatives from his side of the family to *her* wedding. It was galling. If only Bryan had more money, they could have paid for the entire wedding themselves, but between getting a mortgage for their new house and paying off the loan for his Beemer soft-top, they were practically bankrupt, she thought glumly as she trudged across the Millennium bridge and hurried into West Coast Coffee & Co. for a panini. She noticed two smartly dressed young women strolling across the street to the Morrison and gazed at them enviously. Her days of lunching with the girls in the Morrison were well and truly over. She had to watch every cent now. It drove Bryan mad, and she tried not to nag him when he flashed his credit card when they were out socializing. He'd probably invite his friends out to dinner tonight and insist on paying. He'd been talking about trying out Gary Rhodes' restaurant on Capel Street. They just didn't have the money for that kind of flashiness at the moment, but he got into a bad humour when she pointed it out.

Don't think about it now. Focus on what you have to do, she instructed herself as she bolted her panini and latte. She switched on her phone again to ring Bryan and saw her message sign flash up. Ha! Mam, she thought guiltily, knowing she'd been a coward to switch the phone off earlier. She read the message and grimaced:

'Ring your father yourself and tell him you're not coming tonight. Do your own dirty work, Debbie.'

Well, her father could wait; she'd send him a text later. She didn't want him getting all huffy on the phone. Since she'd told him she didn't want him to give her away at the altar he'd been really cool with her, but she wasn't a chattel and, anyway, he'd lost that right a long time ago.

'It's just not me, Dad. I don't need anyone to *give* me away. But I'm sure Melissa will be getting married some time, so you won't be done out of your walk up the aisle,' she informed him snootily when he'd protested that he was her father and it was tradition.

'So is marriage,' she'd wanted to say smartly, but her mother had glared at her and she'd kept her mouth shut.

She dialled her fiancé's number but it rang out. He was probably in a crowded wine bar and couldn't hear it.

She'd want to get a move on. The queues in the bank had made her heart sink, but she needed to lodge a cheque from a cashed-in insurance policy into her current account or there would be a lot of bouncing cheques. Her lunch-time was being whittled away, and lateness was frowned upon in the busy wages and salaries section where she worked. Old Beady-Eyes Baxter was a walking wagon to work for. She was a crabby old spinster who didn't approve of pregnant women getting time off to go for check-ups or married women doing job-sharing. If girls wanted to get pregnant and have babies, that was their look-out; it shouldn't interfere with their work, Judith Baxter often proclaimed. Just being pregnant was not an excuse to be treated differently. Working mothers were the bane of Judith's life. Looking for days off because they had to bring children for injections and health-clinic appointments. Rushing out of work because crèches called to say the darlings were sick. 'Teething problems are not Johnson & Johnson's problems!'

Debbie could just see her supervisor mouthing off in the canteen, oblivious to the fact that she was causing severe stress to at least half a dozen women under her thumb. Or maybe she wasn't so oblivious. Maybe she knew *exactly* what she was doing and enjoyed it. Judith was a bully and a manipulator. She liked being in control. She liked making her underlings' lives difficult, especially the married ones who had children. Well, that wouldn't be her for a few years yet, Debbie vowed, narrowly escaping being knocked down by a cyclist who broke the lights as she went to cross the quays to Merchant's Arch.

She could always leave her job in the big insurance company that she worked for and get another position elsewhere, she mused as she zig-zagged her way across the cobblestones of Temple Bar, ducking and weaving through the lunch-time crowds. But there was no guarantee that she wouldn't end up with another Judith. Besides, the salary was excellent at Johnson & Johnson, and the perks were good. Apart from Judith, Debbie liked and got on well with her colleagues. Moving job was the last thing she needed with her wedding coming up.

She put a spurt on: she only had five minutes left – no time to slip into Marks for some of the hoisin duck wraps that Bryan adored. She'd get them after work, she decided as she raced up the steps of the office just off Dawson Street. She watched with dismay as the door of the lift closed and it began its ascent to the upper floors. The other lift was also in use so she ran up the stairs, panting as she reached the second floor where the big open-plan office she worked in was located. She kept her head down, hurried past Judith's glass-fronted office, which always had the blinds open so the supervisor could view her minions, and flung her bag on the floor before sinking into her chair without taking off her jacket. She was two minutes late and had the beginnings of a thumping headache. Her mobile rang and she saw that it was Bryan. She couldn't take the call. Judith's gimlet gaze was upon her, and personal calls and the use of mobiles were frowned upon.

Sighing, Debbie set her phone to silent. If she got a chance she'd send him a quick text later. She shrugged out of her jacket, slid it on to the back of her chair and bent her head to her keyboard. She could feel Judith staring at her. If you got into Batty Baxter's bad books she could make your life a misery, and that was the last thing she needed.

Oh yes, you may avoid my eye, but you're two minutes late, Miss Adams. Judith Baxter tapped her desk with her pen as she stared at the young woman at the corner desk. Who did she think she was, swanning in from her lunch, late? Just because she was getting married and had chores to do was no reason to neglect her job. These young ones were all the same, no sense of responsibility. Madam was no teenager; she was in her mid-twenties, old enough to know better. But what did she care about her job anyway? Hadn't she far more interesting and exciting things in her life than sitting behind her computer working out wages, salaries, pensions, annual leave and sick leave? Did Debbie Adams even realize how lucky she was to have a sexy boyfriend, her own house, holidays abroad, sex on demand – everything Judith longed for but, realistically, now, had little chance of ever having. Young women these days took so much for granted.

Judith's sigh came from the core of her. Debbie Adams had the lifestyle Judith had hoped she'd have when she started working. She'd had a happy, carefree time for the first five years of her working life. She'd been a 'normal' young woman, she thought bitterly, turning to look out at the rooftops of the city below her, shimmering in the hazy heat of a late May afternoon.

She'd shared a flat with her best friend. She'd had several boyfriends, and then her father had had a stroke. Although she had a brother and a sister, both were married, and it was to

Judith that the whole family had looked, to help her mother take care of him.

'I've got two young children to take care of' was her sister's excuse. Her brother didn't even offer an excuse; he lived in Maynooth, and that was too far out of the city to be of any real use, even if he wanted to be helpful. If she had been married, they would have had to work out something between them, but because she wasn't she'd been well penalized for her single status.

Judith had strongly resisted moving back home, knowing that if she did she'd never have a life of her own again, but her mother had whinged and moaned so much and made her poor father feel such a nuisance that in the end she'd had no choice. Her father had died ten years later, but by then her mother had given in to 'nerves', unable to leave the house except to go to Mass. Lily Baxter had caused such havoc when Judith had told her she was moving out again that she'd had little choice but to stay put. Her mother had taken to her bed for months.

She had been twenty-five, the same age as Debbie Adams, when her life had ended and she'd returned home to live under her parents' roof, to help nurse her father, Judith thought bitterly as she turned to look at the attractive young woman with the luxuriant copper hair and slender figure and the afternoon sun glinting on the diamond solitaire on her left hand.

Judith knew the girls looked upon her as a sour old hasbeen who'd never managed to nab a man. She knew they sniggered at her behind her back when she got dressed up for the company dos. All they could see was the façade; they didn't know the circumstances of her life or that, inside, she was crucified by sadness, loneliness and resentment.

Oh, they thought they knew her, they thought that she was a hard-hearted bitch, and maybe she was now, but she hadn't always been like that. She'd been like them once, carefree and happy, looking to the future with optimism. She remembered once, in a previous job, a celebration lunch for one of the manageresses to celebrate twenty-five years in the job. Judith had been twenty-two at the time and had thought smugly that

that would never be her, she'd be married with children and finished with nine-to-five office hours. She'd be her own boss, coming and going as she pleased with no autocratic supervisors telling her what to do.

That was twenty-seven years ago and here she was, still with a manager and working office hours and not a husband, child or house to call her own. Fifty was looming in a few months and Judith was dreading it. Whatever about being a 'career woman' in her late forties – everyone knew that once you hit fifty you were a no-hoper heading for your pension, she thought forlornly as her phone rang. Her heart sank as she heard her mother's voice on the other end of the line.

'I'll be wanting you to bring Annie up to visit me this evening. I've arranged for you to pick her up at half seven,' Lily Baxter instructed.

'Mother, how often have I told you not to be making arrangements for me without asking me first,' Judith hissed furiously. Lily was forever getting her to collect this relative or that friend without knowing if Judith had made plans to go out herself. Annie, Judith's aunt, lived in Lucan, which would mean crossing the M50 in the rush hour and then having to traipse back with her later that night.

'I'm going out myself tonight. You'll have to tell Annie to get a taxi or get some of her lot to give her a lift,' Judith snapped and hung up. Now she'd have to go somewhere after work and hang around until eleven or else she'd have to drive her aunt home.

She noticed Debbie Adams chatting to one of the accountants. Judith's lips pursed. She checked her computer. The annual-leave and sick-leave record hadn't been sent for her to sign off. She stood up, straightened her pencil-straight skirt and marched out of her office. 'Have you the AL and SL record ready for me to check? I don't have it on my email,' she said curtly, interrupting the pair's chitchat.

'I'm just forwarding it on to you now,' Debbie responded coolly.

'Really!' Judith arched an eyebrow and turned on her heel to walk away.

'What a bitch,' she heard the young woman mutter to the accountant as she clattered the keys on her keyboard.

Judith smiled thinly. *You haven't seen the half of it. I'm just starting on you, you smug little madam.* She scowled as she swept back into her office to check whether the email had arrived.

CHAPTER THREE

Aimee Davenport cursed quietly under her breath as she scanned the monitors and saw that her flight was delayed. She'd assured Barry that she'd be home early to collect Melissa from her friend's so that he could go and meet with his ex-wife to talk about the forthcoming nuptials.

How she hated Heathrow, she thought glumly as she saw the queue at the check-in desk. Bad enough having to fly to London regularly for meetings without having to waste precious time in queues. She scrolled down her phone and dialled Barry's number.

'Hi, how's it going?' She heard her husband's voice down the line, crackling because of interference.

'Not great,' she sighed. 'Flight's delayed by an hour.'

'Aaww, *Aimee*,' he groaned.

'I'm sorry. It's not my fault. Just pick up Melissa from Sarah's, I'll be home as quick as I can,' she retorted tetchily.

'Look, I can't get away before five. I'm going to be stuck right in the rush hour if I've to pick up Melissa, drop her home, wait for you to arrive and then drive all the way out to Greystones. It will be bloody midnight before I get there,' he grumbled.

'Get the Dart and ask Connie to meet you and bring Melissa with you,' Aimee suggested briskly.

'Debbie's going to love that!' Barry retorted.

'Oh, for God's sake, Barry, let her get over herself. She'd want to grow up. You're paying a big whack for that wedding, don't forget that.'

'How could I? You remind me at every opportunity,' her husband barked. 'Leave it with me . . . I'll deal with it, as usual. Bye.'

Aimee heard the dial tone and threw her eyes up to heaven. Just what she needed . . . Barry in a snit. It wasn't her fault the damn plane was delayed. Did he think she liked being stuck in a stale, stuffy, noisy airport with hundreds of people milling around, when her feet were killing her, her head was throbbing, her shoulder was aching from lugging her laptop and she had a report to write and email off before the morning?

Aimee shuffled forward in the queue. Everyone thought she had an exciting career, jetting off to trade fairs and choosing new ranges of marquees and furniture and chinaware and crystal for the exclusive catering company she worked for. They didn't think about the drudgery of travelling to these places that not even flying business class could alleviate. They didn't have to listen to snooty clients moaning and looking for discounts. She'd discovered, since she'd been promoted to Corporate and Private Sales Director of the Irish division of *Chez Moi*, a top-of-the-range catering company, that the more wealth people had, the more parsimonious they were. Some of them were downright stingy. She frowned as her mobile rang and she saw her daughter's name flash up on the caller ID.

'Mum, I don't want to go to Greystones with Dad. You said you'd be home. It's not fair. Why can you never do what you say you'll do?' Melissa raged.

'Honey, I'm sorry, my flight's delayed, it's not my fault—'

'Yes it is. You're just mean. All you care about is your job,' Melissa accused.

'Darling, that's not true.'

'Yes it is. I'm a latchkey kid 'cos you and Dad are too busy to do things with me like Sarah's mum does with her,' Melissa sulked.

Aimee smiled at the familiar emotional blackmail. 'Stop being a drama queen. I've bought you something nice.'

'See if I care. Can't I stay at home on my own . . . pleezze, Mum? Connie doesn't even have satellite TV. It's so *boring* down there.'

'Not at night, darling. Look, I have to go, it's my turn in the queue—'

'Yeah, well, I'm the daughter that has to make an appointment to see her mother – how awful is that?' The phone went dead.

Were all teenagers like this or was it just Melissa? Aimee wondered wearily as she plonked her case on to the luggage belt and handed her passport and ticket reference to the bored-looking young man behind the check-in desk. He yawned rudely. He could do with lessons in customer care, Aimee thought crabbily as she assured him that, yes, indeed she had packed her bag herself and that, no, it had not been out of her sight at any time.

'Flight's delayed an hour and thirty minutes,' he informed her uninterestedly.

'I thought it was just an hour?' she snapped.

'Hour and a half, you haven't been assigned a gate yet – just keep an eye on the monitors,' he informed her, yawning again.

She wanted to rant. She wanted to rave; she wanted to shriek at him as Melissa had just shrieked at her. How deeply satisfying it would be to roar at him to smarten himself up and do his job properly and what sort of a crappy airline was he working for that couldn't even have their flights on time? Aimee resisted the urge with difficulty.

'Thanks,' she said curtly, taking her boarding card, but he wasn't even looking at her; he had turned to talk to his colleague beside him.

'Little ignoramus,' she muttered as she walked towards the long queues that awaited her at Security, wishing that she'd worn a pair of more serviceable shoes, knowing the long trek she had through those drab, grey, hideous tube-like corridors to her as-yet-to-be-assigned boarding gate. She supposed she could make a start on her report in the business-class lounge. Aimee sighed deeply. It had been a very long day; all she wanted to do was to get home and fall into her bed. Maybe it was a blessing in disguise that she was delayed. Tonight she just didn't have the energy for the girls' night she'd planned to have with Melissa or, she was ashamed to admit, to pacify her daughter.

Melissa Adams dawdled towards the changing room feeling utterly browned off. Their basketball team had just lost a home match, she'd fumbled a shot and missed a chance to score an equalizer and then the final whistle had blown and she'd wanted to crawl away and hide. And then, with perfect timing, her father had phoned to say that he was collecting her from Sarah's and that she was going to have to go out to Greystones with him. It wasn't her fault her half-sister was getting married. Why should she have to suffer? Sometimes she considered calling herself Melissa Davenport and using her mother's name just so she wouldn't feel she was related to Debbie. After all, her mother never used the name Adams. She felt Aimee Adams didn't sound as posh as Aimee Davenport. Her dad would be hurt though, and she wouldn't like to do that to him. Her dad was good to her, she thought forlornly as she trudged along.

Worst of all, though, she'd been really looking forward to a girls' night with her mum. They hadn't had one in ages. It was always the same in the summer. There were weddings and parties practically every day, it seemed, and her mother was very busy. When she did get home, she worked on her computer and then fell asleep in front of the TV.

Aimee had assured her that they were going to have a girls' night – they were going to have something to eat in Purple Ocean and then go to the pictures. She'd been *so* looking forward to it. She'd been telling Sarah about it. Sarah thought Aimee was cool. Sarah's mum wasn't really into fashion like Aimee was and Sarah was not allowed to have her computer and a TV in her bedroom like Melissa had. She had to share a bedroom with her younger sister, and that was gross. She had no privacy at all. Her younger sister was always stealing her clothes and make-up and they were constantly fighting.

At least she didn't have to put up with that, Melissa

comforted herself as she headed into the noisy changing room where her team-mates were changing into civvies.

'Hard luck.' Gemma Reilly gave her a friendly pat on the back as she rooted in her sports bag for her deodorant.

'Thanks, Gemma,' Melissa said gratefully, wishing she had a tall, slim figure like the other girl, who was unabashedly standing in her bra and pants, quite unaware of the envy she was stirring in several of her chunkier classmates. Melissa wriggled out of her shorts and hauled on her jeans as quickly as she could, anxious to hide her thunder thighs.

'Pity we dropped down to fifth in the league,' she heard Terry Corcoran say loudly to no one in particular. Terry Corcoran was a snobby bitch and Melissa detested her. She bit her lip and turned away to pull her shirt over her head, wishing she was invisible. Her boobs looked so big compared to Gemma's. Secondary school was much more difficult than primary, she thought dejectedly as an excruciating pain ripped through her tummy.

Perfect, she thought bitterly. Periods. Just what she needed.

She dragged on the tight-fitting black T-shirt that read 'Cool for Cats' which her mother had bought her in Paris.

'Ready?' Sarah came up to her.

'Yep, just got to go to the loo. Got my P's I think.'

'Tsk,' Sarah said sympathetically. 'Hope it doesn't ruin your night with your mom.'

'It won't. It's all off, she's delayed in London and I have to go out to my wicked stepmother.'

'Oh! Poor you. We're going to visit my gran in hospital tonight, otherwise you could have stayed with me.'

'Thanks, Sarah, I know. Just my tough luck. I could stay on my own in the house no probs, but they won't allow me.'

'Bums!'

'Yeah, bums!' echoed Melissa as she made her way through the throng at the door and headed for the loo.

CHAPTER FOUR

Barry Adams drummed his fingers against the steering wheel as the traffic crawled bumper to bumper along the Booterstown Road. The roadworks were a blood-pressure-raising nightmare, and it was starting to drizzle rain. The fine sunny weather of earlier had disappeared and dark clouds massed out to sea. He was on his way to pick up Melissa and his humour was not good. The phone buzzed in the hands-free set and he saw he had a message from Debbie. Perhaps she was running late too. Maybe he should have suggested a rendezvous with her to give her a lift, but she'd been so touchy with him lately he wasn't sure if the offer would have been appreciated.

Barry scowled as a Merc cut in in front of him and broke the red light. 'Idiot,' he snarled, jamming on. Why was there never a cop around when irresponsible bastards like that broke the law? He flicked on Lyric FM and Debussy's 'Nocturne' filled the air. As he waited for the lights to change he scanned the message and his mouth tightened. Debbie wasn't coming to arrange the seating at her own wedding. That was more than a bit rich, he fumed. Madam Debbie's manners left a lot to be desired. She was an ungrateful, churlish brat who ought to know better. He dialled her number and got her voicemail. She'd probably turned off her phone immediately so she wouldn't have to speak to him.

'Debbie, my time is as precious as yours. I *do not* appreciate being stood up at the last minute. And you might have had the decency to ring earlier and speak to me rather than sending a text,' he rebuked curtly and hung up.

Would they ever get on an even keel? Was she going to punish him for the rest of his life? Life really was too short, and he was going to have it out with her one of these days. But not right now, unfortunately. Connie would freak if he caused a row before the wedding. Still, it meant Melissa wouldn't have to come to Greystones tonight, so that should put *her* in a good humour. Would sons have been easier to deal with, he wondered ruefully.

He dialled Connie's number. 'Hi, Barry,' she said cheerfully, and he smiled. One thing about Connie, she was generally good-humoured most of the time. It had been one of the things that had drawn him to her all those years ago.

'Just had a text from Debbie, cancelling. So I suppose we better set up another date, although I'm a bit tied up for the rest of the week.'

'It's leaving things tight, Barry. Look, why don't you come anyway? We can do a rough plan and, if they want to change it, they can,' Connie suggested pragmatically. 'It's not that it's going to be really formal anyway. Barbecues are supposed to be laid-back. It was more to sort out the grandparents and um . . . Aimee and Melissa.'

'Oh . . . Oh. I suppose so.' Barry frowned. He'd insisted on Aimee and Melissa coming to the wedding. Maybe, on reflection, it would have been easier all round if he'd just gone himself.

'Er . . . it's just I've another complication in that regard. Aimee's flight has been delayed and I've to pick up Melissa. Could I bring her with me?' he asked hesitantly.

'Sure. No problem. Will you have eaten?'

'I don't think we'll have time. The traffic is crap. I'm crawling along. We'll grab a sandwich in a garage or something.'

'Don't be ridiculous, Barry, you can't give the poor child a sandwich after a long day at school. I'll stick your names in the pot. Melissa's not a fussy eater, sure she's not?'

'She'd eat yourself,' laughed Barry, feeling more relaxed.

'Look, I can't tell you what time I'll get there, I don't know what the traffic is like on the N11, I haven't heard a traffic update. But if it's anything like here, it's pretty slow.'

'There're plenty of roadworks; I got stuck last Monday just after Loughlinstown. Why don't you get the Dart from Sandycove and give me a buzz and I'll drive down and collect you? It would save you an hour at least.'

'Are you sure? That's putting you out a bit.' Barry felt a tad guilty to have his ex-wife running around after him.

'Don't worry about it. Otherwise it will take you all night and I want to go to bed early, I've an early shift tomorrow,' Connie said briskly.

'Oh . . . OK, I'll buzz you when we're leaving Bray.'

'See you then.'

'Thanks, Connie,' Barry said gratefully and hung up.

He gave a sigh of relief. Getting the Dart and having Connie collect him, not to mention feeding him and Melissa, would make life so much easier. It would take all the hassle out of the evening.

He was so lucky with his ex-wife, he reflected as the lights turned green and he crawled forward another few metres. Connie was a sound woman. He heard such dreadful tales from blokes he knew who were crucified by their ex's demands. Bill Wallis in the golf club had been driven to a heart attack by his ex's selfishness. Sheena Wallis had always been bone idle anyway, Barry remembered. Sheena had given up work the minute she'd got a ring on her finger. She'd had two children and moaned her way through her pregnancies and made Bill feel like a heel. The chap had never had a proper dinner handed up to him when he came home from work; she bought processed meals and pizzas and stuck anything she could in the microwave. If it was sunny she sat out sunbathing all day. She demanded an au pair so she could play golf and 'lunch with the "girls"'. She was always taking off to those spa places for beauty treatments and Bill had endured twenty-five years of hard labour before he met a gorgeous woman who cherished and loved him and had fun with him. When he'd told Sheena he was leaving her there had been ructions. She'd got a hotshot lawyer who'd seen to it that she'd kept the big house in Sandycove they'd lived in and he was paying a whacking big dollop of spousal maintenance, even though the two sons were grown up and living abroad.

Sheena still golfed and sunbathed and went to spas and had no intention of ever doing a day's work. Bill and his second wife were living in a small apartment in Cabinteely, but he told the guys at the club that it was worth all the hassle to be with a woman who really loved him.

Bill wasn't the only one who had to put up with mega hassle from an ex-wife and Barry knew that he'd been really lucky with Connie. When they'd made the decision to split he'd told her that she could have the house and that he'd continue paying the mortgage but she told him that that wasn't fair and she'd take over the mortgage herself, as long as he paid maintenance for Debbie.

'I've never been a sponger and I'm not going to start now,' he remembered her saying firmly. He'd really admired her for that. She'd gone back to agency nursing five mornings a week rather than the part-time hours she'd worked when Debbie was young. Once their daughter had gone into secondary school she'd worked full-time, starting early so that she could be off at four-thirty to be there when Debbie got home from school.

He still sometimes felt guilty about their break-up. When, after months of him withdrawing and distancing himself from her because he felt trapped and unhappy, she'd asked him if he wanted to separate, he'd grasped the chance eagerly. He'd rejected her offer to go to couples counselling, he'd just wanted out. He'd been a selfish bastard really, he acknowledged as he slowed to a halt at the Blackrock Clinic. He'd made no effort to try to save their marriage. They could have struggled through the bad times if he'd been prepared to try and work at it. He'd let it go too easy.

He sighed. If she hadn't got pregnant with Debbie before they got married, things might have been different. He wouldn't have felt *obliged* to propose. They could have travelled, worked abroad, had fun, before settling down.

He remembered the sense of dread and despair that had enveloped him as they'd signed the papers for their first mortgage. He'd felt utterly hemmed in and resentful, but he'd put on a brave face and accepted the congratulations of his friends when he and Connie had thrown their housewarming party.

He *had* tried. And their first years together were happy enough. He'd been very much a hands-on dad and had always mucked in with the housework. When Connie had had a miscarriage when Debbie was three she had been gutted and he'd grieved with her, but a part of him – and he still felt ashamed, when he looked back – had felt relief. Two children would have anchored him very, very firmly.

By the time Debbie was five he felt well and truly in a rut, working nine to five as a copywriter in an advertising company. A couple of bottles of wine on Friday night with friends, sex on Saturday morning, then the fry-up, supermarket shopping or a trip to the DIY, a meal out that night if they could get a baby-sitter. A walk by the sea on Sunday morning and then lunch at either of their parents'. Roast beef, roast lamb or stuffed chicken – it rarely varied. A game of golf Sunday afternoon. Then home to flick through the papers and, before he knew it, it was Monday and the whole boring routine started again. It did his head in and he'd taken it out on Connie and punished her by withdrawing from her. There weren't ugly rows or slamming doors and walk-outs, just coldness and silence.

It had been a relief when she'd suggested a separation, but then she'd always been the brave one. He hadn't had the guts to suggest it first. He'd been a bloody coward, he thought, as he finally took the left turn for Dun Laoghaire, glad that he didn't have to face the mayhem of the N11.

He'd moved out and got a small flat before moving to the States. He'd got a job in Boston in an advertising agency, through a friend who'd moved over there a few years previously. He'd spent two years there, sorting his head out, dating women and sowing the oats he'd never had a chance to sow before he'd married and become a father. On a trip home, he'd hooked up with an old college buddy, Frank, who was the publisher of a string of successful trade magazines. He'd dragged Barry to a launch of a sport and leisure company in a posh marquee in Killiney, and there he'd met Aimee Davenport, who'd overseen the catering end of things. She was tall, raven-haired, supremely confident and utterly driven to succeed. She fascinated him. Her career meant everything to her, and he was challenged.

She was the one who rang up cancelling at the last moment because something had come up at work. She was the one who insisted on driving her car on dates because she liked being in control and hated being driven around by other people. She was the one who couldn't understand how women would want to give up work after having a baby. 'What a waste of a brain,' she'd scoffed when telling him about her boss, who was resigning to stay at home to look after her children after her third pregnancy.

He'd fallen hard. She was so different to most women he met. And marriage was not on her agenda, even though she was in her late twenties.

'Marriage is on every woman's agenda,' he'd assured her when he'd asked her why she was still unwed.

'Well, it's not on mine . . . and never has been. I want to be with someone because I want to, not because I *have* to. And I want them to feel the same. I can look after myself, I can provide for myself. I am *every* man's equal. Marriage changes all that.' He could still remember the sparkle in her green eyes as she eye-balled him.

He had found her attitude very refreshing, especially after his experiences in the US, where most of the women he'd dated seemed frantic for 'exclusivity' and marriage. She'd been equally refreshing about sex.

'You want it, I want it . . . what's the big deal?' she'd said casually, and then proceeded to lead him into her cool, minimalist, mint-green bedroom, where she'd stripped un-selfconsciously and laughed at his reserve. He'd felt happy, free, unfettered, being with her.

Connie had been cool when he'd told her he was seeing a woman at home. Somehow, seeing a woman in Dublin was harder for her to take than knowing he was with someone in Boston. Debbie, as usual, ignored him. Angry and hurt at what she saw as his desertion of her, she wanted nothing to do with him at first. He was always shocked by the changes in her when he came back to Ireland to visit. How tall she got, the smattering of freckles across her nose, the gap in her front teeth just before her Holy Communion that made her look like an endearing little urchin. Each time he came home he had to get to know her all over again, and it was difficult for all of them.

In fairness to Connie, she tried her best to foster good relations between father and daughter but, always, just as he'd begun to make a little headway, it was time to go back Stateside. When Debbie had realized, the last time he'd come home, that he wasn't staying, as she'd fantasized he would, she had, with all the rage and anguish of a devastated child, screamed that she hated him and wished he were dead.

He'd gone back to Boston with his head in a spin. When he phoned Connie, as he did every week, Debbie refused point blank to speak to him, in spite of her mother's entreaties. *That* was painful – much more than he'd expected – and life in Boston began to pall. He missed her breathless 'Hello, Daddy' and all the childish little tales she had for him.

Aimee had kept in touch sporadically and he found himself wanting to be with her and wishing that she wanted to be with him. His father had become ill with heart trouble and he'd flown home several times that year. Debbie refused to see him and Connie had eventually asked him to stop forcing the issue. It was too upsetting for their daughter and very stressful for her. He'd felt completely miserable, frustrated and angry and hadn't tried to see either of them on his last visit.

He'd always linked up with Aimee on his trips home, and his time with her made him briefly forget the other dramas in his life. Frank, the friend who'd introduced them, had bumped into them in the Horseshoe Bar in the Shelbourne one Friday night.

'Just the man I need. That little turd Gavin Clooney has taken a job with a rival publisher and left me in the lurch. I need someone good. I need someone who knows their stuff. I need a new managing editor who can write copy if needs be, and no one can write better copy than you. What do you think, Barry? Do you want to come home and give it a go and sicken that little bastard at the same time?' Frank grinned at him.

Barry laughed. No one in the business had liked Gavin Clooney; he was a self-opinionated, pushy know-all, but he was good at the job.

'I suppose it's something to think about,' he said slowly.

'Come on, it will be fun, just like old times. We'd make a great team,' Frank urged. 'Persuade him, Aimee.'

'My phone bill would be a hell of a lot cheaper.' Aimee slanted him a teasing glance.

'And you could keep an eye on your dad, and spend a lot more time with your little girl,' Frank observed shrewdly, knowing he was pressing all the right buttons.

'Stop! Stop!' Barry held up his hand. 'Overkill!'

'OK.' Frank backed off, laughing. 'Let me email you a proposal, salary, perks, etc. Have a think and let me know by midweek.'

'What do you think about Frank's proposal?' Barry asked Aimee several hours later as they lay spooned together after a lusty session of love-making.

'Entirely up to you,' she murmured drowsily.

'I know that,' he retorted. 'I'm asking you, what do you think?'

'Are you asking about the job or about us?' Aimee turned to face him, her eyes glinting at him.

Barry laughed. 'Direct, aren't you?'

'That's me.' She leaned up on her elbow, her hair tumbling down over her face and shoulders, and smiled at him. 'As I said, my phone bill would be a lot cheaper.'

'And that's it?' he demanded.

'Don't push, Barry. I like what we have. You're a sexy man, you turn me on, we have fun together and it would be nice to see more of you, *but*. And it's a big but ... don't make *me* the reason for deciding to come back to Ireland.'

'Well, that's honest,' he muttered.

'Oh, don't get huffy,' she teased, sliding her hand down his thigh. 'You guys, you're all the same. All needing your egos stroked.'

'You should have been a man,' he growled, kissing her hard.

'I'm glad I'm not,' she laughed, when he lifted his head to look down at her. 'I'm not a girly girl and I never will be. I'm my own woman and don't forget it.'

Barry smiled at the memory. Aimee was still very much her own woman and he knew that she might never have married him, only that Melissa had begged them to get married for years, before they finally tied the knot in a registry office three years ago.

Would he have come back home if Aimee hadn't been on the scene? It was still hard to tell, but he'd taken the job and made a go of it, and become a director and shareholder of the firm to boot. So, careerwise, it had worked out. He and Aimee hadn't moved in together for a year after he returned, until she was 'sure' she wanted to be in a long-term relationship. When she had decided that she should 'do' motherhood, he'd looked on Melissa's birth as a chance to be a proper father, second time around. And this time he really had been hands on. He'd had no choice. Aimee had climbed the career ladder with single-minded determination. She'd been back at work full-time two months after giving birth. Maternity leave had sent her climbing the walls.

Connie and Aimee were chalk and cheese, that was for sure, he reflected as he drove past the yacht club. And, lately, because of the time he'd spent with his ex discussing the forthcoming wedding, he was beginning to appreciate Connie a lot more than he had when he was married to her.

He hoped Melissa wouldn't be surly and rude tonight. It would be good for them to sit down to dinner at a properly set table for a change. TV dinners were not at all satisfying.

He dialled his younger daughter's mobile. 'Hi, love, I'll be with you in five minutes, be at the door,' he instructed as he turned right off the coast road to Sandycove. His stomach rumbled. He wondered what Connie would serve for dinner. She was great at cooking comfort food. He parked on double yellows and hurried into an off licence. A good bottle of wine would be nice. Pity he didn't have time to stop at the florist's. What was the etiquette about bringing flowers to an ex-wife? It wouldn't bother Aimee, but Melissa might be perturbed. She was very protective of her mother when he was with Connie and had once asked him, when she was small, when he and Aimee were having a spat, if he was going to leave them and go back to live with Connie and Debbie. Melissa was such a little worrier, he thought fondly.

He chose a Sancerre and hurried back to the car. It was a bit like going on a date, he thought, half amused at the notion, as he started the ignition and drove off to collect his daughter.

CHAPTER FIVE

'I like it; I love the spherical and cylindrical shapes. I'd say he was inspired by Braque, possibly Fernand Léger and Roger de La Fresnaye and, of course, the ultimate Cubist . . . Picasso.' Debbie hid a yawn as she listened to Andrea Matthews pontificate to a group of Bryan's friends as they stood sipping lukewarm plonk and nibbling on soggy canapés.

How she would have loved to stand up and say, 'I think it's a load of rubbish. A six-year-old could do just as well.' She didn't like abstract art, no matter who painted it. She wondered would Andrea put her money where her mouth was and actually *buy* a painting. Bryan had pointed out one particularly garish geometrical monstrosity and suggested it might be nice over their fireplace and she had hissed, 'No!', aghast. Not only was it a monstrosity, it was an expensive monstrosity. Two thousand euro they did *not* have to spend on questionable 'art'.

'It would be a talking point. No one else would have one and it would be an original,' he urged. 'And it would appreciate in value. It could be an investment.'

'We can't afford it, you know we can't,' she whispered.

'Oh, OK,' he said affably and turned to chat to another friend of his.

She drifted off to the edge of the group and stood at the long narrow window, looking out at the city traffic and fine misty rain which had started to fall. The weather was very changeable these past few days. It had been gorgeous this morning; now it was raining. She hoped against hope that it would be a fine day for the wedding. So much depended on the weather. Her parents were probably pretty miffed with her at the moment, she thought dolefully as she watched a cyclist shake his fist at a driver for cutting him up.

She was feeling a little guilty at not having gone to Greystones to discuss the wedding. It wasn't her mother's fault that the step-family was invited. And it wasn't Connie's fault that Debbie had a thorny relationship with her father either. Her mother had never badmouthed him to her; she'd always tried to keep the peace between them without taking sides.

Debbie chewed her lip. She'd acted childishly and that annoyed her. The only tables that needed seating were those for the grandparents, and some of her relatives and Bryan's family. No more than sixteen people in all, if she remembered rightly. The rest of the guests could free-seat. That was the whole idea about having a barbecue, she thought crossly. Guilt still niggled. It wouldn't have taken more than twenty minutes to sort, and twenty minutes more to go over the plans for the ceremony. But Barry would have started going on about walking her up the aisle, and she just wasn't in the humour for arguing with him. A wedding planner would have sorted all that, she supposed, but they didn't have the kind of money a wedding planner commanded. They'd been at a wedding recently that had cost the guts of fifty thousand. A friend of Bryan's had invited them. The bride and her mother had gone to the Canaries for a week before the wedding to top up their tans so that both would look stunning in their designer frocks. Fake tans were not an option. Ava, the bride, had worn a Vera Wang ivory silk creation that had necessitated three fitting sessions in New York. It was very simple in design and, to Debbie's mind, no different from many of the ones she'd looked at herself. The limo had been as long as a tennis court.

'You wouldn't know it was a designer dress, sure you wouldn't?' one of the girls at work said as they'd viewed the photos a week later.

'Oh, we knew, believe me – we *knew*,' Debbie assured her fervently, remembering Ava's oft-repeated assertion. 'It's Vera Wang, isn't it stunning?' They had covered the cost of the wedding by remortgaging an eggbox of an apartment which they'd be paying off well into middle age, but they'd have the video of the wedding to look at for ever and a day, Debbie thought wryly. She didn't think it was worth being in debt to that extent just for one day in your life.

'What's the matter? You're very cranky.' Bryan appeared at her side with another glass of wine.

'Sorry, it must be pre-wedding nerves. I suppose I should have gone home and met the parents for an hour.'

'Ah, don't worry about them; they'll get over it. That's the reason we're having a barbie, so there'll be no fuss. Stop panicking.' He leaned down and kissed the top of her head and suddenly she felt happy again. He was right. She looked at him, his jet-black hair falling boyishly over his eyes, and his melting cocker-spaniel eyes smiling at her and thought how lucky she was to have met him. Bryan never let things get on top of him; he was so laid-back he was almost horizontal. It was just as well – she got uptight enough for the two of them. He loved clothes and shopping and socializing, and he was the life and soul of every party they went to.

'Come on, let's go and eat and have a laugh with some of the others. They want to go to Yamamori Noodles. That won't break the bank, so you won't have to be worrying about whether we can afford it or not.' He smiled down at her, his brown eyes twinkling. She smiled back at him.

'I love you, Bryan, sorry for being such a nag.' She leaned up and kissed him. That was one great thing about her fiancé: he never held a grudge, and their fights didn't last long.

'Life's too short to worry, I'm always telling you that,' he shrugged, dropping his arm around her shoulders.

'Dad left a pretty cold message on my phone,' she confided.

'He'll get over it,' Bryan said airily. 'Come on, let's go over and chat to Caitriona and Suzy – they've just arrived.'

Typical response, thought Debbie disappointedly. Bryan

hated family stuff. She could never really talk to him about her family issues. His attitude was: ignore the bad things and have fun in life. She wished she could be more like him. He was right: life *was* too short. She was going to have fun with the gang tonight. She'd deal with her parents tomorrow. He was lucky, he was the baby of the family and he was spoilt rotten. He never had to lift a finger. She was finding that out for herself after six months of living with him. He dropped his clothes wherever he took them off. The washing machine was completely alien to him. She'd got him used to filling the dishwasher, but getting him to empty it was proving more difficult. She'd just have to persevere, but it was irritating sometimes, and she was very conscious of not wanting to be a nag.

Debbie swallowed her wine in two mouthfuls and helped herself to another glass.

'That's my girl,' encouraged Bryan. 'Let's party!'

Connie wrapped the aubergine-and-mushroom-stuffed chicken breasts in slices of bacon, drizzled some olive oil over them and slid them into the oven. She'd add the cream ten minutes before she served them. It was a handy dinner; she just hoped Melissa would eat it. She had some new potatoes and a selection of vegetables ready to cook in the steamer.

Miss Hope, her little black cat, curled around her ankles, purring ecstatically. Connie smiled down at her and shook a few treats into her food dish. She didn't have to worry about her cat's appetite, she thought in amusement, hearing the sound of contented munching.

Melissa was such an edgy, sullen young girl. Just like her older sister at the moment, Connie thought as she took out the ironing board and began to press her uniform. She had to travel across town first thing tomorrow. She was doing the weekend on the orthopaedic floor in the Bon Secours in Glasnevin. Only that she liked the hospital so much, she'd have said no. It wasn't handy for the Dart. So she either had the option of driving, or Darting to Connolly and getting a bus. Maybe she'd treat herself to a taxi from town, she decided. She didn't usually work weekends but she needed the extra money for the wedding and for Debbie's wedding present. She was giving her cash because she knew how tight things were, financially, for her daughter.

Until two months ago, Connie had been nursing an elderly lady five mornings a week, and it had suited her. She'd loved having the afternoons off. Rita Clancy had suffered a bad stroke and needed round-the-clock nursing but, fortunately, her family could afford it. She'd been ill for a year and had suddenly deteriorated, developed pneumonia and died. It was a blessing for the family and the poor woman herself, but it meant that Connie was back doing the rounds of the hospitals. Private nursing was a desirable choice at the agency, but there had only been a couple of vacancies, both of them difficult commutes.

Still, she liked orthopaedics, and she liked the Bons, so that was this weekend sorted, but once the wedding was over and she'd made the extra money she needed to cover her expenses, and her holiday to Spain, she was going to cut down on her hours, she promised herself as a tasty aroma wafted from the oven.

She was hungry. It seemed a long time since her lunch with Karen. She hoped that Barry wouldn't be too long. He'd sounded fed up and harassed on the phone. She had the feeling from snippets of conversations she had had with him that life with Aimee wasn't always a bed of roses. Not that it was any of her business now. After all these years she'd got over the hurt, anger and shock of her marriage break-up, and for that she was truly grateful, because there was a time when she'd been eaten up by bitterness and rage and she'd *hated* Barry. It had taken a long time to come to terms with her own contribution to the break-up. Her neediness. Her facility for ignoring her intuition. Her tendency to try to please and placate despite her own feelings of unhappiness and resentment. She'd been a real wimp, but once she'd acknowledged that it wasn't all one-sided and that she'd had a role to play, once she'd taken responsibility for her actions, healing had come.

It had been tough, very tough, she mused, ironing the leg of her navy trousers with more force than was necessary. And she'd certainly never expected to end up on her own. With hindsight, she knew she should never have married Barry while she was pregnant. If things had been left to develop naturally between them, they might have married and stayed married or they might never have married at all. Barry had only proposed because he felt obliged to. That was no foundation for a marriage.

She blew a strand of hair away from her face as she ironed vigorously, feeling a wave of heat envelop her. She remembered how shocked she'd been when the pregnancy test had proved positive. She'd had to sit down on the bed and fight the waves of nausea that engulfed her. Barry was as pale as she was. She'd never been able to take the Pill because of the excruciating headaches she'd got on it. They'd used condoms when she was ovulating but her cycle had been irregular and they'd got caught. She remembered the trapped look in his eye, and she was sure her own expression mirrored his. She felt well and truly trapped herself.

'We'll get married. We can have a small wedding, we'll get a deposit for a house no problem, the two of us are working.' He was pacing the bedroom in his flat.

'Are you sure you want to marry me?' Her voice had quivered when she'd asked the question, knowing that if she said no, he might not push it.

'Of course I do,' he said stoutly. 'I love you.'

'I love you too,' she assured him, relieved beyond measure that he hadn't backed out. Being an unmarried mother was a path she really didn't want to go down.

'You're a nurse! You should have known better,' her mother had said in disgust. Stella Dillon hadn't been at all happy when she heard the news.

Her father, Jim, had been more accepting, and when she'd told him that Barry had proposed, he'd said kindly, 'Connie, don't get married just because you're expecting a baby. Wait for a year or two. You and the baby will always have a home with us.' But Connie, hormones in a heap, and madly in love with her boyfriend, had wanted to get married. So what if they were having a baby; they would have had children at some stage. The main thing was that they loved each other.

When they'd got the keys to their house, on a small estate in Deansgrange, she'd been ecstatic. Every piece in her jigsaw was falling into place, albeit a little earlier in her life than she had planned.

They'd had a modest wedding, and her empire-line cream chiffon dress had hidden her neat bump satisfactorily. They'd honeymooned in Portugal, and as she lay sunbathing on the golden swathe of beach fringed by the frothy white waves of the Atlantic, she'd felt exquisitely happy and she'd persuaded herself that Barry felt the same.

How easy it is to delude oneself, she thought wryly as she hung her uniform on the back of the door and started ironing her sheets.

She had put Barry's moodiness on their return home down to stress of work and, four months later, the stress of a new baby. Over the years she'd made excuses for his gradual distance and withdrawal. He'd been very good with Debbie when she was a baby and, when they'd lost a baby through miscarriage, Connie had felt that he was as upset as she was. But all along, at the back of her mind, she knew something wasn't right, but she'd been afraid to confront her fear.

They'd seemed to have it all. A happy, healthy child. Good jobs. A nice home. Plenty of friends. Why would she rock the boat because she felt their intimacy had disappeared? Sex was perfunctory, but wasn't it like that with most working couples with a young child, she'd comforted herself. It was just that they didn't seem to talk or have fun any more. Gradually, over the years, all they seemed to have to bind them in any sort of marital intimacy was Debbie.

She damped down her feelings of loneliness and frustration as best she could and got on with things, but although she put on a bright façade, Connie was desperately unhappy.

She'd sat at a dinner party with him one evening and watched the interaction of the other couples, all friends of theirs, over the course of the meal. The small gestures and intimacies between them were like a flick-knife to the heart. In that small, intimate tableau in their friends' dining room she saw clearly all that was so lacking in her marriage. The little nudge, the eyes meeting and smiling at each other, the good-natured joshing and teasing. The casual dropping of an arm around the shoulder or the interlacing of fingers. Little wordless gestures that were the underlying bedrock of companionship and affection which was so important in a marriage. The little things that said 'I love you,' 'You're special to me,' 'This is fun and I want you to enjoy yourself and I'm glad I'm with you.'

She'd stroked Barry's hand when he'd made a joke and he hadn't even noticed or, if he had, he'd deliberately paid no attention to her. Cut to the quick, she'd wanted to cry out, 'Don't ignore me. I'm your wife. I'm here and I need to be acknowledged. Stop punishing me.'

That night had been a turning point for Connie. She knew she couldn't go on any more without confronting the problems in their marriage, no matter what the outcome.

'We need to talk,' she'd said bluntly when he came back after walking the babysitter home.

'It's late. Can't it wait until tomorrow?' He had been surprised at her abrupt tone.

'No, Barry, it can't wait. You know as well as I do something's wrong in our marriage. You won't deal with it. I've tried to address it over and over, and you tell me it's nothing or that you're too tired to talk. Well, we can't run away from it for ever.' Once she'd actually started saying what she felt, it had come easy to her. She knew deep down this was the crunch moment for them, and she knew in her heart and soul that, if she gave him an out, he'd take it. Connie was so scared she'd started to shake, but she'd stared Barry straight in the eye and said, 'Do you not want to be married to me?'

'Don't say that,' he blustered.

'Answer the question, Barry, because that's what you're making me feel.'

And then it had all come pouring out. How trapped he felt,

how he hadn't wanted to get married so young. And how he loved her but he wasn't 'in love' with her.

'Is there anyone else?' she'd asked him quietly, stunned at his response.

'No. I wouldn't do that to you,' he'd replied indignantly, and she'd believed him.

'What do you want to do? Do you think counselling would help?' Her mouth was as dry as the Sahara.

'No . . . I'm sorry, Connie, I can't help the way I feel, nothing's going to change it,' he said miserably.

There was no answer to that. He was being honest, and she could see the relief in his face that the truth was out. 'I guess not,' she muttered, realizing that there was no point in prolonging the agony.

'I do love you, I . . . I'm just not in love any more. Can you understand that?' he asked earnestly as he took her hand and caressed it and she thought how ironic it was that such a gesture, one she'd longed for, should signify the end of their marriage.

'I understand.' She swallowed. She wanted to pull her hand away and rake her nails down his face and say, 'Fuck you. I don't want your wishy-washy love. I want you to desire me, find me attractive, I want you to want to be with me, you bastard.' But she'd swallowed her rage down, not wishing to give him the satisfaction of seeing how devastated she truly was.

'Look, I'll sleep on the sofa, and tomorrow I'll go looking for a place.'

He couldn't get out quickly enough, she thought wildly, afraid she was going to start howling.

'What about Debbie?' Her voice sounded disembodied.

'We'll work something out. Don't worry, Connie, I won't ignore my responsibilities towards you and her.'

'Is that right?' she'd said coldly and walked out of the room.

Why on earth were all those horrible memories coming back right now? She bit her lip as she folded a pillowcase. Barry had kept to his word about his financial responsibilities, but he'd run off to America when the chance arose, leaving her with all the practical difficulties of rearing a child on her own. Then he'd come home, just when she was beginning to get on some sort of an emotional even keel, and announced that he was seeing another woman. A year later he'd informed her they were going to live together.

Debbie had never got over that and, when Barry's daughter was born, she'd refused point blank to see her or have anything to do with her. It wasn't poor Melissa's fault, Connie had pointed out to her daughter when Barry had got annoyed at her intransigence.

'I don't care, I don't have to see her and if you make me I'll . . . I'll run away,' Debbie raged. 'I hate them.' She'd just had her first period, her hormones were awry and her resentment of her father and his new family knew no bounds.

'I can't make her want to see them, Barry. I'm doing my best, but you know as well as I do that Debbie knows her own mind. I'm not going to force her and I'd advise you not to either.'

'OK,' he said angrily. 'But they are half-sisters, after all.'

'I know that!' she retorted sharply, and Barry had known by her tone that she wasn't too thrilled at the situation either.

How often had she lain in bed imagining her ex-husband in bed with his glamorous new partner, trying not to feel bitter and twisted and resentful? She missed sex, even though it hadn't been great by the end of their marriage. She missed lying curled up in someone's arms. Would she ever have that again, she'd wondered miserably, trying not to be jealous of Aimee. Men had backed off when she told them she had a child, and she'd finally given up on the idea of dating. It wasn't worth it. She was petrified of making another mistake because of neediness and loneliness. She couldn't put Debbie through trauma because of her failed relationships.

She'd been amazed that Barry hadn't come looking for a divorce before Melissa was born, but when he had, some years later, she was glad to give it to him. She'd always felt she was in some sort of limbo as his separated wife. Once the divorce had come through, she felt relief that she finally had closure. She was a free woman, and she hadn't disgraced herself with bad behaviour. A colleague of hers was divorced also but, even after ten years, the other nurse hated her ex-husband with a vengeance and never lost a chance to stick the knife in. She hadn't moved on at all, and it showed in her drawn, angry visage and tight, agitated body language. She was forever looking for more maintenance and sending him demanding solicitor's letters.

Connie could look herself in the eye and know that she'd kept her dignity and her independence, and she hadn't been eaten up with bitterness.

'Not easy, but you did it,' she murmured as she unplugged the iron and folded up the ironing board. The mobile rang. It was Barry to tell her the train was pulling out of Bray. She poured a carton of cream over the bacon-wrapped chicken breasts, ran a comb through her hair, traced a lipstick over her lips, grabbed her bag and went to collect her ex-husband and his daughter from the train.

CHAPTER SIX

'And then she said, "I don't eat beef, I'm afraid I'd get mad cow disease." She's eighty-five, for God's sake and she *is* a mad cow. And then do you know what she said?'

Judith stifled a yawn as she sat in the Westbury eating a selection of sandwiches and drinking coffee with her 'friend', Orla. She'd phoned her on the off chance that she might like to go for a meal or go to the pictures, but Orla's mother-in-law was staying with her for a week and she'd said that she'd just have time for coffee and sandwiches. Only that Judith had said 'my treat' she probably wouldn't have bothered.

Orla Doyle was in her mid-forties and Judith had worked with her before she joined Johnson & Johnson. She and Orla had kept up the friendship, but sometimes Judith wondered why she bothered. She wasn't a really good friend, like Jillian, her ex-flatmate. Jillian had been there for her through thick and thin, especially when her father had died, but, unfortunately, she'd moved to Sligo when she'd got married to a farmer and most of their contact was through phone and email now. Unlike Jillian, Orla couldn't be described as a friend in the true sense of the word. She wasn't even a fair-weather friend. When things were going well in Orla's life, Judith might not hear from her for weeks. But when she had a drama, as she often had, she'd be on to Judith morning, noon and night, whingeing and moaning. Once Judith heard the words, 'Wait until I tell you what's happened . . .' she knew she was in for an ear-bashing.

Orla suited herself in the friendship. If she felt like going out with Judith for a couple of drinks and a meal, she would, but if she wasn't in the humour or had other plans, she had no compunction about saying, 'It doesn't suit.' She took their friendship completely for granted and made little or no effort, leaving that to Judith.

Sometimes, sizzling with resentment when a phone call or email hadn't been returned or plans had been cancelled, Judith would decide she just wasn't going to bother any more. Orla could go to hell, and the next time she phoned with one of her dramas, Judith would tell her in no uncertain terms to get lost. The fact was, Orla was a user, plain and simple, and tight-fisted to boot. Judith invariably ended up paying for the meal or taxi.

Tonight, though, she hadn't wanted to traipse around town on her own and had hoped that the other woman would be free for the evening. She would use Orla just as Orla used her, she'd decided as she made the phone call. But Orla had informed her that she had to go directly home from work – until Judith had said, 'My treat.'

'Well, maybe for a quick cup of coffee, then,' the other woman agreed, and had then spent the entire evening complaining about her mother-in-law. Judith had tuned out and spent a while studying the distinguished-looking man at the bar. 'I know what's going to happen; she's making plans to come and live with us. She's just sussing it all out,' Orla declared angrily, bringing Judith out of her reverie.

'Hmm, it looks like that. You'd want to nip it in the bud,' she murmured, heartily sick of Orla's moaning.

'I know. I don't want to be stuck with her, the old harpy. She has three daughters of her own—'

'I think we should go and drown our sorrows!' Judith said impulsively, suddenly longing for a drink. 'There's a lovely little cocktail bar off Chatham Street – would you like one?'

'Oh, well, I'd want to be getting on home, I've—'

'My treat,' Judith urged.

'Oh, well, maybe one then.' Orla, true to form, acquiesced.

'Great,' Judith said cheerfully. Maybe she could get Orla tipsy and she'd stay for more than one, and Judith wouldn't have to spend the evening on her own. But even if Orla went home early, Judith could take a taxi home, she could come into town in the morning and collect her car and perhaps do a little shopping. She wouldn't have to drive her aunt out to Lucan, later, because she'd been drinking. A perfectly legitimate excuse. Win, win, she thought with satisfaction, looking forward, now, to a delicious cocktail. Even an evening spent with Moany Orla was better than being stuck at home watching *EastEnders* with her mother.

'Something smells good,' Barry approved as he followed Connie into the kitchen and handed her the bag with the bottle of wine.

'Oh, thanks. There was no need,' she said, placing it on the counter and slipping on a pair of oven gloves.

'It's a Sancerre,' he explained, anxious that she wouldn't think it was a cheap bottle of plonk.

'Oh nice one, stick it in the fridge to chill.'

'Already chilled – would you like me to open it?'

'Sure. There's a corkscrew in that drawer,' she informed him as she slid the roasting dish out of the oven. A burst of herb- and lemon-scented steam sent a tantalizing aroma wafting under their noses.

'I hope you like this, Melissa. Sit down there beside your dad and help yourself to potatoes and veg,' Connie instructed kindly, and Barry felt a sudden surge of affection for his ex. She had a very kind heart and had always been good to Melissa, no matter how ungracious his daughter was.

Gradually, over the course of the meal, Melissa became less surly and tucked in with gusto, accepting the offer of seconds with relish.

Connie had chatted about this and that, and his tension eased as he sipped a glass of the full-flavoured wine and ate the tasty meal set in front of him. For a fleeting moment he thought how nice it would be to be able to have another couple of glasses, spend a while talking to Connie and then, instead of having to travel back to the city, go to sleep in that cosy attic room of hers and not have to get up in the morning.

Melissa stared out of the Dart, watching the fields and houses flash by. She liked looking into the windows and seeing the various little scenes being played out along the suburban railway line. It wasn't quite dark and she could still see the houses rushing by. Various gardens were well maintained, others higgledy-piggledy and full of junk.

Some houses had lovely lamp-lit rooms, others a solitary light, stark and cold. The backs of houses always looked so much shabbier than the fronts; it was all about façades, she supposed. And she knew all about façades. Every day she went to school she had to put on a façade, pretending that she was cool and confident, on top of things, when inside she often felt as wobbly as jelly, scared that her classmates would discover she wasn't confident and brash like them.

Melissa yawned. She was very tired. At least she had a good lot of her homework done. She'd curled up on Connie's squishy sofa with her books and done her maths, English and geography, the three subjects she had first thing Monday morning. It meant that she was free for the weekend, because she didn't have to have a history assignment done until the Tuesday.

Her mother was very strict with her about doing her homework. She wanted her to get high grades, A1's in all her subjects, if possible. Aimee had told her that she hadn't been good at maths and science subjects at school but it hadn't held her back. Aimee felt girls should reach their full potential and only by studying was that achieved. Her dad was much more laid-back and, sometimes, when her mother was on overnighters abroad, he'd do her maths for her so that she got her homework finished faster, then they'd go to McDonald's in Blackrock and have Big Macs and ice-cream, her favourite.

She'd been so cross at having to go to Greystones, but it hadn't been the worst night of her life, she had to admit. Connie had been quite kind to her and given her second helpings of that yummy dinner, and then told her to watch whatever she liked on the TV while she and her dad discussed the wedding. Connie's little black cat had come in and sat on her knee, purring like mad as Melissa stroked her. She had gorgeous green eyes and a cold velvety nose. She was adorable. Melissa would give anything for a pet, and her dad would let her have one, but her mum said no. Apartments were no place for pets and, besides, animals were unhygienic, according to Aimee.

Melissa had been most relieved that Debbie wasn't there. Her half-sister could be very moody. Sometimes she'd talk to her and sometimes she wouldn't bother. It was just as well they didn't meet very often, because Melissa never knew what to say to her. She hadn't wanted to go to the wedding but, tonight, Connie had told her that she could bring a friend. Melissa was *so* relieved. She'd been dreading going, knowing that there wouldn't be anyone of her own age there. Now Sarah could come and they could have a laugh, and there might even be a few fine things there. It was a pity it was taking place during the school holidays, or they could have gone into class the following Monday and boasted about the hunks they'd danced with. They'd just have to wait until September, but they'd take loads of photos as proof.

She felt a frisson of excitement. Bryan must have loads of friends. The reception was going to be a barbecue. Maybe she might even get off with someone. A lot of the girls in her class were going with blokes, and she always felt left out of things when they started talking about snogging and drinking shots until they were out of it. It scared her. She didn't want to get out of her head on drink and not remember what she'd let a boy do to her. She didn't want boys she hardly knew fingering her and sticking their tongues down her neck and making her put her hand on their thing. She'd had a horrible experience the previous Christmas. They'd gone to visit family friends on New Year's morning and while the adults were drinking champagne and nibbling on a selection of canapés, she had agreed to have a game of snooker with Thomas, their fourteen-year-old son she'd known for yonks.

'You want some vodka and cranberry?' he'd asked. 'I've been

skulling it all morning.' He looked a bit unfocused, Melissa realized, as she took the glass he offered her. She spluttered at the strength of the drink but gamely took another sip as he set up the snooker balls. The first game had gone OK, and he'd beaten her even though his play was a bit erratic, but when he'd won the second time he'd grabbed her, muttered, 'Winner gets a kiss,' and stuck his tongue down her throat, thrust his hand under her dress and managed to get inside her knickers, fingering her roughly until she managed to push him away and make her escape.

None of the adults had noticed her red-cheeked distress, being far too busy downing copious amounts of alcohol themselves, and she'd sat quietly pretending to read a magazine, wishing they could go home as her hands shook from the shock and her heart hammered against her ribcage.

Melissa grimaced at the memory. Growing up was *so* scary sometimes. Amanda O'Connell and her gang at school seemed to think scoring and fingering were experiences to boast about. She couldn't for the life of her understand why. She thought the whole thing was too gross for words.

She and Sarah could pretend they'd done all those things at the wedding barbecue and then the slappers at school might give them a bit of peace. The wedding was going to change her life, she decided, as the train clattered along the tracks back towards Dublin. Her father gave a snore beside her. She'd better stay awake, in case they missed their station. He wouldn't be too happy to wake up in Howth!

Melissa stared out the window, seeing nothing and imagining Johnny Depp asking her to dance on a moonlit beach before lowering his head to hers until their lips met in a long, lingering and very romantic kiss.

Connie popped a mug of hot chocolate into the microwave and set the timer. Miss Hope curled around her ankles, purring like a train having just enjoyed a supper of chicken left-overs. Connie bent down and lifted her up, burying her cheek in her silky black fur. 'I think things went well,' she said. 'And if

Debbie doesn't like what we've decided, she can take one big running jump.' Miss Hope purred even louder and Connie laughed as she put her down and took her hot drink out of the microwave. Her fingers hovered over the carton of mini Jaffa cakes. She was trying to lose weight for the wedding, but the day had been so stressful she felt she was entitled to a treat. She'd just have one. She switched off the kitchen light and followed Miss Hope, who was scampering up the stairs to her dormer bedroom. A sudden squall of rain had turned into a steady downpour and it battered rhythmically against the Velux windows.

Connie loved listening to the rain against the windows. It made the room seem so cosy and snug. She loved this room, she reflected, as she slipped out of her clothes and pulled a long T-shirt over her head. The bedroom was decorated in pine and the inviting double bed had a cream and pink patchwork quilt and a big bolster pillow that reminded her of her grandmother's house, where she'd spent many happy holidays as a child. Rose-pink shades on cream lamps cast a warm glow around the bedroom, the light reflected in the big oval mirror of the pine dressing table. Connie yawned as she dived into bed and switched out the lights.

The evening had gone much better than she'd anticipated. Feeding Barry had been a good idea – he'd wolfed his dinner, drunk a glass of wine and become so relaxed that the expected rant about Debbie had not happened. Perhaps he decided against it because Melissa was with him, Connie reflected as she threw the bedclothes off her, beginning to feel a prickly heat. The girl had devoured her dinner as well and made good inroads into the proffered seconds.

'These are lovely,' she'd enthused, spearing a chunk of floury new potatoes.

'I get them from the farmer down the road; they're organic and dug fresh today,' Connie had informed her.

'Wow, cool! Real potatoes. We buy ours ready-mashed from Marks or the Butler's Pantry,' she divulged artlessly, and Connie hid a smile.

She hadn't seen Melissa in a while, and had been a little shocked at the amount of weight the teenager had put on. She could see that a lot of it was puppy fat, but her arms and thighs were chunky and her skin was pasty and full of spots. Debbie had suffered from the usual teenage acne, but she'd played a lot of sport and the puppy fat had melted off her after her first term at secondary. Hopefully the same would happen to her half-sister. Poor Melissa had looked pale and tired and she was ravenous; she'd fallen asleep after doing her homework with the cat curled up against her. Secondary school was hard going. Connie remembered how knackered Debbie used to be. She felt sorry for Melissa, now, having to endure a Dart and car journey home before she would get to bed.

It was while they were arranging the seating that Connie had realized that Melissa would have no one of her own age at the wedding. 'Let her bring a friend, or she's going to be bored out of her tree,' she suggested to Barry, who'd agreed with alacrity.

'It's a pity she couldn't be a bridesmaid,' he sighed.

'Don't even go there, Barry,' she retorted, determined not to let him get on to one of his favourite bandwagons about how the two sisters should be closer.

'OK,' he'd agreed reluctantly. 'But I think Debbie's damn rude and ungrateful not to have come here tonight to make the arrangements with us like we'd planned.'

'I know and I said it to her,' Connie'd said, hoping he'd say no more. She wasn't in the humour for making excuses for their daughter. He'd said nothing else about the matter, for which she was grateful, and they'd ended up talking about the rip-off prices at the wedding fair.

Connie blew a deep breath of air up to her forehead and stared out at the sprinkling of stars that had emerged from behind the drifting banks of clouds as the rain stopped as suddenly as it had started. Barry could be such an ostrich some-times. He couldn't see what was in front of his nose.

He'd want to start taking an interest in Melissa's nutrition, for starters, instead of worrying about her being a bridesmaid. From remarks both of them had made about the dinner it was clear that home cooking was not high on the list of priorities in the Davenport-Adams household. She supposed that Aimee, with her high-powered job, just didn't have the time to prepare home-cooked meals.

Well, thank God it wasn't her responsibility, and Barry wasn't her worry any more, and the great thing was she didn't care. One daughter reared and flown the nest. Once Debbie was married she was a free woman; she might even stop cooking herself and eat out more. Her life was going to change for the better, she was going to cut down on her hours and do things that she really wanted to do.

She'd look on her fiftieth as a birthday of liberation. Going into a new decade didn't have to be a great big negative, even if it was a bit nerve-racking and daunting. The important thing was her attitude to what was happening in her life, the dreaded M-word included, she decided drowsily as she spread herself across the double bed and fell asleep.

Barry lay beside his wife and listened to her deep, even breathing. She'd been asleep when they got home and he hadn't even had a chance to tell her about Connie's kind invitation.

He'd very much enjoyed the evening with his ex-wife, and the dinner had been extremely tasty. He and Aimee should make more of an effort to eat 'proper' food rather than all the frozen processed stuff or ready-cooked meals that took only a few minutes to microwave.

Aimee turned in her sleep, her breast, erotically curved in her flimsy nightdress, nudging his arm. He felt suddenly horny. It had been a while since they'd had sex but he dared not wake her. She'd had a gruelling week and she needed to catch up on her sleep. His hand slid down between his thighs and, as he drifted off into fantasy, a thought struck him. Maybe when the wedding was over he'd ask Connie would she invite Melissa to stay for a long weekend so that he could take Aimee away for a mini-break.

It would be good for Connie and Melissa's relationship to improve and deepen. His daughter had confided to him as they'd driven into their apartment complex that she liked Connie, even if it was a pity that she didn't have satellite TV. And she loved Miss Hope and begged him yet again for a pet. He'd had to say no of course. Aimee was dead set against the idea, but he might suggest Melissa coming visiting with him again so she could see the cat.

That might work very well, he thought: he and Aimee could have the odd long weekend away, knowing that Connie would be the most responsible child-sitter they could ever have.

He tried to visualize Aimee astride him but, for some reason, it was Connie's face that he saw. A flashback of one of their most lusty nights of passion came back to him. A young Connie in her nurse's uniform, open to the waist, her gorgeous firm breasts thrusting towards him. She'd been a dream in that white starched dress, every man's fantasy with the cinched-in waist and her full ass undulating as she walked. The new uniforms with the navy trousers that she wore now weren't a patch on those dresses, he thought as the memory became more vivid and his breathing quickened.

Aimee stretched against him and he realized what he was doing. He was having a sexual fantasy about his ex-wife while his current wife slept beside him.

Barry groaned and tried to summon up an image of Aimee in a floating negligee falling open to reveal her beautifully toned body. He held it for a moment but Connie in her uniform was tempting him. He tried Aimee again and nearly gave himself lockjaw yawning. His desire subsided and he turned on his side. What the hell was wrong with him? he thought tiredly. He had enough complications in his life without having sexual fantasies about his ex-wife.

CHAPTER SEVEN

Judith grimaced in pain as she sat up and tried to figure out where she was. The room swam before her eyes, a jumble of red and orange that made her wince and close them rapidly again. She heard a groan and a snore beside her and her eyes flew open again as she gazed down in dismay at the bearded stranger in the bed beside her.

Oh God! *Who* was he? she thought in horror. She couldn't remember anything of the night before. Her mouth tasted like an ashtray and she smelled like a brewery. She had to get out of there before he woke up, but by the look of him and the smell of him he was in as bad a state as she was.

She slid gingerly out of the bed and shivered in the watery early morning sunshine that penetrated the garish purple gauze curtains. She was naked. Frantically her eyes raked the room looking for her clothes, and she found her panties and her black skirt in a heap on the floor and pulled them on as quickly as she could, moaning in pain as a sledgehammer pounded inside her head. She couldn't find her bra, but she found her maroon blouse draped over a chair in the even more garishly decorated sitting room. She unearthed her shoes under the coffee table and her suit jacket was crumpled in a ball on the sofa. With trembling fingers she fastened her blouse and wondered where in the hell she'd left her handbag.

She edged her way into the bedroom again, nearly gagging at

the stale smell of drink and BO. She needed a cigarette badly and she had the shakes. There was an open bottle of brandy on the bedside locker and she took a swig out of it, gasping as it burned the back of her throat before coursing down into her stomach, comforting her with warmth. She took another swig for good measure and went back to the sitting room, where she found her bag under a cushion, its contents spilling out in disarray.

Bleary-eyed, Judith gazed around, wondering where the bathroom was. She desperately needed to pee. She found the bathroom just off the bedroom. Its chipped enamel bath and cracked dirty-white basin encrusted with a grey rim of shaving cream and toothpaste was an affront, even in her hungover state. Gingerly she squatted over the broken loo seat and tried to hold herself steady as she emptied her bladder. She couldn't bear to wash her hands in the sink so she settled for rubbing them in some loo roll before turning her attention to her appearance.

Two runny-mascaraed, swollen, red-rimmed eyes stared back at her from the mirror over the sink. Her blond-highlighted hair streeled over her face. Her skin was pasty from drink and caked in slept-in make-up. She'd better do some sort of a repair job. No cab driver would pick her up looking the way she looked right now. She wet some loo roll with spit and dabbed at the streaks of mascara that ringed her eyes. It was difficult to get it off.

Judith rummaged in her handbag, found some foundation and smeared it on as evenly as she could. She brushed a dusting of Egyptian Wonder over her cheekbones and traced her lipstick across her bloodless lips. Her hands shook as she attempted to apply her eye shadow and, after a couple of attempts, she gave it up as a bad job.

She looked at herself in the mirror and cringed as she saw the results of her endeavours. God, she looked dog-rough, she acknowledged.

She dragged a brush through her tangled hair and that helped a little. A thought struck her. If only she had her sunglasses, that would hide a multitude. She delved into her bag again and rooted anxiously. 'Yes!' she muttered triumphantly as she took out the dark glasses and placed them on her nose. Perfect. No one would ever know she'd been on the tear. She slipped on her creased jacket and stared at her reflection in the stained, cracked mirror. Fine. No problems there. She looked like a lady.

She let herself out of the front door and found herself at the top of beige-carpeted stairs. The house was very quiet. It was clearly let in flats. Two bicycles leaned against the curve of the stairway down in the hall. The paint on the landing and down the stairs was flaking, the carpet threadbare in patches, and a faintly musty smell permeated the air. There was no one else about. Judith couldn't remember what day it was, but it was obviously early in the morning. She glanced down at her watch: seven forty-five. She'd be in plenty of time for work. She hurried down the stairs and fumbled at the latch on the green front door. She stepped out on to the uneven steps and gazed around. Traffic trundled past. Judith winced as she turned her head sideways and stared up the road, but it was too painful trying to focus long distance so she directed her glance across the road again. She didn't recognize the street. Vague memories of the previous night fluttered tantalizingly close, only to slip away again.

She was on a wide, tree-lined road of tall red-bricked Victorian houses, but where she had no idea. She remembered meeting the bearded guy at the cocktail bar the previous evening. Images slowly drifted back. He was an artist, he claimed, which might have explained the décor of the flat, she thought wryly as she walked down the steps and hailed a passing taxi. She gave the address of the office and slumped into the black leather seat and closed her eyes.

They'd travelled less than a mile when her stomach suddenly turned and she puked all over the floor.

'Ya stupid slag,' the taxi driver roared as he pulled over to the kerb and flung open the door. 'Get out, ya bleedin' tosser.' He pulled Judith out of the car, ranting and raving as he did so. She threw up again, barely missing him. 'Get the fuck out of here, ya alco. I should have known better than to take ya with the stink of ya,' he raged as she tottered off down the street, oblivious to the curious looks she was attracting from drivers. All she wanted to do was to get home and sleep her brains out. She couldn't face work today. She vaguely recognized an imposing grey-bricked church ahead of her. Was that St Peter's? Was she in Phibsboro? Had she been in a flat on the North Circular Road?

She walked on, breathing deeply, trying to calm her heaving stomach. A gush of semen soaked her briefs and she groaned. She'd had sex with that man and she couldn't even remember it. They obviously hadn't used a condom. Bloody hell, she could have caught a disease off him, she thought in panic. What had possessed her?

She couldn't think about it now, she needed to get home. She'd have to go to bed. She could ring work and tell them she was ill. That wasn't a lie, she thought forlornly as a wave of nausea washed over her and tears smarted her eyes.

She was walking past the Mater Hospital when the realization that it was Saturday dawned. Relief swept through her as the pieces began to slot into place. Her car was in Drury Street car park; it would be open by now, and she could collect it and drive home and stay in bed for the rest of the day.

A thought struck her: she hadn't phoned home, her mother would be frantic with worry. She'd better ring her. She rooted in her bag and found her mobile. There were five missed calls listed on the screen. Her eyes squinted in the sunlight as she dialled the number. Hammer blows of pain pounded her temples.

'Hello, Judith, is that you?' Her mother's shrill voice made her hold the phone away from her ear. 'Where have you been? I've been worried sick about you.'

'Don't be worrying, Ma, I stayed with a friend,' Judith lied. 'My phone battery went dead. I'll be home in a while,' she hedged.

'But why didn't you ring on a real phone, has your friend no phone?' her mother demanded stridently.

'It was too late to ring. I'll be home soon. Bye.' She hung up and swallowed hard. The thought of going home to her mother's piercing questions was more than she could bear; she needed to lie down in peace and quiet and sleep off her hangover. Where could she go? The Gresham Hotel wasn't too far away.

She might not get a room so early though, and it would be noisy on O'Connell Street. She could try the Skylon Hotel or one of the bed and breakfasts in Drumcondra. That wouldn't be too far to travel and she'd be near home. All she knew was that she'd rather lie down on the pavement and sleep than go home to endure her mother's cross-examination.

She'd managed to sit in another taxi for the duration of the journey to the Skylon without retching by dint of sucking a Polo mint, although she'd broken out in cold sweats several times. She got a room at the back of the hotel without difficulty, and as she closed the door behind her she burst into tears. What a nightmare she was in, but she couldn't think about it now, she *had* to sleep. Her mobile rang and her nerves were so frayed she jumped. Her mother's number came up. She probably had some shopping for her to do or some tiresome chore. She switched off the phone with shaking hands and dropped it into her bag. She'd pay for all of this neglect later, she knew, but right now she didn't care.

She pulled the heavy drapes and eased herself on to the bed and closed her eyes. She felt dizzy. She opened her eyes but the room swam around her and she closed them hastily. Judith lay very still, willing herself not to barf. Slowly, her breathing deepened and she slept in a stupor of crazy dreams where taxi drivers hurled abuse at her as she ran naked and crying through winding, eerie streets where the buildings were painted in garish, horrible colours.

Lily Baxter was very vexed. Judith had sounded most peculiar and had hardly talked to her at all when she'd finally phoned. It was bad enough that she hadn't slept a wink worrying about her, waiting to hear the key in the lock last night, but when her daughter *had* phoned, she'd been short and abrupt and didn't seem to care at all about the worry she'd put her mother through. And just now when Lily had rung to ask her to get a Mass card for poor Martha Collins, who was having her hip replaced, she hadn't even answered her phone. It was all very trying indeed.

Lily poured herself a cup of tea, sugared it, added milk and took a mini Twix from the jar of biscuits. She needed a little treat to keep her awake, she thought despondently as she walked into her front parlour and sat in her favourite high-backed, wing-tipped chair at the window, from where she could watch the comings and goings of the street. She peered out at the neat row of red-bricked houses similar to her own. Mr Reilly from two doors down was heading across to the nearby park for his walk, before going to the library at the end of the road. Polly Kavanagh was out cleaning her brasses, rubbing them with vigour, a big floral apron wrapped around her ample form. Otherwise the street was quiet. It was early enough on Saturday morning, most people were having lie-ins and a sense of peace prevailed rather than the usual to-ing and fro-ing the weekdays brought. The trees in the park looked fresh and verdant after the night's rain and she could hear childish laughter in the distance as giddy children made their way to the playground. The morning sun streamed in, warming her cheek, reflecting prisms of light in the mirror over the fireplace.

This was her room; Judith rarely ventured in here. Her daughter didn't like the old-fashioned green and gold two-piece sofa or the two glass cabinets on either side of the fireplace that housed all Lily's treasures. The mother-of-pearl fan that her husband had bought her for Christmas one year or the silver salver and the bits and pieces of Waterford Glass they'd got for wedding presents. There were some fine bone-china pieces her mother had given her but which she'd never used, as they were far too delicate.

'Clutter,' Judith called it, but Lily liked polishing and dusting her ornaments. They brought back happy memories, from before her husband had got sick and let her down. And then died on her. She knew it was wrong to resent her husband's death, even after all these years, but if it wasn't for Ted she wouldn't be stuck, a recluse in her own home, living with a daughter who considered her nothing but a burden.

Ted had been a decent, kind husband and a good provider until he had been cruelly struck down with a stroke and she'd been left to fend for herself and take on all the household responsibilities. Then Judith had come back home to help her nurse her husband because it had got too much for her and she wasn't able to manage on her own. Lily, who had always been taken care of, had had to become the carer. No more breakfasts in bed before Ted went to work in the mornings. No more spins in the car on Sunday afternoons and afternoon tea in a fine hotel on the way home. Ted had always paid the bills and done the shopping. She hated big supermarkets and got fluttery and panicky in them. All those responsibilities had become hers and she'd found them burdensome.

Not knowing how to drive had left her very reliant on her children. The two married ones always had an excuse that they couldn't do this or they couldn't do that because they were bringing the children here and there, so she'd grown more and more dependent on Judith. She'd been hard on her daughter, Lily supposed, insisting that she come home to help her nurse Ted, but she hadn't been able to cope on her own.

Her nerves were shaky. None of them understood that. None of them knew what it was like to be the way she was. Edgy, twangy, jumping at her own shadow. Her stomach tied up in knots. It hadn't been so bad when Ted was alive, he had minded her and understood her, unlike any of her three children, who had no patience with her.

When he'd passed away Judith had announced that she was off to live in a flat again. It had all proved too overwhelming for her nerves and Lily had had to take to the bed for months. She felt safe in bed, burrowed down under the bedclothes. She didn't have to talk to anyone, she didn't have to make any effort, she could just lie snug and out of harm's way and take the tranquillizers her doctor had given her.

It was selfish, she knew. And manipulative. She could have

managed if she'd really had to. She wasn't helpless. And if Judith hadn't crumbled, she would have had to get on with it, she supposed. But her daughter had caved in and stayed, and the longer she stayed, the more dependent Lily allowed herself to become. Just as she had with Ted.

She'd known that Judith was very angry with her. She'd known by the banging press doors in the kitchen when her daughter came home from work to find no dinner cooked. Or by the long, moody silences, the snapped retorts, the sarcastic comments. Judith didn't know how petrified Lily was of living alone. When Judith had announced that she was leaving, a fear had gripped Lily all those years ago and that fear never left her, even to this day.

The only way she had managed to keep Judith by her side was by promising her the house when she died. That was their secret. Tom and Cecily thought they were getting a share but they'd get a shock when the will was read.

She didn't care – Judith deserved the house; the other pair didn't deserve a cent, Lily thought bitterly. Oh, they came and they visited with the grandchildren every so often, and Cecily took her to stay in her big house in Dunboyne once a year when Judith went on holidays, but Lily knew she was always glad to see the back of her. She was an intrusion in her daughter's life. Cecily had her routine and having Lily for two weeks was a big deal.

Tom, the eldest, did the bare minimum; he was too busy playing golf and drinking expensive red wines and having dinner parties with his little madam of a wife to bother about his poor old mother. He rang her the odd time and called on Mother's Day, her birthday and at Christmas, with his big bouquet of flowers and two fifty-euro notes in her card. Was she supposed to be impressed? she thought sourly. Buying her off. A sop to his conscience. Her children had turned out to be selfish individuals. Was that her fault for the way she had reared them? Had her selfishness rubbed off on them? But she didn't mean to be selfish. It was just because she was nervous and edgy and needed someone to lean on.

Lily sighed. She could understand why they wouldn't want to be with her. A moany, whingey whiner who wasn't able to stand on her own two feet. She understood Judith's frustration with her, but she could never let on to her daughter that she felt guilty about having tied her to her. Show any weakness and Judith would be gone and she'd probably end up in a nursing home. Judith was used to being bossed around and demands being made of her. That was the way they'd lived all these years. Fighting and arguing, or else in moody, resentful silence.

It was too late to change things, she was too dependent. She'd never been brave enough even to try living on her own in her fifties, and she was in her early seventies now, no age to be considering it. Judith would be fifty soon, and Lily knew that she was dreading it.

Fifty was a hard age for a woman. Neither young nor old but in between, an age for regrets if life hadn't gone the way you wanted it to. And Judith's certainly hadn't gone the way she'd hoped it would. Lily felt an ache of guilt. That was her fault and hers alone. She had prevented her daughter from living her own life because she'd been too frightened to live hers.

Two wasted lives – what a sad legacy to leave behind her, Lily thought as tears blurred her eyes and she gazed unseeingly through the pristine white curtains of her front parlour.

CHAPTER EIGHT

'Sshhh, Melissa will hear you,' Aimee murmured against Barry's ear as he groaned into her hair.

He gave a slow, deep thrust and *she* moaned with pleasure.

'Sshhh, Melissa will hear you.' He raised his head and looked down at her triumphantly.

Aimee slanted a languorous, sultry glance at him and arched her back, tightening her long legs around him. He came with one last shuddering thrust and collapsed, his breath coming in ragged gasps, on top of her as she buried her face in his neck to muffle her own cries of pleasure as she climaxed.

They lay entwined for a few moments before Barry rolled off her on to his back. He lay against the plump pillows, his arms behind his head. 'That was good.' He turned and smiled across at her, thinking how lovely she looked with her hair dishevelled and her cheeks tinged with pink from their passion.

'Hmm.' She sighed drowsily, and he saw the black fans of her lashes sweep down over her cheeks.

'Don't go asleep, I want to talk,' he protested.

'Just forty winks. Go and get the bagels and I'll talk to you at breakfast,' she said, pulling the sheet up around her and turning on her front, her favourite position to sleep.

Barry scowled as he flung back the duvet and headed for the en suite. Would it kill her to spend a little time talking to him? There'd been a time when she'd snuggle up to him after love-making and they'd talk for ages, before making love again. Those days were fast becoming a distant memory.

It was kind of insulting, he thought irritably as he stepped under the powerful jets of water in the shower and began to soap himself. Give me an orgasm and let me go asleep, was her motto these days. If he behaved the same way to her he'd get a right lecture and probably be accused of less than desirable, unmannerly behaviour.

He'd wanted to tell her how Melissa had enjoyed her evening more than she'd expected at Connie's. He'd wanted to discuss a new column he was anxious to get up and running in one of the trade magazines. He'd wanted to ask her opinion on the best writer for the job.

He remembered all the times he'd lain with his arms around her, fighting drowsiness after love-making, listening to her enthusiastic plans for this event or another or her describing the new crystal and linen range she'd selected from some fair she'd been to. Or asking his advice about a colleague who resented her promotion and was giving her a hard time. If he'd had the temerity to drop off asleep he'd get a dig in the ribs and be told to wake up in no uncertain terms.

He made no effort to be quiet as he pulled open drawers and wardrobes to dress, but his wife was beyond being disturbed; she was snoring softly into her pillow, deep in slumber. Work and sleep, that was all Aimee did these days. He supposed he should be grateful for getting a ride this morning. He frowned as he closed the door and walked down the aubergine and cream hallway to his daughter's bedroom. He glanced at his watch. Ten ten – she might be awake.

Melissa was busily texting when he knocked and poked his head around the door of her lilac and white bedroom. She was sitting at her computer in her pyjamas, and when she saw him she hastily closed the site she'd been viewing.

Something she clearly didn't want him to see, he thought, a little dismayed, wondering was she in a chat room that wasn't suitable. Although they had the Net Nanny on it, he wasn't a hundred per cent happy about her having a computer in her room. But they had no space for it anywhere else in the apartment. It would spoil the look of Aimee's red and gold dining room to have a chunky computer sitting in the corner.

'Hi, Dad.' She smiled up at him, her black hair tousled, her cheeks a little flushed.

'Morning, Muffin.' He smiled, too, using one of his pet names for her. 'What are you up to?'

'Just texting Sarah.' She was still a little flustered.

'Working on the computer too, I see. Are you doing a project or just surfing?' he said easily.

'Yeah, just surfing. Is Mom awake?' She changed the subject quickly.

'She's having a lie-in. Want to come and get some bagels with me? We could pop into Hughes & Hughes on the way home and treat ourselves to a book each. Have a quick cup of coffee and a doughnut in the coffee shop, if you like, just to keep us going.'

'Sure, I'll be dressed in five minutes.' She jumped up, grinning at him, the freckles dusting her nose making her look about ten.

He smiled back, his heart full of love for her. Soon she'd be at the age where she wouldn't want to go and get breakfast with him and then who would he have for company? he thought with a sudden pang. 'I'll leave you to it then.'

'OK, Dad, won't be long,' she assured him as she pulled open a drawer and rooted for a T-shirt.

He walked down to the lounge and opened the French doors to the balcony. It was a glorious day, all traces of the previous night's rain gone. He stood looking at the SeaCat churning up the water as she left the safety of the harbour and began her voyage across the Irish Sea. He could hear a Dart clattering into Dun Laoghaire station, and a flock of wheeling, screeching gulls swooped and dived after a fishing boat that was chugging alongside the pier. In the distance Howth was bathed in early morning sun, the tweedy, muted greens, purples and brown fields cushioned in a pale lemony haze that was drifting over the summit. He inhaled deeply, looking forward to the stroll to the bakery and then to coffee and a doughnut. They might have their coffee in Meadows & Byrne or one of the other cafés along the seafront and then go book-shopping. He'd see what his daughter would prefer. He liked living practically on the seafront in Dun Laoghaire. It had a buzz, a cosmopolitan edge that appealed to him. Aimee would like to move further along the coast to Sandycove or, even better, Killiney, or Dalkey, which were far more upmarket and chic addresses, in her view. And the property prices were much more upmarket and chic too, he assured her, and they were at their limit.

'Ready, Dad.' Melissa bounced into the room in a pair of red cut-offs and trainers and a black T-shirt that clung too tightly to her pubescent curves. A little roll of puppy fat could be seen in the gap between her top and trousers. He must get Aimee to have a word with her. She was extremely sensitive about her weight and wouldn't take kindly to him saying anything that could be construed as a criticism. He shouldn't be bringing her for doughnuts, and Big Macs and the likes, he supposed, but she loved her junk-food treats and so did he. Aimee wasn't at all interested in food and could exist on coffee and water biscuits, if left to her own devices.

'Do us a favour? Will you pop down to the recycling bins with the cartons and boxes, and I'll follow you down with the bottles? I just need to make a quick call.' He dropped an arm around her shoulder.

'Sure, Dad.' She walked with him into the kitchen and took the recycling bag out from under the sink. He filled another one with a few empty wine and Amé bottles and a couple of jam jars. As soon as the front door closed and he heard the ping of the lift and the doors swishing open, he dropped his bag of bottles on to the counter and hurried to Melissa's bedroom. He clicked on the keyboard and the screensaver came up. He tapped the Safari icon and scrolled to recent history, anxious to find what his daughter had not wanted him to see. He shook his head as he stared at the site that came to life on the screen when he clicked on it.

She really was still a child at heart, he thought tenderly as

Paper Doll Heaven came up as the last hit. No wonder she'd been embarrassed – she wouldn't want him thinking that she still liked to dress paper dolls at her age. And here he was thinking she was on some iffy chat room. He closed it down, sent the computer to sleep and hurried out of the room feeling a little uncomfortable. He felt like he was spying on his daughter and invading her privacy, but it was important to keep some sort of check on what she was up to. She was on her own a lot because both Aimee and he worked full time, and sometimes it bothered him that he didn't get to spend enough time with her. He'd mucked up with Debbie; he didn't want to make the same mistake with Melissa. He grabbed the bag of bottles and went out to the lift, which she'd sent back up for him. He pressed the button for the basement, knowing that she was waiting for him. Maybe he'd treat her to that new iPod she had her heart set on. She was a good kid, she deserved it, Barry decided as the doors slid open and she stood waiting patiently for him to empty his recycling bag so they could set off on their Saturday-morning jaunt.

'Come on, it's a lovely day – leave that,' Bryan urged as Debbie emptied the linen basket and began sorting clothes for the wash.

'I want to put another wash on, Bryan. Will you empty the washing machine and hang out those clothes while I do this lot?' She tried to keep the exasperation out of her voice.

'We can do it when we come back. Come on – the gang are meeting in the IFSC and we're going for brunch. I told them we'd be there,' he wheedled.

'But, Bryan, we were going to clear out the spare room and strip the wallpaper off the walls. We've got to get working on the house. It's a shambles.' Debbie looked at him in dismay.

'Aw, come on, Debbs, don't exaggerate. It's liveable in, there's no rush – we'll be living here for years to come. I've been incarcerated in the office all week and so have you. We need some fresh air. It's a smashing day. Who wants to be stuck inside on a day like today doing housework?' he retaliated.

'Well, I don't,' she snapped, 'but it's got to be done or we'll be going back to work on Monday and the house will be in an even bigger mess.'

'Look, we'll do it this evening. Let's head off.' He hauled her to her feet and propelled her out of the kitchen, protesting.

'Ah, Bryan, stop it. Look, you go.' She scowled, shrugging off his hand. 'I'll get a Dart to Connolly and join you later. I really want to get the clothes hung out at least, there's great drying out.'

'You sound like a housewife,' he said sulkily.

'Ah, shut up, Bryan. If you want to live in a slum I don't. I'm not your mother, your sister or your cousin. I'm not going to run around after you. We share the chores. That's what couples do. Get used to it,' she flared, stung by his jibe.

'Right! Well I'm going out now and I'll do my share later,' he retorted, picking the car keys up off the hall table, which had a week's post, mostly bills, to be dealt with.

'See you later,' she responded coolly, not letting him see how mad he'd made her calling her a housewife and leaving her in the lurch to go and have brunch with their friends.

'Ciao, baby.' He waved his keys at her and gave an insouciant grin as he closed the door behind him.

'Bastard!' she swore as she flounced back into the kitchen. In a temper she divided the dirty washing into his and hers piles, a determined jut to her chin. He could do his own washing tonight, she thought grimly as she plucked an armful of her clothes and flung them on the floor in front of the washing machine. She emptied the damp clothes into the wash basket with mounting resentment and filled the machine with her dirty washing. She twisted the dial viciously, feeling more furious by the second. Why would she want to marry a selfish pig like Bryan? She sighed deeply as she took the wash basket into the overgrown and weedy back garden and hung her clothes out to dry, leaving his tossed in a heap with the pegs. If he thought she was going to hang his clothes out too, he had another think coming, she thought spitefully as she stabbed a peg on to a pair of black briefs.

Anger fuelled her, and in the next hour she filled a bag for a charity shop, loaded up the green bin, washed out the kitchen and bathroom floors and spent ten minutes on the phone paying bills with the twenty-four-hour banking option before making herself a cup of coffee and a bacon sandwich and heading out on their small deck. Their small, sadly neglected deck, she thought ruefully as she surveyed the couple of dried-out plants in flowerpots, the round table and two wrought-iron chairs. She was really going to have to get to grips with the garden or it would turn into a wilderness. It was only a postage stamp of a garden. If Bryan was any way inclined, an afternoon would sort it out. But that could be a long time coming the way he was behaving at the moment, she thought dolefully.

They'd bought a small townhouse in a quiet cul-de-sac in Sandymount and, although they were stretched to their limit with the mortgage and had spent more than they really could afford, they had wanted a house close to the Dart so that Bryan could take the train to work in the IFSC and she could visit Connie in Greystones without having to drive in the gridlock that plagued the N11.

She should give her mother a call, she thought guiltily. She wondered how the previous evening had gone. She really had behaved badly. Connie was working this morning and would have her phone turned off. Her mother worked hard. She was a great mother, Debbie reflected remorsefully. She hadn't made much of a fuss of her lately; she'd been too occupied with her own concerns. Maybe they could have a late lunch together when Connie was finished work.

That would be nice; it would be her treat to make up for her childishness, and she could find out what seating plan had been arranged. She'd text her so the message would be there for her when she came off shift. She took a bite of her sandwich, and a slug of coffee, starving after her exertions.

The sun was warm and she felt the tension ease out of her body as she raised her face to its beneficent rays. Little puffball clouds scudded across the indigo sky and the breeze lifted the hair off her forehead, cooling her temples in a most refreshing manner. Bryan was not in the slightest bit domesticated, she thought glumly. Perhaps he was right. She should be enjoying a lovely day like today with their friends, but chores had to be done or else they piled up. It had hurt when he had said she was behaving like a housewife. Maybe she *was* acting the martyr, but what did he think – that clean clothes magically appeared in the wardrobe, washed and ironed?

It was his doting mother's fault. She had treated him like a little prince since he'd been born and it was a role he'd grown used to. Debbie liked Mrs Kinsella – she was a kind, warm-hearted woman – but she really spoilt Bryan, who was her youngest child and only son. He was so used to being fussed over, he found Debbie's attitude towards his lack of housework skills hard to understand sometimes.

He had inherited his mother's generous nature and would give Debbie anything she asked for; she just wished he would pull his weight around the house a bit more. She knew his laziness irritated Connie, who couldn't understand how little they had done to the house since they'd moved in. It wasn't easy when the two of them were working. They'd get around to it eventually, she supposed. It wasn't that it was in a very bad state of repair or anything like it. It was just shabby and in need of redecoration. A couple with two young children had lived in it previously and the wallpaper had crayon marks and scuffmarks that couldn't be camouflaged. The carpets were stained, and she and Bryan had decided to get wooden floors put down.

If she had the money she'd have got a painter and decorator in, but they couldn't afford it right now, not with the expense of the wedding coming up. But they *could* afford a few cans of paint, and if Bryan was anyway helpful they could have painted the small bedroom, then at least they'd have a presentable guest room and they wouldn't be so inclined to keep it the junk room it had turned into. Still, the summer was long and, once the wedding and the honeymoon were over, they could turn to and roll up their sleeves, thought Debbie, her optimism beginning to reassert itself.

She finished her coffee and sandwich and sat enjoying the

peace and quiet of the back garden. Birds sang and in the distance came the sounds of a lawnmower and children playing. Someday she hoped that their children would be playing here and she could give up full-time work and take a part-time job somewhere, the way Connie had done when she was small. It would be such a relief not having to face Batty Baxter day in, day out. Her boss was always picking on her lately, and it was beginning to get to her.

It was probably her nerves, she decided, she was very edgy lately; it had to be pre-wedding jitters. She should chill out and start enjoying the lead-up to her wedding. She took her phone out of her jeans pocket and sent her mother a text: *'Let's have lunch, how about Roly's?'*

The restaurant on the seafront was one of their favourite haunts and the fish was to die for, straight from the fishing boat. There was just one drawback: it was a bit too close to where her father lived and they could bump into him. As he wasn't best pleased with her, that could be awkward.

She dialled Bryan's number to let him know of her plans.

'Hi, doll. Are you coming in?' her fiancé asked good-humouredly, and she had to smile. Irrepressibly cheerful as ever.

'I'm going to meet Mam for lunch, and then I'll hook up with you wherever you are by then. OK?'

'OK, whatever. See you when I see you. I love you.'

Debbie's heart softened. 'I love you too,' she echoed, still smiling in spite of herself as she hung up. She carried her dishes back into the kitchen and her phone beeped. It was Connie agreeing to meet her for lunch. Before she left to meet her mother, she put her future husband's dirty clothes in the washing machine and hung out the wet ones she'd ignored earlier.

Bryan Kinsella sat by the riverside café, enjoying the heat of the sun and the sparkle of light on the river as he listened to his friends joshing and ribbing each other as they tucked into a selection of salads, pasta dishes and pizzas. The Liffey shone sparkly-blue in the sunlight and prisms of light reflected off the big, shining plate-glass windows of a new office block on the opposite bank. A small boat chugged down the river, its wash causing waves to lap gently against the quay wall. The sound of laughter and chat blended with sounds of the river, the screeching of seagulls and the steady thrum of the boat's engines.

What a humdinger of a day. Debbs was mad to be stuck at home doing housework, he reflected as he watched a Dart snake lazily across Butt Bridge, the sun glinting on the windows.

He sighed. He wished his fiancée were here to enjoy it; she really needed to lighten up and chill sometimes. Just because they were getting married didn't mean they had to become a boring stay-a-home couple. Ever since they'd bought the house she'd been fussing and fretting about getting things done. Sometimes he was sorry they'd bought the damn place, but they'd both known, the way house prices were going in Dublin, if they didn't get a foot on the property ladder sooner rather than later, they never would.

The responsibility of owning a house and paying the crucifying mortgage had changed the dynamics of their relationship and he was finding it difficult to come to terms with the new responsibilities being a householder entailed. They weren't able to afford things they'd once taken for granted, like frequent dining out, weekends away, going to the races and not worrying about spending a few hundred smackers on bets. Now it was all penny-pinching and expenses and stress and strain, and he felt stifled and under pressure.

And then there was his mother-in-law to be, Connie. She was nice enough, he supposed, but she was always asking him how he was getting on with the decorating and making him feel as though he wasn't pulling his weight. She was different to his mother and sisters; she didn't seem to think a lot of him for some reason. Sometimes he felt that Connie thought Debbs could have done much better for herself, and he wasn't used to that kind of attitude. It was the first time he'd ever come across a woman who hadn't fallen for his charm, and it rankled, he thought crossly as he took a gulp of ice-cold beer.

He'd had a chat with some of his married mates and they'd

assured him that this kind of stuff was all par for the course and that things would settle down once he was married. He hoped so because, much and all as he loved his Debbs, right now he felt like calling it quits.

CHAPTER NINE

'This is nice.' Connie smiled at her daughter as she sipped a soda and lime and waited for her cod and chunky chips. She stretched her legs under the table and leaned back in her chair, glad that her shift was over. It had been a busy morning, and one of the post-op patients she'd been looking after had developed a clot and needed constant monitoring. Getting a text from her daughter inviting her to lunch had been a more than pleasant surprise.

'Mum, I'm sorry about last night. It was mean of me,' Debbie blurted out, and Connie felt a wave of love for her. Debbie always apologized when she was in the wrong and their tiffs never lasted more than a day or two.

'Your dad was a bit put out.' Connie stifled a yawn.

'I know, I got a fairly tetchy text from him,' said Debbie contritely as she fiddled with the condiments. 'Did you sort out the seating arrangements to your satisfaction?'

'Yeah, we sorted the families and grandparents, and we're going to put Aimee and Melissa at Karen's table. I told Melissa she could bring a friend with her – the poor kid would be bored out of her tree otherwise.'

'You might have asked me.' Debbie pouted, annoyed. It was, after all, her wedding, but it seemed that, between them, Connie and Barry were taking over.

'Ah, stop it, Debbie. What age are you now? Six?' her mother grumbled.

'Sorry.'

'I should think so. Don't worry, you won't have to pay for her meal, I'll look after that,' Connie said tartly. 'Melissa's not a bad kid, and I'm sure the last place she wants to be is at your wedding.'

'Well, then, she shouldn't come to it, or Aimee, either. I won't be the slightest bit insulted. I hate the hypocrisy of playing happy families, pretending we're all lovey-dovey. All Dad is thinking about is himself. He has this notion that we're all going to be one jolly extended family, and it's never going to happen, no matter how much he kids himself. It's all to ease his conscience. Well, tough, I have to be true to my feelings too, you know. I never wanted those people in my life and I don't want them now. What's so awful about that?' Debbie said crossly.

'He means well, Debbie, he has your best interests at heart and he's trying to make life as easy as possible for all of us.' Connie sighed.

'You're entitled to your opinion, Mum, and I'm entitled to mine. I just don't want that pair at my wedding. I know I'm a bitch but that's the way I feel.'

'Can't you just let it go, Debbie?' her mother urged. 'It's not good to hold such bitterness and resentment. Sometimes I feel I've really failed as a mother when I hear you talk like that. I tried very hard not to let any negative feelings I had about your father influence your feelings for him—'

'Mum, he did that all by himself, you aren't to blame for anything,' Debbie insisted vehemently. 'You're a great mother.'

'I don't know, honey. If you're still feeling so bitter and angry towards your dad at this stage of your life and after all this time, I've failed you in some way. Maybe I should have arranged some sort of counselling for you when you were younger. I should have seen your difficulties. I guess I was just too engrossed in dealing with my own stuff,' Connie said tiredly.

'Mum, stop! It's not *your* fault.' Debbie reached across the table and grabbed her mother's hand. 'They're my issues, I have to deal with them, and I have, and you don't need to feel guilty. I'm just not pushed about having any of them in my life. It's as simple as that, and you and Dad don't seem to be able to grasp that. Who says I have to like them? Can't I just let them get on with their lives and get on with my own life without having anything to do with them? Is that so awful?'

'I suppose it isn't,' Connie conceded. 'But it's a shame. Barry *is* your dad and it's not Melissa's fault the way things turned out. Aimee, I can take or leave.' She made a face.

'I can certainly leave her, snooty bitch. She thinks she's so superior. She looks down her nose at us, you know.'

'Don't say that,' Connie remonstrated.

'She does. She adopts this "tone" when she's talking to us; she's so supercilious, just because she's this high-flying businesswoman. High-flying up her own arse.'

Connie snorted, laughing. 'Stop it and don't be so mean. Don't forget she came into your father's life after we separated. She had nothing to do with our split.'

'I still don't like her. Why he went for the likes of her when he had you I'll never understand. And you're so loyal to him, Mum. He doesn't deserve it,' Debbie declared.

'He's not the worst, Debbie, he was more than fair in his financial dealings with us and he would have played a much bigger part in your life if you'd let him.'

'I didn't want him then, and I don't want him now. It's as simple as that,' her daughter reiterated firmly. 'If he wasn't at my wedding, it wouldn't bother me one whit.'

'Look, Debbie, I want your wedding to be a lovely day, the best day of your life. I don't want it ruined for you because you don't want Aimee and Melissa at it. I want you to make your peace with your dad and just move on. Couldn't your wedding day be a fresh start for you, darling? Let all the bitterness of the past go and don't let it ruin the most important day of your life,' Connie implored. She delved in her bag and brought out a book. 'One of my patients gave me this book. Would you please, please read it. There's a lot in it about forgiveness and letting go of stuff – it might help.' She thrust it at her daughter.

'All right, Mum, I'll have a flick through it. Now can we not talk about it any more, let's just enjoy our lunch,' Debbie urged as the waitress arrived with two steaming plates of golden battered cod and chips. She shoved the book in her bag, sighing.

'Debbie, you can't run away from things all your life. Because the things you run away from have a habit of catching up with you at some stage,' Connie advised, realizing that she was getting nowhere.

'Mum, just let me deal with things my own way,' Debbie ordered, pronging a satisfyingly chunky chip with her fork. 'I'm not talking about it any more.'

'Is Bryan doing up the spare room?' Connie asked, changing the subject. Debbie had spoken of plans to redecorate at the weekend, so that was safer territory for discussion, she decided.

'Nope, we decided it was too nice to be stuck in, so after lunch I'm going into town to hook up with him and some of the gang,' Debbie said off-handedly.

'Oh right,' Connie murmured. She should have known better than to think that that slacker was stripping wallpaper. 'The cod is scrumptious isn't it? It's so fresh.' She smiled at her daughter, who smiled back at her. They ate companionably in silence for a few moments and then Connie saw Debbie's face fall as something caught her eye.

'Oh shit, just my luck,' she groaned, and a frown darkened her face.

'What's wrong?' Connie turned around to see what the problem was and saw Barry, Aimee and Melissa walking through the door.

Barry saw them almost immediately, his face lighting up as he waved across at them.

He murmured something to the maître d' and headed across to their table. 'Hi, you guys, what a nice surprise. We popped in on spec, hoping there'd be a table but it seems pretty crowded still – may we join you?' He smiled at Connie.

'Sure, why not?' she agreed, feeling it would be rude and churlish to refuse.

'OK with you, Debbie?' He glanced over at his daughter.

'Yep,' she answered shortly. Barry beckoned to his wife and daughter, who made their way to the table.

'Aimee, Melissa, hi! There's plenty of room – why don't you

sit here beside me, Melissa?' Connie invited, wishing she and Debbie could have been left to enjoy their lunch in peace.

'Hiya, Connie, how's Hope?' Melissa slid on to the chair next to her and cast an uncertain glance at her half-sister across the table.

'Hello.' Debbie's greeting was polite but cold and Connie felt like kicking her under the table.

'Hope's fine, pet, I left her snoozing on my bed this morning while I had to get up for work. I bet when I get home she'll be out snoozing in the sun. She just loves snoozing, that cat.' She smiled at the teenager, who smiled back at her.

'Aimee, how are you?' she asked the other woman, who was slipping out of a taupe linen jacket to reveal beautifully tanned and sculpted upper arms in her lemon, figure-hugging vest. Connie tried not to feel envious, and the chips that she'd been enjoying made her feel irritatingly guilty.

'I'm very well, thank you, Connie, and you?' The younger woman nodded graciously. She clearly wasn't too thrilled to be dining with the other half of the family either.

'Great.' Connie regretfully pushed aside the crispy golden batter she'd been looking forward to.

'Are you all sorted for the wedding?' Aimee arched a perfectly shaped eyebrow at Debbie.

'Yes, thank you.' Debbie avoided her father's gaze.

'Excellent,' Aimee said coolly, not even looking in Debbie's direction as she moved slightly to accommodate the waiter, who was adding three place settings to the round table they were seated at.

'So how did work go?' Barry smiled at Connie.

'Busy. I'm going to go home and flop on my lounger for an hour or two, I can tell you.'

An awkward silence descended on the group.

'What are you going to have?' Barry asked his wife and daughter as they perused the menu. 'Was the fish good?' he asked Connie.

'Really fresh,' she informed him, longing to eat a forkful of batter.

'I don't think I'll have the fish and chips, too laden in calories for me,' Aimee said crisply. 'I'll just have a Caesar salad, dress- ing on the side and no starter,' she instructed her husband. 'You're brave to be eating fish and chips so close to the wedding. Aren't you afraid you'll put on weight?' She focused her stare in Debbie's direction, eyeing her up and down.

'God, no. I couldn't bear to live the life of a twiglet.' Debbie's eyes flashed disdain.

'What's that? A chocolate bar?' Aimee asked, confused, a tiny frown trying unsuccessfully to crease her Botoxed brow.

'No, it's one of those silly women who look like a twig, who push a lettuce leaf around their plate and fret about their calories and cholesterol, and bore the pants off people talking about their diets and their non-existent figures,' Debbie said sweetly.

Connie almost choked on the soda and lime she'd been sipping. Barry's mouth tightened, and he glowered at his elder daughter as, once again, a strained silence descended on the group.

'I see. Well, I guess no one could accuse you of looking like a . . . um . . . "twiglet",' Aimee drawled.

'Thank goodness for that!' Debbie responded, ignoring the implied insult.

'Did you ask your friend to the wedding, Melissa?' Connie interjected hastily, breaking out in a sweat that, for once, wasn't a hot flush.

'Not yet. Her mobile's off, I'd say she's run out of credit, but I think she'll be able to come.' Melissa glowered at Debbie; she understood perfectly well that her half-sister had subtly insulted her mother.

Debbie ignored her glowers.

'What are you going to have, Lissy?' Barry asked, using another of his pet names for her. He was beginning to realize that joining Connie and Debbie for lunch was not the best move he'd made that day.

'Can I have the fish and chips, please?' she said sulkily, fishing her phone out of her bag and beginning to text.

'That's rude at the table, darling,' Aimee remonstrated.

'It's important.' Melissa shrugged and carried on texting.

Aimee pursed her lips and looked to Barry for support. He kept his gaze firmly on the waiter who was heading in their direction.

'Darling, I've asked you to stop texting. It's bad manners. Now put the phone away,' Aimee commanded in clipped tones.

'Lissy, do what your mother asks, please,' Barry said wearily.

'It's OK, if the message is important,' Connie ventured, aware that the young girl beside her was absolutely mortified.

'That's not the point, Connie,' Aimee said sharply. 'Put your phone away *now*, Melissa.'

Beetroot-red, Melissa shoved her phone into her bag and blinked hard. Connie could see the brightness of unshed tears in her eyes.

'Would you care to order?' the waiter, who had been hovering, inquired discreetly.

'A Caesar salad with dressing on the side, two cod and chips, a diet Coke and two white-wine spritzers please,' Barry said briskly.

'Excuse me, I need to go to the loo,' Melissa muttered, standing up abruptly and making her way between the tables to the toilets at the back of the restaurant. Connie knew she was going to have a cry and felt sorry for the young girl. Aimee had been way too sharp with her, especially in front of herself and Debbie. Teenagers were so sensitive. Things were awkward enough between the two families; she could have been a bit more tactful.

'Are you having dessert and coffee, Mum?' Debbie asked and Connie knew her daughter was willing her to say no.

'Thanks, but I think I'll have coffee out on my lounger at home, if you don't mind, hon. I'm tired – it's been a hard day at work.'

'Fine, I'll go up and pay. I'll have coffee with Bryan when I meet up with him.' Debbie got to her feet with indecent haste and hurried over to the cash desk.

'Well, enjoy your lunch, folks. If you'll just excuse me, I need to go to the loo too.' Connie got up and made her way to the toilets.

'That was great,' Aimee hissed. 'You could have given me a bit of support.'

'And you needn't have acted so heavy-handed, Aimee. You went over the top and made us all feel uncomfortable,' Barry retorted. 'And you were way over the line commenting on Debbie's meal and weight. That was completely uncalled for.'

His brusque tone stung. How dare Barry treat her like a child? 'Well, she was damn rude to me but I didn't notice you jumping to *my* defence.' Aimee's eyes were glacial as she stood and picked up her jacket and bag. 'I guess I'm just not hungry. I'm going home.'

'Oh, for God's sake, Aimee, don't be so childish.' Barry could see Debbie looking at them.

'Deal with it,' Aimee spat and turned on her heel and walked out.

'Great,' muttered Barry. 'Just great.'

'You OK in there?' Connie called as she stepped into the cubicle next to Melissa's.

'Yeah,' came the muffled reply.

'Well, we're just heading off, so I wanted to say goodbye and please come and visit Hope any time you want to, she really likes you,' Connie said kindly as she did a quick pee.

'Thanks, Connie.' She sounded so subdued next door that Connie wanted to put her arms around her and give her a hug.

'Mind yourself, pet,' she said warmly as she washed her hands. She came back into the restaurant just in time to see Aimee marching out the door.

'Where's Aimee gone?' she asked Barry, who had a face like thunder.

'Home,' he said shortly as Debbie rejoined them. 'And you, Miss, could do with a lesson in manners. You were very rude to Aimee,' he barked.

Debbie was about to give a heated response but a glare from Connie stopped her.

'Don't start, the pair of you, I'm warning you,' she hissed. 'I'm fed up to the back teeth of the carry-on between you two. Sort yourselves out before this damn wedding or I'm not going to it.

Thanks for lunch, Debbie. I'll see you, Barry.' She stalked out, leaving father and daughter glaring at each other.

'This is supposed to be the most wonderful time of my life and it's already a disaster. But what's new? Nice one, Dad,' Debbie said tearfully, before hurrying after her mother.

For the third time in less than five minutes Barry watched a furious woman walk out on him.

He groaned. What the hell was wrong with them? Were they *all* pre-menstrual? Was the lead up to all damn weddings as fraught as this one? he pondered gloomily. It was time he faced facts: they were never going to be one happy family, no matter how much he wanted it. This wedding was not going to mend fences as he'd hoped. If anything, the chasm between Debbie and his other family was wider and deeper than it had ever been.

CHAPTER TEN

Debbie sat on the Dart as it headed towards town, twisting her engagement ring around her finger. This day was a real bummer so far, she thought despondently as they flashed past Lansdowne Road. Connie had been in no humour to talk when she'd caught up with her and had told her in no uncertain terms that her behaviour was rude, childish and unacceptable.

'I'm ashamed of you. And whatever about being rude to Aimee, there really is no excuse for the way you treat Melissa. That young girl has done nothing to you. None of this is her fault, just as none of it was yours. She's only a child and you're supposed to be an adult. Whether you like it or not, she's your half-sister, you should give her a chance. Grow up, Debbie,' she'd fumed, before marching off to the car park looking tired and fed up.

Her mother had a point, she thought wearily: she was twenty-five and she was acting like a five-year-old throwing a tantrum. She knew she was behaving badly and yet she kept at it, kept pushing her father to see how far she could go with him. Was she hoping that if she was obnoxious enough he'd butt out of her wedding and her life?

He'd been absolutely furious with her, she had seen the disgust in his eyes, but she didn't care. It was all very well for her mother to go on about putting the past behind her, but you didn't switch off your feelings just like that. She'd lived with these feelings most of her life – they were like old friends, even though they were negative and bitter – but they were the feelings that came up whenever she had prolonged dealings with her father. They were all she knew. Those emotions had been with her since childhood; just because she was getting married was no reason for them to change.

Even to this day she could still remember listening to her mother's muffled crying in her bedroom when Barry had left them and gone to live on his own. She'd been afraid. Mothers were supposed to be strong; they weren't supposed to spend hours crying into their pillows. She'd felt somehow that it was up to her to look after her mother now that her father was gone. She had to find a way to make her happy, to make things OK again. But what could she do to make her Mum's hurt go away?

She remembered how truly fearful she'd felt when her mother had told her that her dad was going to live in America. Who was going to mind them? Who was going to fix things when they went wrong? That's what daddies were for, her childish reasoning went. She remembered Connie struggling to pull herself up into the attic to set a trap for the mice which had been rampaging over their heads like little elephants the winter after Barry had gone, and that same winter when the car wouldn't start, trying to push it with her shoulder and steer it at the same time. Debbie remembered her sense of frustration and rage watching her mother's futile efforts, and knowing that Connie had been presented with yet another problem to deal with on her own.

She'd bet a million dollars that Madam Aimee would never have to climb up into an attic to deal with mice or push her car by herself to try and get it to start. She'd bet, too, that Melissa would never endure half the heartaches and anxieties she'd had as a child. 'Lissy' her father had called her, kindly, gently. They always seemed so close when she saw them together. They had a strong bond. When she was younger she'd felt searing pangs of jealousy towards Melissa. She knew that it wasn't the younger girl's fault and she did feel she was a bit of a bitch for the way she treated her. Connie was right, she thought with a little dart of shame. She could give Melissa some leeway. But Barry? He could forget it.

Things were different now. She felt as if *she* was the one with the power. Her father wanted to get close to her and she wouldn't let him. It was a revenge of sorts, she supposed. And he deserved it. Spoilt, cosseted Melissa would never endure the torments that had taken the good out of *her* childhood. Even now, sitting on a train heading into town, the memories were still vivid.

Most of the other girls in her class had fathers who'd brought them to school and did their homework with them sometimes, especially maths. Connie wasn't good at maths and she hadn't been a great help. Debbie remembered the knots she used to get in her tummy doing her arithmetic, wondering if it was right. The teacher, Miss Kelly, used to make anyone who got less than six sums right out of ten stand up for the last five minutes of class. Debbie spent a lot of time standing up. Once or twice she was the only one, and Miss Kelly had told her she'd have to speak to her mother. She remembered the sick feeling of dread she'd had going home to tell Connie that her teacher wanted to speak to her because she was a dunce at maths.

'Don't mind her, so am I.' Connie had hugged her tightly and Debbie remembered thinking that Miss Kelly had never saved someone's life by giving them mouth-to-mouth resuscitation and heart massage after they'd collapsed, the way she'd seen her mother do once in a supermarket when a middle-aged woman had crumpled over in the aisle.

Connie had given the teacher a piece of her mind and told her that just because someone didn't have a flair for maths didn't mean they were thick and that Debbie should concentrate on the subjects she was good at. Miss Kelly had not been impressed by her attitude and had made life even tougher for Debbie.

That teacher had been the bane of Debbie's life; she used to feel sick going to school, and, thinking back, she realized with a shock that the woman was very similar in manner to Batty Baxter. Great, she thought, a bully of a teacher had ruined her schooldays and a bully of a supervisor was trying to ruin her work life. Well, she was damned if she was going to let that happen. She had enough crap to deal with, without taking it at work.

Tears smarted in her eyes and she blinked rapidly. What on earth was wrong with her? Why in the name of God was she bringing up these old hurts, griefs and long-buried memories to torment herself with? That's what spending time with her father and his second family did to her. It was always the same after dealing with them en masse. She was better off having nothing to do with them for her own peace of mind, no matter what Connie said about making fresh starts. You couldn't make a fresh start when there were years of hurt to get over. It was impossible, she felt sure.

And, besides, why would she want to have to spend time with a snooty consequence like Aimee? She just couldn't imagine having anything in common with the woman. She shouldn't have bothered to even respond to her ill-mannered questions in the restaurant. Where did she get off? Imagine being so rude as to comment on what someone was eating and asking if they were concerned about putting on weight. It's a pity she wasn't as concerned about her own daughter. Melissa was positively chubby. Nothing was said about *her* ordering the cod and chips. She'd really thrown a few filthy looks in Debbie's direction when she'd made her smart comments in response to Aimee's impertinence. She supposed she could understand the younger girl's anger. If someone had had a pop at Connie, Debbie wouldn't be too happy about it. She could identify with her half-sister's annoyance and respected her for it but, even so, it had felt good to knock the superior sneer off Aimee's face by saying that *she* didn't want to be a twiglet.

That had hit home, she thought with satisfaction as they came to a halt at Grand Canal Dock. Childish but immensely satisfying. A thought struck her. Why on earth would Aimee possibly want to come to her wedding now? Surely after this little spat she might decide not to come. It might be worth it after all. If she could only annoy her dad enough he might not show up either and she'd have the day that she really wanted.

95

Aimee's breath came in short, controlled rasps as she clocked up her tenth kilometre on the treadmill. She'd spent three-quarters of an hour doing a work-out and was finishing off with a run on the treadmill. The backs of her calves ached as she slowed the machine, and it was a relief to step off it, do a few stretches and head for the shower. She was still fuming about the lunch episode; she hoped Barry and Melissa didn't come home until she'd managed to regain some sort of equilibrium.

The nerve of Debbie to speak to her the way she had. How dare she imply that there was something silly about watching your diet and figure? The term 'twiglet' had stung.

She'd been so tempted to retort that there was no danger of Debbie turning into one, she was more at risk of turning into a 'piglet'. But that would have been an insult too far and there'd have been uproar. Most girls who were getting married didn't sit stuffing chips and battered fish into their gobs like Debbie had been doing in Roly's. If she wasn't careful her dress wouldn't fit her and that would be a fine disaster on her wedding day.

Recently Aimee had been organizing the catering at a huge wedding in a big pile in Ballsbridge and there'd been mayhem upstairs because one of the bridesmaids had put on seven pounds since the last fitting for her dress and the zip wouldn't close. The designer, bride, bridesmaid and bride's mother had been in tears, and the wedding had been delayed for an hour until the designer had let out two side seams. Miss Debbie would want to be careful the same thing didn't happen to her.

Aimee sighed: it was so difficult dealing with her surly, ill-tempered step-daughter. She was lucky, she supposed, that they didn't have that much contact. She knew Barry wanted them all to be closer but it wasn't going to happen – and he couldn't see why not. It wasn't as though she had come between him and Connie – Debbie couldn't hold that against her – so what was her problem?

Aimee could understand perfectly how Barry had got bored in his first marriage. There was no get up and go in his first wife, she wasn't one bit ambitious or go-ahead. Connie had been content to be a run-of-the-mill housewife. Aimee couldn't understand that attitude.

Connie was putting on weight too and it didn't seem to bother her. Didn't she want to do something more with her life? Couldn't she go back to college and study and move up the career ladder? Why would she not consider going into hospital management? What *was* the attraction of nursing? Aimee could never figure it out. She hated being near sick people and disliked hospitals. If Barry got sick she had to struggle to hide her annoyance, and she was no good at mollycoddling him. She didn't have time to be doing the tea and sympathy bit.

Didn't Connie want to have a relationship with someone? she mused as she unlaced her runners. Didn't she miss sex and intimacy? She was in her late forties now. Was she content to slide into frumpy middle age? Aimee gave a shudder. That was one thing she would not do. She'd never give in to ageing. She'd never let herself go. She despised women who did. It was a lack of pride and discipline, and she had those in abundance, she thought with satisfaction as she stood under the powerful jets and let the hot water sluice over her supple, toned body.

She couldn't ever imagine Connie doing ten kilometres on the treadmill. She was probably being a bit of a bitch, she thought wryly as she massaged shampoo into her scalp. Connie had done well to rear her daughter and she had taken on the mortgage for her house. In fairness, she hadn't been too much of a limpet on them, financially. She didn't dislike the other woman – she was pleasant enough – but Aimee was not the girly type and watching Connie and their sister-in-law Karen giggling and laughing together when the clans gathered always made her irritable. Gaggles of women tittering and guffawing were definitely *not* her scene. She preferred intelligent, informed, stimulating conversation, and she didn't do 'girls' nights' the way Connie and Karen did. She just wasn't like them and she had no desire to be. She dried her hair, dressed and strolled home, beginning to unwind. She always felt de-stressed having done a good work-out.

Twenty minutes later she lay in a sheltered corner of the

wraparound balcony of their penthouse smoothing sun-tan lotion over her limbs. She was still angry. Barry hadn't even phoned to see if she was OK. He was behaving most uncharacteristically lately, she reflected gloomily, and his timing was crap. She needed his support; she needed their life to be on an even keel so that she could give all her energies to work.

Ever since this wedding had come over the horizon he'd been distracted. Why couldn't he simply accept that Debbie didn't want him there, even though he was paying more than his fair share? It was unseemly the way he was running after her and Connie, turning himself into a doormat. He should have given Debbie her answer at the table. He should have stood up for *her*, Aimee thought crossly as she slid a pair of sunglasses on to her nose and settled down.

She tried to relax but her thoughts kept returning to the lunch. Typical, too, that it would be the one day that Melissa would get thick and disagreeable. She hadn't covered herself in glory either. It was infuriating for her to have made a show of herself, in front of that other pair. It grated that Connie had been so sweet and nice to her. Her lips tightened as she remembered how the other woman had butted in and said that the text message might be important. Aimee had cut her off very sharply. She'd felt like saying, 'You leave the rearing of my daughter to me. She's not going to end up like the bad-mannered brat that you reared.'

Aimee grinned as she gazed up at the cobalt sky. She wished she'd had the nerve to say it. How wonderful it would be in life if you could say exactly what you felt at any particular time and not give a hoot about the consequences.

'Get over yourself, Debbie, and grow up.'

'Keep your nose out of my business and my family, Connie, and go and get yourself a life.'

'Barry, I'm not going to that bloody wedding, and you're an idiot if you go and I don't like being married to an idiot. And while we're at it, stop being so lavish with our money.'

It would be bliss indeed to speak as she wished, she thought as the conversations raced around her brain.

She might have the conversation with him about not going to the wedding yet. What was the point? She wasn't wanted and that didn't upset her in the slightest. If she could manage it at all, this was one wedding she definitely wouldn't be attending.

Barry sat in a chair, tucked up in the non-fiction section of the big, airy bookshop. Melissa had gone off shopping with a friend and he didn't want to go home to his wife after the disastrous episode at lunch.

He flicked through a biography of Conrad Black, the Canadian media baron who had come a cropper. He read about his wife, Barbara, who had clawed her way up the social ladder with a single-minded determination that was rarely seen. Aimee flashed into his mind. She was pretty single-minded, he supposed. But he couldn't possibly compare his second wife to the status-seeking Barbara Amiel, he thought guiltily. There was no comparison. Why would he even think like that?

What was wrong with him lately? he wondered. He felt so dissatisfied. It was this bloody wedding. Up until this, life was flowing placidly along and he was going with the flow of it. It was only since he'd started spending more time with Connie that he'd become unsettled.

Why could he not stop thinking about her? Why had he started comparing her to Aimee? It made him feel extremely uncomfortable and disloyal. They were completely different women and, the older he got and the more time he spent in her company, the more he realized that his ex-wife had some sterling qualities which he'd never really appreciated when he'd been married to her.

She was very, very understanding, especially when dealing with Melissa. Aimee should not have made such a song and dance at the table today the way she had. Lissy had been humiliated and upset and Connie had seen it and gone out of her way to be kind. Not that Aimee had appreciated it; she'd been very sharp in her response to Connie and, to his shock, that had rankled. He'd felt like telling his wife to be quiet. He'd immediately wanted to take his ex-wife's side.

He'd felt like telling Debbie to be more than quiet. She was being totally insufferable. He'd never felt the vibes so toxic between them. No matter what he said or did, she wasn't happy. She loved trying to make him feel guilty. How could she keep it up after all this time? He'd done his best, he'd always looked after her financially and been more than generous but she'd kept those barriers up so high, no matter what he did to try and repair the damage between them. But what was even worse was the cold way she treated her half-sister. Only that Connie sometimes warned him to go easy on her due to wedding nerves, he'd let her have it. When the wedding was over he was going to confront Debbie and have it out with her once and for all. It wasn't all about her. He was a damn good father despite what she might think and it was time she grew up and copped on to herself.

He put the book back on the shelf and ambled over to the café, ordered a latte and started the *Irish Times* crossword. There was no point in going home – Aimee would be in a snit with him, and if they started a row things might be said that could cause real trouble.

He might as well sit here and relax with the paper for another hour or so and let things calm down.

'My mom was like, so mean, she just kept on and on about it being rude to text at the table, in front of them, and I was like, nearly crying inside I was so embarrassed. How could she do it in front of them? She was just showing off and I hate her. She had her snooty show-off voice on that she uses when she wants to impress people.' Melissa sipped a diet Coke as she sat on a seat on the promenade and poured her heart out to Sarah, who was tucking into a Big Mac and a milkshake.

'Parents are just so annoying sometimes, that wasn't very nice. What did Debbie say?' Sarah oozed sympathy.

'Nuttin.' Melissa sighed. 'She never says anything. She's *so* unfriendly. I think she hates me.'

'Don't say that,' her friend protested.

'She does. And I know why. It's 'cos I live with our dad and she's jealous of us. I heard my mom and dad talking about it once. They didn't know I could hear them. My dad was saying how he'd really like us to be friends and my mom told him he was wasting his time. Debbie doesn't want to be friends – she's too angry with him for splitting up with Connie when she was small.'

'I suppose it makes sense – I wouldn't like my dad to live somewhere else with another daughter,' Sarah said matter-of-factly, licking the sauce off her fingers.

'I don't care, it's not my fault. Once this wedding is over I won't be seeing much of her,' Melissa said sulkily.

'It's a pity though, in a way. She's your only sister. You could have fun with her. You could go and stay with her at weekends and meet all Bryan's cool friends,' the other girl pointed out.

'Yeah, well, that's never going to happen so we better make the most of the wedding. She'll be so busy she won't bother us on the day.'

'It was very kind of them to ask me to it.' Sarah's eyes lit up.

'Connie's pretty OK, actually. I'm starting to like her the more I get to know her,' Melissa admitted. 'We had a good time in her house last night, even though I didn't think I was going to enjoy it. I played with her little black cat for ages. She's a good cook too. Those new potatoes we had were scrumptious. They were straight out of the ground and she cooked them lovely. She stood up for me, too, at the lunch today. She told my mom that the text might be important, but my mom wasn't having any of it. Then, later, Connie came into the loo and asked me if I was OK. And when I came out Mom had gone home in a huff so my dad and I ate our lunch on our own, and he's gone to Hughes & Hughes, even though we were in it this morning. Thank God you were able to meet me. It won't be much fun at home for the rest of the weekend.' She chewed the inside of her lip.

'And I can't ask you to mine because my granddad's going to be staying while my grandma's in hospital and my mam's in a tizzy and not in very good humour either. *And* she's got PMT! Our house is no fun. Let's go up to the market and have a look around, will we?' Sarah suggested.

'OK. I want to have a look at the jewellery, I got a cool bracelet there a few weeks ago – remember the one I showed you?'

'Yeah, it was beautiful. You should wear it to the wedding.'

'Mom wants me to wear a dress. I told her no way.' Melissa finished her Coke and threw the can in a bin as they began to stroll towards the People's Park.

'Look, we have to look grown-up – maybe she's right? A dress with very high heels and black tights can look great. Look at Kate Moss; she looks dead cool in dresses,' Sarah advised. 'Don't forget we want those hot guys to dance with us so we can take loads of photos of them.'

'Yeah, you're right,' Melissa agreed eagerly, seeing the sense of her friend's words. 'We'll show them around the class when we go back to school after the summer. We can pretend we're dating and that might shut that minger Terry Corcoran up. She's always asking me have I ever had a boyfriend and have I ever done it and she knows very well I haven't. Do you think she's done it or is she spoofing?'

'Don't know, she's a tart, though, so she could have. Lenny Dunlop said he's done it with her after they'd smoked a joint at Lena Conway's party.' Sarah shrugged. 'I don't know how they could keep smoking it, do you remember the way it made us puke after a couple of goes? I was scared. I wouldn't try it again.'

'Me neither,' Melissa said in heartfelt agreement, remembering how violently ill she'd been in Lena's garden after attempting to smoke her first joint. She'd felt so woozy and out of it. Sarah said she'd actually turned green. She'd felt green, she thought guiltily. She definitely wouldn't be experimenting again. 'Do you think it was because she was out of it that she did it?'

'Maybe, I don't know. She's always messing with boys, she's a slapper,' Sarah said dismissively.

'I'd be afraid to do it. I bet it would hurt; it hurts putting in a tampon.' Melissa grimaced.

'A tampon's tiny compared to a mickey,' Sarah scoffed.

'I know.'

'Pretend your tampon is Johnny Depp,' giggled Sarah as they strolled along, laughing, all their worries temporarily forgotten.

'And then she had the nerve to ask me was I not worried about putting on weight because I was eating the cod and chips. How rude is that, Bryan? I felt like smacking her. But I gave her her answer, I can—'

'Stop! Enough! I don't want to hear any more. You know what I think, Debbs? I think we should call the whole thing off, it's causing nothing but trouble. *They're* not happy. *You're* not happy. You're stressed out. We don't seem to be having any fun lately. It's just not worth it.' Bryan took a slug of beer and studied his fiancée to see her reaction.

'What! You want to call it off?' Debbie stared at him in horror.

'Yeah, I do. It's no fun any more. You're totally stressed out and that's stressing me out. Everything's a big deal. That's not the way it should be.' Bryan ran his fingers through his hair and shrugged.

'Don't you *want* to marry me?' She could hardly speak. She felt as though he'd punched her in the solar plexus.

'Yes I do, of course I do.' He leaned across the table and took her hand. 'But not this way. Not with all this fighting and arguing, not if every single minute is going to be consumed so much by this frigging event that we don't have a life any more.'

'But, Bryan, these things happen in life. I need to know you're supporting me. I need to know I can depend on you when things are tough for me, the way you know I'm there for you when things are tough for you.'

'I *am* there for you,' he protested. 'I just don't think this is very enjoyable for you and I think we should not go through with it. Or maybe do it differently further down the line. We could go to the Caribbean and get hitched in a ceremony on the beach, just you, me and some of the gang.'

'But Mum would be very upset if she wasn't at my wedding.'

'Well, she could come then.'

'And what about Karen and my cousins?'

'See, there you go, Debbie, I'm trying to simplify things and you start causing complications straight away,' he said angrily. She couldn't see his eyes – they were hidden behind his sunglasses – but she knew they'd be almost black.

'I don't know what to say,' she whispered, gutted, and then she could contain her tears no longer and she put her hands up over her face and cried.

'Aw, don't do that, Debbs – people are looking,' Bryan said uncomfortably.

'Let them look. I don't care,' she sobbed, as the couple at the next table looked at them curiously. They were sitting outside a bistro in Temple Bar, and the streets were full of shoppers and tourists wandering around the cobbled square.

He handed her a serviette. 'Here, use this,' he said awkwardly. 'I didn't mean to upset you.'

'Are you mad, Bryan? Of course you've upset me,' she snapped, pulling her hand out of his, suddenly furious at him. 'One minute we're getting married and the next we're not, because you can't cope with the hassle. Well, life's full of hassle, whether you like it or not. And if you can't deal with it, there's nothing I can do about it. I'm going home. You better give me the keys of the car. You've been drinking. You don't want to get caught drinking and driving, that might be too much for you to cope with,' she raged tearfully. She grabbed the keys off the metallic silver table, stood up and hurried in the direction of the quays, tears streaming down her face.

Today was the worst day of her life, and it was all Barry and Aimee's fault. If they hadn't gatecrashed her and Connie's lunch, she and Bryan would never have had this conversation and the wedding would still be on.

It was typical of Bryan to back off when things weren't going smoothly. She just couldn't depend on him sometimes. What was the point of marrying someone you couldn't depend on? She emerged through Merchant's Arch and crossed the road to where the car was parked.

The seats were hot when she got into it but she kept the roof up. A guy in a hoodie had thrown his empty Styrofoam coffee carton into the passenger seat once when she'd been driving and it had put her off driving on her own with the top down when she was in town.

She drove along the quays in a daze, turning right to cross the Liffey to come back down the other side.

'*I think we should call the whole thing off.*' Those shocking words kept twisting around, tormenting her, frightening her. If Bryan wanted to call off the wedding, maybe he was unsure of his love for her. A cold, fearful dread engulfed her. Maybe he wanted to end it completely. When he said he wanted to call the whole thing off, did he mean the engagement as well? She couldn't imagine her life without Bryan. He was what made it worth living. She had never had as much fun with anyone as she did with her fiancé. He made her laugh; he brought out the giddy, girlish, carefree part of her. Maybe he was right. She was turning their wedding into an angst-filled nightmare and all the joy had gone out of it for them. And she had to shoulder the blame for most of it.

Her parents were trying their best. Barry wasn't mean, she had to give him that much. But if she had just taken all that he'd offered and pretended that nothing was wrong and everything was hunky-dory she wouldn't have been true to herself. She would have felt such a hypocrite.

She drove in turmoil, trying hard to concentrate in the heavy traffic. She veered from sorrow to anger. How dare Bryan treat her like that? How dare he suddenly announce that he wanted to call the wedding off? Had he no consideration for her feelings? What did he expect, that she was overjoyed at the suggestion? He'd just sat there, coolly and calmly, and hadn't even reacted when she'd got upset, except to tell her not to cry. Well, she could manage fine without him. She had a good job, she wasn't dependent on him, he could stick his wedding, she raged, as she passed the riverside restaurant where he'd had brunch with his friends earlier. He was such a self-centred bollix. He wanted everything in life to suit him. He was always taking and she was always giving. Well, she should have given him his ring back while she was at it. If he didn't want to marry her now, what guarantee was there that he'd want to marry her in the future?

It was going to be embarrassing telling everyone that the wedding was postponed. Connie would freak and Barry probably wouldn't be too pleased either. They'd lose their deposit for sure with the hotel. And some of their friends had already bought them wedding presents. Well, *he* could tell them it was all off. He wasn't going to get away with any more crap. If he made decisions, he was going to take responsibility for them and not leave her to do all the dirty work.

Her heart contracted. How could he do this to her? Didn't he love her? Was that what all this was about? He was looking for an escape route and he'd found it. Blaming her stormy relationship with her father for backing out. Why didn't he understand? She wept as she crossed the river at the Point.

Didn't anyone understand where she was coming from? Bryan was the one who was supposed to understand most of all, and he just didn't want to know. Now he'd pulled the rug from under her. Maybe that was what men did, she thought wildly: her father had done it to her and now Bryan was doing it too, pulling the rug from under her just when she needed it most. Well, two could play at that game. All she needed was courage.

'Oh God, help,' she whispered as she paid her toll for the East Link and drove home.

CHAPTER ELEVEN

'Well, Miss Hope, my lunch was a disaster, but I know that you'll enjoy yours.' Connie smiled as she spooned some tuna, a rare treat, into her little black cat's dish, and was rewarded with ecstatic meowing and rubbing against her leg. She patted her pet's furry head as she bent down and placed the dish in front of her. Cats were so easy to please: tuna and cuddles, and they were happy.

Her left knee gave a twinge of pain as she stood up and she grimaced. She was getting old and decrepit, she thought gloomily. She certainly felt it today. She walked upstairs to her bedroom and began to undress, stepping out of the red and black floral skirt that she'd worn to lunch. She pulled the black shirt she'd teamed with it over her head and caught sight of herself in the mirror and groaned. Toned and supple she certainly was not. Aimee had looked fabulous at lunch today. So slim and fit and tanned. Her boobs pert and firm, her arms with not a hint of wobbly flesh.

Connie studied herself. She was around five foot seven, and her legs were in reasonable shape due to the walking she did on the beach. Her waist was still there but had thickened – she couldn't deny it – and a soft little wobble of tummy was unmistakable under her black briefs. Her boobs, tragically, could no longer, under any circumstances, be called firm and pert, she observed wryly. 'Ripe' and 'full' could describe them, she wouldn't pass the pencil test like she used to a few years ago, but they were still shapely for a woman on the wrong side of forty-five. She turned sideways and felt even more depressed as she studied her bum. Definitely a question-mark ass! Drooping and starting to spread, there was no denying it. A far cry from Aimee's tight buns.

She sighed deeply and sat down on the bed. No matter how hard she dieted or exercised, she was never going to have a body like Aimee's or even a body like she'd had herself, ten years ago. For the first time she actually *felt* middle-aged. Sometimes, especially when she'd begun to notice that she couldn't see the small print on packets and was beginning to have to use her glasses more than occasionally, she'd realized that the ageing process was at work, but it wasn't something that she'd dwelt on. She'd noticed her periods being a bit erratic, and that the hormonal headache that often accompanied them was becoming more intense and sickening, but it wasn't until her sister-in-law had teased her over lunch and told her that she was peri-menopausal and probably having a hot flush that it really hit home that her youth was gone.

A wave of grief overwhelmed her. Life certainly hadn't turned out the way she'd planned. She was middle-aged, with a failed marriage behind her, living on her own with just a little cat for company. Her body, no longer youthful, was now a reminder to her that time was passing and her options were diminishing. She cried for what was never going to be. No partner to start a new family with, the way Barry had done with Aimee. Always at the back of her mind had been the hope that she would meet and fall in love with someone that Debbie would like, and they would have lived together and had children and been very happy.

Instead, she was alone, with no realistic likelihood of having another child. Having reared a daughter, and given her what she had hoped was as normal a childhood as possible, it was painful and worrying to realize that her daughter was, at the age of twenty-five, still full of rage, anger and bitterness because of the failure of her parents' marriage. That *had* to be her fault.

She'd failed completely as a wife, a mother and now her feminine womanly bits were falling apart too. All she had to look forward to was a lonely middle-age and God only knew what sort of an old age.

Old age was cruel, she reflected, thinking of the elderly patients she'd nursed over the years, suddenly feeling that it was much closer than she'd ever imagined.

A lump the size of a melon lodged in her throat and she swallowed hard, and then she was crying again, her heart breaking as waves of despair and anxiety swept over her and she curled up in a ball on her bed, weeping like a child.

Seeing Barry and Aimee with Melissa as they walked over to their table had made her feel empty and thrown her life into sharp focus. She knew it was pointless and unproductive to compare and contrast, but they looked so affluent and glamorous – the family that had it all. Barry had held Aimee's chair out for her and Connie could see that it was force of habit. He obviously did it for her every time they were out.

Even after all these years that little gesture had given her a pang. Her ex-husband had never been attentive to her like that, even when things had been good between them. He'd never treated her with the respect he treated Aimee, she thought sadly. If he had, and just made more of an effort, they might still be married. She felt pretty sure that Aimee didn't have to put up with the moody silences that had so dominated the latter part of their marriage. She probably wouldn't stand for it. Aimee was a sharp cookie who wasn't afraid to voice her feelings or opinions. She wouldn't let Barry off the hook because she was afraid it might cause upheaval in her marriage, Connie felt sure.

In comparison, she'd been far too wimpish about speaking up. What good had repressing her emotions done? None. Her marriage had failed, in spite of her appeasements, she thought bitterly, disgusted with herself and suddenly feeling very angry. What in the name of God was wrong with her? What on earth was she doing? Hadn't she dealt with all of this stuff? Why was it all coming back to haunt her? She was as bad as Debbie.

She heard Hope patter up the stairs and jump up on the bed

beside her. And then a cold nose rubbed hers as her cat gazed at her with green-eyed affection. 'Oh, Hope, I'm a middle-aged failure and a disaster of a mother,' she gulped, and snuggled her face in the cat's silky black fur. She felt the heat of her solid little body and the steady beating of her heart against her cheek. Hope gave her a comforting lick and curled herself in against her, and that made Connie cry even more. She lay with her arm around her cat, crying bitterly as the late afternoon sun streamed in through the window, warming her back and shoulders.

The phone rang and she struggled to compose herself. 'Go away,' she muttered, but it kept on, insistent, jangling her nerves and, eventually, she answered.

'Hi, what are you up to? Fancy a walk later?' It was Karen.

'Hi, Karen,' she managed, before bursting into tears again.

'Hey! Hey! What's up? What's the matter?' Her sister-in-law's concerned tone came down the line.

'Oh Karen,' wailed Connie.

'What! Tell me what's wrong?' Karen said sharply, getting really worried.

'Aw, just had a disaster of a lunch with Barry and his gang, and Debbie was so rude I was mortified, and I just feel I've failed completely in bringing her up. She's so angry and bitter and it's all surfacing now. This wedding's going to be an absolute fiasco.' It all came pouring out.

'You had lunch with them? Was it planned?'

'No. Debbie was treating me to lunch in Roly's and they walked in and the place was still full so what could I do? Only ask them to join us?'

'Oh dear. Was Aimee thrilled?'

'What do you think? As thrilled as I was,' Connie said dryly.

'And is that why you're crying?'

'Oh, don't mind me, I'm menopausal, according to you. I don't know what's wrong with me, it must be my hormones.' Connie cleared her throat, trying to compose herself.

'Ahh. Look, don't tell me any more. I'll come over and we'll have a natter. I'll be with you in about an hour.'

'Haven't you loads to do?' Connie said weakly.

'Oh yeah, a week's washing and a report for my boss on the impact of the green-bin collection in my catchment area. Why do you think I'm looking for an excuse to escape?' Connie knew her sister-in-law was smiling.

'OK,' she sniffed. 'See ya.'

'Chin up, honey, we'll sort it,' Karen promised.

Connie wiped her cheeks with the back of her hands and sat up. Having a good friend was such a blessing. Karen was a great support to her, she could tell her anything. She unhooked her bra and wriggled out of it, and her briefs, slid on a black swim-suit and wrapped a beach robe around her. She might as well catch a few rays. They could have their tea on the patio when Karen arrived. It would be good to see her, she thought, her mood lifting as she hurried downstairs, followed by Miss Hope, purring like a train at the prospect of more grub.

She shook some dried food into the cat's dish, placed two mugs on to a tray and spilled a few chocolate snacks on to a plate. Might as well have another few calories to add to the thousands she'd consumed with her fish and chip lunch. She'd better be careful though. She knew what she was like when she got down in the dumps. She could go on an eating jag and put on a half a stone in the blink of an eye, and she couldn't afford to do that with the wedding coming up.

She went out to her small utility room and took two lounger cushions out of the press she kept them in. The sun was warm and comforting, and she lay down on one of the loungers and stretched her tired body. Maybe she might be able to have forty winks before Karen came. She'd been up since five forty-five this morning, and it had been a long and eventful day.

She felt the tension slowly ebb out of her body as she squirted Ambre Solaire on to her arms. The garden was coming into its summer glory. It was winding and higgledy-piggledy, full of flowering shrubs and apple and damson trees. There were two cottages on either side of her and a meadow at the end of it, so she wasn't overlooked, and high, evergreen hedges gave her complete privacy. Pots of petunias and geraniums lent colour to the patio and jasmine and wisteria tumbled over the trellises on either side. The garden was her haven, the place where she came to think and wind down; it was the garden that had drawn her to the house, even though it had been a wilderness when she'd viewed it. But she'd imagined what it could look like and she'd worked hard in it over the years until it became her small paradise.

She had moved from Deansgrange to the seaside town of Greystones, in Wicklow, to be near to Karen and her family. Debbie loved her cousins and they all got on extremely well, and Connie hadn't felt so isolated, particularly while Barry had been in America. Having the Dart made commuting to Dublin much easier, especially in the last few years when the patient she'd been nursing had lived very close to a Dart station.

Even though it was now firmly in the commuter belt and new apartments and houses were springing up everywhere, Greystones still retained the village-like atmosphere and friendliness that she'd found when she'd moved there all those years ago.

She lay back and raised her face to the sun. She adored lying in the sun. It relaxed her, calmed her spirit. She hoped it would perform its magic on her today, because her mind was in turmoil, her thoughts racing from Debbie to Barry and back to herself and her own woes.

She wondered had Barry and Aimee made up yet? Who would apologize to whom first? Right now they were possibly cuddling together, discussing Debbie's rudeness. She'd seen the look of disdain on the other woman's face as Debbie had wittered on about 'twiglets'. Why couldn't her daughter have stayed quiet and behaved with some dignity instead of making herself look churlish and infantile? She'd acted just like Melissa on a bad day.

Debbie knew that Connie was pissed off with her. And rightly so. Connie had enough on her plate without worrying about her daughter's bad behaviour. Her eyelids drooped as tiredness swept through her and her body jerked as her muscles began to relax and she fell asleep.

She awoke to find her sister-in-law stretched on the other lounger grinning over at her.

'How you doin', sleepyhead?'

'Karen! How long are you here?' Connie yawned and nearly gave herself lockjaw.

'About twenty minutes. I came in through the side gate because I guessed you'd be out here and you were flakers and I didn't have the heart to wake you up. I know you were up at the crack of dawn.'

'That's for sure.' She struggled up into a sitting position and ran her fingers through her hair. 'What time is it? Tea? Coffee?' She arched an eyebrow at Karen.

Her sister-in-law held up her hand. 'It's quarter to seven. Stay where you are. I brought sustenance with me.' She grinned.

Connie laughed. 'Did you now?'

'Lie back there. I'll be out in a minute,' Karen instructed.

Connie lay back against her cushion. It was lovely being pampered, especially after the day she'd had.

Five minutes later Karen appeared with a tray laden with nibbles. 'We have pâté and crackers, smoked salmon and cream-cheese rolls, chorizo, olives and sun-dried tomatoes, and some fresh crusty bread slathered in butter,' she announced. She laid it down on the table and winked. 'Liquid sustenance on the way, plonk your ass in the chair and tuck in.'

'Thanks, Karen, you're such a pal.' Connie hauled herself up and gave the other woman a hug and was warmly hugged in return.

'You've done it for me many's the time. A nice glass of chilled wine?'

'Why not? I won't be going anywhere tonight.'

'Great. I took the precaution of getting John to drive me over and he'll collect me whenever I ring, being the good husband that he is. So I can join you. Aren't I kind to myself?' She laughed as she went inside to get the glasses and the wine.

'This is lovely and tranquil, Connie, it's a real little oasis of peace. You've done a great job of it,' Karen remarked as she handed her a glass of Chablis a few minutes later.

'I know, I love it myself. But I've no one to share it with.' Connie bit her lip.

'Is that what this is all about?' Karen's grey eyes were kind and understanding.

'Yeah, a bit,' sighed Connie, nibbling on an olive. 'When I saw Barry and Aimee and Melissa in Roly's today, for some un-fathomable reason I felt terribly empty. I never thought I'd end up living on my own. It's been hard getting used to Debbie going. At the back of my mind I suppose I'd always hoped that I would find someone else and have another child with them, and that's not going to happen now.'

'Well, perhaps not the child, but there's nothing to say that you won't meet someone, a gorgeous woman like you. Why wouldn't you?' Karen declared.

'Oh come on, Kar, I'm a middle-aged nurse, who's going to look at me?'

'Now *stop* it. Stop this middle-aged stuff,' Karen rebuked sternly as she bit into a slice of bread and chorizo. 'Why are you thinking of yourself as middle-aged, for crying out loud? What's brought all this on?'

Then it all came pouring out in a torrent of words and emotions as she spoke of her fears, of her loneliness, her worries and guilt about Debbie, her envy of Aimee's youth, her resent-ment of Barry leaving her, which she had thought she'd long put behind her.

'But, honey, why are you surprised to feel like this?' Karen asked when the whole sorry saga was finished. 'Your daughter is getting married; of *course* things are going to surface. Weddings are life-altering occasions. Yours and hers. You're only getting used to living on your own. That's not easy. And Debbie's up to ninety too. You're very hard on yourself. It's only natural that you'd be feeling fragile.'

'I know, but today was dreadful and she *was* rude.'

'Well, it sounds to me that Aimee was *as* rude.'

'That's no excuse. I was raging that she let herself down in front of her.' Connie frowned.

'I know. Even though they're old enough to get married, you

still think of them as children and you want them to be on their best behaviour.'

'Poor old Melissa got a telling-off too, I felt sorry for her. Behind that surly exterior she's a nice enough kid.'

'Aimee was feeling about Melissa the same way you were feeling about Debbie. I'm telling you, kids do it to their mums every time.'

'Yeah, but Debbie's twenty-five. I'm at my wits' end with her, Karen. She's never going to give Barry a break and I feel sorry for him. He doesn't deserve the way she's treating him, in all fairness.' Connie took a slug of her wine.

'She's very stubborn. I won't deny that. But I think the run-up to the wedding's exacerbating everything. She's stressed and she needs to dump on someone and it can't be Bryan and it can't be you, so it's going to be Barry. Things will calm down,' Karen assured her, refilling her glass. 'Look at you today, upset and all in a tizzy, when usually you take things in your stride.'

'I know, but Debbie's stuff is deep and ingrained. I should have been more aware of it, maybe brought her to counselling after we split up or something,' Connie berated herself.

'You did your best and, besides, marriage break-up wasn't as prevalent then as it is now. There wasn't that much in terms of counselling and support to be had. Stop beating up on yourself, it's not deserved, Connie.' Karen leaned across the table and squeezed her hand.

'I'm worried about her. And I'm worried about their marriage. I don't think Bryan's the right one for her. It's all too one-sided. She's the one who does everything. That's all very well now when there's just the two of them, but what happens when children come along? Will he pull his weight then? Or is she going to be left trying to juggle everything while he goes to the races and his art-gallery openings and the likes?' she fretted.

'Connie, you can't spend the rest of your life worrying about them. Let them lead their own lives and you start leading yours. These next few years are going to be all about *you*, and make the most of it. And if you want another relationship – and I think you should try and find someone – go for it,' her sister-in-law counselled. 'Take stock, move on, and try something different. That's what life's all about.'

'If I was ten years younger maybe.' Connie made a face.

'Well, you're not, live with it,' Karen retorted.

'I'm trying to but, cripes, fifty is looming and it scares the hell out of me.'

'Me too! I'm petrified. I keep forgetting things. I can never find my car keys; I forget words in the middle of sentences. My head goes woolly. My eyesight's going, my hair's as grey as a badger behind the hair dye. I have to use KY sometimes. I'm getting those lines around my mouth! Everything's gone south – boobs, ass, belly. Oh God, it's the pits! I keep seeing all these lissom young beauties coming into the house with Jenna, and I hate them, prancing around in their belly tops and short skirts, and I wonder how John can still want to make love to me, and is it just habit or do I still turn him on? And I wonder do these flighty young things realize how lucky they are that they don't wake up with aches everywhere, feeling like old women. They aren't a bit grateful for their youth and their soft, unlined skin. They just take it for granted. And have you noticed, or is it just me, that there's loads of ads about the menopause on the TV these days? I never noticed them before, because they've never been on before. They're just rubbing my nose in it! And what about those ads for over-fifties insurance? Or active friggin' age? That's going to be me in a few years and I just can't believe it . . . See . . .' She grinned. 'I can throw a wobbly and rant away just as good as you can!'

Connie burst out laughing and Karen joined her, guffawing heartily.

'That's *exactly* the way I feel, apart from the making-love bit. When I came home yesterday I went to the alarm panel, saw the numbers and keyed in 1234 and couldn't understand why the alarm wouldn't turn off. I stood in a daze before realizing I hadn't keyed in my code.'

'The joys of getting older! Aimee, eat your heart out,' Karen said wickedly. 'She's having Botox done, I'd swear it.'

'Well, she looks great on it. I wish I had the nerve to do it.'

'Me too, but I'd be petrified to put that poison into my body. Who knows how it's going to affect her in years to come?'

'She looks fantastic though,' Connie said wistfully.

'Yes, she does, but at what cost? Look at poor old Melissa. Aimee's so busy working, and working out, that child gets fed processed foods and fast foods and, as far as I'm concerned, is sadly neglected. I wouldn't dream of letting my kids have satellite TVs and computers in their bedrooms. God knows what she's watching and surfing. She has all the games and the gadgets, the clothes and make-up, but she's one of those kids whose parents are cash-rich and time-poor. We made time for our children, our careers didn't dictate our lives. Aimee and Barry's careers are paramount.'

'I think they're quite strict with her though,' Connie observed.

'When it suits them. I called one evening to leave a birthday present in for Melissa, and she was in that apartment on her own eating a pizza at five o'clock in the afternoon. Aimee was in that posh gym in Dun Laoghaire and Barry wasn't home from work. I think that's appalling. The child should have a decent dinner when she gets home from school.'

'I know, I gave her some new potatoes the other evening when she and Barry called over, and she told me she'd never had them before, they get their mashed potatoes in Marks or the Butler's Pantry. Aimee never cooks, that's why she's a bloody twiglet,' Connie grumbled.

'Lucky wagon.' Karen tucked into crackers and pâté. 'I wish I could get away with that with my crowd.'

'We're bitches, aren't we?' Connie gave a wry smile.

'Yep, jealous bitches, but at least we're honest about it.' Karen giggled. The wine was beginning to hit. 'Here, have another glass?' she held up the wine bottle.

'Just one more, I'm working tomorrow. I don't want to be on the wards with a hangover, that's all I'd need.'

'What are you moaning about? I've to write a report and do a Sunday lunch for two sets of grandparents as well as my gang. I invited them ages ago in a moment of madness. I'm telling you, Connie, don't be too quick to give up your peaceful life.

There's a lot to be said for it,' declared Karen as she topped up their glasses again.

She had a point, Connie admitted. She was feeling better already. Whatever miasma had overcome her earlier was drifting away on the kindness of friendship. Sitting companionably beside Karen in the balmy evening breeze as the sun sank between the trees in a last glorious display, the loneliness that had seemed so all-encompassing earlier lessened, and her angst was almost manageable.

Her sister-in-law's common-sense reassurances eased her worries. She was getting herself into a heap about things she had no control over and there was no point in that. Perhaps tomorrow she might have one last attempt to try and smooth things over with Barry and Debbie. If she could get them sorted she'd feel a huge sense of achievement.

And she'd go into a health store on Monday and buy some supplements and fish-oil tablets in an effort to ward off the worst symptoms of the menopausal tidal wave that was beginning to envelop her whether she liked it or not. She'd start her diet on Monday, she decided as she helped herself to more smoked salmon. This was her last fling. The last supper, so to speak. She might as well enjoy it.

CHAPTER TWELVE

Judith lay in the bath, immersed in bubbles, soaping herself with the small bar of hotel soap. It was after seven and she was ravenously hungry. She had slept until the afternoon and woken up, dazed and disorientated, not having a clue where she was.

Slowly, as she gazed around the hotel bedroom, it all came back to her and she groaned. She still felt sick and her head was pounding, but it was nothing in comparison to the way she'd felt earlier.

She'd struggled off the bed and made herself a cup of tea and eaten a biscuit, and that had helped settle her tummy. Rooting in her bag she'd found a packet of Solpadeine, taken two of them, and had another cup of tea.

She knew she was going to have to go home, but it was comforting to lie on the bed drinking tea, flicking the TV stations aimlessly. Her eyes started to close again and she undressed and got into bed properly and had fallen asleep again. She'd woken around five and lain in her little cocoon, unwilling to get up. Flicking channels again, she found an episode of *Stargate*. Judith lay looking at the ruggedly handsome Colonel Jack O'Neill and felt horny and lonely. Jack O'Neill was her type of man – lean, rangy, strong, with a good heart behind his sardonic exterior. She wouldn't mind a one-night stand with the likes of him.

What was she like? Imagine having sex with a stranger, like

she'd done last night. And what was even worse, having sex and having no memory of it. She hoped she'd enjoyed it, because she could remember nothing of it. From what she'd seen of her sleeping partner, he'd been nothing much to look at. Stocky, bearded and balding. A far cry from the ruggedly handsome colonel on the TV.

It was two years since she'd had anything like a similar episode, although that night she hadn't been so hammered out of her skull that she couldn't remember any of it. It had been on the night of her forty-seventh birthday. She'd been at a reception for a work do and had bumped into an old colleague from a previous workplace who was at a conference in the same hotel. He was one of the systems analysts, a skinny, lanky guy with lemonade-bottle shoulders and greasy hair. He hadn't changed much, just gone grey and puffy-faced, but he'd been pleased to see her and she'd always got on well with him.

She knew she was looking good, in a black velvet cocktail dress that showed off her figure to its optimum. They'd gone into one of the bars and had a drink and she'd caught up with all the gossip. Another couple of drinks had led to the offer of supper, and when he'd suggested going up to his room she hadn't demurred. She knew that he was married and felt a niggle of guilt, but the longing for male contact and intimacy, for however fleeting a moment, had overcome her scruples and she'd been as eager as he was. In the cold light of day she'd felt dismayed at her weakness and disappointed in herself. But when he'd phoned her at work a week later and asked her out for a drink she'd agreed. They'd booked into a room in Jury's Inn on Christchurch Place, but he'd left her at three a.m. with a promise to phone her the following week and she'd lain awake listening to the sounds of the city outside and never felt lonelier.

She'd refused to meet him again. Being alone was easier to live with than having sordid encounters in hotel rooms with a married, middle-aged man who was really only looking for available sex, no matter what way it was dressed up.

Well, she'd really surpassed herself this time, Judith thought grimly, as she watched her hero dive athletically through the stargate and wished she were going with him, away from this nightmare of a life living with her neurotic mother, working in a dead-end job, going on alcohol binges and having sex with strangers.

She'd watched the news, and then hunger had forced her out of bed. A club sandwich was the snack that appealed to her most on the room-service menu, but she knew she had to have a bath before she ordered. She stank to high heaven and she had no robe; she couldn't face getting back into her clothes until she'd washed. Her mother was going to have a hissy fit, but she'd stayed out this long – another couple of hours wouldn't make any difference to the ear-bashing she was inevitably going to have to endure.

The need to eat drove her out of the bath and, wrapped in a skimpy towel, she rang room service to order her meal. She'd hung her blouse and jacket on the shower rail, hoping that the steam of the bath would help shake out the creases and reduce the smell of smoke and BO.

It hadn't made that much difference and she wished she had a robe so that she could eat in comfort. Those clothes were such a reminder of her night of shame. At least she was clean and her hair smelled nice again, she comforted herself as she towelled it to remove the excess water. She was dressed and had her hair blow-dried by the time the young Eastern European waiter knocked on the door. She tipped him and fell on her food, glad that she'd ordered chips on the side.

She ate her dessert, a gooey gateau concoction, and poured her coffee. In a strange way, she'd grown fond of her room; it offered her shelter from her life, and she didn't want to leave. She felt as if she were in a bubble, detached from real life. Once she closed the door behind her, she would be back to its harsh realities. And the first harsh reality she had to face was getting a taxi across town to collect her car from the car park.

Eventually, she could put off the moment no longer, and with a deep sigh of regret she picked up her bag and reluctantly walked out of the room.

*

Lily Baxter's stomach was churning. It was after seven thirty in the evening and she had heard no word from Judith since her short, sharp phone call that morning, and her phone was turned off. Maybe she'd had an accident somewhere, Lily fretted, but surely the guards would have contacted her if that were the case. They'd be able to get her address from her reg. plate.

She wondered should she ring her son or daughter and tell them. But if Judith came home and found out that she'd phoned the other two wondering what to do, she'd be as mad as hell and there'd be a row.

Lily twisted her wedding band around her finger. 'Oh Ted, Ted, where are you when I need you? What did you leave me for?' she asked in her oft-repeated refrain. She was too tense to eat; she'd managed a few crackers around four thirty but hadn't bothered to cook a dinner.

Maybe Judith was looking at a flat with her friend. Maybe she'd had enough and was going to move out. Lily's heart started to race in panic. 'Don't get into a fluster,' she whispered, rooting around in her paper rack for her Oxendale's catalogue. She liked flicking through it. It was a lifesaver for her. She could buy all her clothes without having to step foot outside the door.

She turned the pages, but she found it hard to concentrate and her gaze kept swivelling between the clock on the mantelpiece and the road outside. Every time she'd hear a car her heart would leap, only to sink in disappointment when it wasn't Judith's.

She nearly jumped out of her skin when the phone rang. A wave of relief swept through her when she heard her daughter's voice. 'I'm on my way home. Have you eaten?' Judith asked, as if everything were normal.

'Of course I haven't,' snapped Lily. If Judith was pretending everything *was* normal, so would she. 'I was waiting for you to come home to see what you wanted.'

'I've eaten. Would you like a snack box or Chinese?' came the curt response.

'A snack box, please, and get a litre of milk while you're at it, we're running low.'

'Right.' The phone went dead, and Lily's mouth thinned. Not a word of explanation. The cheek of her, putting her mother through such a torment of a day. Well, she'd get a fine lecture for herself, Lily decided as she hurried out to the kitchen to set a place at the table and to warm her plate in the oven.

Twenty minutes later she heard Judith's key in the door, and the smell of chips wafted into the kitchen. She composed her features in a stern expression, lips pursed, eyes narrowed. If Judith thought she'd got away with this carry-on she'd do it again, and Lily's nerves just wouldn't stand it.

'Well, you're a fine one.' Lily launched into her attack immediately, taking the brown bag and the milk from her daughter and glaring at her. 'What sort of a way is this to treat me? Ringing me in the morning after staying out all night, telling me you'd be home later and then not arriving until this hour of the evening? You should be ashamed of yourself. Ill-considerate and ill-mannered was not the way you were reared.'

'Mother, eat your chicken and chips and don't annoy me. I'm not feeling well, I'm going to bed,' Judith growled and marched out of the kitchen, leaving Lily with her mouth open.

What was wrong with her? She looked very pale. And what was she wearing her sunglasses for at that hour of the evening? Maybe she had a migraine. That must be it. Sometimes, three or four times a year, Judith would get a headache that would force her to stay in bed it would be so sickening.

Lily hoped that was it. But she wasn't sure. She was uneasy. She gazed out at their small back garden. Clematis tumbled riotously along the back wall that divided their garden from their neighbours'. A marmalade tabby sat staring at her with half-slitted eyes. She hated cats. Sneaky creatures slinking around.

'Get out of it.' She shook her fist angrily, but the cat ignored her and began to wash his face. More disrespect, came the irrational thought. Was there no respite for her? Lily thought wearily as she ate her dinner alone at the kitchen table.

That hadn't been too difficult, Judith decided as she undressed and rolled the clothes she'd been wearing into a bundle. She'd never wear them again. She didn't want to be reminded of the lowest point yet she'd sunk to in her miserable failure of a life.

She sat on her bed and rubbed her temples. The headache was still there, dull and aching. She'd tell her mother she'd had one of her migraines and couldn't drive. She'd seen the pinched look of worry and apprehension in her mother's face and eyes. It had been cruel, she supposed, to leave her worrying all day. But she wasn't a ten-year-old. She was a grown woman. She should be able to come and go as she pleased, she thought resentfully, feeling the bars of her prison closing in on her again.

The evening light had softened and the last rays of the sun slanted in through the top left-hand corner of the window. She had the back room and it faced west so she always got the evening sun. It was a soothing room, papered and painted in shades of ochre and buttery cream. Her wardrobe, chest of drawers and dressing table were cream and nothing was out of place. She had no ornaments or trinkets on view, just a jewellery box on the dressing table and a small TV on the chest of drawers, where she could escape from her mother's interminable soaps and quizzes.

One thing Judith could not stand was clutter. Her mother drove her mad with all the knick-knacks and bits and bobs she surrounded herself with. Her bedroom and sitting room had no surface uncovered, no order or clean lines, just disorder, un-tidiness and confusion. They were so different in taste and personality. Judith was more like her father. The strong depend-able type, she thought gloomily, wishing that she'd been born feckless and irresponsible.

The rays began to diminish and fade as she lay against the pillows, worn out and disheartened. When she was a child she'd always liked watching the sun's progress around her room in the evening, seeing the beams on the wall opposite the window get smaller and smaller as the shadows of dusk encroached.

Today's dimming sunset was a metaphor for her life the way it was now, she supposed. Middle age was encroaching rapidly, and what had she to show for her life before old age diminished her completely? Very little. She didn't even own her own house. She felt so restless and stifled and tied down. A prisoner to her mother's neurosis. If only she'd had the guts to walk away all those years ago. Her mother would have had to learn to cope and it probably would have been a greater kindness to her. Bitterness rose in her. Her sister and brother had abandoned her to her fate with little concern or kindness. They were practically strangers to her now, apart from their occasional visits. They never rang her and she never rang them. She wasn't close to her nieces and nephews. She didn't buy gifts for them at Christmas and birthdays, nor they for her. She was quite alone really, when she thought about it. Her chance to have children and a family life of her own was gone; she was past her sell-by date for sure in that department. And what man would ever want her now? He'd be taking on her mother as well, and no man was ever going to be interested enough in her to do that. If it hadn't happened in her late thirties early forties, she may as well stop daydreaming about it. She had as much chance of getting a man as she had of Col. Jack O'Neill knocking on her front door. She was on her own and that was the be all and end all of the matter.

Judith started to cry, great gulping sobs that she hastily stifled in her pillow in case her mother heard.

'You're very late getting home, miss,' Aimee snapped as Melissa sauntered through the door.

'It's only nine o'clock and it's Saturday night. All my friends are allowed stay out until eleven,' her daughter retorted sulkily.

'And don't back-cheek me either, we had enough of that at lunch today. That was a fine performance you put on in front of Debbie and Connie. I was mortified. Your father and I didn't raise you to be bad-mannered.'

'Oh, for God's sake, Mom, give me a break. I was only texting, not belching or farting. Get real! You're doing my head in.' Melissa glowered at her mother, stung by her criticism.

'Go to your room.' Aimee's eyes flashed with anger as she pointed an elegant, manicured finger towards the door.

'Well, I'd prefer to be there on my own than here with you,' Melissa said rudely, stalking off.

Aimee was furious. That young madam was getting her pocket money docked for her attitude, she decided as she walked out to the kitchen and poured herself a glass of wine. She took it out on to the balcony and sat on her lounger. Dusk was settling, and in the distance the lights of Howth and Dublin Bay began to twinkle and shimmer.

She wrapped a pashmina around her arms and shoulders. The night air had cooled and, even though it was still balmy, she didn't want to catch a chill. She needed to be at her peak for the next few weeks. She had a very important wedding coming up. The *crème de la crème* of Irish society was going to be there, and both she and the wedding planner were in constant contact. She was seeing more of him than her own family lately. She smiled at the irony of it. The wedding she was catering for was of far more concern to her than her step-daughter's, if only Barry knew it. A ship sailing out to sea from Dublin glided serenely across the flat, calm sea, and for a moment she wished she were on it.

She felt far from serene as she sipped the chilled wine. Melissa was beginning to get terribly cheeky ever since she'd started secondary school, and Aimee didn't like it one bit. This summer coming was worrying her. A childminder had taken care of their daughter until she had left primary school, picking her up from school and bringing her to her house until either she or Barry had collected her. This year Melissa had begged them to let her stay at home on her own for the summer holidays. She was thirteen, she was old enough, she'd assured them but, nevertheless, Aimee felt apprehensive.

Barry had agreed after much pleading and begging but, then, their daughter was able to wrap him around her little finger, and he could rarely say no to her. That was all very well, but it usually meant that it was Aimee who had to lay down the law and then suffer the backlash of resentment. They had set strict rules. Only Sarah and her other friend, Clara, were allowed to visit the apartment. One misdemeanour would be one too many and they would be reviewing the position, she'd been warned.

Aimee's mobile rang and she groaned as she recognized the number. It was Gwen Larkin, a friend of hers whom she hadn't been in touch with for ages. She kept meaning to ring her, but she was so busy these days, she had to prioritize. Gwen was very good for keeping in touch. If it had been left to Aimee, the friendship would have fizzled out long ago, she thought guiltily.

'Hi.' She put on her bright, breezy voice. 'I've been meaning to ring for ages. I'm just up to my eyes, you know how it is?'

'I'd probably faint if I got a phone call from you,' the other woman retorted, but Aimee knew she was smiling.

'So! What's happening?' She settled back on her lounger, ready for a chat; she'd nothing better to do so it would be nice to gossip and catch up.

'This is a quickie, actually,' her friend informed her, and Aimee felt a little put out. 'Ellie is home from Australia for a couple of weeks and a few of the girls were planning a farewell lunch on Tuesday. We wondered if you'd be able to come.'

'Oh, I didn't know she was home. No one told me,' Aimee said in dismay.

'Oh! Right! You see, we all met up and went for coffee after Kim's mother's funeral, and Kim told us she was coming home, so most of us have seen her, but you'll see her if you can come to lunch. I know it's short notice, but she went to stay with her sister in Kilkenny for a few days and we weren't sure when she was coming back,' Gwen informed her cheerfully.

Aimee knew in her heart and soul that none of them expected her to go to the lunch and that phoning her had been an afterthought. 'Where is it?' she asked casually.

'One p.m. in Bianconi's on the Merrion Road, opposite Vincent's Hospital. There's a car park in the grounds of the church beside it. Parking in town is so horrific we decided against meeting up there.'

'Just let me check my BlackBerry – I'll call you back in five minutes,' said Aimee briskly.

'Talk to you then,' the other woman agreed and hung up.

Aimee hurried into her bedroom, which was also accessible from the balcony, and scrolled through her BlackBerry. She had meetings at ten and eleven thirty. She could make the lunch at a push if she really wanted to. She dithered. She hadn't gone to Kim Lynch's mother's funeral. She hadn't even sent the girl a Mass card. That was going to be awkward. She could always pretend that she hadn't got the text about it. Aimee sighed, irritated. She had enough on her mind without having to worry about making excuses about a funeral she hadn't had time to attend.

But it would be a good opportunity to catch up with her college group. It would take the pressure off for a while about meeting them for coffee or drinks. A sop to friendship, she thought, realizing how cynical and detached Gwen would think her if her friend knew how her mind was working.

Did none of them realize how busy she was? Did they think she had time to be sitting at her computer answering emails or texts? Some of them regularly met up to go to a film and have a meal afterwards. She'd gone once, but the film had bored her and she'd stopped concentrating on it and had spent the remainder of the film planning a Holy Communion brunch she'd been asked to organize. She hadn't gone to any more film nights and eventually they stopped sending her the emails about them and she'd been relieved at not having to make any more excuses.

Should she go to the lunch? Could she afford the time? It would be nice to see Ellie again though. She'd always got on well with her. Impulsively, she picked up the phone and dialled Gwen's number.

'Hi, I might be a few minutes late but count me in,' she declared gaily.

'Am I hearing right?' Gwen teased. 'I think I *am* going to faint.'

'Stop,' Aimee warned. 'So what's the news? What's happening?'

'Sorry, don't have time to chat, I'm on my way out the door. Tony and I are meeting Kim and Richard in the Four Seasons and we're late. I'll see you at lunch and we'll catch up then. Byeee,' Gwen said cheerily and hung up.

'Oh!' Aimee stared at the phone; usually Gwen would have loads of gossip for her. She wasn't used to being given the brush-off. So they were all off to the Ice Bar in the Four Seasons, and Gwen hadn't even asked if she and Barry would like to come. They really were out of that loop, she thought, a tad miffed. Gwen had always been the one urging her to come and meet up with the others, and even she hadn't bothered this evening. Maybe it was time to make a bit more of an effort. Gwen was a good friend. Aimee always enjoyed telling her about work. Her friend was a stay-at-home mother, one of the reasons she had so much time on her hands to be texting and emailing. Aimee knew her friend was impressed by her high-powered career. It always made Aimee feel good to tell her about her achievements, and Gwen was always encouraging and lavish in her praise. Aimee would have enjoyed telling her about the O'Leary/Weldon wedding.

She went back out to the balcony feeling unaccountably grumpy and dissatisfied. It was dark now and Aimee noticed that Melissa's curtains were drawn. Her daughter hadn't even bothered to say goodnight.

It was a pity Barry hadn't witnessed her display of cheek earlier. It would be good to have more back-up from him some-times. And she certainly hadn't had much of that today, she thought sourly.

He'd had to go to a function and, because she was annoyed with him, she hadn't accompanied him. She'd phoned the babysitter and cancelled her, telling her husband that she was going to have an early night.

'Suit yourself,' he'd said coolly, but he'd been displeased. She knew by the jut of his jaw and the grim expression on his face. Well, let him be annoyed. Support worked both ways. It was quid pro quo. And she'd be telling him again in no uncertain terms before the weekend was out what she felt.

Aimee stared out to sea. Her daughter wasn't talking to her, her husband was off enjoying himself, her friends were out socializing and she was sitting alone on her lounger sipping luke-warm Chardonnay. A great way to spend a Saturday night, she thought morosely as she picked up her BlackBerry and began to fire off emails to her secretary concerning the forthcoming high-society wedding.

Bryan stepped back from the heaving mass that erupted out of the Dart, as he stood on the platform in Tara Street waiting to board. He was slightly apprehensive about going home. He hadn't heard from Debbie since she'd raced off in tears hours ago when he'd suggested calling off the wedding. He felt a bit of a heel. He should have phoned her at least, but he just couldn't face the hassle of it. Weeping women made him uncomfortable.

He'd felt mean after Debbie had gone but he didn't want to go home himself so he'd hooked up with a few friends and they'd rambled around the galleries in Temple Bar before heading to the IFC for coffee and to see what films were showing.

'Where's Debbs? Is she coming in later?' one of the girls had asked and he'd suddenly felt a spasm of guilt. His fiancée was probably at home crying her eyes out. She was such a softie really, and she'd been terribly hurt. He'd seen the pain and fear in her eyes when he'd landed his bombshell suggestion on her.

'No, we're going to work on the spare room tonight, decorating stuff,' he'd heard himself saying. 'I'm going to head off – enjoy the film, you guys.'

They'd bid him goodbye and disappeared into the weaving throng of film-goers that flocked through the foyer and long narrow corridor and he'd made his way outside. He'd inhaled the cool breeze, which was a respite after the stuffy heat of the film centre. On impulse he'd phoned Debbie's mobile to tell her that he was on his way home, but she hadn't answered. He'd dialled their landline, but it had gone straight to the answering machine. Apprehensiveness enveloped him and, as he waited impatiently to get on to the Dart, he took out his phone and dialled her number again. Still no answer. Perhaps she'd gone home to Connie, or to see Jenna, her cousin, who was going to be her bridesmaid. She was probably crying on Jenna's shoulder right now.

Again he felt bad. Not because he'd suggested calling off the wedding – he still thought it was a good idea – but he should have gone after her when she grabbed the keys and hurried off. He should have told her that he loved her and always would. He could have been more sensitive to her feelings.

Bryan sighed as he slumped down on to a seat and gazed unseeingly out the window as the apartments and houses became a blur as the train picked up speed. Dusk was falling. He hadn't realized it was so late. He felt impatient each time the train came into a station. The journey seemed to be taking for ever, even though it was a relatively short one of a half a dozen stops or so. He walked fast from the Dart station, anxious to make amends. At least to reassure his fiancée that he loved her. He felt uneasy. It wasn't like her not to answer her phone. He turned the corner into their small cul-de-sac and saw that the car wasn't in their parking space. Where had she gone? he wondered as he put his key in the lock.

His stomach lurched at the sight that met him. His big sports bag was packed at the bottom of the stairs and there was a note on the hall table, folded over with his name scrawled on it.

She was kicking him out! Bryan shook his head in disbelief. She had one bag packed for him and a note to tell him to go with no discussion whatsoever. That was a bit bloody high-handed. He couldn't believe it. Now there was going to be a whole big thing about selling the house and each of them getting their share, and he was going to have to find somewhere else to live.

He looked around the hall and saw the scuffmarks on the wallpaper, at buggy level, which had pissed her off; she'd planned on painting the hall cream and pale green, and he'd liked that colour scheme. It was elegant and tasteful. And now it wasn't going to happen. He could see into the kitchen through the half-open door. Everything was tidied away. Even the fruit bowl on the middle of the table was empty, and he was generally the one who ate fruit. His eating habits were much healthier than hers. If she'd thrown out the fruit, she definitely wasn't expecting him to be eating at home. He could see a bulging black sack ready for the bin by the back door. Was she getting ready for house buyers to come and view already? God, she didn't waste much time! Was this what was meant by the old saying 'Hell hath no fury like a woman scorned'? It looked like she was going to make him pay . . . big time.

Bryan felt a deep sense of dread as he viewed his bag lying at the bottom of the stairs. His hand was shaking as he picked up the note and read what Debbie had written.

Chapter Thirteen

'Morning.'

'Morning.'

'What do you want to do today?' Barry looked over at his wife, who was reading a report on the other side of their super-kingsize bed.

'I'm not fussy. I've to work on this.' She waved the papers at him.

'You missed a good night last night.' He yawned and rubbed his stubbly jaw.

'Barry, I need to discuss something with you, and I'm not going to spend the day skirting around it. I know we spoke briefly about it, but I want it sorted.' Aimee sat up, her hair tumbling over her shoulders.

'Fair enough,' Barry said warily. He knew what was coming. He knew that Aimee was not going to let yesterday's lunch fiasco go without sorting it to her satisfaction. It was one of the things he admired about her. When she had something to say she said it straight out, no matter how unpalatable. And then, when it was sorted, she'd forget it and move on. No emotional dramas. No silent, bubbling resentments. It was much less wearing on the nerves, even if the going was rough for an hour or so. He sat up and leaned back against the pillows and waited for her to offload.

'I told you that I felt you could have supported me at yesterday's lunch,' she said bluntly, 'but I don't think you really took it on board. You could have spoken to Melissa earlier than you did, and backed me up *immediately* she didn't do as I asked. And you certainly shouldn't have let Debbie speak to me the way she did. It was the height of rudeness, and you just sat there and let her insult me. Whether she likes it or not, I *am* your wife and I'm entitled to respect.' She eyeballed him, her chin up, her shoulders squared.

'Well, again I'm saying, I think you went over the top with Melissa, frankly, and I *did* tell her to do what you asked. And as regards Debbie . . . if you don't mind my saying so, you started it by commenting on what she was eating. It was none of your business. I could see why she responded the way she did to what she considered rude. I didn't like what she said. It was childish and silly, but I could see where she was coming from.' He was equally blunt.

His response took her aback. He could see the surprise in her eyes. She stared at him, her eyes cold. 'You know something, Barry? That hurts. And you know something else? She doesn't want me or Melissa at the wedding. Well, Melissa can make up her own mind, but I've decided I'm not going. You'll be perfectly fine without me. I'm sure Connie will take care of you, no problem.' She flung back the duvet and got out of bed.

'Connie's not my wife, you are, Aimee. And if you don't want to be at my side at my daughter's wedding, there's not much I can do about it. But support works both ways and, if you expect it from me, I also expect it from you.' He got out of bed and walked into the ensuite after her.

'Fine, Barry, we both know where we stand.' She kept her back to him.

'So are you coming to the wedding?' he demanded.

'No!' Aimee turned and shook her head. 'What's the point? The only person who wants me there is you.'

'Well, that should be enough for you then,' he retorted, turning on his heel and marching out, slamming the door behind him as he went.

Aimee stared at herself in the mirror. Some very fine lines

were beginning to cobweb around her eyes, and the lines around her mouth were deepening. Probably because she was scowling, she thought crossly as she smoothed some replenishing cream on to her face. She needed to book another Botox treatment. She should pencil it in before the O'Leary wedding so she'd look her best for the biggest event her firm had ever had on its books.

This damn wedding of Debbie's was causing nothing but trouble. Why Barry wanted her to go was beyond her comprehension. Well, she wasn't some trophy wife to be trailed along and trotted out. She was her own woman, and he knew that. He needn't go trying to get her to change her mind with emotional blackmail because it didn't work on her. She'd made her decision. She wasn't going to that bloody wedding and if he didn't like it he could get over himself.

Barry ran the electric razor over his jaw, furious with his wife. The one thing that he wanted – for her and Melissa to be at his side at Debbie's wedding – was increasingly unlikely to happen. She'd turned him down yet again. It was happening more and more often these days. Last night had been an important social function for the company. All the other executives were there with their wives and he'd stuck out like a bloody sore thumb. Now it was going to be the same at Debbie's wedding. Had she no loyalty? Why did she always have to put herself first? Just because he hadn't let her get away with her behaviour yesterday, she was punishing him. As if he were some kind of child, not her husband, her equal partner.

Aimee could be incredibly stubborn sometimes, and nothing that he could say or do would change her mind. It used to be a trait that he found attractive, once, but now it was becoming irritating and off-putting. He valued loyalty. It was a great quality to have in a relationship. Connie had never badmouthed him to Debbie and had always stood up for him as a father. How ironic that his ex-wife was showing him more loyalty right now than his current wife was. What did that say about the state of their marriage? he thought despondently as he walked down the hall to the main bathroom to take a shower, unwilling to use the ensuite while Aimee was in the bedroom.

'Yikes! These cobbles are hard on the feet,' Debbie moaned as she walked across Dam Square with her fiancé.

'I can't believe we're in Amsterdam. I can't believe that you organized this trip so fast. You're some woman!' Bryan exclaimed delightedly, lifting her up in the air and kissing her.

'Let me down,' she squealed. But she was beaming from ear to ear.

'I swear to God I thought you were throwing me out.' He laughed, putting her down and slipping an arm around her shoulder. 'When I came home and saw that bag at the end of the stairs and saw the note on the hall table, I sure did think I was a goner.'

'You nearly were.' She grinned. 'But what the hell? I'd never have as much fun with anyone else.'

'When I read the note and found out that you'd booked us a cheapie flight to Amsterdam and that we had to be at the airport at four a.m., you could have knocked me down with a feather. I was gobsmacked. I can't believe we're here,' he repeated.

'Well, believe it,' she said as they stopped to let a tram pass. 'We're young, free and in Amsterdam on a sunny Sunday morning, and I'm dying for a cup of coffee.'

'And maybe something else,' Bryan grinned, looking forward to a hash brownie. Two hours later, stoned and woozy, they fell into their hotel bed for a nap, giggling and laughing as all the stresses and strains of the past few months slipped away and they fell asleep, arms entwined.

They woke up late in the afternoon and made love, happy to be together with two more full days stretching out ahead of them like an oasis, cocooning them from real life and all its problems.

'What made you book this? We can't really afford it . . .' Bryan raised himself on his elbow and looked down at his girlfriend.

Debbie reached up an arm and stroked his cheek tenderly. 'Well, first of all I was going to throw your ring back at you and tell you to get lost, and then, when I calmed down, I realized that what you said was true. There was no joy in it, it was all hassle, and we weren't having fun any more. I'm sorry, Bryan, I didn't mean to be such a drag. It all got to me.'

He leaned over and kissed her. 'And I'm sorry too. I know I could help more around the place. I know you only want the best for us. It's our home, and I want it to be nice too. And I'm sorry about yesterday, about the way I suggested calling off the wedding. It was insensitive of me. You know I love you more than anything and I *do* want to marry you, I just want it to be a good time for us.'

'I know that.' She smiled happily, snuggling into him, mightily relieved that all was well between them and that they were back on an even keel as a couple. The wedding wasn't the most important thing about their relationship, she acknowledged as she traced her fingers along his hip. This . . . togetherness . . . was what was important and if they never got married she didn't care, as long as they didn't lose what they had right now.

Later, they showered and dressed and went strolling around the buzzing, vibrant square, exploring side streets until they found a little restaurant beside one of the canal bridges. They sat outside and ordered their meal and, watching Bryan, relaxed and smiling across the table, Debbie knew that her instincts had been right. Her fiancé didn't respond well to arguments and hassle. He hated confrontation. She knew him so well. Bryan could bury his head in the sand better than anyone she knew, she thought fondly as she sipped her red wine and nibbled at the bread and olives on the table in front of her.

A couple sat down at the table next to them; they were bleary-eyed and stoned. Although she and Bryan had enjoyed their hash brownie, they'd decided they didn't want to spend their time in Amsterdam in a drugged haze or pissed out of their skulls. It would be a complete waste of money. Tomorrow they were going to explore, visit some art galleries, take a trip on the canals, visit Anne Frank's house. The options were endless. It was going to cost money they could ill afford but, if the wedding was off, it wouldn't be such a problem.

Bryan smiled at her and reached across the table and took her hand. 'I'm having a ball. Thanks so much, Debbs, you're the best.' He squeezed her hand tightly and Debbie squeezed back happily.

She'd chosen the right path to go down. Had she gone down the road of resentment and anger, which had been her first reaction, she wouldn't be sitting here with him, happier than she'd been in a long, long time. He was happy too, full of enthusiasm for making the most of their stay in Amsterdam.

A thought struck her. It was the road of resentment and anger that had led to a dangerous crack in their relationship. It was because of those negative emotions she felt towards her father that she'd lost sight of what their wedding should be. Her mother was right: she needed to move on and let go or she'd never be happy. It was time to sort things out with her father. Time to forgive and forget. She couldn't run away from it for ever.

'You're where?' Connie couldn't believe her ears. When she'd called Debbie's mobile and heard the unfamiliar tone, she'd thought something was wrong with the phone. 'You're in Amsterdam! When did you decide this? You never said anything.

'Spur of the moment,' she echoed. 'Right. Well, enjoy yourselves. Call me when you get home, OK?' Connie shook her head in disbelief as she hung up. Debbie and Bryan were in Amsterdam on a mini break, a month before their wedding. It was crazy. Irresponsible to be getting into even more debt. She wasn't going to tell Barry – he'd explode, and rightly so. Weddings were so expensive these days, the least they could do was to share the financial burden as much as they could. Even with cheap flights and accommodation, breaks to Europe cost money, money Debbie and Bryan didn't have. There was no point in talking to them. Why was she sitting worrying about them? she thought crossly as she plugged in the iron to press her uniform. Karen was right. It was time to start living her own life.

CHAPTER FOURTEEN

Judith sat at her desk, shuffling papers in front of her. It was a wet Monday morning, after the sunny weather of the previous day. She'd wanted to cry coming into work this morning. The same familiar grind, the same faces, the same old, same old. The week stretched out like an eternity ahead of her.

A sheet of paper caught her eye. It was Debbie Adams' yearly assessment form – dependent on which was her increment. Madam Adams hadn't appeared yet. She was half an hour late. Judith ticked the box marked 'poor' on the form beside the question about her punctuality.

Her phone rang. A man's voice came down the line. 'This is Bryan Kinsella, Debbie Adams' fiancé. Debbie won't be in today or tomorrow; she has a bug. She'll be back Wednesday if she's OK.'

Judith wasn't sure, but she thought she heard a giggle in the background.

'Fine,' she snapped. 'Thank you for calling.'

'You're welcome,' he said politely and, this time, Judith knew she wasn't imagining things. There was definitely a woman giggling in the background.

'Poor', she ticked in the box marked attendance. If Debbie Adams thought she was going to get an increase in salary this year, she had another think coming. The day dragged on and sheets of rain battered her office window, making her feel even gloomier.

She wondered where Debbie and her fiancé were, probably stuck in bed, at it like rabbits. She no more had a bug than the man in the moon. Judith felt a surge of irrational hatred for the younger woman but, with an enormous effort, she dragged her concentration back to the stack of files on her desk that needed her attention.

Tuesday was no better. It had been an effort to crawl out of bed and get ready for work. Her heart was heavy as she stepped into the crowded lift and pressed the button for her floor. Debbie Adams' empty desk mocked her. A peach mini-rose plant bloomed gloriously on her desk and a photo of a tall, handsome young man sat beside it. Her fiancé, no doubt. A calendar of love poems hung from her noticeboard. How soppy, thought Judith with a sneer of derision. The desk appeared messy with all the personal bits and pieces. There was too much to divert attention from work. What was the little liar doing today? she wondered nastily as she let herself into her office. The smirk would be swiftly removed from her face when she discovered that she was not going to get her increment.

Loneliness enveloped Judith as she closed the door behind her. Her own desk was immaculate but impersonal. Sterile even. Not for her plants and photos of lovers or children, which some of the other women decorated their desks with. Well, she had neither, she thought with a wave of sadness. Unaccountably, Judith felt close to tears. She swallowed hard as two big ones plopped on to the desk. Frantically, she blew her nose and tried to compose herself. What on earth was wrong with her? Why were her emotions in such upheaval? Why was she so weepy, she who rarely cried? It had to be hormonal, menopausal stuff, Judith rationalized as she stood up and stared out the window. Ever since her one-night-stand she'd been weeping like a willow.

She should go and see a doctor, go on HRT or something. Was it her hormones or something much deeper in her psyche? What could lift the shroud of gloom and depression she felt so mired in these days? What could take away that awful, heavy, anxious dread that seemed permanently lodged in her stomach? Would tranquillizers take the edge off the restlessness she felt? Was she heading for a nervous breakdown? she wondered wildly. She'd heard that the Change could do strange things to women, make them depressed and anxious. That was exactly how she felt, she thought with rising panic. Maybe she was more like her mother than she knew. Fear seized her. *That* thought was scary. She studied the big plate window with the side opening. Would it hurt much if she jumped? she wondered recklessly.

'Get a grip on yourself,' she muttered. Imagine if someone walked into the office and saw her in this state? It would be around the building like wildfire that Judith Baxter was cracking up.

Aimee could hear the laughter as she pushed open the door to Bianconi's, and then she saw them right at the back, seated at a round table, laughing uproariously. How very girly, Aimee thought irritably. Two sharp-suited businessmen nearby turned to look at them. No wonder women got a bad name, she reflected as she made her way past the counter filled with luscious goodies, down to the table at the back wall, her high heels click-clacking against the wooden floor.

She remembered being at a working lunch with a group of businessmen, once, and a party of women beside them had drunk bottles of champagne and got louder and louder as their meal progressed. 'Silly wimmen talking about silly wimmen's stuff,' her florid-faced, pinstriped table companion had remarked scathingly. No doubt these two suits were thinking along the same lines.

'Here's Aimee,' she heard Gwen say, and they all turned to wave at her. Ellie jumped out of her chair and hugged her.

'Hi, long time no see – you're looking terrific,' her old friend remarked admiringly, looking her up and down.

'Thanks. You look pretty good yourself.' Aimee smiled, hugging her back. The other woman looked tanned and healthy, and she'd cut her long, black hair and wore it short and feathery. 'The hair suits you.'

'Do you think? I do so much surfing and watersports it's just easier to manage,' Ellie explained as she sat back down.

'Hi, you guys.' Aimee greeted the other two women at the table, and sat down in the empty chair beside Gwen.

'Well, we're honoured,' Sally, another friend, teased. 'You were able to fit us in.'

'Ah, stop it,' Aimee retorted. She gave a double take. 'You're pregnant!' she said accusingly. 'You never told me.'

'Well, you're always so busy these days. I'd never ring you at work now; I gave it up as a bad job. You're always at meetings or out of the office,' Sally responded lightly, buttering a piece of walnut bread.

'Ring me at home then.'

'I did a few times and you weren't there.'

'I do travel a fair bit,' Aimee said defensively. 'How far along are you?' She changed the subject briskly.

'Twenty-six weeks, but who's counting?' Sally grinned.

'Well, rather you than me, but I know you're happy about it. You're glowing.' Aimee shook out her napkin. 'Where's Kim and Jill?' She looked around the table.

'Kim's little one's got a tummy bug so she had to cancel. And Jill's in the loo,' Gwen informed her.

'Aw, that's a shame,' Aimee murmured, but secretly she was relieved. She had been dreading the awkward moment of offering her sympathy on the death of the other woman's mother.

'What are you having to drink? We've cracked open a bottle of Veuve Clicquot.' Gwen waved a half-full champagne flute at her.

'Better not – I'm driving,' Aimee demurred.

'Aw, Aimee,' Ellie remonstrated. 'It's our girls' lunch. God knows when we'll have another one.'

'Well, maybe half a glass, then. Have you ordered?'

'No, we waited for you.' Gwen handed her a menu. 'The basil mash is very tasty, and they've got the monkfish wrapped in Parma ham on today, that's lovely as well, if you want to go for a fish dish.'

'Hmmm.' Aimee gave it a quick glance. 'A Caesar salad with

dressing on the side for me,' she said, ordering her usual. She wasn't into fish and pasta was too fattening.

'Are you having a starter?'

'Is everyone else?' She looked around the table, hoping the answer was no.

'Of course,' said Sally. 'And dessert . . . some of us don't get out to lunch as often as others, you know.'

Was it her imagination or was Sally needling her a bit? Aimee wondered.

'*Definitely* dessert. The florentines here are to die for,' Gwen agreed emphatically, and the others laughed. Aimee's heart sank. It was clear they were here for the long haul.

'Fine, I'll have the soup,' she said crisply. She had no intention of staying for dessert. A two-course lunch in the middle of a working day was long enough for anyone. Gwen and Ellie wouldn't be in that much of a rush, granted, but Sally worked in a busy architectural office. Surely she had to get back to work.

'Are you taking a long lunch?' Aimee asked her, nibbling on a bread stick.

'I had to go for a check-up this morning, which was very convenient timing, so I rang them at work and said there were delays and I'd be back late,' Sally replied nonchalantly.

Typical, thought Aimee, disgusted. No wonder Sally had never progressed beyond being a secretary/receptionist with a work ethic like that. She had barely scraped through her exams at college and had been far more concerned with finding a husband than climbing up the career ladder.

'Hello, stranger,' a voice behind her said, and Aimee turned to find a tall, leggy brunette looking down at her.

'Hey, Jill, what happened to you?' she exclaimed, seeing the other woman's arm in plaster and a sling.

'Had a collision with an over-eager defender on the basketball court,' Jill said wryly.

'You're not still playing basketball!'

'Of course I am.' Jill eased herself into her seat. 'Have to keep fit somehow.'

'I can think of easier ways. So you can't drive. How are you managing?'

'With great difficulty.' Jill made a face. 'At least I can work from home a lot, and Gwen and Sally have been great, ferrying me around. It's true what they say about a friend in need. I'd be lost without them.' She smiled affectionately at Sally and Gwen.

'And what about Bob?' Aimee looked at her in surprise, wondering why she'd be so dependent on the girls.

'We've split up.' Jill shrugged. 'I found out he was seeing someone else on the side, so I kicked him out.'

'Oh . . . oh . . . I didn't know. I'm sorry,' Aimee murmured, thinking it strange that Gwen hadn't told her. 'Did it happen recently?'

'About three months ago. Crap timing.' She pointed to her arm.

'Umm. Tough,' Aimee said sympathetically, thinking that, apart from the quick call to arrange the lunch, it had been at least three months since she'd spoken to Gwen, so no wonder she didn't know.

'Yeah, but tell her about the gorgeous referee that took you to the hospital,' Sally urged wickedly.

'Look, will you give over about that.' Jill threw her eyes up to heaven.

'Well, you know the old saying . . . To get over someone you have to get under someone else,' Sally said matter-of-factly.

They all hooted with laughter but, as the conversation ebbed and flowed between them, Aimee realized with a sense of dismay that she had little in common with her old friends now. Men, children, family were their main concerns; there was little about their careers. They'd listened to her talk about the big wedding she was working on and shown interest but soon the conversation drifted back to Jill's search for the perfect relationship.

What was wrong with her? She was a high-achieving, intelligent, smart woman. She ran her own successful au pair agency, owned her own house, drove a BMW convertible and felt a complete failure because some idiot of a man had broken her heart and left her feeling inadequate and, even worse, living on her own.

Sometimes female stupidity irritated the hell out of her, Aimee thought, eating a crunchy crouton and listening to Sally advising her friend to accept the hunky referee's invitation to dinner.

Aimee would never, *ever* let a man bring her down. She loved Barry, but he wasn't the be all and end all of her life, that was for sure. Even Ellie had given up a promising career as a caterer to follow her boyfriend to Australia. Sally had been in the same job for the past three years and wasn't the slightest bit interested in progressing. Gwen was content to live off her husband's salary and raise her children.

Aimee knew she'd never be able to exist without her own salary. Her independence meant everything to her. Jill was the one she would have most in common with but, having heard her moaning and whingeing about her broken heart, she couldn't help but feel a tad contemptuous. She listened to her friends swapping tips on interior decorating and her thoughts drifted. The cream, gold and crimson colours in the restaurant worked very well, she thought idly, studying her surroundings while keeping one ear on the conversation. It was a somewhat similar colour scheme to her dining room. The dramatic crimson wall behind them was a very strong focal point and contrasted extremely well with the cream and gold. The carvings were most effective and she loved the use of bamboo as a wall decoration. That was a look that worked. Something similar would be striking on her dining-room walls. She must keep an eye out for suitable wall hangings.

By the time it came to desserts and coffee she was getting impatient and more than ready to leave. She slipped a fifty-euro note under her plate, pushed away her chair and stood up. 'Girls, it's been great, but I'm a little pushed for time. I've a meeting in twenty minutes so I need to get going.' She leaned down and gave Ellie a hug. 'It was lovely to see you. Safe journey back to Oz tomorrow.' She smiled at the others. 'Thanks for the lunch invite, I'll be talking to you.'

'See you, Aimee, I'll give you a call,' Gwen said.

Sally arched an eyebrow at her. 'I suppose it will be another year until we see you again.'

'If you're lucky,' Aimee riposted. 'See you!' She raised her hand in farewell and strode briskly out of the restaurant. That was her girly bit done for the foreseeable future. It was a relief to get back to work and real life.

'I suppose we were lucky that she honoured us with her presence,' Jill drawled sarcastically as they watched the heavy glass door close behind Aimee.

'Ah, don't be like that,' Gwen said uncomfortably.

'You always stand up for her. Sometimes she can be such a superior bitch. She looks down her nose at us. You know she does. She thinks we're silly because we get together and have a laugh and a chat.' The other girl's tone was belligerent. She'd noted Aimee's boredom when the conversation wasn't centred on her.

'Bet *she'll* never have another bun in the oven,' Sally remarked dryly. 'Would interfere with her plan for world domination.'

'Ah, stop, she's not that bad. Aimee's always been focused on her career. There's nothing wrong with that,' Gwen argued.

'She never even sent Kim a Mass card, let alone went to the funeral. Kim was really upset about that. She never answers emails and texts. She's just downright rude. You're too soft, and too nice, Gwen,' Jill retorted. Alcohol always made her aggressive.

'She's very busy,' Gwen murmured.

'We're *all* very busy. But at least we keep in touch and give a helping hand when we're in a fix,' Jill pointed out, taking another slug of champers.

'Buckle up . . . here we go,' Gwen murmured to Sally as Jill continued to rant. Aimee and Jill had always had an edge between them, but it usually emerged only after drink had been taken.

'Did she even offer to do anything for me? Did she even *ask* could she do anything to help? The trouble with that girl is that she's so centred on herself we don't even exist for her. I can guarantee you by the time she's sitting in her car we'll be out of her head and she won't give us another thought until one of us gets in touch again. She won't even ring to find out if Sally's had the baby unless one of us tells her. Trust me. Career, career, career, that's all that matters to her. To have a friend you have to be a friend, and I'm not going to bother my ass with her any more. Did you hear her saying to me, '*You don't need a man, you have everything you need in your life!*' she mimicked. 'God, I wonder does she even ride Barry any more she's such a cold fish? I'd like to see *her* if he was having an affair with someone. She mightn't be so smug and high and mighty then.' She burst into tears.

'Aw, Jilly! Stop. Don't cry. He's not worth it,' Gwen exclaimed as they hastened to comfort their inebriated pal, without another thought for Aimee and her failings as a friend.

CHAPTER FIFTEEN

'Bryan, look! Look at the name of the bar!' Debbie giggled, pointing down a narrow arcade where a red and green sign reading WYNANDFOCKINK flashed on and off. 'Could you imagine that in Sandymount?'

'It's a pity we don't have time to pay a visit. The few days went fast, didn't they?' Bryan said regretfully.

'I know. I bet Batty Baxter will be giving me a few glares tomorrow. Oh, look, there's some great shops down this street. Look at this one with the Buddha and the Chinese fans. Oh, let's go in.' Debbie didn't wait for an answer but hurried into an Aladdin's cave of carvings and ornaments and oriental treasures.

They spent a happy half-hour browsing and emerged with a carved laughing Buddha and two rectangular candle-holders with an intricate dragon design that was most unusual.

A small jewellery shop across the street caught Debbie's eye, and with a whoop of delight she hurried over and spent twenty satisfying minutes admiring fabulous bling before buying a pair of fake diamond earrings for twenty euro.

'I better get out of here,' she exclaimed, looking longingly at a cross that was really dressy and would go with so many of her tops. Reluctantly, she left the shop, followed by Bryan, who pointed out a cheese shop on the same side as the oriental shop.

'That looks interesting!'

She glanced at her watch. 'If we're going to have something to eat before we head off to the airport, we better get a move on. You go into the cheese shop and I'll go into the Leonidas one and get some chocs for Mum.'

'OK,' Bryan agreed, focusing on the inviting array of cheeses and olive oils on display in the window.

Debbie inhaled deeply as she walked into the luxury handmade-chocolate shop. Bryan was far more of a gourmet than she was. He'd probably emerge with something smelly and weird-looking that would stink out the fridge for a week.

She spent a while looking at the tempting array of chocolate delights, which left her mouth watering with anticipation. She might as well treat herself to a few as well. Now that she was well and truly maxed out on her credit card she'd be having very few treats in the foreseeable future.

'I'll have some of those white ones, and some of those light chocolate ones.' Debbie pointed to the creamy-brown chocolate whirls that lay so temptingly beneath the glass counter. She left ten minutes later with two beautifully wrapped boxes of chocolates. Bryan was still studying his cheeses. A pang of hunger hit her as the aromatic smell from a shwarma and kebab takeaway wafted up the street.

'Will we have a kebab in that place and have a cup of coffee in that big hotel with the funny name around the corner?' she suggested.

'Sure,' he agreed. 'Except we don't even have to go around the corner, there's a side entrance to the hotel where WYNANDFOCKINK is.'

'You're so observant,' she teased him, linking her arm in his as they walked over to the takeaway. Half an hour later they were sitting in the red and cream lounge of the Grand Hotel Krasnapolsky sipping coffee and eating a selection of delicious cakes. They had a fine view of Dam Square. The Royal Palace opposite them was an imposing, impressive building that dominated its surroundings. She found it easy to imagine another era, when the elegant square was filled with horse-drawn carriages as the crowned heads of Europe gathered at the magnificent palace. Or young maids in their long white caps buying produce for their mistresses from the marketplace. The paintings of Vermeer, Rembrandt and Frans Hals came to mind and she was glad they'd been able to view some of the Dutch Masters at the Rijksmuseum.

It was such a diverse city, Debbie mused, watching cyclists weaving their way across the cobblestones and the trams rumbling along the tracks that traversed the big square. The atmosphere was generally friendly, but, when they'd wandered off into some of the side streets, it had changed and become faintly sinister. Drug addicts, raddled and emaciated, and prostitutes, eyes glazed and empty, were numerous, and Debbie had been shocked by the bleak, sad, total emptiness in one young girl's face. A girl not much older than Melissa. She looked like a walking corpse. It gave her the shivers and she'd told Bryan she wanted to go back to the square.

They'd taken a cruise along the canal the previous night which had passed through the red-light district and, while it was fascinating to watch the ladies sitting and posing in the windows, many of which had red lamps, adding to the air of seedy decadence, she wasn't sure if she'd like to come back to visit again. Underlying the gaiety and buzz of the city was an air of seedy sadness and hopelessness that didn't appeal to her, and she found the blind-eye attitude to the very prevalent drug culture disheartening.

She knew that easy accessibility to drugs was part of the attraction of the city and she and Bryan had enjoyed their brownies, knowing they weren't breaking any laws, but, even so, the wretchedness and soullessness of the poor unfortunate addicts seemed to seep out of the cobblestones.

That young girl had disturbed her; she couldn't get her defeated expression out of her mind. She gave another little shiver. She must have PMT, she thought as she watched women in their finery and elegant men in their tuxes make their way through the foyer into the renowned Winter Garden restaurant for a glittering function.

How lucky was she to be sitting here on a mini break with the man she loved, knowing she had a nice home to go back to, a job that paid her a good salary and a family that loved her? Easy to forget these things until you were brought up short, she thought with a jolt of shame.

She was glad she'd bought the chocolates for Connie; she knew her mother would enjoy them immensely. They were one of her weaknesses. She was such a good mother, even though she could let rip sometimes, thought Debbie affectionately as a flood of love swept through her.

'We'd need to be getting a move on, I suppose.' Bryan interrupted her musings.

'It was a great few days, wasn't it?' She caressed his hand.

'The best time we've had in ages. This is the way it should be, babes.'

'I know,' she agreed.

'Back on track?' He grinned.

'Back on track,' she echoed, laughing.

'Maybe we won't postpone the wedding then,' he said easily.

'It's up to you.' Debbie stared at him.

'It would be a pain in the ass telling everyone, wouldn't it?' Bryan ran his fingers through his hair.

'I guess so,' she agreed, heartily relieved at what she was hearing.

'Let's go then.' He stood up and held out his hand. She took it, and he pulled her up and kissed her lightly. Arm in arm they strolled through the famous five-star hotel and out into the hustle and bustle of Dam Square.

'Are you going to sort things with your dad?' Bryan asked as they walked down the marble steps.

'I suppose I better,' she sighed.

'I was just thinking that he might appreciate some cheese. They had a great selection in that shop and it's just around the corner. Do you want to get him some? It would be a nice peace offering.'

'Oh Bryan, that's very thoughtful, he'd like that.' Debbie hugged her fiancé, appreciating his good nature.

'Come on then, I'll help you pick something ripe and stinky,' he teased, as they turned left on to the street that led off the square, to the cheese shop. The assistant was extremely helpful and made up a small selection in a presentation box for them and, to her surprise, Debbie found herself looking forward to giving the gift to her father, knowing that he'd be flabbergasted, at the very least. She was a bit flabbergasted herself. She'd never imagined this scenario.

Later, as they sat on the shuttle bus taking them to Schiphol airport, her fingers hovered over the keys of her mobile. She had to take the first step in reconciliation. It was up to her. Her father had tried his best to meet her more than halfway and, as her mother so bluntly put it, it was time for her to 'grow up'.

'We're at the airport already – look at the landing lights,' Bryan exclaimed in surprise. 'That didn't take long.'

Debbie put her phone away. She'd send the text later, she thought, a little relieved to be able to postpone the moment. Once it was gone she was committed, and she felt nervous, knowing that the meeting with her father would not be easy for either of them if she was going to be completely honest with him about her feelings.

An hour later, they sat in one of the small coffee bars watching their green Aer Lingus airbus move smoothly to the gate, the setting sun reflecting off its shiny fuselage. Bryan drank a glass of beer while she sipped a frothy cup of hot chocolate. She was tired but very happy. They'd had a wonderful, loving time and soon they'd be home, sleeping in their own bed with their trauma sorted. It was a pity she had to get up for work in the morning, but she'd taken two days casual sick leave. If she stayed out another day she'd need a cert, and her GP wasn't great at handing them out. Still, it would be Wednesday and she'd only have three days to work until the weekend, she comforted herself.

'Tired?' Bryan put his arm around her.

'Whacked!' she admitted.

'Me too, but it was worth it. It was great having the whole day to play around with. A night flight was perfect. We can have a snooze on the plane.' Bryan stretched his legs out in front of him and closed his eyes. He was asleep in minutes. Typical, she thought fondly, he went asleep while she waited to hear their boarding call. It would be a while yet – the passengers were still disembarking from the incoming flight.

She rooted in her bag for her phone and scrolled to the Create Message icon. She bit her lip and looked up at the ceiling. What would she say to her father?

She took a deep breath and her fingers moved swiftly over the keypad. It didn't take long, and when she was finished she switched the phone off. Whatever response he made, she'd get it tomorrow. For now, she'd taken that first hesitant step of letting go and moving on.

'So how did the lunch go?' Barry lay sprawled on the sofa surfing the channels. It was drizzling outside and he hadn't felt like going for his usual walk along the pier.

Aimee lifted her head from her BlackBerry. 'Just let me finish this email and I'll tell you,' she said.

Barry flicked again and saw that an episode of *Frasier* was on. He settled in to enjoy the banter between the two snobby social-climbing brothers.

'That's your phone. You're getting a message.' His wife cocked an ear towards the hall.

'I'll get it in a minute. I'm too lazy to budge.' He yawned.

'It could be important!'

'Lissy's in her room, you're here. Whatever it is, it can wait.' He shrugged.

'Right.' She continued keying in her email. Barry grinned. He knew he was annoying her by not taking the message. They were so different. If her phone went, she checked it. She might not answer the text, depending on who it was, but she'd check her messages immediately. He always put his mobile on the hall table the minute he came in the door and forgot about it. A mobile phone was for work, as far as he was concerned, and he did enough of that in the office without bringing it home.

He laughed as Roz whacked Bulldog in the goolies after he'd swatted her ass. Aimee, seeing she had a window of opportunity, kept on with her emails. She was flying to Milan in the morning and she needed to be on top of her office work. Ten minutes later, seeing that he was still entertained watching *Frasier*, she slipped out of the room and went into their bedroom to pack her case. She packed with practised ease, her staple travel ensembles: sharp, tailored black trousers, smart tops that didn't crease and her silk underwear.

She was undressed and in her nightdress when Barry came into the room with a mug of steaming low-fat cocoa. He always made cocoa for her when she had an early start, to help her sleep.

'Thanks, darling.' She took it gratefully and sipped its chocolatey creaminess. She laid it on her bedside locker and slid between the sheets. She was tired. It had been a busy day and she had a hectic couple of days ahead of her.

Barry sat on his side of the bed, kicked off his shoes and lay back against his pillows.

'So how did the lunch go? How are the girls?'

'They're probably still there,' she said a tad sarcastically.

'Why not, if they're having fun?' Barry put his hands behind his head and looked at her.

'I can only take so much of it. I left before dessert,' she confessed.

'What did you do that for?'

'I was busy. I had a meeting.' She turned to look at him.

'For goodness' sake, Aimee – you meet them once in a blue moon, surely you could have stayed for dessert and coffee. That wouldn't have killed you. You need to chill out a bit more.'

'Barry, you know me, I'm not into girly lunches, I'm not into talking about kids and men and all the other daft stuff that some women love to twitter on about. I was bored, to be honest with you.'

'But Gwen's a very interesting woman, and so's Jill. Sally's a bit scattered, I suppose, but I wouldn't call any of them boring by a long chalk,' Barry remarked.

'Well, half the lunch was spent discussing Jill's emotional

traumas because she's kicked Bob out because he two-timed her—'

'That doesn't surprise me! I never really liked him,' Barry interjected.

'She's in bits. In a complete heap! I'm telling you, Barry, I'd never let a man do that to me.'

'Well, that's good to know,' he said caustically.

'Sorry, darling, but not even you would reduce me to a whiney, whingey emotional wreck. I mean, she has everything going for her. She doesn't *need* him. She's got a successful career, a—'

'A career doesn't put its arms around you at night,' he pointed out.

'Oh, for heaven's sake! I'm going to sleep. You'll be reading romantic novels next if you're not doing it already,' she scoffed as she drained her cocoa.

'You're speaking from the safety net of a loving relationship.' He ignored her jibes. 'You might look at things differently if you were on your own. And don't be too quick to diss your friends, you might need them sometime.'

'You've been watching too much Dr Phil,' she jeered. 'Who was your message from?'

'I never opened it.' He got up off the bed. 'I'll go and lock up.'

He went around the rooms switching off the lights and checked to see that the light was off under Melissa's door. She'd spent most of the evening in her room. Aimee had docked her pocket money and she was in a snit with her mother. He'd slip her a few euros when his wife was in Milan. Aimee would freak if she knew he was doing that but he felt she could be too strict at times. Melissa was a good kid.

He was walking down the hall towards their bedroom when he remembered his phone message. It would be an act of mercy if he told Aimee who it was from. He scrolled into his messages and saw that it was from Debbie. He certainly hadn't been expecting a message from her, he thought grimly as he remembered their last fraught encounter.

'*Hi Dad, could we meet? It's important. Thanks. Debbie,*' he read.

What was all this about? It was an extremely polite message, not like the terse texts he was used to.

'*When and where? Dad,*' he texted back as he walked into the bedroom.

'Who are you texting at this hour of the night?' Aimee looked over at him, surprised.

'A beautiful woman who wants to meet me,' he teased.

'Smarty,' she riposted, but she was curious.

'Actually, it's Debbie. She wants to meet me.'

'For what?' Aimee couldn't hide her surprise.

'Haven't a clue.' Barry pulled his Lacoste jumper over his head and started to unbutton his shirt.

'She probably wants more money for the wedding. Well, tell her in no uncertain terms that we've contributed enough. I'm not working my ass off for her to bleed us dry,' Aimee grumbled, turning over and pulling the duvet up over her shoulder.

Barry paused. That was a smart dig. Aimee had earned more than he had last year and it irked him, although he tried never to let on.

'Whatever is spent on the wedding will come out of my salary, Aimee,' he said coldly.

'Oohhh, don't get huffy! I didn't mean it like that,' she groaned, in no mood for a row.

'I'm not getting huffy, I'm just telling you. That's the way it is. Your hard-earned money is quite safe,' he said stiffly.

'Don't be like that, Barry,' she remonstrated.

'Go to sleep, you've an early start,' he growled, wrapping his dressing gown around him. He walked out of the bedroom, and she lay staring up at the ceiling, cursing Debbie Adams. Since she'd decided to get married there'd been nothing but rows and dissension. And she was damned if she was going to watch her p's and q's talking to Barry about it. She felt very resentful that their money was going to pay for a wedding for that spoilt, ungracious daughter of his. She tossed and turned, pummelling her pillows into shape, but still she couldn't sleep.

Barry sat in the kitchen drinking peppermint tea. He was

exasperated and aggrieved with Aimee. There was no need for her to be so bloody rude about Debbie's wedding. When it came time for Melissa to marry, he'd be spending as much if not more on her big day. For the first time in their marriage she'd made him feel their money was no longer jointly shared but his and hers. And that made him very uncomfortable. They both had their own personal accounts as well as a joint account but, since she'd begun to earn more than he did, he was conscious of matching every lodgement she made into the joint account.

He sighed deeply. If they ever bought another house, and it looked as if Aimee would like to, she'd be the one whose salary would get them the bigger loan and she'd be the one paying the lion's share of the mortgage. He hated the idea of it. It made him feel less of a man somehow. He knew that was a ridiculous notion in this day and age, but deep down he couldn't deny that that was the way he felt. Not that he'd ever admit it to a sinner. Was it just him, or did other men in his position feel the same?

He couldn't stay skulking in the kitchen for the rest of the night. He had a busy day ahead of him and he was tired. He rinsed his cup, switched off the light and walked back down the hall to the bedroom. He lay near the edge of his side of their bed, wishing that Aimee was in Milan so that he could have the bed to himself. They lay with their backs to each other, each seething with resentment, until weariness overcame them and they slept, not touching once for the rest of the night.

He heard her alarm clock go off at five but he pretended to be asleep as she moved quietly around the bedroom. For the first time in their marriage he let her go without raising his head from the pillow for a goodbye kiss.

Sometimes his wife was too cocky and too judgemental for her own good, he thought angrily as he heard the front door close and silence descend on the apartment.

CHAPTER SIXTEEN

'A word with you, please, in my office,' Judith Baxter said coldly as Debbie clocked in and headed for her desk. Debbie's heart sank. She hadn't been at work for two minutes and already Batty Baxter was on her back. She was certain sure Judith didn't want to ask how her health was.

'Certainly, Judith,' she said with exaggerated politeness, which wasn't lost on the older woman, whose lips thinned into a straight line as she marched into her office. Debbie followed, throwing her eyes up to heaven as she caught her colleague Carina Brennan's sympathetic gaze.

'Close the door please,' Judith instructed crisply.

Oh no! thought Debbie, obeying reluctantly. *This is going to be a real telling-off.*

'Sit down please.'

Debbie was tempted to say that she'd prefer to stand, but there was no point in antagonizing her boss even further. Judith had it in for her for some reason, and taking two days sick hadn't helped. But she could have been sick, for all Judith knew, she thought sourly as she composed her features and faced her boss.

'I trust you're feeling better.' Judith arched an eyebrow.

'Actually, no, I still feel a bit ropey, to tell you the truth,' Debbie said calmly. She wasn't lying. Her stomach was fluttering like a thousand butterfly wings, although she wouldn't give

Judith the satisfaction of knowing that she was making her feel nervous.

'Hmmm.' Judith was clearly unimpressed.

What she wouldn't give to barf right in front of her, Debbie thought nastily, fighting the urge to fidget. This was worse than school. An old memory of being told to stand for the rest of her maths class came back to her, and her tummy lurched. It was a horrible feeling, being at someone's mercy.

Judith lowered her reading glasses down her nose and stared out over the top of them. 'I'll get to the point, as you have a lot of catching up to do today. As you probably know, it's time for your staff review and assessment for your annual salary increment and, having given the matter a lot of thought, I cannot, in all honesty, recommend that you get one this year. I'm recommending deferring it for six months, at least, to see if your performance improves.'

Debbie was stunned. This was the last thing she'd been expecting.

'Why?' she demanded. 'I'm a very good worker, Judith. I was depending on that money. I'm getting married this year. I need the extra cash. I was banking on it,' she said heatedly.

'I'm afraid your personal life is no concern of mine, Debbie. But your work behaviour is. You're constantly running in the door, late. You chat too much to your colleagues and you've taken five casual sick days this year and it's only May. That's not the type of behaviour I expect from an employee in this department and I would be failing in *my* duty to the company if I were to recommend you for a raise. As I say, I've suggested a six-month postponement to give you a chance to improve your performance.'

'That's not fair. Why are you picking on me?' Debbie jumped to her feet. 'I don't deserve this. I'm very conscientious in my job. This will go on my record if I want to go for promotion.'

'*Precisely*,' Judith said icily. 'You don't just swan into positions in this company. You *earn* your promotion and, when you've proved to me that you've earned your increment, you'll get it. *And* I object both to your tone and your term. I do not *pick* on people. Now, I suggest you go out to your desk and start your day's work.'

Debbie bit her lip. She wanted to shriek at the other woman and tell her she was a mean, spiteful bitch but she knew that would be fatal. She needed her job more than ever after the extravagances of the past few days. Judith Baxter had her over a barrel whether she liked it or not, and she had no option but to put up with her crap.

'Well! What are you waiting for? I have work to do, if you don't,' Judith said coldly and bent her head to a file in front of her.

Debbie picked up her bag and walked out of the office, trying hard not to cry. She wouldn't give that bitch the gratification of seeing her crying. Carina winked at her, but she was too upset to wink back, and she hurried to her desk and logged on to her computer.

'*Everything OK?*' Carina's email winged its way to her.

'*No, that fucking bitch has stopped my increment, I hate her guts,*' Debbie emailed back.

'*Poor you. I'll treat you to lunch. Don't mind the frigid old cow,*' Carina emailed back sympathetically. Judith's door opened and Debbie hastily deleted the email; she knew by Carina's bent head that she was doing the same to hers.

'Debbie, I need you to make sure that the correct amount has been paid into these six bank accounts for employees who will be getting their increments next week. Please change the payroll amounts to correspond with these figures,' Judith ordered sweetly, handing her a sheet of paper.

'Certainly,' Debbie said brightly. 'No problem. I'll attend to it straight away.'

Judith's eyes narrowed at her defiant tone. 'See that you do,' she snapped and stalked back to her office.

Debbie Adams was a cheeky little bitch, that was for sure. Judith scowled as she sat behind her desk and stared out at the other woman, who was busy keying in figures at her computer.

It had felt good telling her that she was withholding her

increment. Judith could see the frustration and anger in Debbie's eyes as she'd fought not to argue back, afraid of where that might lead. She'd enjoyed watching her struggling to compose herself. And the sense of power she'd felt, seeing the desperation in Debbie Adams' eyes when she began to realize that she was not going to get the money she'd been expecting.

She was only doing her job, Judith told herself. If she went around giving out increments willy-nilly, to employees who didn't deserve them, she'd have to do some explaining to her own department head. If Debbie Adams was as conscientious as she maintained she was she'd have got her raise without question. It was time for her to pull up her socks and prove that she deserved it, Judith thought self-righteously, trying to forget the younger woman's indignant accusation that she was 'picking' on her. It rankled, even though she wouldn't admit it and, suddenly, the buzz of reprimanding Debbie faded and Judith felt utterly weary.

What a bummer of a day it had been. Debbie sighed as she trudged out of Sandymount Dart station and headed home. Losing her increment for the next six months was a mini disaster. The increase would at least have paid the interest on her credit cards and kept them at bay. She'd better keep that news to herself. Bryan was still on a high after their trip to Amsterdam. If she started whingeing and moaning he'd come crashing right back down and probably suggest postponing the wedding again, and she wasn't going through all that again.

Her father had texted her to tell her that Aimee was away and he needed to pick up Melissa. He'd wondered could she oblige him by meeting in Costa Coffee close to his apartment around eight p.m., if it suited her. She was more than welcome to meet at the apartment if she wished.

She'd hastily texted back to say that Costa Coffee would be fine. It would be much easier for her to say what she had to say on neutral territory.

Her stomach was tied up in knots at the thought of the meeting. Should she have just left things as they were and pretended to Bryan that all was OK between herself and her father? But what was the point of that? It wasn't going to be much of a marriage if she kept having to hide things from Bryan. It was bad enough not being able to have a good moan to him about her increment. She'd give her cousin Jenna a ring later and arrange to meet her for a drink and get it all off her chest. She could tell Jenna anything, she thought gratefully. She was lucky to have her in her life. She was like a sister.

She let herself into the house and hurried upstairs to shower and change. What did you wear to a make or break meeting with your father, she wondered as she flicked through her wardrobe. It was cool and overcast so she decided on a pair of white jeans and a loose black knitted top. The shower helped ease away the tension that was tightening the muscles around her neck and shoulders and she stood, eyes closed for a minute, in the steaming heat and felt herself relax a little. Meeting her father couldn't be any worse than her encounter with Bitchy Baxter, she sighed as she reluctantly turned off the water and stepped out of the shower.

She was just putting the finishing touches to her make-up when she heard Bryan's key in the front door.

'Hey, babes, you still here?' she heard him call.

'Yeah,' she called back and smiled as he bounded up the stairs.

'Nice!' he whistled. 'What time are you meeting your dad?'

'Eight. In Costa Coffee in Dun Laoghaire.'

'Will I drop you over?'

'I think I'd be as quick on the Dart – the traffic looked pretty heavy when I was coming home.' Debbie traced some lip-gloss over her lips.

'Just as well I know it's your dad you're meeting or I'd be jealous,' Bryan teased as he watched her spray some Eternity on her neck and wrists.

'Well, I'd need to wear some perfume, one of those cheeses is stinking. I'll probably have a carriage to myself on the train.' She grinned as she picked up her handbag.

'You've plenty of time. Come on and have a glass of

wine with me, it will relax you a bit. I know you, you're tense.'

'How do you know?'

Bryan took her left hand; her fingers were curled tightly in her palm, the nails digging into her skin.

'Chill, babes, it's only your dad,' he said kindly as they made their way downstairs.

'*Only* my dad,' she repeated as she sat at the small circular table on the deck while Bryan poured the wine.

Its cold tartness was refreshing and she sipped it appreciatively, wishing she could spend the rest of the evening sitting with Bryan, relaxing and drinking wine. Ten minutes later she stood up to go – she wanted the ordeal to be over. The sooner she met her father, the sooner she'd be home.

'I'll cook us some fajitas. Text me when you get on the train in Dun Laoghaire, OK?' He hugged her.

'OK,' she agreed, wishing she could tell him that she'd changed her mind and that she didn't want to go, and wishing she could tell him about losing her increment.

'Great stuff,' her fiancé said cheerfully, and she knew that the minute she was out the door he'd be sitting at his computer playing Sudoku games with not a care in the world.

Her palms were sweating as much as the cheese in the gift box that she'd taken from the fridge. She sniffed, wrinkling her nose as she paid for her return ticket in the Dart station. The monitor said there'd be a train in four minutes, so she walked slowly down the platform knowing that it would be easier to get a seat in the carriages near the front.

She felt terribly nervous. What would she say to him?

Her phone rang and she rooted in her bag, hoping that it might be Barry cancelling. It was her mother.

'Well, you're back,' Connie said crisply. 'Did you have a good time?'

'Yeah, it was great, Mum. I have a present for you. It's just something small but you'll like it,' Debbie assured her.

'Debbie, you shouldn't have bought presents,' Connie chided. 'You'll need your money for your wedding.'

'It's just something small, honest, Mum, don't give out,' Debbie said plaintively.

'OK, I won't.' Connie's tone softened and Debbie wished it was her she was going to meet. She saw the train curving into the station.

'Mum, I'm just getting on to a Dart. Can I call you later?'

'Sure,' Connie said. 'I'll talk to you then.'

'Bye, Mum. I love you,' Debbie said, before she hung up. She didn't want to say anything to Connie about her imminent meeting with Barry, just in case it didn't work out. There was no point in tormenting her mother. She'd had to put up with enough all these years.

The tide was in and the evening sun glinted on the gunmetal sea. She could see Dun Laoghaire in the distance. The sun was trying to break through the silver-grey clouds, and she wondered if it was an omen. They slowed into Blackrock, and then the train was picking up speed, Dun Laoghaire grew inexorably closer and her palms grew damper.

You're an adult not a child, she chided herself, but she had those same fluttery feelings she'd experienced that morning while standing in Judith Baxter's office. Would she ever feel in control of things? she wondered as the train juddered to a halt.

She took a deep breath and hurried on to the platform and up the stairs of the pedestrian bridge. As she stood at the traffic lights waiting to cross the street she could see his penthouse and the building where they were meeting. Was her father there already?

The lights turned red and the traffic came to a halt. Debbie raised her chin and lifted her shoulders. She was in control. She had initiated the meeting. This time it was all about her.

'And where's Melissa?'

'In the penthouse.'

'On her own?' Aimee's voice rose an octave.

'No, Sarah's with her – but it's just eight o'clock, it's broad daylight. I can see it from here, Aimee. Stop getting excited over nothing,' Barry said coldly, unimpressed with his wife's agitation.

'I'm not getting excited, Barry. I just don't like the idea of Melissa on her own at night.'

'Aimee, give it a rest – she's not on her own. It's bright. I'm close by. You've left her alone while you've gone to Crunches and there hasn't been a word about it. OK?'

'There's no need to be like that,' she snapped.

'You're the one who's over-reacting, *dear*,' he retorted. 'I see Debbie coming up the stairs. I'll talk to you tomorrow. Goodnight.' He hung up before she could answer.

He watched his daughter climb the curving staircase and thought with a little shock how like her mother she looked with her copper hair tied back in a ponytail.

What did she want to talk to him about? he wondered anxiously. He'd been as apprehensive as hell all day about their meeting. It was so unusual for Debbie to want to meet him voluntarily. If it was that she needed more money, as Aimee had suggested, he'd give it to her, but he was keeping it to himself. Aimee would not be made privy to that piece of information, he decided as he stood up to greet his daughter. His heart softened as he saw the smattering of freckles over her nose that no amount of make-up could disguise.

'Hello Debbie,' he smiled, not daring to give her a kiss in case he was rebuffed.

'Hello, Dad,' she said quietly. 'Can we talk?'

CHAPTER SEVENTEEN

'I'm always happy to talk to you, but let me get you something. Tea? Coffee?' Barry said easily. He could see that his daughter was nervous. His heart sank.

Oh, no, please don't let her tell me she's pregnant. She's too young, just like I was, he thought with a lurching sense of dismay.

'Aah . . . um . . . a latte, please.' Debbie sat down.

'Anything to eat – a muffin, cookie, shortbread biscuit?' He tried to keep his tone light, but watching her tense, pale face his heart was heavy. 'Back in a sec.' He made his way up to the counter and ordered their coffee. 'We're over at that table.' He pointed and paid the bill. The young girl nodded at him. She didn't look much older than Melissa, he reflected as she handed him his change. Young women didn't notice him any more. He felt middle-aged. It was dispiriting.

'So! What's the problem?' He came back and sat down opposite his daughter. Might as well get to the point and make it easier for her.

Debbie cleared her throat. 'Actually you are,' she murmured.

'Sorry?' He wasn't sure he'd heard right.

'You're the problem,' she said, and this time her voice was stronger, accusatory almost.

'What do you mean, I'm the problem? Do you not think I'm giving you enough towards the wedding? I thought I'd been reasonably generous,' he responded, trying to keep his tone level.

She really expected a lot from him, he thought in exasperation.

'No, it's not that. It's us. It's *our* relationship, Dad. I need to talk to you about how I feel,' she burst out.

'Oh . . . oh . . . OK,' he said warily. He supposed he should be glad she wasn't pregnant, but talking about their relationship wasn't going to be a cakewalk. He tried to hide his dismay as the young waitress arrived with their coffee. He tipped her and gave his most charming smile but she simply mumbled a quick 'thanks' and was gone, immune to his charm.

Idiot! He cursed himself silently. How middle-aged was that? Trying to flirt with a girl young enough to be his daughter. Even worse, behaving like a prat while his elder daughter was sitting at the table trying to talk to him about their abysmal relation-ship. He was a sad git for sure. A sad git having a mid-life crisis. Suddenly Barry felt very sorry for himself. He didn't want to hear what Debbie had to say. He knew it was going to be far from complimentary.

'Dad, I've been dreading my wedding and it's all your fault,' Debbie exclaimed heatedly when the waitress was gone. She was sitting rigid, twisting her engagement ring around her finger.

'Oh! How so?' He was completely taken aback at this full-on assault.

'I haven't really wanted you there from the beginning. I've felt you've no business being there. It's only because you're paying something towards it, and because of Mum, that you're involved,' she said bluntly, and he could see the anger sparking in her eyes.

'I guess I'm not completely surprised by that. Your behaviour has been anything but appreciative, and less than civil,' he said, his own anger beginning to rise.

'And why do you think that is?' she demanded.

'Look, Debbie, I know we don't get on. I know you've never forgiven me for breaking up—'

'*Walking out*,' she hissed. 'You walked out on Mum and me and left us to our own devices. You went to America and didn't give a toss how we managed. And that's why I hate you, Dad.

You abandoned us.' Her face was bloodless, waxy and he could see how her hands shook as she raised her mug to her lips.

He felt his mouth turn dry. This moment of reckoning had been a long time coming. Barry took a deep breath. 'Debbie, in fairness, I never stinted on paying for your upkeep and, if your mother needed anything, she only had to phone me,' he protested, unnerved by the raw blast of anger she'd unleashed on him.

'Oh, for God's sake, Dad, anyone can write a cheque, how easy is that?' Her lip curled and he saw the contempt in her eyes. He felt himself shrivel inside. No one had ever looked at him with such disdain and that it should be his own daughter was crucifying.

'Where were you when Mum was crying herself to sleep and I had to listen and feel helpless because I could do nothing to make her stop? Where were you when I couldn't do my maths and needed help? Where were you when the car broke down? Or when there were mice in the attic and Mum had to climb up and set traps? Where were you when she got mugged in town and her bag was snatched and she got a black eye because she fought with the druggie that attacked her? Where were you on Christmas Eve and Christmas Day? Where were you on my birthdays? All my friends had their fathers to help them blow out their candles. I just had Mum. A *cheque* doesn't cover all that, Dad. What were you going to do? Fly over from America every time we were stuck?' Bitterness laced her tone, and her eyes were bright with hostility.

'I was only gone for a couple of years,' he countered, shocked by her vehemence.

'Yeah, and then you came home and moved in with Aimee and we were pushed aside.'

'Ach, Debbie, don't be so dramatic. You *weren't* pushed aside,' he argued heatedly, feeling she was being extremely unfair. 'I did my best to try and build up a relationship with you when I came back to Ireland but you just wouldn't let me. You were determined to keep me at arm's length; no matter what I did it was never right. You have to accept responsibility for your part in it. It wasn't all one-sided.'

'For God's sake, I was a child. You left me when I was very young . . . walked out of my life. One day you were my daddy living with us, the next you were gone and I only saw you a couple of times a week, and then you were completely gone. How do you think that made me feel? Then you came back and expected everything to be OK again. I was twelve when you had Melissa. How do you think *that* made me feel? How do you think I felt, watching how close the two of you were? How loving you were with her when you'd turned your back on me?'

'But I would have been like that with you if you'd *let* me,' he said earnestly, leaning across the table to take her hand. For one awful moment he felt she was going to snatch it back but, after a moment's hesitation, she left it in his clasp.

'Debbie, I'm sorry that you felt betrayed and abandoned. In a marriage break-up everyone gets hurt, that's the way of it.'

'But some more than others,' she murmured, tears welling in her eyes.

'Oh, Debbie, Debbie, please don't cry, I'm truly sorry for the hurt I've caused you and your mother. Connie's forgiven me long ago – can't you try?' he pleaded.

'I want to. I just can't help the bitterness that's in me. I feel overwhelmed by it.' She was crying now, trying to avert her face. 'It ruined my childhood. I was in turmoil all the time. I felt it was all my fault. I felt there was something wrong with me, that I must be horrible and you couldn't love me and that's why you had to leave. I'd torment myself over and over in bed at night, listening to Mum crying and feeling it was because of something I'd done.' Other people were looking at them now.

'Please stop, Debbie.' He squeezed her hand, trying to swallow the lump in his throat that was causing him grave discomfort. Her words were like the cut of a thousand knives to his heart. He was horrified.

'Was it because you had me, was that what made you leave?' Her eyes were pools of pain, and he almost flinched as she focused on him.

'No, Debbie, no, no, no. It was me, it had nothing to do with you.' He shook his head vehemently. 'I did love you. I do love you. And I do regret splitting us up. I was young, immature, I—'

'Would you have married Mum if she hadn't been pregnant with me?' Debbie brushed her tears away with the back of her hand in a gesture that made him think of Melissa. 'Please tell me the truth, Dad.'

'Aw, Debbie! It was a long time ago. What's the point in revisiting it?'

'Because I think, if she hadn't been pregnant with me, you wouldn't have got married.'

'So what you're still saying is *everything* is your fault?' he said brusquely.

'I suppose so,' she agreed.

'Why would you want to lay all that on your shoulders, for God's sake?' He couldn't hide his frustration.

'Children do that. No one asked me about how I felt. I had no say in anything. I had no control over anything.'

'And you've felt this all along?'

'Yes,' she agreed miserably.

'Debbie, people make mistakes. That's what living is all about. Making mistakes and growing from them. It wasn't your fault, it wasn't your mother's fault, and it wasn't my fault. There's no point in trying to apportion blame and indulging in "if only"s. We've got to work from where we are now. And it didn't turn out so bad. We're all reasonably happy. You're getting married. Your mum has a lovely home and—'

'Mum's lonely, especially since I've left home,' she interrupted, 'and she's not as young as she used to be. She should have a lot more than what she has. She sacrificed having relationships because of me, so don't say we're *all* happy, Dad,' Debbie snapped angrily.

'Debbie, you know, you really should get off the cross. If your mum had met someone who was right for her not even you would have prevented her from being with him, much as you might like to think otherwise,' Barry said crisply, deciding he wasn't going to be the fall guy for everything.

'Just like you met Aimee.' Debbie pulled her hand away.

'Yes, just like I met Aimee,' he said evenly.

'She's so different from Mum. What was wrong with Mum that you had to leave?' Her tone was sulky and surly, and again he was reminded of his younger daughter.

'There was nothing *wrong* with your mother, Debbie. Look, if you want to apportion blame, fine, I'm happy to take responsibility. I wasn't ready to get married when we did. If it was today, I guess we wouldn't have got married for a while, we could have lived together before making any decisions. Connie is a wonderful woman, I wasn't half good enough for her, but we've made our peace with each other, Debbie. You're the only one unwilling to move on and there's nothing else I can do,' he said wearily. 'If you don't want me at your wedding, I won't come. I don't want to ruin your day.'

'Oh!' Debbie hadn't been expecting that and it threw her. Her father was giving her what she'd wanted all along. Why did she suddenly feel empty and hollow? She had an opportunity now to evict him from her life for good. He was on the ropes. She'd won. She looked at him and saw how tired he looked, how dispirited. Grey streaked his black hair and he had bags under his eyes, which were dull and red-rimmed, as if he hadn't slept too well the previous night.

She remembered the book her mother had given her, *Applications for Living from Conversations with God*. Did she want to hang on to all her dramas with her father? Did she want to hang on to her fury and resentments? They had nourished her since childhood. A phrase she'd read came to mind: '*That was then and this is now.*' Now could be her fresh start. All that negativity wasn't good for her physically, emotionally or spiritually. All that horrible anger that twined around her insides like ivy poisoning her. She could carry it on and punish herself as well as her father or she could get off that particular roundabout and channel all that energy into something positive and enriching in her married life.

Debbie took a deep breath. It was time to make a decision. Did she want Barry in her life or out of it?

'Well, um, that wasn't really why I came, you know . . . to ask you not to come . . . that wasn't the reason . . .' she stuttered, half amazed at herself.

'Well, what was the reason?' he asked, perplexed.

'I just wanted to tell you how I felt. I wanted you to know why I've been . . . well, not very friendly, I suppose. I wanted you to know how deeply it affected me. You never seemed to acknow- ledge that . . .' She trailed off.

'So what are you saying then?' He eyed her warily.

'Mum thinks I should let go of the past, put it behind me and make a fresh start for my wedding.'

'Mum talks a lot of sense, but it's not Mum we're talking about here, it's you. What do *you* want, Debbie? Let's put our cards on the table now that we're getting down to the nitty- gritties of our relationship – or non-relationship, as the case may be.'

'I suppose the grown-up thing would be to let bygones be bygones and start afresh.' She shrugged and gave a little smile.

'Aw, forget the grown-up thing. What do you want to do? What's your gut telling you? Is it to tell me to get lost and that you don't want to have anything to do with me? If that's what you want – and I hope it isn't – I'll respect your wishes. And after what you've said to me I'll understand why. And I certainly won't blame you. I never realized how awful it was for you, and I'm sorry, desperately sorry. I wish I could go back in time and try and change how you felt but I can't. So it's up to you . . . You're the boss.' He smiled wryly at her, relieved at last that it was all out in the open. If she told him to get out of her life, he wouldn't blame her at all, and at least he was finally giving her a chance to be in control of some decision concerning their relationship.

'Well, I brought you a present, actually.' Her cheeks flushed with embarrassment and he felt an even worse heel, that his own daughter would be embarrassed because she had brought him a present. 'Bryan and I were away for the weekend. I thought it might be a peace offering.' She leaned down and picked up the bag with the box of cheeses in it and handed it to him.

'*Oh!* This *is* unexpected.' His face creased in a smile in spite of himself as he pulled out the straw-filled presentation box. 'I love cheese, it's a real weakness of mine,' he exclaimed, sniffing the pungent Gorgonzola. 'That was very kind, Debbie. Very kind. Thanks.' He was genuinely delighted and, surprisingly, she was pleased at his reaction.

'Bryan suggested the cheeses,' she explained, wanting to give her fiancé his due. 'He loves cheese and crackers himself.'

'A man of good taste then. Tell him thanks – he chose well.'

'I will.' She gave a real smile this time, and for an instant her face looked unguarded and carefree and she looked so like Connie when he'd married her.

'So could we make a fresh start, do you think? Is this a true olive branch?' he asked hesitantly, still not too sure what her response might be.

'We could give it a try, I suppose,' she agreed. 'But I still want Mum to give me away,' she said hastily, afraid he might take advantage.

'I understand. It's certainly her right, she reared you. One thing I would like to say – seeing as we're being very frank with each other.' He arched an eyebrow at her.

'OK,' she said cautiously.

'It's about Melissa. You know our circumstances are not of her making and she *is* your half-sister. Could you manage to be a little kinder to her when we're together? She's a good kid; she just seems surly because she feels awkward. She probably has her own insecurities about our situation,' he said delicately. Having heard what Debbie had to say, he felt he should make it his business to see if his younger daughter had any issues that she might be keeping to herself. He didn't ever want to go through an experience like this again.

Debbie swallowed hard. 'I realize that, and I suppose it wasn't fair to take it out on her. It won't happen again,' she said, suddenly feeling very ashamed of herself.

'Good stuff. I really appreciate that, Debbie.' He reached out and squeezed her hand again, and this time she gave a little squeeze back.

'I suppose you wouldn't like to pop in and say hello. Aimee's travelling and Melissa's over in the penthouse with her friend Sarah, who's coming to the wedding. You've never been to visit. Do you want to come up for a couple of minutes, or are you tied up?' he asked on impulse.

Debbie looked a little startled at his invitation, but to his surprise she agreed and stood up to follow him downstairs.

It was a windy evening and tendrils of her hair blew around her face as an easterly breeze gusted up from the seafront. 'Hope the weather's a bit better than this for the barbecue,' Barry remarked as they walked briskly towards his apartment block.

'It just means we'll have to eat in the hotel rather than the courtyard, but I'd much prefer to eat in the open; it's more laid-back and that's what we want,' she said.

'It's in the hands of the gods, unfortunately,' Barry replied as he walked towards the big glass-plated doors that led to the foyer of his building.

'Should you have phoned Melissa to say we're coming? I don't want to land in on top of her.' Debbie was beginning to feel uncomfortable as they stepped into the lift that carried them to the penthouse.

'So she can get rid of the boys and hide the vodka bottle?' Barry chuckled. 'She knew I was only five minutes away. They won't be getting up to much. I don't believe she would go behind our backs anyway. As I said before, she's a good kid.' The lift glided silently upwards and moments later she was following him into a small entrance hall that led to a cream panelled door.

'Welcome,' he said as he opened it for her, and she walked into a tastefully decorated hall with various doors leading off it. He showed her into a large, airy sitting room that had floor-to-ceiling windows facing on to a large, wraparound balcony. The views of the bay were stunning and Debbie had to admit that Aimee had decorated with style and excellent taste. It was very minimalist, even a little sterile, she thought as she gazed around and studied the elegant pieces of furniture, which seemed to have been bought more for aesthetic impact than creature comfort.

'Hey, Dad ... oh! Oh hi, Debbie.' Melissa looked flabber-gasted when she walked into the room, followed by her friend, and saw Debbie standing with her father. Her face darkened into her usual scowl.

'Hello, Melissa, um, Dad asked me up. I've just met him for a coffee in Costa Coffee.' She smiled uncertainly at her half-sister, ignoring the scowl.

'Oh ... right. Were you talking about the wedding?' the younger girl said awkwardly, taken aback that Debbie had actually talked to her.

'Yeah, that's what we were talking about,' Debbie agreed, smiling at the other teenager who was standing behind Melissa. 'Hi, you must be Sarah; I believe you're coming to the wedding.'

'Yes, I am. Thanks for asking me.' She smiled, showing a mouthful of braces and Debbie remembered her own teen years and all the anxieties and uncertainties associated with them.

'You're welcome. I hope you enjoy it. Dad and I were just say-ing we hope it won't be this windy – you know we're having a barbecue?' She turned to Melissa.

'Cool. I didn't know that. I love barbecues. It should be fun.' The scowl was gone and her eyes lit up at this news.

'Well, that's why we decided to have one. We didn't really want everyone sitting around designated tables – well, except the family,' she amended. 'Mum and I just felt the grandparents and family might be happier sitting at tables with people they knew. Sometimes older people prefer that.'

'But can we sit where *we* like?' Melissa looked at Debbie. 'Or have we to sit at family tables?'

With the parents was the underlying question. Debbie grinned, understanding perfectly where her half-sister was coming from.

'You can sit wherever you want,' she said.

'Hey, thanks, that's cool.' Melissa grinned back, their eyes met and for the first time in their lives a connection sparked between them. Barry, watching the interaction, gave a little prayer of thanks. Maybe at last after all these years his daughters might be at the beginning of the journey that would bring them close to true sisterhood.

'Would you like a drink?' he asked impulsively. 'A glass of champers to toast the wedding . . . and em . . . fresh starts?' He stood smiling at her, and she could feel him silently urging her to say yes.

How typical of her father, she thought with a flash of irritation, one glass of champagne and everything would be fine, all the past erased. He really had no idea of how deep her feelings ran. Certainly, until today, he had had no conception of the depth of her anger or pain. She looked at him standing there, smiling broadly, and couldn't help the notion that in some ways he was a lot like Bryan. He liked everything to be hunky-dory. He liked to brush things under the carpet and pretend that problems didn't exist. Was she marrying a man just like her father? The idea shocked her and she pushed it away.

'Can we have some?' Melissa interrupted her train of thought.

'I'm allowed to drink champagne, I had some for my gran's birthday,' Sarah said eagerly.

'One glass?' Barry gave Debbie a quizzical look.

'Why not?' she heard herself say. What was the point in refusing? Whatever issues she had, she had to deal with them herself.

'Terrific,' Barry exclaimed, and went out to the kitchen to do the honours. Aimee always liked to keep a couple of splits of champagne chilling and this was the very occasion for a champagne moment.

'What's your dress like?' Melissa asked shyly, unused to conversing with her half-sister.

'It's not a fussy meringue – it's got a lacy sort of top and a plain satin skirt. It's very simple really. I hate frills and ruffles,' she explained.

'Are you wearing a veil?' Sarah asked.

'I wasn't going to, but when I tried it on it looked good, and I suppose it made me feel really bridey.' She was about to say 'You only get married once,' when she remembered whom she was talking to.

'Here we are.' Barry appeared with a tray of champagne flutes. 'Girls, the half ones are for you. I'm not sending you home intoxicated, Sarah.' He smiled at her.

'OK.' She giggled, taking a glass and handing another to Melissa.

Debbie took hers and watched the bubbles bursting up through the golden liquid.

'To you, Debbie, to your wedding and to family.' Barry raised his glass.

She saw Melissa and Sarah raising theirs to her. Melissa caught her eye. Debbie took a deep breath. It was up to her. Things could stay as they were or she could leave the past and all its grief and resentments behind her and walk a new path.

She looked into her half-sister's youthful blue eyes and saw Melissa looking back at her with anticipation. Debbie sighed; she was, after all, the older sister, the one to lead the way. She raised her glass and studied the younger girl intently.

'To family,' she toasted.

'To family,' echoed Melissa, solemnly clinking her glass to Debbie's.

They smiled at each other and, for an instant, Debbie felt it was just the two of them in the room. This moment must have been made for them, because Debbie knew if Aimee had been home she wouldn't have agreed to come up to the apartment. She knew it was special and she knew Melissa felt the same. She was only a kid. God only knew what worries and anxieties she had. Debbie hoped with all her heart that she hadn't caused her half-sister any angst with her unfriendly behaviour. That would be horrible. Her mother and father were right: Melissa was an innocent party in all of this.

It had been petty and childish of Debbie to blame the younger girl for the problems in her relationship with her father. She was suffused with shame as she looked at the young teenager. It was clear that she wanted to be friends. That surly façade had obviously been her defence mechanism for Debbie's cold attitude towards her. She would have to make amends and take the lead.

'To sisters,' she said softly, impulsively, and clinked her glass with Melissa's again. Melissa went pink.

'Yeah, to sisters,' she muttered, but she was smiling.

Her father touched his glass to hers. 'To fresh starts,' he said, and she wished that Connie were here beside them to share the moment of reconciliation.

'To Mum,' she said, and took a sip of the golden liquid. If it wasn't for Connie she'd never have taken the first step in asking to meet her father to talk. If Connie hadn't given her that book to read she might not have had the wisdom to change her thinking. If anyone deserved to be drinking champagne it was her mother.

It would be a pleasure to tell her about this evening. And when she did tell her, she'd make sure they had a bottle of champagne to celebrate, Debbie decided, observing the pleasure in her half-sister's face as she raised her glass in toast to Connie.

Chapter Eighteen

'Well done, darling,' Connie exclaimed. Debbie had phoned her on her way to the train station to tell her of the evening's events.

'It was the book you gave me,' she told Connie. 'It made me see things differently. One phrase kept coming into my head. *"That was then and this is now."* It's very true, I suppose. Anyway, I'm glad I did it. And Melissa was pleased, so thanks for the lecture and sorry for being so childish about inviting her to the wedding.'

'That's OK, but it's good to move on. Life's hard enough without carrying all that baggage. I'm delighted the book helped. I must tell my patient. I liked what I read of it and I hoped it might resonate enough with you to help you take that step and change a negative into a positive,' Connie praised. 'I'm proud of you. It's a *great* way to start your married life.'

Debbie smiled. She knew her mother was pleased as punch by her news.

'I just wanted to get it over and done with, I wanted to feel better about myself,' Debbie said as she reached the traffic lights at Meadow's and Byrne. She hoped a Dart wouldn't race into the station across the street before she got there. Luck was with her: the lights changed to green and she hurried across the road. She slid her ticket into the turnstile as they talked and hastened out on to the platform and scanned the monitor. Two minutes to wait for the train. Not bad, she thought happily, longing to get home to tell Bryan the news.

'And I'm particularly relieved for you and Melissa. Blood is thicker than water at the end of the day and family *is* important, and I like the child,' Connie continued. 'I think you'll feel much happier in yourself. Was Barry delighted?'

'He was pretty pleased all right, he invited me up to the penthouse and we had a glass of champers.'

'*Really!* Was Aimee there? What's it like?' Connie sounded incredulous.

'No, she wasn't. She was travelling. I wouldn't have gone if she was there. It's elegant, but not really homely as such. Look, I'll tell you all when I see you. I'll ring you tomorrow, Mum. I hear the train coming. I want to give you your little present from Amsterdam.'

'Why don't I treat you to a bite to eat? It would mean I didn't have to cook dinner when I get home. I could meet you in Dun Laoghaire. We could go to Purple Ocean for a change, if you like?' Connie suggested.

'Lovely, they do a good early bird—'

'To hell with the early bird, we're going the whole hog. We've a lot to celebrate.'

'Well, the champagne will be my treat,' Debbie said gaily. She was on a high.

'You're on,' agreed her mother. 'Talk to you tomorrow. And well done, pet.'

'Night, Mum, I love you. Thanks for everything.' Debbie smiled as she pressed the button to open a carriage door.

'Night, Debbie, I love you too,' Connie said before hanging up.

Debbie settled in her seat feeling drained but exhilarated. It had been a rollercoaster of a night, but she'd finally had her say and left her father in no doubt about her feelings. It had been a liberating moment for her. The shock on his face had been a balm of sorts after all the years of secret anguish. Even verbalizing it had brought back those sad, distressing memories, and unexpected tears glazed her eyes. She'd felt so out of place as a child, especially when she saw the happy unit that Karen and John made with her cousins.

Even though he'd been stunned and dismayed, she felt Barry still had no real conception of how abandoned, betrayed and frightened she'd felt at his leaving. Blaming it on his immaturity had been very convenient, she thought as the train pulled out of the station. There was still anger in her but at least it wasn't suppressed any more. She'd faced it and had her say and now she was going to try hard to forget about it and focus on the good things in her life. She was realistic enough to know that just by talking it out with her dad didn't mean that those feelings would disappear overnight. But she'd taken the first step towards reconciliation and the first step was the hardest step of all.

'So he liked my choice of cheese. I thought he would,' Bryan said smugly as he handed her a bowl of crisp baby salad leaves sprinkled with stilton and pear wedges to carry to the table.

'It was inspired. It really broke the ice. Thanks for thinking of it, because I never would have,' Debbie confessed, leading the way to the candle-lit table. 'This is lovely. Thanks, hon.'

'Anything for you, babes. This is a night to celebrate. You've made up with your father and half-sister; you can enjoy your wedding now. No more angst! Life's peachy,' Bryan declared, pouring her a glass of wine.

'I took the first step, Bryan, it's not going to be as easy as that,' she murmured. 'I can't deny my feelings. They're still raw.'

'Forgive and forget, don't wallow in it, Debbie. Life's too short,' he said cheerily, feeling an edge of irritation at her reservations. She could be a little bit of a drama queen if he indulged her. His attitude was 'Get on with it.'

'Cheers,' he said, raising his glass, ignoring the frown that creased her brow. 'Eat up, I slaved over a hot pan for ages,' he teased as he tucked into his steaming fajita.

'Thanks,' she said quietly, wishing he wouldn't dismiss her feelings so lightly. Men just seemed to do that to her, she thought irritably.

'So, has Aimee got taste? What's the Taj Mahal like? Does she sit on a golden throne?' Bryan demanded, determined she wasn't going to go quiet and huffy because he wouldn't humour her need for angst.

Debbie giggled in spite of herself. Bryan felt relief wash over him. He hated all this family stuff. Rows and scenes were to be avoided at all costs and he'd certainly be steering clear of them to the best of his ability. Life was to be enjoyed, and he intended to enjoy it to the full and Debbie's family weren't going to get in the way of that.

Good girl, Debbie, Connie thought with pride as she rearranged plates in the dishwasher to try and accommodate a dirty lasagne dish. It took her five minutes, moving dishes around like chess pieces on a board, before everything finally fitted, and her knees ached from sitting on her hunkers. She pulled herself up stiffly and set the cycle. She'd missed her walk these last few days and she was beginning to seize up, she thought crossly as she stretched her neck and shoulders.

She opened a press door and took down some IQ oil tablets. They were supposed to be good for memory loss. She should start taking Udo's Oil to lubricate her joints as well, she supposed, feeling indignant that her body was beginning to let her down. Just at a time in her life when she could start cutting back on work and taking it a bit easier, all this peri-menopause, or whatever the hell she had, had to start kicking in.

Her thoughts turned to the perfectly toned and supple Aimee and she felt irrationally resentful. No wonder she was toned and supple with the hours she spent at the gym while her child was home alone eating pizza for her dinner. Wasn't it well for her that she had Barry at home to mind Melissa while she travelled around Europe for work? Much chance she'd had for travelling when Debbie had been a child.

Her sense of injustice increased as she flung dirty tea towels and dish cloths into the sink. It must be great to be able to afford to have champagne in your fridge so that you could pop a cork at the drop of a hat. Just seeing them walking into Roly's in their designer gear – Barry in his Polo shirt and Ray-Bans and Aimee with her Dolce & Gabbana shades and Pierre Cardin bag – looking effortlessly affluent and chic had made her feel frumpy and dull in her M&S reliables and her black leather shoulder bag that was donkey's years old. She'd have to make sure she got something really dressy and upmarket for the wedding. It wouldn't do for the mother of the bride to be upstaged by the second wife! Karen was coming shopping with her to pick her outfit.

Wasn't it ironic? Debbie had confronted Barry about her feelings, and the issues that Connie had felt she'd dealt with years ago were surfacing for no apparent reason. It must be, as Debbie had angrily declared before the reconciliation, that contact with the other family brought up restless, angry feelings.

Connie knew she was being unreasonable but these days she was often angry for no apparent reason as if she had permanent PMT.

She should read up on the M word, she thought grumpily, as she tossed in a cup full of bleach and filled the sink with cold water. Or was she better off knowing what to expect, or would reading up about symptoms make her imagine she had them? Was not knowing protection in itself? Nothing had prepared her for this . . . this high and low of emotions, this achy crucifixion of joint pain, this lack of concentration that made her feel she was losing her marbles.

She could take HRT, she supposed, but a doctor had said something once that stuck in her mind, that she was of the opinion that it wasn't normal to put a young hormone in an ageing body. Besides, there was breast cancer in her family and Connie wasn't going to risk it. The oestrogen withdrawal was just going to have to take its course and she'd give that herbal remedy Black Cohosh a bash, she decided, heartily sick of herself.

On impulse she picked up the phone and dialled Barry's number.

'Hello?' He sounded subdued.

'It's me, what's wrong?' she asked. 'I thought you'd be in

good form after meeting Debbie. She rang me and told me she'd had a chat and that you'd asked her back to the penthouse and had champagne. That's a big step forward, surely.'

'Yeah it is.' He sighed heavily. 'It's just I didn't realize how much my leaving had affected her, and it's made me feel bad about myself.'

'Why, what did she say?' Connie probed, not expecting this response at all.

'She told me that she was in torment as a child. That she felt unloved and unlovable. She felt it was all her fault that we split up. She told me about listening to you crying yourself asleep and feeling helpless about not being able to make things right.'

'She said *that*! Oh God!' Connie was equally shocked.

'Yeah and much more. I never realized, Connie.'

'Like what?' Connie said, dismayed beyond measure.

Barry relayed the conversation down the line and Connie's heart was caught in a vice-like grip. 'Oh, my poor daughter. Poor Debbie, I never realized it went so deep.' Connie was devastated. 'I knew she was angry and bitter but I felt that was normal in the circumstances. Oh God!' She started to cry.

'Don't do that, Connie,' Barry said miserably.

'But I used to give out to her for not being nice to you, I used to tell her you were very generous—'

'Oh, I had that thrown at me,' Barry interjected dryly. '"A cheque doesn't make up for anything", and she's right, I suppose.'

'Oh Lord! I never acknowledged her feelings; I never affirmed that they were justified. When people asked how we were getting on, I always said we were getting on fine and brushed our difficulties under the carpet. I'm a shite mother,' Connie wept. 'No wonder she was so angry and resentful. I should have brought her to counselling. I should have listened more and not told her she should grow up. She was only a child.'

'You're *not* a shite mother, Connie. You're a great mother,' Barry said fervently. 'It was all my fault; I behaved like a selfish, thoughtless bastard. I'm the one to blame. Please stop crying, Connie.'

'Look, I'm going to go, Barry. I'll talk to you again.' Connie gulped.

'Do you want me to drive down? I'll try and get a babysitter,' he suggested helplessly. 'Aimee's away.'

'No . . . no, I'll be fine. It's just distressing to hear.'

'Are you sure?'

'Yeah, I'm sure. Goodnight, Barry,' she managed. She put the phone down and collapsed into tears on the sofa.

Memories brought her back to those years when Barry had left them, and she remembered with painful intensity Debbie's big blue eyes full of hurt and anger on her birthday when she realized that he wasn't going to be there.

'Where's your daddy?' one of her little classmates asked.

'He's sick,' she'd lied. 'He's in hospital. I'm bringing him cake later.'

'No he's not,' said another. 'You don't have a daddy, he went away.'

Debbie had gazed at Connie in consternation, silently pleading with her to say something.

'Of course Debbie's got a daddy, Brenda, don't be silly. He's working in America, and he couldn't come home because he's got a chest infection and can't fly.' Connie wanted to smack the smug little madam standing in front of Debbie. 'Now go and play and be a good girl.'

'Well, my mammy said—'

'I don't care what your mammy said. Enough,' Connie snapped, vowing that Brenda Cullen would never be invited to their house again. But it had ruined the party for Debbie, she'd been subdued and clingy; and when everyone was gone she'd proclaimed, 'I hate my daddy' before stomping off to bed.

The pain of it convulsed her. She'd buried those memories deep, almost banished them. No wonder her daughter had been in torment. Connie had been in bits after Barry left and she was an adult – how much worse was a marriage break-up for a child? Guilt shrouded itself around her. If she hadn't married Barry when she'd got pregnant and fooled herself into thinking it was what he wanted too at least Debbie wouldn't have known what it was like to live with her father and she would have been spared the agony of the break-up. Connie had deluded herself into thinking that their daughter had coped well. Tonight's revelations made a mockery of that. She was as much at fault as Barry for the heartache their child had endured, and that truly grieved her.

She switched off the lights and trudged upstairs. She might as well go to bed, she thought miserably as Hope shot ahead of her and jumped up on the bed, green eyes glittering almost black in the moonlight.

Maybe a lavender bath would help relax her, she decided as she absentmindedly stroked her cat's silky black fur. Her mind was whirring like a washing machine on spin; she'd never sleep in the frame of mind she was in. She ran the bath and poured in some rose oil and lavender drops. The scent filled the bathroom and she sank down into the bath and felt the hot water welcome her body and ease the aches in her joints. She lay back and felt some of the tension seep out of her.

Just when it seemed everything was finally going right all this had come up. Now *she* was the one flooded with guilt and sadness.

Connie poured some liquid soap on to her sponge and wished heartily that she hadn't phoned her ex-husband.

'But where is he gone?' Aimee asked, perplexed. Barry hadn't said anything about going out tonight when she'd spoken to him earlier in the evening.

'He said he had to go and see a chap and he'll be back in a couple of hours. It's no big deal, Mom,' Melissa assured her airily.

'But he didn't leave you on your own?' Aimee said, horrified.

'Don't be silly, Mom. He insisted on getting a babysitter, as if I was six years old. Helen's here. But I could stay here by myself anyway. I'm old enough now.'

'Not at night, Melissa,' Aimee retorted. 'So what did you do for the day?'

'Went to school. Boring. Came home, did homework. Boring.

Then Sarah came over and Dad went to meet Debbie in Costa, and then they came back here and we drank champagne and did toasts to family, and then Debbie and I clinked glasses and said, "To sisters."

'You did what?' Aimee said faintly, wondering if she'd heard right.

'Dad brought Debbie back and he opened champagne and we did toasts,' Melissa said patiently, as if explaining to a child.

'He brought Debbie back to the penthouse and you had champagne?' Aimee repeated.

'Yep, it was great. Sarah and I had a glass, Dad said we could.'

'A whole glass? Is Sarah allowed to drink alcohol?' Aimee asked in dismay, wondering what the hell had been going on while she was away.

'It was a half a glass and she's allowed to have champagne; she had it at her gran's birthday.'

'And why did Dad bring Debbie back to visit?' Aimee quizzed.

'I dunno. They were talking about the wedding, I think. She was very nice actually. I liked when she said, "To sisters." And she told Sarah and me we could sit where we liked at the barbecue. I didn't know it was going to be a barbecue. I think it's going to be totally cool – Sarah and I are *really* looking forward to the wedding now.' Melissa bubbled down the line.

'That's good,' Aimee said distractedly. 'Don't stay up too late; I'm going to ring Dad on his mobile. Goodnight, darling.'

'Night, Mom, see ya,' Melissa responded cheerfully and hung up.

Aimee gazed at the phone, stunned. Barry had brought Debbie up to the penthouse and opened a bottle of champagne. And Melissa and she had drunk to sisterhood. That was some turnaround. What on earth had gone on at their meeting? She felt extremely miffed that he hadn't phoned to tell her about it.

She always phoned at night when she was away to say good-night to Melissa. She hadn't expected to be told that Barry was out meeting someone, or that her step-daughter had visited while she wasn't there. It rankled! She hoped that the place was tidy and that Melissa and Sarah hadn't got their bits and pieces strewn around. Barry must have agreed to give Debbie more money, she surmised – what else would account for the unexpected détente? Her lips thinned. Shallow little money-grabber, she thought nastily, remembering how cold and rude Debbie had been on occasions. Barry could be such a fool sometimes. She hung the phone back in its cradle. She always used hotel phones when she rang home, even though it was more expensive, but she used the mobile so constantly for work she hated ringing home on it, listening to the echo of her own voice when she was abroad.

Aimee lay back against the pillows of her double bed and wriggled her toes. Her feet were killing her. Milan's cobblestone streets were far from kind and she'd been wearing high heels all day. The room was stuffy. The air-conditioning wasn't working. It was humid and sultry out and, in the distance, she could hear low growls of thunder. Aimee yawned; she was exhausted. The very early start, the queues in Dublin airport and a long day's work had her wrecked. People thought travelling to work in European cities was glamorous. There was nothing glamorous about this, she mused, as she sipped some Perrier from the mini bar and wiped the beads of perspiration from her forehead. She had a report to write and then she was going to have a quick bath and go asleep, but first she *had* to ring Barry and see what he had to say about what had gone on back home. She rooted in her bag for her BlackBerry and dialled his number.

'Hello,' he said briskly, and she knew he was driving by the background noise.

'Where are you off to? I've just been on to Melissa,' she said, deliberately keeping her tone light. She wasn't going to indulge his wounded ego after their spat the previous evening.

'Aw, there's been a bit of a glitch with one of the magazines and it goes to print tomorrow, have to get it sorted.'

'Oh . . . right.' This wasn't anything out of the ordinary even if it was rather late.

'How are you?' His tone was polite, businesslike.

'Fine. Busy day. Same tomorrow. The air-conditioning isn't working in the room, which is a real pain in the ass. It's very humid here, there's thunderstorms,' she informed him, waiting for him to say something about his meeting with Debbie.

'Get them to change you to another room.'

'There's no other room available. There's a conference on so the place is booked out. I'm waiting for a fan. Housekeeping told me they'd send one up but everyone else is looking for one too, so I'll be lucky,' she said mournfully, feeling a little sorry for herself.

'Have a tepid bath,' he suggested.

'How did the meeting with Debbie go?' she asked, unable to contain her curiosity any longer.

'Good,' he said non-committally.

'I believe you brought her back home. That's a first.'

'Yes, we sorted a few issues out and I thought it would be polite to bring her up. She made a nice effort with Melissa, and I appreciated that.'

'I heard you all had champagne. Pity I wasn't there,' she said a little tartly.

'There'll be other times. Look, I'm just about to park. I'll talk to you tomorrow. Hope you get your fan,' he said. 'Night.'

'Night,' she echoed, then he hung up and, for the second time that night, she was left listening to the dial tone.

Her husband hadn't been very forthcoming. What issues had been resolved? How much more money had Debbie wangled out of him? She'd never find that out now, she supposed. Whatever he was going to pay her would be from his own account and, unless she went snooping in his bank statements or chequebook stubs, she'd never know.

That bloody wedding had caused nothing but divisions between her and Barry. Debbie Adams was a cool, calculating customer, and how clever of her to get Melissa onside as well. Madam Connie was probably orchestrating it all. The nice façade couldn't be real – she was probably as two-faced as they came.

Aimee sighed. She didn't have time for all this. She had her own big wedding to concentrate on. It was the biggest, most prestigious event the company had ever catered for, and the success or failure of it was all down to her. She needed to be at the top of her game, and Connie and Debbie weren't going to scupper that with their piddling little affair, she thought angrily, stalking into the bathroom to fill the bath.

'Good film, isn't it?' Helen turned to Melissa, who was sprawled at the other end of the cream leather sofa yawning her head off. They were watching a DVD of *Bridget Jones* while drinking hot chocolate and eating Jaffa cakes.

'Brill,' agreed Melissa, who couldn't decide who she preferred, Hugh Grant or Colin Firth. Johnny Depp was her absolute favourite of course, but she rather liked Colin Firth when he was being stern and manly. She yawned again. She was bushed. It must be the champagne that was making her sleepy, even though she hadn't had that much. She knew she wasn't going to last until the end of the film but she didn't mind, she'd seen it before.

'I think I'll go to bed, Helen. Night.' She hauled herself off the sofa, gave her babysitter a casual wave and padded off to her bedroom. She was too tired to brush her teeth; she'd do it in the morning when she was having her shower. She was in bed in five minutes, snuggling down into the middle with her arms tucked around her favourite teddy-bear.

Today had been a very good day on balance, she decided as she rewound the events of the last twelve hours in her mind. Miss Horan, her religion teacher, had been out sick and they'd had a free period in the library. She detested Miss Horan with her long, beaky nose and squinty-up beady eyes which viewed her pupils as though they'd crawled out from under a piece of particularly mouldy cheese. Witchy was her nickname and it really suited her.

Then Evanna Nolan and Niamh Samson, two of the nerdiest snobs in the class, had had a fight that had turned physical, as they prepared to debate 'Pride and Prejudice, meretricious rubbish or literary novel?'

Evanna, a lanky beanpole with straight, greasy black hair who liked to think of herself as an intellectual, had had her glasses broken in the brawl and had been led weeping to the head-mistress by her fawning coterie of like-minded snobs while the rest of 1B cheered and hollered until the arrival of their English teacher curtailed their revelry. They'd all thoroughly enjoyed the sight of Turdy Samson turning on Evanna, who was particularly obsequious and two-faced and loathed by the majority of the class.

Then, this evening, her dad had brought Debbie home and they'd all drunk champagne. Best of all, Debbie had said, 'To sisters.' Melissa repeated the words to herself as she lay in bed listening to the sound of the boats' riggings clanking in the harbour.

'To sisters.' It sounded really cool. It made her feel not alone any more. She had an older sister just like her best friends Sarah and Clara. Maybe she and Debbie would become very close and she could stay over in her house. What would be very nice would be if Debbie had a baby. Then she'd be an auntie. How mega cool would that be? When Debbie had smiled at her it had given her a real good feeling. Today had definitely been one of the best days of this year, probably even her life, she thought drowsily as her eyes closed and she fell asleep.

Barry took the Greystones slip road off the N11 and yawned. He was tired. It had been a long day and, because he hadn't slept well the night before, he'd found it hard to concentrate on his driving. Fortunately, the N11 was a great road to drive when there was no traffic and he'd made the journey from Dun Laoghaire to Greystones in twenty minutes.

He wished Aimee hadn't phoned. He'd found it difficult to lie to her but how would she understand his motivation for going to comfort Connie? Lately she was extremely over-sensitive wherever Debbie and Connie were concerned. That was more than evident in her crack last night about how much the wedding was costing. He'd found himself unwilling to dis-cuss his meeting with Debbie with her, partly for his daughter's sake – he didn't want to breach her privacy – and partly for his own sake. What Debbie had divulged to him didn't show him in a very good light. He was sensitive as to how his wife would view the disclosures.

For the first time in their marriage he felt distanced from Aimee, and it was unsettling. Her work was definitely a factor in the chasm that seemed to be opening up between them. This big wedding she was working on was all-consuming. He'd never seen her so focused or worked up about an event before. She was on her BlackBerry permanently, and it was beginning to get irritating. If he did what she was doing he'd be given a real ear-bashing. Aimee was driven to succeed, but at what cost, he thought resentfully as he negotiated a tricky bend on a narrow part of the road. They didn't have time to talk any more. They barely had time to make love. Work, sleep and the gym were her main priorities lately. He and Melissa were coming a poor fourth.

His thoughts turned to his ex-wife. She'd been distraught at his revelations about his conversation with Debbie. He should have kept his big bloody mouth shut, he thought guiltily. It had been unfair to dump it all on her shoulders. Only a cold-hearted rotter would have left her on her own tonight without trying to bring some ease to the situation. He hoped that she'd be comforted by his surprise visit. Barry turned down the small winding road that Connie lived on. He felt uncharacteristically nervous as he pulled up outside his ex-wife's house, wondering what sort of a reception he'd get.

CHAPTER NINETEEN

Who on earth was knocking on her door at this hour of the night? Connie wondered as she hurried into Debbie's old room and peered out the window. The moonlight glinted on to a silver Merc and she recognized Barry's car. She opened the window and stuck her head out. 'Hold on, I'm just out of the bath, I'll be down in a second,' she called, and saw her ex-husband look up.

'Oh Lord,' she muttered, wiping her hands on her bath towel. She'd been rubbing body moisturizer on her arms and legs and her hands were greasy. His timing was crap! She hurried down the stairs and opened the front door.

'Hi,' she said. 'Come in. You shouldn't have bothered coming down. I just got upset when I heard what Debbie had said to you. It brought back sad memories, I suppose.' Her voice trembled and she cursed her weakness as tears filled her eyes.

'Aw, don't, Connie.' Barry closed the door and turned to take her in his arms.

'Sorry, sorry,' she sobbed against his shoulder. 'I feel I've let her down terribly. I didn't deal with it properly. I was too intent on being independent and standing on my own two feet. I wanted her to be the same, but it was far different for her and I didn't make enough allowances for her. No wonder she was so angry. I used to give out to her and tell her to let go of it. Easy for me to say, the poor little muppet.'

'Will you stop it? You're being too hard on yourself. It was *my* fault,' he protested, stroking her hair, which had escaped from the scrunchie she'd tied it up in.

'It doesn't matter whose fault it is – we mucked it up and she's the one who's suffering,' Connie said angrily, drawing away from him.

'Well, at least it's all out in the open and she and I have some hopes of getting back on some sort of an even keel,' Barry declared.

'But we ruined her childhood.'

'No we *didn't*, Connie. You gave her very happy times. And I know she doesn't rate it very much, but I wasn't mean with money and she didn't suffer financially, she had all the material things other kids had, so it wasn't a complete disaster.'

'I know that. I'm not saying or never have said you were mean, Barry.' Connie wiped the tears away from her cheeks. 'Go and put the kettle on until I put my dressing gown on, I feel a bit daft standing here in my bath towel.'

'You look fine,' he assured her. 'Nice tan. Is it fake or real? You can never tell these days.' He leaned down and sniffed the nape of her neck. 'Real.' He grinned. 'Those fake ones always smell.'

'Back garden.' She smiled back, remembering how he always used to tease her for being a sun-worshipper.

'Milk no sugar – see, I remember,' he called up after her as she made her way up the stairs.

She pulled a short cotton nightdress over her head and wrapped a matching robe around her and rewound the scrunchie around her hair. She didn't even bother to look in the mirror. He could take her as he found her at this hour of the night, she thought, yawning so widely her jaws ached. She hoped he wouldn't stay too long, she was tired. Still, it was thoughtful of him to come and see if she was OK. It was nice to know he cared enough about her to do that much.

He was munching on a chocolate Kimberly when she came into the kitchen. 'I helped myself – I hope you don't mind,' he said, pouring the tea into two mugs. He stirred in a drop of milk and handed it to her. 'Biscuit?'

'Not for me, thanks, I'm trying to make sure I fit into

something for the wedding.' Connie shook her head. 'Come on in and I'll light the gas fire, it's a bit nippy at night, isn't it?' she said, leading him into the sitting room off the kitchen. She turned on a side lamp and bent down to switch on the fire. Blue flames licked around the coal pieces, gradually turning to yellow as the fire took hold.

'They're so realistic now, aren't they?' Barry commented as he sat down on the squishy blue sofa that faced the fire. She sat beside him, tucking one of the big creamy cushions at her back.

'Is your back at you?' he asked, noticing what she was doing.

'I was lifting an elderly patient the other day and I felt it give a twinge. I guess I'm just not as young as I used to be,' she said wryly.

'Join the club. At least you're not fifty yet. I'm a geriatric compared to you.' He threw his eyes up to heaven and sipped his tea. 'Listen, I'm sorry about this evening, I should have kept my mouth shut. I never meant to upset you,' he said earnestly.

'I know that,' she sighed. 'I should have been more aware of Debbie's feelings when she was younger. I just didn't face it, I suppose.'

'You had enough on your plate,' he said gruffly, and she noticed the bags under his eyes and the deep lines grooved along his mouth. He looked tired, dispirited, and her heart softened.

'Look, we can't do anything to change the past. And we can't keep beating ourselves up about it. We both made mistakes and we have to live with them and try and do the best we can from now on.' She reached out and squeezed his hand.

'You always had a kind heart, Connie,' he said gratefully. 'You don't hold grudges. Some of the chaps I play golf with are scourged by their exes. You've never done that to me.'

'What's the point? It gets you nowhere and just leaves you bitter and twisted. I'd hate that. But I'm no saint, I've had my moments,' she said acerbically, remembering her bile towards Aimee earlier that evening.

'Trust me, Connie, I've seen the way some ex-wives behave, and you're nowhere near their league. Some women think marriage is a ticket to the good life without ever lifting a finger to earn a penny.'

'Well, I guess you were lucky with Aimee,' she murmured.

'Yeah, she works hard. It can go to the other extreme too.' He pulled a face.

'Oh!' It was the first time he had ever offered the faintest criticism of his second wife. All wasn't perfect in paradise then.

'At least Debbie got it off her chest and had the guts to tell me how she felt.' Barry changed the subject. 'And she really did make an effort with Melissa. Perhaps some good will come out of it. It would be great if they became close. I wouldn't feel that I had two 'only' children, if you know what I mean.'

'I know *exactly* what you mean, and it *would* be great if they became friends. Pity there's such an age difference.'

'When you and I are gone, they'll be there for one another,' he reflected.

'Cheerful Charlie,' she retorted. 'I'm not planning on kicking the bucket for a while.'

'You know what I mean,' he said sheepishly.

'What does Aimee make of it all?' Connie arched an eyebrow.

'She's in Milan at the moment, on business, but I'm not going to say too much of what Debbie said to me. It's our business, and I think it's only fair to keep it like that,' he said slowly.

'You're probably right. It will cause less hassle all round. You know Debbie – how private she is, and how touchy.' Connie nodded, glad that the other woman wouldn't be too involved in her daughter's emotional upheaval. 'I'd say she'd go mad if she knew we were even sitting here talking about her.'

'I know. Maybe you shouldn't even let on to her that we've had this discussion,' Barry suggested.

'I worry about her, Barry,' Connie confessed, feeling an enormous relief at being able to share her concerns about her daughter. 'What do you think of Bryan?' she asked bluntly.

'Er . . . um, he seems a nice enough chap,' he hedged. 'You'd know him a lot better than I would. Why?' His eyes narrowed as he studied her intently.

'I don't know,' she said slowly. 'I don't think he makes enough of an effort. She's the one who does all the running around. He seems to swan around having a great social life while she looks after the house, does the shopping, all that kind of thing. I don't think he pulls his weight enough.'

'Do you not like him?' he asked in dismay.

'Not really,' she admitted.

'Does Debbie know?'

'She knows I have concerns, but any time I've ever even tried to broach the subject she cuts me off very sharply. She just doesn't want to know.' Connie shrugged.

'I can't really say anything or that would be the end of us, and we've barely started to talk.' Barry chewed the inside of his lip.

'I just don't want to see her ending up miserable.'

'She seems happy with him. He's got a good job. The office design business is booming. He can be thoughtful – he selected a box set of cheeses she brought me as a present, so he has some pluses,' remarked Barry, disturbed by what she'd said.

Connie said nothing; she couldn't say to him that she felt Debbie was repeating a pattern with her choice of husband. Bryan was similar to Barry in some ways, that streak of me, me, me, for example. Having heard what Debbie had said to her father about not feeling worthy to be loved, Connie feared that she'd take any kind of bad behaviour from Bryan and let him walk all over her. But if she said any of this to Debbie she'd be the worst in the world. It was a terrible dilemma to be in. Or maybe it was just her, perhaps because she didn't like Bryan she was looking for faults.

'At least there's divorce in the country, she won't have to stay with him for ever if it doesn't work out,' Barry said pragmatically.

'If that's the case I hope there'll be no children involved,' Connie said sarcastically.

'And maybe it will all work out for the best. Who knows what the future holds?' Barry took a slug of tea and leaned back into the sofa, which was decidedly comfy. Far more relaxing than the leather one at home.

'We'll see. I could be barking up the wrong tree, I hope so,'

Connie yawned, patting Hope, who had wandered into the room. The cat purred loudly and jumped into her lap.

'That cat sure does love you,' Barry grinned, reaching over to stroke her silky fur.

'Just as well someone does,' she said tartly.

'Ah, don't say that,' he reproved.

'Melissa is very taken with her.' She switched topics smartly, annoyed with herself for sounding needy.

'She'd love a pet but apartments aren't really suitable. Maybe if we move house Aimee might relent.' Barry tickled Hope under her ear and she purred ecstatically.

'Are you moving?' she asked in surprise.

'I'd say we will eventually. Aimee wants to. I quite like Dun Laoghaire. Who knows?'

'Oh . . . right.'

'I guess I should be going,' he said reluctantly. 'This is a lovely cosy room, Connie. You did a great job with the place.'

'I love it. It's home.' She smiled.

'It's a long time since we've had such a good chat about things. We should do it more often,' he proposed.

It was a relief being able to confide her fears about Debbie to him. Sharing the burden was strange after so long carrying it alone. And he was right: it had been a nice, relaxing interlude with no tensions between them; at least they'd long gone past that stage of their relationship. 'That would be nice. Let's hope there aren't any more tumults like this. It was a relief to talk things over, Barry,' she agreed.

'Any time.' He stood up and pulled her to her feet. 'Sorry for keeping you up so late.'

'It's only quarter to eleven, it's not that late. It's just I've an early shift tomorrow. Thanks again for coming down. You didn't need to,' she told him.

'I know that. I wanted to,' he said, giving her a hug. 'I didn't mean to hurt you, now or ever. I'm sorry, Connie,' he murmured against her hair.

Her arms tightened around him. 'I know,' she said, feeling the roughness of his cheek against hers. They held each other in the firelight, the soft golden lamplight bathing them in a warm glow. It was the closest they'd been since their break-up all those years ago. It was a peaceful moment.

He drew away and looked down at her and then, before she could react, he'd bent his head and his mouth touched hers, lightly at first and then hungrily as she responded involuntarily.

'Barry!' she exclaimed, stunned. 'Stop.' She pushed him away.

'I don't want to stop,' he said huskily, his eyes glittering as he drew her close and kissed her again. He slid his hand beneath her robe and cupped her breast, caressing her nipple with his thumb through the light material of her nightdress.

'No, Barry, *stop,*' she protested again, shocked when her nipples hardened and a frisson of desire scorched through her. It had been so long since she'd been touched by a man she'd almost felt all that side of her had shut down. 'Barry, you're married. What about Aimee?'

'Just for old times' sake,' he muttered against her mouth, and then he was kissing her again, and this time she was kissing him back, hungrily, running her fingers through his hair, revelling in the sensations he was unleashing in her. At the back of her mind she knew she should stop, knew it would be disastrous to allow him to continue, but she threw caution to the wind, fed up of always being the responsible one. She'd reminded him that he was married. That was his judgement call.

Her body was coming alive, reminding her of what she'd missed during all these years of unwanted celibacy. Reminding her of her femininity, her womanliness, and her earthy, lusty side, which had been dormant for so long. When he took her hand and led her upstairs she was glad to follow him, wanting to pull him down to her in the big double bed and wrap herself around him with wild abandon. It was passionate and quick and they came, groaning and arching almost simultaneously. Connie lay beneath him with her eyes closed, and gave thanks that her body had behaved so wantonly and youthfully and she wasn't a write-off quite yet.

Her reactions shocked her. Where was her guilt? she

wondered as Barry lay on top of her panting, whispering her name over and over. She felt no guilt; she felt exhilarated.

'That was fantastic,' her ex-husband exclaimed.

'Let's do it again,' she urged with a wild light in her eyes, her hair tousled, her cheeks flushed, remembering how they had often made love twice in a row when they had been married, the second time always better than the first.

'Ah, Connie, I would if I could,' he groaned. 'I'm a middle-aged man, remember,' he said, withdrawing from her and lying back against the pillows.

'Oh,' she said, disappointed. 'We shouldn't have done it even the once, I suppose.' She leaned on her elbow and looked down on him, thinking how puffy he had become, how slack his jaw had grown, how grey his chest hair had got in the intervening years since their marriage.

'Old times' sake,' he said, giving a deep sigh, his eyes closing.

'Don't go asleep,' she warned.

'I won't. I wish I could. I wish I could stay the night,' he sighed as his breathing slowed.

Connie lay wide-eyed. Would she want him to stay the night? Would she want to wake up with him in the morning? Would she like to be married to him again?

No, no and no, she decided firmly. She cared about Barry but she didn't love him any more. If he thought there was going to be a repeat of this in the future, he was sadly mistaken.

She smiled. She felt strangely empowered. Alive again. He had done her a great service although he didn't realize it. She might be the wrong side of forty, but she'd just reawakened to the fact that she was still a vital, sensual woman and it was time she did something about it instead of galloping into middle age, depressed, defeated and defunct.

'Barry.' She nudged him in the ribs as he began to snore. 'Wake up.'

'Do I have to?' he groaned, drawing her to him. He kissed her and she kissed him back, wishing he would revive. She'd love another ride, long and slow, she thought wistfully, but he was as dead as a dodo.

Typical, she thought, frustrated: Barry, true to form, had let her down again.

'You don't want to keep your babysitter up too late,' she reminded him as she leaned out of the bed and picked up her dressing gown from where it had been flung on the floor.

'Oh hell, yeah, I forgot about Helen,' he grimaced as he ran his fingers through his hair and threw off the bedclothes.

'Should I apologize?' he asked self-consciously as he stepped into his boxers.

'Don't bother,' she retorted. 'I didn't do a lot to stop it.'

'It was good, wasn't it? Fast and furious.' He grinned boyishly.

'That's not the point really. We shouldn't have done it and we won't be doing it again,' she warned.

'Of course,' he agreed. 'Strictly a one-off.' He pulled up his trousers and fastened his shirt.

'Are you going to tell Aimee?' she asked from the other side of the bed, tying the belt of her robe.

'Are you *mad*!' he exclaimed, turning to face her.

'I was just wondering. Men get urges to confess to these things, and you were never great at keeping things to yourself. They always came out eventually.'

'This little episode is strictly between us.' He gave her a sheepish smile.

'Fine,' she said airily. 'I just don't want Aimee having a pop at me ever, if I'm not prepared for it.'

'Don't worry, that's not going to happen,' he assured her, knowing full well that if he confessed to Aimee that he'd slept with Connie he'd be out on his ear. 'We never used a condom.' He frowned as he bent down to put on his shoes and socks.

'No, we didn't,' she said slowly. 'And we talk about kids being irresponsible. But I don't think there's much likelihood of me getting preggers at my age.'

'No, I suppose not.' He straightened up. 'This has been one hell of a day and a night!'

'You can say that again,' she agreed, with a little smile as he came over to her and leaned down to kiss her.

'That was fantastic. Did you enjoy it as much as I did?' He studied her intently.

'Do you have to ask?' she said dryly. He laughed. He'd forgotten how wild Connie had been in bed when things were good between them.

'I suppose not. I just wouldn't like to think it was all one-sided. And it was great talking to you as well,' he asserted, anxious that she wouldn't think he'd used her for sex. 'I'll call you.'

'Don't feel you have to. I won't be waiting by the phone. I'm not twenty-two any more,' she said crisply. 'As you said, this was strictly a one-off, Barry. Go home now, and drive carefully.' She felt almost maternal as she kissed his cheek and patted him on the back. All her desire had ebbed away and she knew with certainty that she would never have sex with her ex-husband again, enjoyable and all as it had been.

CHAPTER TWENTY

Barry lay on his side of the spacious bed he shared with Aimee and couldn't figure out whether he was more shocked by his infidelity with Connie or his lack of guilt about it. Was it because Connie was his ex-wife and he still felt some indefinable bond between them? Or was it because he was pissed off with Aimee because she had made him feel less of a man with her smart comments and he'd wanted in some way to get his own back, and he'd done it by doing the thing that would probably hurt her most if she ever found out about it.

Whatever his reasoning, it had been great sex and Connie had enjoyed it as much as he had. Probably more, he thought smugly. He had regular sex, which she didn't, so no wonder she'd been up for it. She'd been like a firecracker. Barry smiled in the dark, remembering her passion.

He hadn't showered before he went to bed. He wanted to keep her scent on him, that faint citrus perfume, which, combined with her own scent, had brought him back all those years when they'd been young, unfettered and carefree.

He'd wanted to stay and feel her arms around him, her body soft and curvy compared to Aimee's more sculpted angularity. When was the last time he and Aimee had sat in front of a fire just talking without the ubiquitous BlackBerry making an appearance? He sighed. The very things that had attracted him to Aimee – her drive, independence and ambition – were now the very things that were irritating him. And those he'd found boring and stifling in his relationship with Connie were, ironically, the very things he now craved. It must be an age thing, or was he just a contrary bastard? he thought gloomily, knowing one thing was for sure, if Aimee ever found out that he'd slept with Connie she'd have his guts for garters. And then she'd walk for sure.

What was even worse and made him wonder about the state his marriage was in was the knowledge that he'd welcome another interlude like the one he'd just enjoyed with his ex-wife, and he felt quite sure she'd feel the same.

The musky tang of sex was still on her, and Connie's body tingled as she rinsed their tea mugs and left them on the drainer before switching off the light in the kitchen. For the second time that night she climbed the stairs to go to bed, but this time in a far different frame of mind. Yes, she still had the worry and sadness she felt about Debbie to deal with, but now she felt she wasn't on her own with the problem. That in itself was a huge relief. Whatever happened between herself and Barry, she felt sure that from now on he would be a support to her emotionally in her concerns for their daughter, even though, after the wedding, she would no longer need anything from him financially.

And then there was the *après*-sex frame of mind. Connie grinned as she picked her nightdress off the floor. 'Well done, bod,' she declared as she untied her robe and slid it off her. Who would have thought that it would have come back to life so confidently and pleasurably as it had? Certainly not her.

'So you're not past it, and you're still sensual and sexy and not a dried-up old prune,' she assured herself as she pulled her nightdress over her head and got into bed. It was very, very reassuring.

The full moon shone down through the Velux window, casting its melon-yellow rays on to her pillows. Less than an hour ago she'd been romping lustily in the bed with her ex-husband. She blushed thinking how she had asked him to do it again. No doubt he thought she was gagging for it. But her own response had taken her by surprise and cheered her up enormously.

Connie gazed up at the moon, now partially hidden by a sullen encroaching cloud. What did it say about her that she'd had sex with her ex-husband knowing full well that he was a married man with a child? True she'd initially pushed him away, shocked that he'd kissed her, but after that she'd joined in enthusiastically. In fairness to herself, she'd pointed out that he was the married one. So, technically, it *was* up to him to desist. She was single and free, she comforted herself.

It was a pity it had been over so quickly, she thought regretfully, remembering how her body had flamed with an ache that she'd long thought dormant. Barry had come very quickly: did that mean that she'd *really* turned him on or that he wasn't getting much at home? His comments tonight had suggested a discontent of sorts in his marriage that surprised her. She'd never heard him make even the smallest criticism of Aimee before but clearly, from his remarks, he wasn't happy with how much time she spent working or with her desire to move house.

How would the other woman feel if she knew that Barry had slept with her? She was such a cool, reserved lady it was hard to know just how badly she'd take it. Well, she might be a hugely successful career woman with a fabulous toned body, but her husband had strayed and, what was worse, strayed with a woman she looked down her nose at and patronized every time they met.

Connie knew it wasn't nice or very moral – in fact it was totally immoral – what she'd done earlier, but she couldn't bring herself to feel very ashamed. Had it been any other woman, yes she would have felt disgusted with herself, but Aimee had looked down her superior aquiline nose at her once too often.

'Would you not think of going into the management side of things, become a director of nursing perhaps, instead of working on the wards?' Aimee had asked her once when they'd been chatting at Barry's mother's birthday party. The woman had no clue of the amount of studying that would entail. The reason Connie hadn't done more college work was so she could be there for her child when she came home from school. She'd wanted to help Debbie with her homework and ask her how her day had gone, not some childminder, she'd informed the other woman, and that had shut her up quick enough. Connie knew when she was being condescended to, and Aimee was a master at it. So, no, she decided, she didn't feel that guilty at all. 'Deal with it, Ms Davenport.'

Connie turned over and felt the moonlight on her cheek bathing her in its pale yellow light. She didn't remember going asleep and slept so soundly she never even felt Hope jumping up on the bed to snuggle down beside her.

'You did *what*?' Karen exclaimed as she sat, the following day, having coffee and a cake with Connie in the coffee shop in Vincent's Hospital. 'Ohmigod!' She was staggered.

'Ssshhh,' murmured Connie, but no one was looking at them and she giggled at the expression on her sister-in-law's face.

'*Desperate Housewives* has nothing on you pair.' Karen took a gulp of her latte. 'What possessed you? Tell me *all*!'

Connie gave her the gist of the night's events, adding a little defensively, 'Well, he did kiss me pretty passionately and I *did* make some effort to get him to stop and told him he was the married one, but then I just joined in, sort of,' she admitted.

'Why wouldn't you, you've been deprived for years? But did it *have* to be with Barry? That could cause complications if it ever got out,' Karen pointed out.

'I know and, believe me, it won't get out. I won't be saying anything and he certainly won't be either. And it won't happen again,' Connie assured her.

'Well, not with Barry, but I sincerely hope that now you've got the hang of it again, you'll go off "riding" into the sunset with some hunk,' Karen said mischievously, biting into a muffin.

'At least I know I can do it and that everything's in full working order and the dreaded M hasn't affected me. It was very reassuring, trust me. I don't feel half as old as I did this time yesterday, before it all happened.' Connie cupped her mug in her hands and remembered how youthful she'd felt the previous night.

'Your eyes are sparkling. Was it good?'

'It was over very fast, tragically.' Connie threw her eyes up to heaven and Karen guffawed.

'That *is* a tragedy – how very inconsiderate of him. And you having waited all these years for a decent seeing-to. I'll ring him up and read him the riot act.'

'Don't you dare!' Connie exclaimed.

'Just joking, dearie. How did you feel? You're not going to fall in love with him again, are you? I don't think that would be a wise move.' Karen eyed her over the rim of her coffee cup.

'Absolutely not. Don't you worry about that, Karen,' Connie said firmly. 'I suppose I felt safe with him. I knew him – it wasn't someone I was doing it with for the first time, and because of that I wasn't inhibited. I used him as much as he used me and, now I know everything's still functioning satisfactorily, that was the best part of it for me. I felt alive and vibrant and horny and womanly.' She grinned. 'I suppose I should feel bad about saying this, but it wasn't about my feelings for Barry. I didn't even want him to spend the night. I care about him, but I don't really *love* him any more and I certainly don't feel his emotional needs are my responsibility. Is that horrible of me?'

'Not at all,' Karen assured her. 'I know a lot of exes who are sleeping together now and again. The Dentons see each other regularly. It's well known in the bridge club. Half the separated men in this country are sorry they separated and petrified their wives will give them a divorce. And half the divorced ones wish they were back with their wives, the Dentons being a case in point.'

'Really! I never knew that.'

'And, my dear,' Karen arched an eyebrow, 'you know the way Rosa Elliott has resisted for years giving Jeremy a divorce so that he could marry Ella?'

'Yesssss . . .' Connie sat up straight, knowing a particularly juicy piece of gossip was about to arrive. 'Every time I see Ella she's spitting feathers about something Rosa's done or said. They do hate each other's guts, don't they?'

'Indeed they do,' grinned Karen. 'Seemingly Rosa's got wise. She told Jeremy he could have his divorce. He nearly had a heart attack, because it's been his great excuse not to marry Ella. Now she wants the full palaver – wedding, dress, veil, bash, honeymoon.'

'Oh crikey! Jeremy's never going to marry her. If Rosa was bad to be married to, Ella would be a thousand times worse and he wouldn't have the escape route he's got now.'

'*Exactly!* I rest my case.'

'Well, you needn't worry, I have no intention of resuming any sort of intimate or emotional relationship with Barry,' Connie asserted.

'What was he doing anyway, trying it on with you? What's wrong in the Garden of Eden? Not casting any aspersions on your undoubted magnetism.' Karen smirked at her sister-in-law.

'He did say that Aimee works too much and that she wants to move from Dun Laoghaire and he doesn't. I just felt there was an undercurrent and that everything wasn't running as smoothly as it usually does.'

'I think it bugs him that she earns as much as he does. Barry's quite traditional behind it all.'

'He's married to the wrong woman then.' Connie made a face. 'And you know what? I don't care. Let them work it out between them. I won't be getting involved.' She looked at Karen and made a face. 'Er . . . we didn't use anything, but I'd say I'm safe enough at my age, wouldn't you?'

'Oh Connie,' Karen groaned. 'This is an iffy time for you. I read somewhere that the ovaries know that they're on the slippery slope, and they produce more eggs to have a last fling, so to speak. What part of your cycle were you in?'

Connie shrugged. 'Who knows at this stage? Sometimes I think I'm ovulating and then I think I'm going to have a period and it doesn't come.'

'Well, that would put the friggin' cat among the pigeons,

wouldn't it? Could you imagine everyone's face if you told them all you were up the duff?'

'Stop it,' Connie said in alarm, not knowing who would be the most shocked, her parents, Debbie, Aimee or Melissa. It was too unthinkable to contemplate. 'Could you imagine Mam and Dad? I'm a big enough disappointment to them, being a divorcée and all that. To get pregnant out of wedlock twice would be the last straw! It doesn't bear thinking about.' A thought struck her. 'Technically, I suppose, in the eyes of the church, seeing as we didn't get an annulment, I'm still married to him. I could use that argument with my parents if the worst came to the worst,' she joked.

'Ha ha! You better have a few hot baths,' Karen advised.

'It's not going to happen.'

'Don't take risks again, that's all I'm saying.'

Connie gave a little laugh. 'Imagine being an unmarried mother at my age! Aimee'd freak if Barry had to start paying maintenance for another child now that he's almost finished forking out for Debbie.'

'I'm thinking more of nappies and teething and school runs – that type of thing,' Karen said dryly. 'There, I knew that would knock the smirk off your face. I better get back to work.

'Seriously, though,' she wagged her finger, 'get out there and get a nice man for yourself. If last night gave you confidence, imagine what great sex with a good man could do for you.'

'Easier said than done.'

'Give it a try, you vamp you.' She smiled.

'Thanks for not judging,' Connie said warmly.

'Why on earth would I do that? You've had it tough and you're very hard on yourself too. I just want you to be happy and I'd love to see you with someone. You deserve every good thing that comes to you. And every fine thing too,' she teased as they finished their coffee and walked towards the exit.

'And pigs will fly,' Connie retorted. 'Thanks for meeting me for lunch – I was bursting to tell you. It was handy being here in Vincent's today and that you were only fifteen minutes away.'

'Wild horses wouldn't have stopped me meeting you after

your text. For God's sake, don't let it slip when you meet Debbie tonight,' Karen warned as Connie reached the lift to take her to her ward.

'I won't. I'm going to give it one last bash to try and get her to change her mind about marrying Bryan.'

'Rather you than me. Good luck,' Karen said as they hugged before Connie stepped into the lift and the doors whooshed closed.

'Debbie, there are three mistakes in the sick-leave entitlements, and Maurice Henderson is on half pay not full pay. This is a serious error. Your mind is obviously elsewhere and this is just not good enough.' Judith Baxter glowered down at Debbie.

'Oh . . . oh sorry, Judith.'

'For goodness' sake, get your mind on your job and do it properly, or I'll be suggesting that your increment be withheld for a full year and not six months,' Judith snapped, before walking over to Gina Andrews' desk to remonstrate with her for making an error in overtime payments.

'Incompetent idiots,' Judith muttered as she closed the door of her office and walked over to the window. She knew what was wrong with her. She'd got her period when she woke up and a very small part of her was disappointed. The irrational, dissatisfied part of her had hoped that she might be pregnant. Even though it was a very faint expectation, a pregnancy might have given her an excuse to change her life. Move out and set up a home of her own with her child.

She stared out over the skyline and wished she was anywhere but where she was right now. She knew, too, why she was angry, and it was all over a damn letter she'd read in an agony aunt's column from a woman who had her own house but whose boyfriend only stayed with her one night a week because he was looking after his elderly mother and he felt guilty if he wasn't at home with her.

Judith went to her bag and took out the letter, which she'd torn out of the magazine. And read it again, frowning where the woman said her boyfriend felt responsible for, and had a huge commitment to, his mother.

The agony aunt hadn't given the answer Judith had been expecting. Not at all. There was no *Poor you, this is difficult and you have made a huge sacrifice and so has he.* No *He's a wonderful man to be minding his mother.* No indeed. The agony aunt had briskly suggested that the boyfriend, now in his forties, was not sacrificing his life for his mother at the expense of his patient girlfriend but had made a conscious choice very decisively to stay with his mother and live his life around her needs. It was a set-up that suited him. The hard-hearted agony aunt went on to suggest that the boyfriend was not a victim, that there was recompense, clear advantages, in it for him, and that was why he was choosing not to be with his girlfriend. *Deal with it* was her attitude, more or less.

Judith had read the letter three times, with a growing sense of despair. Putting herself in the boyfriend's position. Yes, she had sacrificed her life for her mother. Yes, she felt guilt and a sense of responsibility for her but, when she had had the chance to reclaim her life after her father's death, she'd chickened out and come back for more of her mother's emotional blackmail. What did that say about her? Had she been afraid to take her chances out in the real world? Was her mother just an excuse for not living her life? And, even worse, was she more like her mother than she'd realized? Full of fear and timidity. Afraid to venture forth and live life to the full.

Her heart began to hammer against her chest, and fluttery butterflies of panic flapped their wings in her belly. She felt dizzy and nauseous. Was this a panic attack? she thought agitatedly as heat suffused her and she felt she couldn't breathe. She opened the window and took in deep, gulped breaths of air. Her phone rang. She swallowed hard and managed to compose herself enough to answer it. It was Personnel enquiring about someone's retirement date.

Judith dealt with the query, relieved to have something to focus on. She'd just put the phone down when it rang again.

'Judith. Can I help you?' she said automatically.

'It's me,' said her mother. 'My eye specialist's secretary was on and they've had a cancellation, so they're offering me the chance to go and get my cataract done tomorrow. I have to be admitted today for blood tests and the like. You'll have to take a half-day to bring me, and I'll need you to get me a new pair of slippers. The ones I ordered from Oxendale's haven't come,' Lily went on. 'I know it's short notice – if you can't do it, I'll ring up and say it doesn't suit.'

For one moment she was tempted to suggest her ringing Tom or Cecily and telling them to take a day off; let them go and buy slippers – but she restrained herself. After all, she'd made the choice to look after her mother for some sort of emotional pay-back, hadn't she? Judith thought angrily, despising herself even more for acting the martyr.

'I'll take the afternoon off. What time do you have to be there at?'

'Between two and four. I don't want to put you out. Maybe I'll call and say I won't go,' Lily twittered agitatedly.

'Don't do that. You might as well go when you have the chance. And it means you won't be worrying about it for weeks to come,' Judith said in a more affable tone. Her mother was working herself up into a state.

'But I don't have slippers.'

'I'll get them. Stop worrying about it now and calm down – you don't want your blood pressure to go up,' Judith warned.

'Get blue ones to go with my dressing gown. And get me some tissues, some Nivea, and some talc.' The list began to grow.

'Right. I have to go, I'll be home by one,' Judith said sourly, and hung up. She'd go to Marks for the slippers; she could get the other items in a pharmacy.

She'd known her mother's eye operation was coming up and she'd planned to paint the kitchen while she had the place to herself. Now it had come earlier than expected and she didn't even have the paint in; she'd have to go and get that tonight.

Her heart lifted a little. Judith loved painting and decorating. Three days of peace and quiet without her mother would be like a mini holiday. Just what she needed to try and regain her equilibrium. She had plenty of time up on the clock for the half-day today; that wouldn't be a problem. A thought struck her. She might as well take tomorrow off as well. She hadn't taken any of her annual leave so far this year. She should make the most of having the house to herself.

She'd treat herself to some nicies out of the Food Hall, and a bottle of wine to go with them. She wouldn't bother cooking. The weather was supposed to pick up, she'd get some bedding plants for the garden and plant them up and do the window boxes, and that would take care of that much for the summer. Then, in a week or two, when her mother was on the road to recovery, she was going to ring her brother and sister and tell them that she was going away for a few days and to hell with them. She *was* going to go away with Jillian to a spa and be pampered. They'd been promising themselves they'd do it for ages, she decided as she clicked on her computer and had a look at a few hotel websites to see what was on offer.

Lily's heart was doing a tap dance as she folded her new, blue lightweight-cotton dressing gown into her small case. When Mr Burton's secretary had phoned to say that, because of a cancellation, he'd be able to fit her in for her cataract operation earlier than planned and would she be available to be admitted to hospital that afternoon, she'd stuttered a 'yes'. Mr Burton had been kind enough to think of her; it was the least she could do.

'Admission time is between two and four,' the secretary had said kindly before hanging up, leaving Lily trembling at the other end of the phone. She didn't mind so much going into hospital, she always felt safe there; it was the idea of having the operation on her eye. If it went wrong she'd be in a fix, she thought as she took her new toilet bag from the drawer and placed her toothbrush and paste in it.

She hoped she would have a room to herself – she'd forgotten to ask if it was possible when she'd been talking to the secretary. Judith hadn't been too cross about taking the afternoon off. That was a relief. You just couldn't tell with her lately what sort of humour she was going to be in. She'd been a little snappish at the end of the conversation as Lily gave her a list of her requirements. She'd wanted to ask her to get a packet of cloves or mints to suck in case she got a ticklish cough, as she sometimes did in the evening. Her hand hovered over the phone on her bedside locker; she could ring her, she supposed. Lily sighed and let her hand drop. There was no point in pushing her luck. She didn't want the nose taken off her; she didn't think her nerves could stand it, not with the ordeal that was ahead of her. She took a deep breath and lifted her little framed photo of Ted off the locker. He was coming with her. She always said goodnight to her husband before switching off the light at night. Maybe it was foolishness but she felt he was there. She smiled down at him and kissed the cold-glassed photo before wrapping it carefully in a couple of linen handkerchiefs and placing it on top of her dressing gown. *Let God grant in His Mercy that I'll wake up seeing him better than I've been able to see him*, she prayed as she closed her case, fumbling with the lock as the bleary haze of the cataract reminded her yet again of how much of a nuisance it had become this past year.

'This pâté is gorgeous – have a taste.' Debbie offered her mother a triangle of toast smeared with a mixture of rich pâté and Cumberland sauce.

'Here, you have a piece of Brie.' Connie transferred a chunk of crispy Brie, melting and creamy in the middle, on to her daughter's plate. They were sitting in Purple Ocean, overlooking the harbour, and the evening sun was glinting on an enormous purple crystal in a display case behind Connie, which was part of the unusual décor of the airy restaurant. It was full of sparkling angel decorations, which could be bought, an unusual touch that had appealed to Connie the first time she'd eaten there.

'This is the life,' Debbie sighed as she forked some of the creamy mixture into her mouth. 'What a nice end to a bummer of a day.'

'Why? What was wrong with it?' Connie enquired.

'Oh, my boss, Judith, never loses a chance to find fault with me, and unfortunately this morning I gave her plenty of excuses. I made three different mistakes in the payroll and Eagle Eyes spotted them.'

'Oh dear. I suppose that's what she's paid for. What's wrong – can't you concentrate?'

'I suppose I was still thinking about last night with Dad,' Debbie said.

'Oh . . . yes,' Connie replied faintly, unable to stop the blush that rose to her cheeks.

'At least I got it off my chest,' Debbie blurted, not noticing her mother's discomfiture. 'I told him *exactly* how I felt. I spared him nothing, so at least he knows now why I was so . . . so distant with him.'

'Could you not have told me?' Connie said gently. 'Debbie, when your father told me some of the things you'd said to him, I . . . God, Debbie, I feel I failed you terribly. I wanted to think you were coping because it made life easier for me. I'm so sorry, darling; I only ever wanted the best for you. I—'

'Mum, Dad shouldn't have told you what I said, that was for his ears only,' Debbie said heatedly.

'No . . . he was right to tell me and I apologize to you, Debbie. You were the child, I was the adult. I should have known better. I wish you'd told me how you felt when you were young.' She reached across the table and squeezed her daughter's hand.

'I didn't want to add to your worries. You had enough on your plate, Mum, and it was Dad I was angry with, not you.'

'You once asked me had I done something bad to make Dad leave us,' Connie reminded her with a smile.

'Did I say that? Sorry, Mum. I guess I just wanted to blame someone – isn't that what kids do?'

'You were a great child, Debbie, I never had any trouble with you, apart from the time you went through your Goth phase – you were pretty obnoxious then – but on the whole we did well, didn't we?'

Debbie smiled at her, a big grin that reminded Connie of when she was about fifteen, and carefree because she'd met her first boyfriend and she felt part of the scene and she seemed to have come to terms with her father's second marriage. It had been a happy time in her life and Connie remembered that summer with pleasure. 'We did fantastic, Mum!' her daughter assured her.

Connie took a deep breath. If she didn't have her say now, she'd never say it and, if anything went wrong in her daughter's marriage, she knew she'd live with the guilt for the rest of her life.

'Debbie, there's just one more thing I want to say. I want you to think very carefully about getting married. Sometimes . . . um . . . when I look at Bryan, I see a little of your father in him, when he was that age. And I just wonder if he's ready to get tied down? Don't make the mistakes I did. There's no rush to get married. Live together a while longer. I just want you to be happy, you know that,' she said earnestly.

'Bryan makes me happy, Mum. He's not at *all* like Dad,' Debbie protested. 'No way.'

'I know he makes you happy, but is that enough? Marriage is hard work sometimes – mortgages, babies, the day-in-day-out sameness of living together knock the romance out of a relationship.'

'I know that, Mum. Trust me, I'm not wearing rose-tinted glasses,' Debbie said dryly. 'Bryan and I will be fine, don't you worry. I've no intention of having a broken marriage.'

'Ouch!' Connie grimaced. *Smug madam*, she thought irritably. *You should have seen what your father and I were up to last night.* She let it pass; there was no point in going on about Bryan. Nothing that she said was going to change her daughter's mind.

'. . . Bryan's a good guy, Mum, and he loves me, so stop worrying and let's look forward to the wedding.'

Connie turned her attention to what Debbie was saying. 'I just wanted to say it. Honey, I wanted to make sure you've no doubts.'

'No doubts at all. Now let's have a glass of champers and enjoy our meal.' Debbie was emphatic.

'Right,' said Connie meekly, feeling more like the child than the mother.

As she sipped the sparkling liquid she wished she could put her fears aside, but the niggle of unease still remained. Bryan Kinsella still had to convince her he was good husband material, no matter what Debbie said about him.

CHAPTER TWENTY-ONE

'It's a pity I couldn't have a room to myself – did you really try to get them to change me?' Lily whispered.

'I did, Ma, but they told me they're chock-full,' Judith told her for the umpteenth time.

'It's not good enough, I pay the full VHI,' grumbled Lily. 'I had my own room the last time I was here, you know. That should be on their records.'

'I told them that too, and they apologized but there's nothing they can do. At least it's a two-bed and not a four-bed,' Judith said briskly as she took her mother's nightdress and dressing gown out of the case.

'They might have a private room for me if I come back another time. This was a cancellation, you know.'

Judith threw her eyes up to heaven. She didn't know why Lily was whispering; they were in the room by themselves. Lily was lucky, she was in the bed by the window and the second-floor room had a lovely view of the hospital grounds and the vista looking south to the Dublin mountains. Her mother had nearly driven her mad since she'd got home earlier, and it was not improving.

Do this, do that.

Where's this? Where's that?

Get me this, that, and the other.

Lily was highly agitated and had taken a half a Valium to

calm herself down. When she'd discovered that she had to go into a two-bed ward she'd been mightily displeased and had wanted to go home, only that Judith had persuaded her to stay.

She'd got upset because she couldn't see the VHI form properly, even with her glasses and Judith's help, until the very kind admissions officer had calmed her down, telling her that she had all her details on the computer from her previous stay for varicose veins a couple of years ago.

By the time Lily had finally got to her ward Judith had felt like taking a couple of Valium herself. A man sitting in a chair beside the other bed greeted them politely. Lily flushed and muttered a response.

'The nurse will be with you in a while,' the admissions officer had said kindly, pulling the curtains around her bed.

'I'm not staying here,' Lily had whispered to Judith when she was gone. 'I'm going home.'

'No, no, you're here now, you might as well get it done.' Judith tried to keep the irritation out of her voice.

She heard the door open again and, from where she was standing at the end of the bed, she could see a plump, grey-haired woman in a green dressing gown enter.

'You might as well go,' she heard her say to the man in the chair. 'I've to go off and have physiotherapy.' She smiled at Judith and Judith smiled back.

'She looks like a nice lady,' she said to Lily when the two of them had left. Lily was twisting her wedding ring around her finger, staring out the window.

'Who does?' she said distractedly.

'The woman you're sharing the room with.'

'It's a *woman*? Are you sure? Was it not that man that was sitting beside the bed?' Lily stopped twisting momentarily.

'Of course not, Mother, what would you be sharing a room with a man for?' Judith was baffled. Where on earth had Lily got that notion?

'Martha Kelleher was in a ward with two men on either side of her down in Wexford,' Lily informed her tightly. 'It was a terrible ordeal for her. I'm sure it hastened her end, too, because even when she went home she was always terrified that she'd have to go into hospital again and have the same thing happen.' Lily burst into tears.

'Mother, please don't upset yourself, there aren't mixed wards in this hospital,' Judith said awkwardly, patting her on the back. 'You'll be home the day after tomorrow, and just think how good it will be to be able to see properly again,' she urged as she handed Lily a tissue. 'Stop crying now or your blood pressure will go up. Go in and get undressed for bed and I'll finish unpacking your case.'

'I still think it's a disgrace that I don't have my own room, and I'll be ringing the VHI to tell them so. They're going to get a piece of my mind, and I'll be wanting a refund.' Lily was not to be mollified as she took the clothes Judith handed her and stomped into the bathroom.

Judith swallowed her exasperation with great difficulty. Trying not to be tetchy with her mother was difficult under normal circumstances, but she always found it extra trying when she had her period and was more likely to fly off the handle. She was furious with her sister and brother. Tom hadn't even the decency to respond to her text, and Cecily had texted back that she wouldn't be able to visit until tomorrow and what were the visiting times. Judith hadn't bothered to answer. Let her ring the hospital herself and find out, selfish cow.

She unpacked her mother's case, hung her towels and face flannel on the shelf behind the locker and took Ted's photo out of its covering of linen handkerchiefs. She looked at her father's picture and felt a spasm of sadness. The grief she'd felt after his death had lessened to a great extent, but there were still times when a deep sorrow would suffuse her and she would have a moment of empathy with her mother, knowing how truly bereft Lily was by his death. Nothing had prepared Judith for the shock and loss she'd felt at her father's passing.

'Oh Dad,' she whispered. 'I miss you.' A tsunami of memories almost took her breath away. That stomach-lurching call to work that Friday evening telling her that her father was in A&E and that she had to get there fast. The terror and sense of

220

absolute helplessness as she sat stuck in rush-hour traffic on the quays knowing that her father was dying and she might not make it in time to say goodbye. The thumping of her heart, the knotting of her stomach as she'd searched frantically for a parking space, and then the racing as fast as she could into A&E, trying to find him, stuttering his name at reception, hardly able to talk.

The momentary sense of relief when she'd found him on a trolley hooked up to a plethora of machines, with Lily sobbing and Tom fidgeting restlessly, afraid. Her father had looked at her and she'd seen fleeting recognition and had felt the merest pressure when she'd taken his hand and squeezed it. 'I'm here, Dad,' she'd said, amazed at how calm she sounded. 'Don't worry about anything.' How pale and fragile he looked as his eyes closed and he gave a little sigh as if of relief that she was there to take charge.

'He's very ill,' a nurse said quietly to her as she changed one of his drips. 'You know that, don't you?'

Judith nodded, her throat constricted. Was he dying? She wanted to ask but couldn't, even though she knew in her heart of hearts that he was. Lily sobbed uncontrollably.

'Mam, do you want to go home? I'll stay with him.' Judith had put an awkward arm around her weeping mother.

'That's a good idea. I'll take her.' Tom jumped at the chance of escape. A weeping mother was easier to deal with than a dying father. 'Come on, Mother.'

Lily stared at Judith, her eyes raw and red-rimmed. 'Should I stay?' she asked tremulously.

Judith took a deep breath. 'I don't think Dad would want you to be so upset, I think he'd be glad if you went home,' she managed, knowing that her mother needed permission to leave, needed someone to make the decision for her. *How can you leave him?* she wanted to rant. *Don't you want to be with him for the last hours of his life? Can't you put someone else first for once?* But she swallowed it all down.

Lily had made her way out through the white curtains, followed by a clearly relieved Tom. A drunk shouted and moaned in the next cubicle, and then the sound of copious puking and the stench that accompanied it. A woman at the desk yelling, 'It's a disgrace, you can't leave her sitting in that chair, she's been in it for five hours and she's eighty-two.'

'Sorry, it's very busy. Friday evening, people get fraught,' the nurse said to Judith as a monitor beeped and she made an adjustment to the saline drip.

Judith made some non-committal response. She'd been in A&E a few times over the years with her father, and mother. She knew the nightmare of it. She knew it hadn't changed in the last ten years, even though the economy was booming. She'd seen the politicians lying through their teeth, saying that improvements had been made and waiting hours were lessened. None of *them*, with all their perks and privileges, ever had to endure a trip to A&E. How could they know what it was like or what those hard-working nurses and doctors had to endure on a daily basis?

'Could you just step out for a moment? We need to do a few things for your father,' the nurse said gently as another nurse appeared at her father's bed.

'Sure,' Judith acquiesced, stepping out of the cubicle, seeing an elderly woman crying in fear in her S-shaped chair as a nurse berated a drugged or drunken man to get up off the floor and a policeman and security man struggled to put him on a chair. Two orderlies weaved their way past with a trolley that had a sort of aluminium container over it. A green see-through sack with clothes rested on top of it. God! she thought in horror, was there a body under that? It looked like a sardine tin. Tears smarted her eyes. What a place to end your life. No privacy, no dignity, only for the utter and incomparable kindness of the nurses and doctors this place was hell on earth. She was suffused with rage that her father, who had worked hard all his life, paid his considerable taxes and never owed a penny or taken a bribe – unlike some of those very politicians who had the nerve to dismiss the problems in the health service – should have to endure this nightmare.

'You can go back in now.' The nurse had tapped her gently on the arm.

'Can you not get a bed for him?' she begged.

'We're doing our best, but it could be a while yet. We've made him as comfortable as we can, he has no pain,' the tired-looking nurse assured her kindly.

'Thanks,' she had muttered, afraid she was going to break down. She didn't even have a chair to sit on, so she leaned on the rail at the side of the trolley and took his hand in hers. 'I love you, Dad,' she whispered, wondering if her father, who was unconscious and breathing heavily, could hear her.

Later, seeing his condition deteriorate, they had moved him to a quieter section of the main A&E area, and Judith had known that he was going to die. The harsh fluorescent lights shone down on his waxy features and she had been glad her mother wasn't here, glad that she'd never have these memories, the way Judith would have when she remembered his last hours.

A chaplain, a lovely sympathetic woman, had come and blessed him and prayed over him as Judith strained to hear her words over the noisy hum of a ventilator in the next cubicle. The cupboard behind the chaplain's head was open and Judith stared at the contents, willing herself not to cry. Could anything be worse than this? she wondered. She had asked was there no room that he could be brought to where he could die in peace with a few candles lighting and no unending cacophony. 'I'm sorry,' the nurse had said sympathetically. 'We're still trying to get a bed for him, but it's a busy night, as you can see.'

When she had phoned Tom, he had said: 'Do you want me to come back in?'

He shouldn't even have had to ask. He should have wanted to be with their father. Didn't he and Cecily care? Had they no feelings for Ted? Had they no feelings for her that she was left on her own to deal with the most painful event anyone could ever have to deal with?

'No,' she had said. Her father would only have a loved one at his side, she thought bitterly as she stroked his thin, bony hand, remembering how strong and vibrant he'd once been.

'Just go, Dad, any time you want to; you've fought it long enough. Rest now,' she whispered, and had been rewarded by a surprisingly stronger grip, and she knew that he had heard her.

He'd breathed his last so quietly that she hadn't realized he was gone until the nurse had told her gently that it was over. She'd felt numb as the nurse led her to the family room and brought her tea and sat with her, stroking her hand, until she felt composed enough to go home.

The non-stop business of the next few days, making the arrangements, organizing everything, had kept her going. Everyone had turned to her. What do we do?

'Why are you asking me?' she had wanted to yell. 'There's three of us. Someone else do something.' But she wouldn't let her father down and leave him now to her siblings' devices.

Only for Massey's and their kind professionalism she would have cracked completely. They had led her through the arrangements with quiet compassion and treated her father's remains with great dignity. Lily, drugged to the eyeballs, had managed to get through the funeral and burial and then collapsed and, though Judith had tried to make the break away a month later, knowing that if she didn't she was doomed never to cut the ties, it had been next to impossible to leave Lily alone and not be overwhelmed with guilt.

'If you don't do it now, Judith, you'll never do it,' her friend Jillian warned, and she'd been right. Lily had become dependent on her, and she only had herself to blame.

Judith sat on the bed holding her father's photo and stared out the window, unseeing, tears streaming down her face. It had all come back so real, so vivid. It must have been seeing the clean, comfortable, airy ward Lily was in, in contrast to that awful place her father had died.

Recently she'd heard a senior government minister saying dismissively that health problems were only 'peripheral'. She'd been incandescent remembering the drunk shouting and puking next door to her dying father. She would have liked to bury the cheesy, grinning, made-up face of that smarmy so-called 'man of the people' in that drunk's puke and say, 'How peripheral is that, you bastard?' She was damn sure he would never end his days on a hospital trolley, nor any of his relatives either. The bitterness she felt over her father's place of death and the conditions he'd died under had never been assuaged. Many elderly people were more afraid of A&E than they were of dying, and rightly so, Judith thought bitterly. Only once had she heard a politician from the opposition say that drunks should be treated separately from the very sick and elderly, and she wholeheartedly agreed, after her experiences, but of course it never happened. If anything, the system had got decidedly worse under the government that was still in power since her father had died. Judith wiped her eyes and struggled for composure. If Lily saw her crying *she*'d start.

She supposed that she should come back in to visit her mother tonight. It looked as though neither of her siblings were going to bother. She should call Annie, Lily's sister, and let her know that Lily was in hospital, but she was going to make it abundantly clear that Annie would have to sort out her own lifts. She wasn't going to spend her precious free time as a taxi service for the relations.

She could come back and visit for an hour and then go home and wash and prime the kitchen walls for painting. Her mother was being operated on in the morning and would be sedated, so there would be no point in visiting until the evening. She'd have a full day to herself to do what she wanted in the house. A rare treat.

'Hang these up for me please, Judith.' Her mother padded out of the bathroom in her new slippers and handed Judith her clothes.

'Are you going to sit in the chair?' Judith asked as she hung the tweed skirt, blouse and cardigan in the wardrobe and folded her mother's underclothes neatly and placed them in the drawer.

'I think I'll get into bed,' Lily decided, and Judith could see that she was already in patient mode as she eased herself under the bedclothes and lay back against the pillows.

'Let me pour you a glass of water,' she offered, softening as she watched her mother rubbing the bad eye. 'Look, here's the menu for tomorrow; we'll fill it out. You'll probably be fasting in the morning, but I'm sure you'll be able to eat lunch or tea; you don't get a full anaesthetic, so you'll recover much quicker.' She read out the selections offered and placed a tick in the box when Lily decided what she'd like.

'Are you having a rest for yourself?' A dark-skinned nurse swished back the curtains and smiled at Lily. She was foreign. Lily gave a little tight smile. She hoped all these foreign nurses were well trained, she'd said to Judith as they'd waited to be admitted earlier. She was very worried in case any of the house doctors examining her might be foreign and she wouldn't be able to understand what they were saying. She had so many worries it was no wonder she was in a tizzy, Judith thought glumly as she saw the concerned look on her mother's face.

'I want to take your medical history now, pet, and your TPR,' the nurse said in perfectly understandable English.

'I should go.' Judith stepped aside to let the nurse move up beside her mother. She wouldn't be needed to translate!

Her mother flashed her a look of panic. 'Will you come back later?' she asked hesitantly.

'Yes I will, don't worry. Ma, if you think of anything you need, ring me on the mobile.'

'I will. Make sure you come back now.' Lily, pinched and apprehensive, was nearly as pale as her pristine white pillows.

'Relax, Mother, I'll be back,' Judith assured her, feeling a smidgeon of sympathy for her. Sometimes Lily was like a child, a very dependent child.

'Off you go so, I'll be here with your mother for a while, she'll be fine.'

The nurse took charge and, with a sigh of relief, Judith closed the door behind her and walked down the hospital corridor with a sudden exhilarating sense of emancipation. For the next few days the responsibility was no longer hers, and she intended to enjoy this brief respite as much as she could.

She heard the self-important footsteps striding down the corridor. A pause, the door handle turned and then Mr Burton was standing beside her bed, all red-faced and pompous as he pulled the curtain half closed.

'A little touch agitated, I hear, Mrs Baxter. No need to be troubled at all, you know. I'll get them to give you a little sedation, I think. There's nothing to worry about – as I've explained before, it's a very common procedure, so don't concern yourself. I'll see you in theatre at ten fifteen.'

He gave her a small bow, nodded condescendingly in the direction of Mrs Meadows, the other patient, turned on his heel and strode out of the room.

'Pompous little git, isn't he?' the other woman remarked matter-of-factly.

Lily managed a smile. 'I suppose he has a lot of responsibility.'

'Responsibility my hat. Some of that lot take themselves way too seriously. My fella, now, Mr Heeney, comes in and sits on the side of the bed and has a good chat with you and he's a right laugh. There's no nonsense out of him. That Burton is a stuffed little shirt. But he's good though. He's done two friends of mine and they're right as rain.'

'Is that so?' Lily said interestedly. Mrs Meadows was a fount of medical knowledge. She was in for a bladder repair but had had a hip and knee replaced and several other minor procedures. She'd introduced herself to Lily when she'd come back from her session with the physiotherapist and had sat in the chair beside Lily's bed and chatted away.

Not for them the immediate familiarity so widespread among a younger age group. They used each other's titles, *Mrs* Meadows and *Mrs* Baxter with ease, but the bond of widowhood and shared generational experiences opened the doors to mutual confidences.

Widowed like Lily, Kitty Meadows had two sons who were married. She lived alone, she informed Lily, and wouldn't have it any other way. She wasn't going to be a burden on any of them, good and all as they were to her and, if it got to the stage that she couldn't look after herself any more, she was going to sell the house and go into a nursing home and she'd told them that too.

'But you hear terrible things about those places,' Lily exclaimed. The other woman, who was a year older than her, had great spirit compared to her, she thought, ashamed of her own timidity.

'Not at all.' Mrs Meadows dismissed the notion. 'I've one or two friends living in them, and some of them are fine places and give great care. Some of them are a disgrace, I'll grant you, but keep looking until you find one that suits you.'

'And don't you mind living on your own? Don't you feel nervous?' Lily was curious.

'What's the point in being nervous?' the other woman scoffed. 'You'd spend your life waiting for something to happen. I get into bed, I say my prayers and I sleep like a log. Life's what you make it, Mrs Baxter. It's up to you. That's my motto,' her companion declared robustly as the rattling of a trolley outside heralded the arrival of tea.

Lily had just finished her tea when the door opened and her son marched in with a large box of chocolates and a bottle of Lucozade.

'Hello Ma. Judith sent me a text to let me know you were here. How are you, all ready to go under the knife?' he said jovially, plonking down on the chair beside the bed. 'I can only stay for ten minutes. We're going to an open night for Jonathan in Walton College. It's so important to pick the right school for them now. I know it's fee-paying, but it will be worth it in later years when he's going for one of the professions. Still, at least I made the effort to get in to see you, even if it *is* only for a few minutes,' he said, plucking a couple of grapes off the bunch Judith had brought for Lily. He picked up the paper from the end of the bed.

'Just want to check the ISEQ and see how my shares are doing. The bloody property market's in trouble in Spain,' he informed her as he flicked open to the business pages.

Did I spawn that stuck-up snob? It's far from stocks and shares and fee-paying colleges he was reared. There was nothing wrong with the secondary school that his father and I sent him to, Lily thought in disgust as her pinstripe-suited son sat stuffing his face with her grapes, his head buried in the paper.

'While I'm at it, Mother, you've made a will, haven't you? It's always good to have your affairs up to date.' He studied her over his bifocals, eyes narrowed.

She looked at him sharply. 'Of course I have. I don't need you to be telling me about my affairs,' she snapped.

'Don't be like that now. I'm your son – it's my duty to look out for you,' he blustered. His hair was beginning to recede, making his nose look beakier, and his blue eyes beadier and smaller. He was skinny, too, which didn't help.

'Judith looks after me very well,' Lily said pointedly.

'I know that, Mother. She's very good at the day-to-day stuff—'

'She's very good at *everything*. She's painting the kitchen tomorrow, I'll have you know. Something *you* should be doing!'

'Now, Ma, you know I'm up to my eyes. Why doesn't she get someone in to do it?' Tom exclaimed in exasperation. 'She doesn't have to act the martyr.'

'These things cost money, Tom,' Lily shot back acerbically.

'She's on a good salary, Mother, and you have a decent pension – you should spend a bit of money on yourselves,' her son lectured, pointing a bony finger at her.

'Only for her I'd be lost,' Lily said tartly.

'Sure, what other responsibilities has she?' Tom derided. 'If she had to put three kids through college and worry about expanding a business, she'd have plenty to worry about. It's not easy out there now,' he moaned. 'Thank goodness Glenda has that part-time job in the boutique to pay for the holidays and her car.'

Lily listened to him rabbiting on about his expenses and the cost of maintaining the apartment he had in Spain, which wasn't just a frivolous holiday buy, he assured her, but a long-term investment so that he'd have money to give his children to put deposits on apartments when they were of an age. If the property market was crashing over there, he could be left with negative equity.

Listen to him now, she thought crossly. The boasting he'd done about that place in Spain. Every Tom, Dick and Harry in the golf club had been invited over to visit but not his elderly mother. Good enough for him if it went sour.

What did he want to know had she got her will made for? He'd never been so blunt about it before. Did he think she was going to die on the operating table? He needn't think he was going to find out what was in it. That was none of his affair. Judith was getting the house. And if he didn't like it he could go ... he could go and live in Spain with his negative equity, she thought acidly, wishing he hadn't come to visit her at all.

Tom Baxter drummed his fingers on the steering wheel as he negotiated his way on to the slip road for the M50. He could see the traffic crawling along on it and he groaned. Glenda would go through him for a short cut if he was late for Jonathan's open night. He'd sent her a text saying he'd meet her there and it hadn't been replied to. She was obviously in a snit already. She probably wanted to arrive in the BMW; it would make more of a statement than arriving in her Polo. That's what she'd be thinking. He had to admit she was right. Image was everything these days.

His mother had been in a very fractious mood. Not at all grateful that he had made the effort to come and see her. Lauding Judith to the skies. There was no need for his sister to paint the kitchen herself; that sort of nonsense annoyed him. Judith was always trying to make him feel bad because she was the one taking care of their mother. What was her problem? She had a nice cushy number. A good job, no mortgage, no children to worry about. And Lily was very healthy for her age and well able to cook and look after herself. His sister would get a right land when Lily was gone and the house was sold and the proceeds divided between the three of them. Then she'd get a taste of real life and she'd have to go and get herself a mortgage and live like the rest of them.

Lily had jumped down his throat when he'd enquired about her will. He just wanted to suss out if she'd made one. Any operation carried a risk at that age. If the will wasn't made, would Judith claim possession of the house? He needed to talk to his solicitor about it. That house would pull in 500,000 euros easily.

Drumcondra was a little goldmine for property. It was close to the city centre and the airport. The proposed Luas line was going to add enormously to the price of property. Judith could go and take a hike if she thought it was all going to her. There was no mortgage on the house and he wanted his share. Hell, he was relying on his share to pay off that damn mortgage in Spain and free up his money to invest elsewhere. Maybe not in property – property markets were taking a hammering, as were stocks and shares. He'd go for blue-chip commodities perhaps.

Investing was such a risky business, and it was nice to know he had a safety net under him. Or so he'd thought. He bit his nails as the car sat idling in a mile-long tailback. He'd always assumed that the house would be left to the three of them to sell and divide up the spoils, but making assumptions could be a disaster. Better to know the full story. He might just take a meander over to the house tomorrow on the pretext of helping with the painting and see if he could have a little snoop in his mother's room to see if he could find the damn will. Forewarned was forearmed.

'Your brother wanted to know had I made my will, Judith. What do you make of that?' Lily plucked agitatedly at the blanket. 'He must think I'm going to kick the bucket. Hundreds of people have this operation at my age, don't they? My nurse' – Judith was amused at the possessive noun – 'tells me it's extremely common, and so did Mr Burton.'

'Of course you're not going to kick the bucket, Ma. What nonsense.' She held on to her temper with difficulty. If she could get her hands on Tom she'd let him have it. It had been at least six weeks since he'd seen them. He hadn't even called over at Easter, and now he was at Lily's bedside wondering if she had her will made. What a crass bastard. 'What else did he have to say for himself?' she queried, wishing her mother would stop fidgeting.

'Ach, do you know where he was off to? Going to an open night in some posh fee-paying college. Wouldn't they give you a pain? That Glenda one always had notions. Then he was going on about his property in Spain, a place you or I will never be getting an invitation to. I told him you were at home painting the kitchen and told him he should be doing it. He scarpered pretty fast after that.' Lily sniffed.

'I suppose you were lucky to get a visit. Any word from Cecily?'

'I got a phone call to say Daisy has the chickenpox and she won't be visiting. Convenient, if you ask me. I thought she had that a few weeks ago.' Lily lay back against her pillow. She looked tired. 'Feck the pair of them anyway,' she said. 'My memory is long.' She reached out her thin, birdlike hand and caught Judith's in a surprisingly strong grip. 'Never you fear, Judith. I've told you you're getting the house, and he can mind his own business about my will. You've stuck by me and I know it wasn't easy for you. Now I'll stick by you.' Lily had two pink spots on her cheeks, and her eyes were momentarily bright with determination, despite the sedative she'd been given.

Judith felt strangely moved at her mother's little speech. It wasn't easy for Lily to say those words. But it was reassuring to hear her mother confirm their agreement. A tendril of unease wound its way around her gut. Tom was a very determined character, and Judith had never actually seen her mother's will. She couldn't very well ask her where it was right now. That would be as insensitive as Tom had been, but it was something she needed to make sure was definitely in order or else she could have a very nasty battle on her hands to keep the home she'd lived in all her life.

Judith sighed deeply. Why was there no respite? Why was everything an uphill struggle in her life? 'That's good to know, Ma,' she said and was rewarded with another tight grasp. She hesitated. Did her mother expect a response? This was uncharted waters for them. Judith couldn't remember the last time there had been physical contact between them. She gave a little squeeze back in return. Lily's eyes met hers in unspoken agreement. Tom could do his worst; in this instance Lily and Judith were as one.

*

'I'll have the green gnocchetti piemontese style and the sword-fish scallop, please,' Aimee ordered, handing back the menu to the rather dishy waiter, who gave her a white-toothed smile that reminded her of a young Antonio Banderas.

'A good choice, señora,' he approved. 'And to drink?'

'I think the Arnesi?' She glanced over at her dining companion, Roberto Calvari, a rep with one of her main suppliers.

'*Perfetto.*'

They were at the window table in the small room in Il Coriandolo, one of her favourite restaurants, in the heart of Milan and just a stroll from her hotel. Aimee wriggled her toes under the table. Today had gone very well and she was pleased with her selections of crystal, cutlery, china and napery. A day's work well done, she decided as she sipped her perfectly mixed G&T with pleasure.

At least she didn't have too early a start in the morning. Her flight was at 11.35 and arriving at 13.10, so she'd miss the Friday rush hour.

'Roberto, would you mind if I stepped outside for a moment to ring my daughter? I always like to say goodnight to her,' Aimee asked her dining companion, who waved expansively in the direction of the door.

She keyed in Melissa's number as she stepped through the big arched doorway and stood in the shade of the beige brick walls dappled gold in the light of the evening sun.

'Hi Mom, Sarah and I are walking along the pier. We're on our keep-fit mission – we want to be skinny for the wedding,' Melissa confided breathlessly.

Aimee smiled. 'That's excellent, darling, keep it up. Exercise is *so* important.'

'And Mom, will you get me some MAC make-up in the duty-free? I really like their Barbie Loves MAC eye shadows. The Magic Dust and the Playful, if you can get them, and some kohl and Barbie Lipglass?'

'If I can, darling.'

'Thanks, Mom, that will be cool.'

'And what's Dad doing?'

'He's having a decaff in Costa and reading a book. He wanted to go and play golf but Helen couldn't come and baby-sit. I told him, like, there was no need for her to come. Mom, I'm really old enough to be by myself now.'

'Maybe next year,' soothed Aimee, pleased that her daughter was exercising and seemed perky; she'd been so sullen lately. Stepping up her challenges to Aimee's parental authority. It was a relief to have a conversation that wasn't a battleground.

'Enjoy your walk, darling. I'll be home tomorrow and I'll see you then.'

'Bye Mom. Love you,' Melissa declared before hanging up.

Aimee smiled as she re-entered the restaurant. It was good to know all was well at home. Barry was probably pissed off that he couldn't go and play golf. She'd ring him from the hotel later. If he was in a grumpy humour she didn't want to know. Right now she was going to enjoy a well-earned glass of wine and real Italian food.

She was pleasantly relaxed three hours later as she lay on the bed and dialled home.

'Hello?' Her husband sounded fed up.

'Hi, how are things? Did you get your problems sorted out last night?' she said airily, having drunk half a bottle of wine plus her pre-dinner G&T.

'Oh . . . oh . . . yeah . . . it's sorted. A computer glitch. How are you? How did your day go?'

'Terrific. I've sourced some really classy stuff. I'm very pleased. It was a good trip all round,' she assured him. 'And I had a delicious Italian meal in my little restaurant, drank a half-bottle of wine and am ready for bed.'

'Sounds good,' he said sourly. 'I was hoping to get a game of golf in but I couldn't get Helen to baby-sit. So my evening was pretty dull.' Self-pity oozed down the phone.

'Well, I'll be home tomorrow – perhaps we might go to dinner, my treat. We could try out the Saddle Room in the Shelbourne. I haven't been in it since it's been revamped,' she suggested.

'Oh, OK, that sounds good,' he agreed with not much enthusiasm.

'Will you ring for a reservation? And see if Helen can come tomorrow?'

'Right. Sleep well. See you tomorrow,' Barry agreed, before hanging up.

Aimee stared at the phone. He wasn't very chatty. Just because he couldn't go for his bloody game of golf. It annoyed her that she'd felt she had to appease him in some way, hence the offer of dinner in the Shelbourne. It was hard trying to juggle everything and keep everyone happy. If he was away on business it was no big deal and she was expected to arrange her work schedule to mind Melissa. When she was away it was viewed as a jaunt and, if he had to miss his golf, Aimee was the baddie. She was travelling much more than she'd been when Melissa was young and she knew it grated on Barry.

She picked up her BlackBerry and began to scroll through her emails. There was one from Gwen, a chainmail with jokes about marriage. Did her friend think she had nothing better to do than to be reading rubbish emails, she thought irritably, as she deleted it without reading it. The woman hadn't a clue. Easy for her to be sitting at her computer forwarding daft emails when she had nothing to do all day except look after her children.

Her fingers danced over the keys as she responded to an email from the wedding planner for the high-profile wedding she was working on. This was the biggest project she'd ever been entrusted with. Her brief: to showcase the best of everything Irish. Food, crystal, tableware, linen. Roger O'Leary wanted to impress big time. He'd been at several high-society weddings, and he had to make as much of an impact with his bash. To outdo his peers would be an even better scenario, he'd hinted. Aimee understood perfectly.

She and the bride, Jasmine, had decided on fine bone Royal Tara tableware with a delicate blue floral motif. Aimee had told the florist she wanted the blue and white theme right through the marquee. Delicate arrangements of tiny white rosebuds, forget-me-nots, baby's breath and trailing ivy would decorate the tables, and the cake, a five-tiered affair, would be decorated tastefully in the same colours. Everything was taking shape, but she was concerned that the florist was going over the top in some of his suggested table arrangements. '*NB. Discreetly elegant!!! This is not Posh and Becks!!!!*' She typed swiftly. Engrossed, Aimee forgot Barry and his grumpy humour and Gwen and her silly email and focused her mind on the real priority in her life . . . her work.

CHAPTER TWENTY-TWO

That shade worked a treat, Judith approved as she stood back to admire her handiwork. She'd chosen a Farrow and Ball pale-green paint called Arsenic which contrasted beautifully with the cream kitchen presses. It completely changed the kitchen. She hoped Lily liked it. She hadn't shown her mother the paint colour, afraid she'd nix it and go for a yellow shade similar to what had been on it.

It hadn't taken that long to paint. The kitchen wasn't very big, and she'd got up at the crack of dawn to start. It had been peaceful at that hour of the morning and as she swished up and down the walls with long, even brush strokes, she'd felt uncharacteristically tranquil. Wearing jeans and an old T-shirt added to her air of relaxation. It was such a relief not having to dress in one of her sharp work suits. And not having to wear make-up. Her mind had been totally focused on what she was doing, and all her anxieties and dissatisfactions faded away. She felt like she was in a little bubble of dipping and brushing and dipping again with the sounds of early morning and birdsong drifting in through the open back door.

She'd phoned the hospital at eleven thirty to be told that her mother was back from the theatre and was asleep. Everything had gone very well and she'd be able for a visit later that evening. Her hours of freedom glittered like unclaimed treasure and she resumed her painting with vigour, anxious to have some time to herself to relax and make the most of her solitude.

Later, when she had finished and was waiting for the paint to dry, she took a stroll down to the library to collect a book she'd put on reserve. She'd got a phone call about it, and she was looking forward to reading it. It was about the great Roman orator Cicero, and the reviews she'd seen of it led her to believe she was in for a gripping read.

Judith loved Roman history. Her father had been an avid reader and one of his abiding interests was Greek and Roman civilizations. He'd given her Graves' *The Twelve Caesars* to read as a thirteen-year-old, and from then she'd been hooked. They'd watched the magnificent Derek Jacobi bring the stuttering Emperor Claudius to life in the powerful series *I Claudius*, and the bond between father and daughter had grown even stronger as they sat together, gripped by the machinations of the promiscuous Messalina, his third wife, and the cold cunning of Agrippina, his fourth. Ancient civilizations had fascinated Ted, and from him she'd learned about the Minoan and Aztec worlds, and so much more. Reading had been his great escape from the tiresome demands of his wife, which he bore stoically.

He would have thoroughly enjoyed this acclaimed Robert Harris book that she was about to borrow. He would have read it and they would have discussed it over cups of strong, sweet tea at the kitchen table. When he'd had his stroke she'd often read aloud to him, inwardly grieving at the state of him as he grew more helpless. Part of her had been glad when death had claimed him, glad that at last he was free of the cruel imprisonment of his body. Judith truly felt his spirit had soared away to a new realm where he was healthy and reading and enjoying learned discussions with all those Romans, Minoans and Aztecs who had gone before him. Often she wished too that she was free and, in the darkest recesses of her mind, when her life had been very difficult in the months after his death, she'd been very aware that her mother had a selection of prescription sedatives and other drugs that would have been easy to swallow down some night. The odd thing was that it was this very knowledge that there was a way out that kept her going. Even to this day

238

that was still a little safety net for her. If things got really unbearably awful there was a solution.

Today, though, she had no need for safety nets. It felt strange to be walking down past the verdant park on a Friday morning. It was like playing hooky. Judith took a deep breath. The trees looked so fresh and vibrant, the tracery of light and shadow dappling her face as she walked in their shade. She crossed Milmount Avenue to the red-brick and cream-painted library building, thinking that she could bring her lunch to the park if she wished and read a chapter as reward for her exertions earlier. She pushed open the big heavy wood and glass doors and was instantly transported back to her childhood by the smell of beeswax polish. Beams of light shone from the high rectangular windows down on to the old, round wooden tables, which gleamed from their polishing. The library had hardly changed since her childhood, apart from being computerized, and it was quiet that Friday morning, with only an elderly man and a young mother and toddler in the small children's section to the right of the desk. The assistant scanned her books, and she gave him the name of the one they were holding for her. She was tempted to go in and start browsing, but if she did she wouldn't have time to have her lunch in the park, and now that the idea had tempted her she was inclined to do it.

She smiled at the young man, feeling decidedly carefree, and left the building and walked briskly past the health centre and small cottages to emerge on to the busy, fume-filled, traffic-jammed Drumcondra Road. It was amazing how a couple of yards could make such a difference, she mused as she waited for the lights to change. Moments ago she'd been in a small tranquil backwater; now she was in noisy madness. That was the nice thing about her area, she supposed – very close to the city centre, yet in the small streets and park it was quiet and peaceful with only the muted roar of the traffic beyond to give an indication of how close they were to town. The lights changed green and she hurried across to get herself a roll and coffee to take back to the park.

Ten minutes later she was sitting under a spreading

horse-chestnut tree, leaning against its thick, gnarled trunk, munching on a cheese, bacon, lettuce and mayo crispy roll and drinking hot, reviving black coffee.

This is the life, Judith thought, relishing her lunch, far from the concerns of her life, far from the irritations of her workplace and far from the vice-like imprisonment of being her mother's unwilling carer. The park was still, with a light breeze weaving and whispering through the trees making a shushing sound that reminded her of the sea. A mother with a toddler in a pushchair and an older child skipping beside her walked along the path opposite as they headed towards the brightly coloured play area. Some students from the nearby teaching college lay on the grass chatting and joshing. An old man nodded asleep on a park bench further down.

Judith gave a sigh of contentment. Who would have thought this day would have turned out so pleasurable? It was one of the nicest days she'd had in a long, long time. She opened her book and was immediately drawn into the life of Tiro and his master Cicero, and everything else faded away. An hour later she stretched and shook the crumbs off her lap. Her little interlude was over; she still had plenty to do at home.

Might make an onslaught on the garden, she decided ten minutes later, looking out at the jungle of lawn which badly needed cutting. It was a warm, sunny day; the fresh air would be good for her, she told herself, trying to psych herself up to cutting the grass, a job she loathed. It didn't help that her back was beginning to niggle, a dull nagging ache from period pain.

She'd have a cup of tea and a chocolate biscuit first, she bargained with herself, filling the kettle. She always craved chocolate with her period. A Cadbury's snack would assuage the longing. It was strange; she kept expecting her mother to appear in the kitchen with some request or other. The house was unusually silent. Lily was an avid radio listener, and Pat Kenny and Ronan Collins were her favourites. Judith hadn't bothered turning on the radio as she worked, and it was taking her a while to get used to the silence in the house.

She was just adding milk to her tea when the doorbell chimed.

Judith went to open it, expecting it to be one of the neighbours checking on her mother's condition and got the surprise of her life to see her brother standing at the door, his black BMW parked outside. She nearly asked, 'What do you want?' but restrained herself.

'This is a surprise. A visit on a weekday!' she remarked a trifle acidly as she walked back into the kitchen.

'I took a few hours off. Ma said you were painting the kitchen and I came to give you a hand,' Tom informed her magnanimously.

In your pinstriped suit! I don't think so, Judith thought nastily.

'That was very kind of you. As you can see, I've just finished.' She waved a hand around the kitchen.

'Very nice job. Good colour. Is there tea in the pot?' Tom enquired, studying her work with a judicious eye.

'I'll make you a cup,' she said ungraciously. This was her precious day off, and she didn't want to be wasting her time entertaining her brother. Tom hadn't come out of the goodness of his heart, she knew that, and alarm bells were beginning to ring.

'I'll tell you what, seeing as I've finished the painting and as you were so kind as to come over and offer to help out, why don't you go out and give the grass a cut? It was getting on Ma's nerves, and I was too busy to do it,' she suggested sweetly.

'Oh . . . er . . . right.' He frowned.

'The lawn mower's in the shed, and the clippers are hanging on a nail on the wall. I'll have the tea made for you when you're finished.' She held the back door open for him and walked down the garden path to unlock the shed.

'This isn't a very convenient time for me.' He glanced at his watch.

'But I thought you were going to paint,' she said innocently.

'Why the bloody hell didn't you get someone in to paint, Judith? And why don't you get someone in to do the garden?' he said irritably. 'You don't have to act the bloody martyr, you know.'

'I'm not acting the martyr,' she retorted, stung. 'And why

241

don't you do a bit more around here if that's the way you feel? Or else, *you* pay for a gardener.'

'I have a business to run and a wife and family to look after,' he snapped.

'So therefore *I* have to do everything. I'm to be penalized because *I'm* not married with children. Well, I have news for you, Tom, I'm fed up of it, and you and Cecily can start pulling your weight a bit more. If you had done so years ago, I might have had a family of my own to look after and you'd be stuck with Ma on your hands a lot more,' she exploded, marching into the kitchen in high dudgeon.

Tom was thoroughly put out as he pulled the lawn mower out of the shed.

'Good enough for you,' muttered Judith. She knew him well enough to know that the purpose of his visit would be revealed eventually, as it wasn't out of good-natured charity that he had come to offer his assistance. He was damn sorry now after her little outburst. He was so smug, self-righteous and self-centred that she'd felt like socking him one in the jaw.

She watched him push the lawn mower through the long sward, his face reddening with the effort. He took his jacket off and hung it carefully on the shed door. Why Glenda let him out in pinstripes, Judith could not fathom. Did he think it gave him gravitas? He was too skinny for them, and they only emphasized his scrawny, skeletal frame. Just as well he wasn't tall or he'd look like a pin-suited cadaver, she mused as she heard him curse as the blades got stuck in a clump of grass.

'I need to have a slash,' he told her when he'd cut the grass and put the lawn mower away.

'Go ahead,' she said edgily. She heard him hurry upstairs and the bathroom door close. The phone rang. It was Annie, her aunt, who wanted to know how Lily was getting on. Judith gave her the progress report.

'I was hoping Nina would bring me in to see her but she can't make it, she's got to go to town for a pair of shoes to wear to a do. Would you be able to come over and collect me?' Annie asked hopefully.

'No I can't, Annie. I'm painting the kitchen for Ma and I want to have it finished before she gets home,' Judith said very firmly. Her aunt had a neck and a half, and she was damned if she was going to go running after her when she had family of her own to ferry her around.

'Oh dear, I might not get in so. Hmmm. That's a pity.'

'Yes it is, Annie, but if you don't get in to see her you can always call over for a visit when Nina is free,' Judith suggested airily. 'Now, I really must go. Byeee.' She hung up the phone and glanced at her watch. Her aunt had kept her gabbing for ten minutes, and her precious free time was getting whittled away. A thought struck her. It couldn't take that long to piddle. What was Tom up to? She walked quietly into the hall and heard him moving around in her mother's bedroom. She raced up the stairs just in time to see him walk out on to the landing. He looked as guilty as hell.

'What were you doing in there?' she demanded aggressively.

'Keep your hair on, Judith, I was looking to see did Ma's room need painting.' She knew he was lying. Anger ignited in her.

'Is that right? What's the interest in house-painting all of a sudden, Tom? And while we're at it, what were you asking Ma if she'd made her will for last night?'

'I just wanted to make sure,' he bristled. 'At her age anything can happen having an anaesthetic. I wanted to make sure all her affairs are up to date.'

'She wasn't having a general and, even if she was, what difference does it make to you?' Judith demanded.

'If she dies without making a will, it could cause a lot of complications.' He couldn't look her in the eye.

'For whom? You?' she said sarcastically. 'This is my home, Tom, whether you like it or not. Get over it. You've left it far too late to get involved now, so you needn't think you're going to be reaping any rewards for all your years of neglect. This place is *mine*. I deserve it.'

'Don't be too sure of that, Judith. If I were you I'd start looking out for a place of your own while you're still able to get a mortgage. Why should you end up with everything?'

'Because I've stayed here and looked after Ma because you and Cecily wouldn't bother your arses,' she said heatedly, furious that she even felt she had to defend her position.

'No one asked you to; if you'd have gone she'd have had to look after herself. There's nothing wrong with her, she's good and healthy, and it just suited you. A nice cushy number, and no rent or mortgage to pay, so don't give me that, Judith,' her brother retorted angrily.

'You fuck off out of here, Tom Baxter,' Judith screeched, incensed. 'You're a selfish, horrible little toad and you always were. And I hope nothing ever happens to you that you're left depending on your children because, if they're anything like you, you'll be a sad, sorry little streak of misery with no one to look after you.' The gloves were off and she didn't care what she said. Her stomach was in knots and she felt sick. She'd never been good at confronting her family.

'It takes one to know one,' he snarled, brushing past her down the stairs. 'You always had a big mouth on you. No wonder you never got married. No one would have ya. And what a lucky escape the male species had.'

'And what did you get? A tarty little peroxide blonde that can't cook to save her—' The front door slammed behind him, leaving the remainder of her sentence hanging in the air.

Judith stood trembling halfway up the stairs. That had been pretty vicious. She and Tom had never got on as kids. They'd more or less kept out of each other's way as they'd got older, but an underlying antipathy still simmered between them.

It had certainly erupted today in a lava flow of insults and invective that would be hard to row back from. Her brother had shown his true colours, she thought as her heartbeat slowed back to normal and the shaking began to subside.

He'd been up snooping in Lily's room looking for the will. She'd never stoop that low. She'd never thought she'd have to. Now she was going to have to find out what her legal position was. Had she sacrificed the last twenty-five years of her life for nothing?

'Oh stop, you sound like a real bitch, she's your mother, for

God's sake!' she said aloud in disgust. She was bringing herself right down to Tom's level thinking like that. Just look at what had ensued. A slanging match where she'd been reduced to a screeching fishwife. And at her age. What did that say about her state of maturity or her ability to handle herself in arguments? What would those young ones at work think if they saw her now? How would Debbie Adams view her, shaking and trembling and near to tears because of an argument with her brother? She felt completely disempowered. Yet again.

The old saying was true: families *were* worse than enemies. Tom had gone and ruined her precious long weekend. That elusive magical feeling of well-being and serenity was gone, to be replaced by sick anxiety. She felt like getting hammered. But how could she? She had to go in to the hospital and visit Lily. If she arrived in stinking of alcohol it would cause her mother great distress. It's all Lily's fault anyway, Judith raged impotently. Why shouldn't she go on the piss if she wanted? The words in that agony-aunt article came back to her. She'd made the choice herself for a pay-off. That was why she'd reacted so violently to her brother's accusations. She needn't have stayed. If she'd had the guts to stand up to her mother's emotional blackmail and go her own way, none of this would be happening and her life could be far different.

Feeling utterly trapped and frustrated, Judith sat on the end of the stairs and bawled her eyes out.

'Hello Connie, I felt I should ring. Er . . . are you OK after our er . . . encounter,' Barry said awkwardly.

'I'm fine, Barry,' his ex-wife said crisply and he had a feeling that she was smiling.

'I just wanted to make sure,' he reiterated, a little put out that she didn't seem to be taking it as seriously as he did. She was making him feel like he'd had a one-night stand or something, he thought indignantly.

'Well, I'm fine, but I think the best thing to do is to forget about it and put it behind us. It should never have happened.' Her tone was so matter-of-fact and businesslike Barry was taken aback. He was right. She *was* treating it as a one-off of no importance.

'I suppose you're right,' he said slowly. 'But it did happen and I'm not sorry, Connie. It meant a lot to me.' It was out before he knew it and he held his breath waiting for her response. He heard her clear her throat.

'Barry, we've been apart for a long time, you're married. That's the end of it. OK?'

'OK,' he said disappointedly.

'Let's get through the wedding as best we can and make life easy on all of us,' Connie instructed. She was so much more assured and self-possessed than when she'd been married to him, he reflected as she bade him goodnight and hung up.

If Aimee didn't come to the wedding as she'd threatened he was going to try and seduce his ex-wife again, Barry decided defiantly. Connie had been well up for it the other night. With a few drinks on her and feeling maudlin because of their daughter's marriage, she'd fall into his arms. She might not be so quick to dismiss it a second time. He didn't like their interlude being considered a one-night stand. He'd hoped it was much more than that.

Barry stretched out on the sofa smiling to himself. If there was one thing he loved it was a challenge. And they had been few and far between lately. It was clear Connie was feeling guilty. The irony was, he was the married one and he didn't feel that bad. It might be different when he actually saw Aimee tomorrow, but he didn't think so. It was all very fine for her to be ringing him from Milan telling him about her delicious Italian dinner and her successful day's work but, if his wife wanted to devote her time to her career and become a workaholic, she should be prepared for the consequences.

At least the phone call had been made and they'd spoken about the events of the other night. Connie had the strangest feeling that Barry was disappointed by her response. What did he want, she thought irritably, to have an affair of some sort with his ex-wife? What did he think she was? Desperate! She wasn't the slightest bit interested in going down that road. She wasn't sorry it had happened, she admitted. It had given her a kickstart, to stop thinking of herself as a middle-aged has-been, but that was all, she decided firmly as she opened a sachet of cat food for Miss Hope, who was gazing up at her with wide-eyed adoration.

'And I love you too.' She smiled, patting the cat's velvet black head. Barry could read all he liked into the encounter but, once this wedding was over, she was going to start living her own life free from all encumbrances, and who knew where that path would lead her – and even with whom, she thought, feeling exceptionally optimistic.

'Can you not go and see the priest on your own, Debbs? It really isn't my scene,' Bryan said sulkily, lazing on the couch slugging a can of beer while she ironed her blouse for work the next day. They had an appointment to see the priest the following evening and she'd suggested they meet up in town.

'Don't be like that,' she protested. 'It's our wedding ceremony.'

'I'd have been just as happy to go to the registry office, babe, it was you who wanted the whole church thing,' he pointed out.

'Right, I'll go by myself,' she snapped, banging the iron up and down the sleeves.

'Do my shirt while you're at it, babes, will you?' her fiancé requested as he flicked channels and caught a snooker match in progress.

'Do it yourself, I'm busy,' Debbie retorted, marching out of the room with her crisp white blouse. She flounced upstairs feeling thoroughly disgruntled. Why couldn't Bryan be more enthusiastic . . . more involved? Her mother's words came to mind as she stood in the bedroom staring out at the neat little cul-de-sac of townhouses where they lived. The orange sodium lamps spilled light over the footpath in front of their house, casting rusty shadows on to the soft-top car. That car was a ridiculous luxury they could ill afford but, when she'd suggested trading it in for a less expensive one and paying off some of the loan, he'd been peeved and she'd said no more, afraid there might be more talk of cancelling the wedding.

The paint on the windowsill was chipped, and she flicked at it, wishing that they could get their bedroom decorated. It was painted dark blue and white and she thought them cold colours which made the room look even narrower than it was. It needed a neutral shade – oatmeal or buttery yellow would look nice, she'd said to Bryan – but he kept putting it off. The house would feel more their own if it was painted in their choice of colours. The wardrobe was bulging with clothes and shoes. They definitely needed more storage. If he'd do up the guest room they could put another wardrobe in there and their bedroom would look tidier. So far nothing had been done, or was likely to be done the way Bryan was going on.

Was her fiancé a bit like her father as Connie had so hesitantly suggested? Was he ready for marriage? Was she making a mistake? She still had time to change her mind.

Debbie sighed, watching the clouds obscure the moon. All she'd ever wanted was to be happily married. Was that too much to ask? Thousands of people managed it. Many of their friends were very happily married and never seemed to have the rumbles of discontent that seemed to permeate her and Bryan's relationship.

Were her expectations too high? Had Connie's expectations been too high? Had she pushed Barry away by constant nagging and whining?

The wedding was getting closer and closer. Everything was in place. If they didn't go ahead with it now, it might never happen. It was her choice. Debbie bit her lip. Maybe this was par for the course. Didn't all brides wonder if they were doing the right thing and get jittery with pre-wedding nerves? She'd go to the priest herself. Bryan was right: she was the one who'd pushed for the church wedding. She shouldn't be surprised at his attitude.

Once the ceremony was all over and they were enjoying the rest of the day with their friends with a honeymoon in New York to look forward to he'd be fine again. Then their lives could

248

get back on an even keel and all the stresses and strains of planning a wedding would be a far-distant memory.

He could still iron his own shirt, though, she decided as she hung her blouse on a hanger and began to undress for bed.

THE WEDDING

CHAPTER TWENTY-THREE

Thank God it's not raining, Debbie thought gratefully as a muted beam of early morning sun filtered through a gap in the curtains. She was in bed in her old bedroom in her mother's house on the morning of her wedding. There had been torrential rain for the past three days and she'd been extremely pessimistic about having a good day for the wedding. But it looked like the gods had been kind. She glanced at the clock beside the bed. Six forty-five. Not bad. She'd slept surprisingly well considering that she, Connie, Karen and Jenna had been up chatting and reminiscing until well after midnight. She picked up her phone and began a text: *'Morning, darling, I love you so much, what a beautiful day for our wedding. See you later. I'm so happy, Love D xx.'*

Debbie hesitated as her fingers hovered over the send key. It was too early to text. Bryan would be fast asleep, and he'd only get tetchy if she sent a text that woke him up. That would not be the best start to married life, so she curbed her impatience and saved the message to be sent later.

They'd hugged each other tightly when she'd left the previous evening to spend the night at her mother's. 'Don't keep me waiting too long,' he'd warned her, and she'd assured him that she wouldn't be a minute late. 'The next time you come back here you'll be a wife and I'll be a husband,' he remarked as he lifted her overnight case into the boot of the car. 'Weird, isn't it? Sort of middle-aged and respectable.'

'Not us at all – we'll never be respectable.' Debbie grinned as she kissed him and ran her hand over his ass.

'The neighbours will see us.' Bryan laughed, grabbing her in a bear hug.

'We might as well shock them while we can then,' Debbie said mischievously, kissing him again.

She smiled at the memory as she lay in bed listening to the birds making an outrageous racket, twittering and whistling. Some people loved the dawn chorus; it had always driven her mad, waking her out of her precious slumber. She didn't mind being woken up today though, this was the most exciting day of her life and she wanted to enjoy every second of it. She turned her head and saw her wedding dress, swathed in layers of tissue and covered with cellophane, hanging on the door of her bedroom.

By the time she stepped out of it tonight she'd be Mrs Bryan Kinsella and a whole new chapter in her life would begin. All the planning and worrying for the big day would be over, and that would be a huge relief, she thought as she slid out of bed and padded over to the window.

Yesterday she'd got a call from the hotel to say that their meat supplier had let them down and they were going to have to source their steaks from a new supplier, who charged more, so the bill would be higher than they'd budgeted for.

The violinist had phoned to tell her she'd broken her wrist but had managed to secure a replacement. Debbie could only hope that the replacement was a first-rate violinist, not having had a chance to hear her play. It would be a disaster if she had to walk up the aisle to the sound of an out-of-tune, caterwauling violin.

'No negativity,' she told herself firmly as she tweaked back the curtains and saw a clear blue sky and a pearly hued orb cresting the tips of the fruit trees at the end of the garden.

It truly was a glorious morning, she thought happily, watching Hope washing her face methodically, sitting in one of her favourite spots, an old stump of a tree trunk that was smooth to the touch and a real little sun trap for a cat that loved sitting in the sun.

She felt a pang of loneliness as she looked out at Connie's beloved cat. Today would be a real cutting of the ties with her mother. For almost as long as she could remember it had just been the two of them, their own little unit. Now she was making a new unit and Bryan would be the main focus of it while her mother would inevitably drift to the periphery. Debbie hoped with all her heart that Connie would not feel that she was being abandoned or sidelined.

It had been hard on her mother having to adjust to living on her own. It had to be lonely for her, Debbie reflected as she got back into bed for another little while. Barry was lucky he had a second family to grow old with. Connie had drawn the short straw in their relationship for sure. Debbie sighed as she pulled the duvet up over her shoulders. She hoped neither she nor Connie would cry when Connie handed her over to the care of Bryan. What would they be like, sniffling at the top of the altar? She'd have a chat with her over breakfast and issue stern instructions that there were to be no tears under any circumstances.

She stretched cat-like, glad now that the day was finally here. All the tensions that had knotted her neck and shoulders in the past few weeks had melted away, thanks in part to the relaxing massage her mother had given her the previous night. A phone call from Barry had also helped when he had told her that he wanted her day to be as happy as it could possibly be and how delighted he was that she had accepted his offer to drive her to the church.

She and Bryan had agreed when they started making their wedding plans that they didn't want a traditional wedding. They didn't want a limo. 'Too tacky for words and a waste of money,' Bryan said as they had a look at the prices and decided they could spend their money in other ways. He was arriving at the church on his best man's motorbike, and the original plan had been for his brother to bring Debbie and Connie to the church in the convertible but, after her reconciliation with Barry, there had been a few phone calls between them and, during the course of one of their conversations, her father had made his offer to drive her to the church. She'd discussed it with Bryan, who had urged her to accept.

'If you're not going to let him give you away, at least let him drive you to the church; it would mean something to him to be part of it, as well as paying for it,' her fiancé had pointed out as she dithered.

Put like that she felt it would be churlish to refuse.

Connie had been so pleased with the news that Barry was driving them to the church, relieved that Debbie had taken another step forward in their ceasefire. Debbie knew her mother felt it would be a real moment of closure for the three of them to arrive together. It *really* did feel like the end of one chapter and the start of a new one, she mused as she turned on her tummy and buried her head under the pillow to drown out the noisy, chirruping racket outside.

It had been strange sleeping in her old single bed. She'd missed the comfort of having Bryan's body close to her own; she loved waking with his arms around her, especially on cold, frosty mornings in winter, when his leg or arm would be thrown across her in sleep. Being part of a couple gave her great comfort. As she'd got older she often wondered how her mother had lived for so long without the intimacy and companionship of a man. It was as if Connie had shut down all that part of her life.

When she was a child Debbie had often hoped that her mother would bring her home a new daddy so that she would be the same as everyone else in her class. She'd fantasized about walking down the street with Connie and her 'new' daddy and bumping into Barry and seeing him crestfallen, gutted, as they all turned their backs on him.

As she'd got older and seen other families in circumstances similar to her own she'd been just as pleased that it was only the two of them. Two girls that she knew had step-parents, and their lives were far from happy. Their loyalties were pulled one way and another, they had to get used to new partners and, in one case, new step-brothers and step-sisters, and it all seemed very troublesome and complicated. Because she'd refused outright to go and stay with Aimee and Melissa for weekends, and because her parents hadn't forced her, she'd avoided that kind of scenario.

Connie was a brilliant mother, she thought gratefully. She'd always tried her best to shield her from the fall-out of the break-up. She hadn't been at all pushy about the wedding either. Her colleague Denise had had a very frustrating experience. Denise's mother had insisted on inviting many of her own friends to her daughter's wedding. She'd interfered so much that Denise had spent her precious wedding day seething with resentment. Marianne Kenny had been so intent on impressing her friends and neighbours, she'd lost sight of her daughter's needs and wishes and, because she was quite an overpowering and domineering woman, she'd steamrollered her way to having the wedding *she* wanted.

The only tiff Connie and Debbie had had was the one they'd had about her not showing up to meet Barry when it had been arranged, and that had been all her fault, Debbie admitted. Otherwise, she and Bryan were having exactly what they wanted – a small, intimate but out-of-the-ordinary wedding, with just close family and their own friends. It was a very different type of wedding from the big, boring, expensive occasions they'd been invited to over the last couple of years, which had cost an arm and a leg and left their friends in debt up to their ears. They could have had a destination wedding, she supposed, but it was nice to get married at home.

No one was going to call their wedding boring, Debbie thought confidently as her eyelids drooped and she fell asleep again.

So it was here at last, the day of her daughter's wedding. What a blessing that the sun was shining. Debbie would be able to have the barbecue she'd so set her heart on in the courtyard of the small hotel.

She had to give credit to her daughter and Bryan for planning a wedding that was unique to them. Bryan had surprised her with his choice. She'd felt he'd be one for the big, flashy occasion, but both he and Debbie had been adamant that they wanted a change from the Keep Up With the Joneses type that they'd attended over the years.

Soon after the engagement had been announced, she and Debbie had attended a wedding fair and left after an hour, horrified at the hype and pressure, and rip-off prices. To give him his due, Bryan had agreed that it was crazy stuff. Two weeks later Debbie informed her that they had decided to have a barbecue in a small hotel off Stephen's Green. It had a huge courtyard that would be ideal for their needs. They were going to marry in University Church, have their photos taken in Stephen's Green, stroll back to the hotel to a champagne reception and then have a real hooley with no speeches, fuss or bother.

'A barbecue, no speeches, you walking her up the aisle. I suppose we should be lucky they're getting married in a church!' Connie's mother sniffed when she heard the sort of wedding her granddaughter was having. 'Have you no say in the matter?'

'It's their wedding and I want them to enjoy it.'

'Let's hope it works out better than yours did,' Stella said tartly, unable to resist the sly dig.

'That's uncalled for, Mother. In fact it's downright nasty,' Connie flared.

'Well, I don't understand why the pair of you couldn't have worked a bit harder to save your marriage. Your father and I had our ups and downs but we stuck it out because we made vows on our wedding day. Couples nowadays give up too easily,' Stella said crossly. It still rankled that she had a divorced daughter. The only divorcée on her side of the family.

'You know something? I'd far prefer to be with someone, and have him be with me because we *wanted* to be together, not because we *had* to be together. I couldn't think of anything worse. You might as well be in a prison.'

'You were always the great one with your smart answers,' her mother retorted, reminding Connie of how glad she'd been to move to Greystones, far from the hazard of unwanted visits and constant lectures. In the early months of the break-up she had caught Stella telling Debbie that it was a bad thing for her parents to part and she should try and get them back together. She'd been furious, and there'd been a stand-up row. She'd vowed never to let Stella interfere like that again and had been vigilant in not allowing a repeat performance. It had strengthened her resolve to distance herself from her mother's damaging influence on Debbie, and it had given her the impetus to move out of Dublin, a move she'd never regretted.

She had brought Debbie to visit her grandparents every week when she was young. She'd felt it was important for her to have a sense of family and a relationship with them but, as Debbie got older, the visits had become monthly, with phone calls becoming more the norm.

She was a dutiful daughter but not a particularly loving one to her mother, Connie admitted. But Stella's lack of support and her anger at Connie's failed marriage was toxic and had caused a rift that had only been papered over, but never really addressed, over the years. It was probably the underlying wounds of her experience with her own mother that had made Connie urge Debbie to try and resolve the differences with Barry.

She was a bit of a hypocrite really, Connie supposed. She wanted everything rosy in the garden with Debbie and Barry and yet she had never got to grips with the problems that laced her own relationship with her mother. Well, at least today Stella would see that, marriage break-up or not, Connie, Barry and Debbie would be together and happy on this most important day.

It would be one of the few times that Stella and Barry would have seen each other after all these years; she hoped her mother would behave herself and at least try to be civil. Aimee would probably get a few frosty stares, but there was nothing Connie could do about that. The other woman would just have to deal with it. Barry's mother, Hilda, and her sister would be coming with Karen, as his father was dead. Connie liked her ex-mother-in-law, who, she knew, really appreciated the fact that Connie had always made sure that Debbie kept in contact with her. Many grandparents lost out on a relationship with their grand-children because of marital strife, but Connie had not been mean and petty in that regard.

It was certainly going to be a wedding with a few jagged edges, Connie reflected as she heard Debbie's bed creak next door. She'd heard her moving around but then get into bed again, and silence descended. Debbie was right to go back to bed: it was early yet – there was no rush to get up. She yawned and threw back the duvet to go and sit in the small dormer window seat to look out over the garden. The old country say-ing that the sunrise was God's statement and the sunset His signature had never seemed more appropriate, she thought as she gazed at the glorious blue sky which portended a splendid day to come.

Thank you, Lord, for bringing Debbie and Barry together for this most special day. Let her and Bryan be happy together, put your loving arms around them and let their love last, she prayed earnestly, wish-ing that her niggles of doubt about her daughter's imminent marriage would evaporate and leave her in peace. She'd done her best to try and advise Debbie. There was nothing more she could do. It was time to let go.

She turned to look at one of her favourite photos of her precious daughter. Debbie was six, gap-toothed, grinning, freckled and pigtailed, her big blue eyes smiling into the camera, looking carefree and happy. In spite of what Barry had told her about what Debbie had said of her childhood, there *had* been many carefree, happy moments, and this had been one of them. She'd done her best to be a good mother; there was no point in tormenting herself now.

Had her own mother had feelings like this on Connie's wedding day? she wondered. Apprehensive because she wasn't sure if she was marrying the right man, relieved that her responsibilities for her daughter were over. Hoping that the day would pass without incident. But then Stella had had the extra worry of knowing that Connie was pregnant as she walked up the aisle. That had been the elephant in the room at her wedding, and she knew for a fact that her mother hadn't enjoyed any aspect of the day, she'd been so concerned about later having to tell family and friends that her daughter was expecting a baby and knowing that people would be counting backwards and not coming up with nine months.

Connie sighed, wishing that she could be just an observer rather than a participant in today's wedding. It would be interesting watching the interaction between the two grannies, the ex-son-in-law, the second wife. No doubt Aimee would be making comparisons between her high-end weddings and Debbie's far more modest do. Connie wasn't going to let it bother her. If she did, her day would be ruined. Debbie and Bryan had planned a small, tasteful wedding and it was what they wanted: that was the important thing. Madam Davenport could turn up her nose as much as she liked. Aimee hadn't been too impressed when Debbie and Bryan had turned down her offer of assistance and a discount on catering if they went the marquee route, according to Barry, but it was ridiculous to take it as a snub. They had their own plans for their wedding. It was decent of her to offer assistance, Connie reflected, but far from desired. Aimee and Debbie had no relationship whatsoever. What had made Barry's second wife think that such an offer would be welcome? She'd probably done it for Barry's sake, Connie thought, trying to be fair-minded. That she could understand.

Thank God for Karen – she was going to have Aimee, Barry and his mother and aunt at her table, so Connie wouldn't have to worry about them. Connie would have her parents, two aunts and two cousins to entertain. Bryan's parents and his grandmother and sisters would be at another table, while the bride and groom planned to table-hop and spend time with everyone.

Melissa and Sarah were really taken with the free-seating idea for the other guests and had plans to sit beside the best-looking guys, so Barry had informed Connie on the phone when they'd discussed the driving arrangements. She might get lucky herself, she thought with a grin, imagining Barry's reaction if he saw her flirting with a young man half her age. It would show him that she was still able to pull, in case he felt that their one-night stand was the best she could do.

She'd have to face Aimee, she reminded herself. She wasn't particularly looking forward to it, but she wasn't going to make a big deal of it either. Barry could take responsibility for his own marriage. She hadn't gone out of her way to seduce him. He could have stopped any time he wanted. He'd chosen not to, and it was up to him to question the reason why.

Connie's stomach rumbled. She was starving. She'd gone on a porridge and brown bread diet for the last week in an effort to drop a few pounds and it had worked. One thing she was sure of, she was going to tuck into the wedding feast, and no matter what dramas were going on around her she was going to enjoy it. She deserved it.

Typical, she grimaced. She was such a comfort eater. Why couldn't she reward herself in other ways? Why did it always have to be with food? If she had the answer to that she'd be a millionaire. Half the women she knew had the same disastrous impulse. She was going to have to deal with it some time, she acknowledged dolefully. The older she got the harder it was to lose weight. If she'd done the porridge and brown bread diet fifteen years ago or even ten, she'd have lost three quarters of a stone no problem. She'd been lucky to lose the six pounds she had lost. Once this wedding was over, her life was going to be all about her and she was going to start a brand-new keep fit and healthy regime. Middle age would not get its claws into her yet; she still had a lot of living to do.

It was such a gift of a day she decided to go for a walk along the beach before breakfast. She could bring a banana to keep the hunger pangs at bay, as she wanted to have breakfast with her daughter. She dressed quickly in jeans and a sweater. The breeze would be cool coming off the sea; a brisk walk would set her up for the day and fortify her for when the madness began.

Bryan Kinsella woke to the appetizing aroma of bacon and sausage wafting up the stairs. He yawned, stretched and glanced out the window. Sun was shining. Perfect! The whole tenor of the barbecue would have changed if it had been raining and they'd had to eat indoors, as they'd feared would be the case after the atrocious weather of the past few days.

These were his last hours of freedom. It was a weird feeling. He loved Debbie, of course he did, but there was this unaccountable sense of loss as he reflected on all the things he'd wanted to do, and achieve, and hadn't.

He'd wanted to ride from the Atlantic to the Pacific coast on a Harley or any bike he could have afforded. He'd wanted to stay in college and study art and design and open an art gallery. He wouldn't have minded being a film critic. What a great job to get paid to go to films and film festivals and write reviews of them. Office design, planning and fit-outs didn't exactly set his creative side on fire.

Instead he was bound by a house and a mortgage and a well-paying job that only half engaged him. How had he got himself in such a position? he wondered, idly studying his nails, which were badly in need of the manicure he'd booked for eleven. Once he and Debbie had got engaged everything had mushroomed. They had to get a house, they had to plan a wedding – it all seemed to snowball until he was enveloped in an avalanche of responsibilities that at times made him feel trapped and helpless.

Then, other times, he was happy enough with his lot. He relished being in a relationship. Debbie understood him more than any other girl he had ever dated. She knew he was a free spirit and, until they'd hit their rocky patch coming up to the wedding, she'd always given him a lot of leeway.

Once the stress of the wedding had worn away and they'd paid off the bills they'd get back into their own easy rhythm. They could get cheap flights all over Europe for weekends away like the one they'd had in Amsterdam. That had been a terrific break. His spirits rose to their usual levels of optimistic cheer just as his mother arrived with a breakfast tray laden with a hearty fry-up and toast dripping with melting butter. Not great for his cholesterol but, what the hell, it was his big day, he rationalized, hauling himself up against the pillows.

'Now, son, get that into you to set you up for the day ahead. I'll run a bath for you when you're finished. Your shirt is ironed and there's clean underwear and socks for you on the chest of drawers.' She set the tray on his lap and kissed the top of his head.

'What would I do without you, Ma?' he said affectionately. 'It's like old times having you looking after me so well.'

'Any time you need looking after, you come home to me,' Brona Kinsella said as she picked up his dirty clothes and put them in the linen basket. She liked Debbie well enough but she felt she could do more about taking care of Bryan. She wasn't one for putting herself out that much. Bryan had to do his own washing and ironing and he seemed to do much of the cooking, from what she gathered. Young women nowadays didn't know what it was to be a good wife. They were far too interested in their careers and their lavish lifestyles and putting themselves first.

Maybe it was the way Debbie had been brought up. Connie Adams had a broken marriage and had to work to support herself and Debbie; that had to have some sort of effect, she supposed. Connie was a very brisk, no-nonsense woman from what Brona had seen of her. Brona was about ten years older than Connie and their attitudes were very different. Bryan wasn't overly enamoured of his new mother-in-law and Brona could see why, having met her on a couple of occasions. Still, as long as she didn't interfere and put her spoke in, things would be all right. And if, and when, children came on the scene, Brona Kinsella was determined that she wasn't going to be sidelined, as many mothers of sons were.

'Mornin', son. Enjoy your last hours as a free man.' Phil Kinsella stuck his head around the door. 'Just going to collect your grandparents, I'll see you later.' His father gave him a cheery wave and then clattered down the wooden stairs, glad to escape from the pre-wedding frenzy.

'See you, Dad. We'll have a pint at the wedding,' Bryan called after him before tucking into his breakfast. He usually ate quite healthily, so a fry-up was a rare treat, and breakfast in bed even rarer, these days.

He was looking forward immensely to the wedding reception, once the church bits were over. A registry-office wedding would have done him, but Debbie and Connie wanted the full church palaver despite the fact that his fiancée rarely attended church. A lot of his friends had done the same; they didn't go to church but they'd been determined to marry there. He found it rather phoney and had said so when the matter had come up for discussion. Connie had said it was up to them to decide the issue, but he felt she'd put the pressure on Debbie to marry in church. It had been another mark of disapproval against him on her debit and credit sheet. He wasn't under any illusions that his new mother-in-law had a high opinion of him; he got on better with his father-in-law to be; on the few occasions they had met he'd liked him. He could quite under-stand why Barry had left Connie. She'd drive any man away with her bossy behaviour. She could try and boss him around, but she wouldn't get far, he assured himself as he bit into a hash brown and turned to other, more welcome observations.

He knew their married friends would be comparing and contrasting his and Debbs' wedding with their own, but he was quite confident that the wedding programme they had put together would be one to remember. His message alert rang and he opened it with anticipation and smiled when he read his bride-to-be's text.

'*I love you too, babes. Can't wait,*' he texted back as his mother arrived with fresh coffee and another batch of hot buttered toast. The day was starting swimmingly, and it was only going to get better, he thought with satisfaction as he took a slug of coffee and demolished a mouthful of golden sausage and crispy bacon slathered with ketchup.

Chapter Twenty-four

'Where are you going?' Barry yawned as he woke up to find his wife dressed in a grey trouser suit and a white cami and inserting a pair of gold earrings into her ears.

'Work,' Aimee informed him. 'I've got that big McNulty christening in Howth. I want to throw an eye over things. Don't worry – I'll be back in plenty of time to bring Melissa and Sarah to the wedding, seeing as you're not driving us.' There was an edge of sarcasm to her tone, but he ignored it. Although she hadn't said anything, he knew Aimee wasn't at all impressed that he was driving his daughter and ex-wife to the wedding and leaving her and Melissa to fend for themselves.

'What time will you be home at? I'll be heading to Greystones around twelve. You'd want to have a taxi ordered for quarter past two by the latest to give yourself plenty of time to get into town for three,' he advised.

'Don't worry about what time I leave at. I'll be there,' she said sharply and marched out the door.

He heard her high heels click-clack down the hall and scowled. He supposed he should be glad that she'd changed her mind and was coming to the wedding with him, but she wasn't being particularly helpful.

He'd hardly seen her in the past few weeks; she'd been so consumed by work. She'd had a half-dozen Holy Communion bashes, each of them costing between twenty and fifty thousand, she'd told him, and there'd been two weddings as well as the O'Leary one, which was coming up the following week. With the arrival of the Celtic tiger, the nouveau riche had been splashing out lavishly on every conceivable occasion, and Aimee's company, an up-and-coming player in the events and catering business, had been reaping the rewards. His wife was working far longer hours than when he'd first met her and earning far more money too.

When she'd arrived home from Milan two days after he'd had sex with Connie, he'd had a flash of disquiet when she'd walked in the door that evening. She'd gone straight to the office from the airport, anxious to catch up, and then got stuck in the Friday-evening rush hour, which left her snappish and in bad form when he'd spoken to her on the mobile to find out if she could pick Melissa up from a basketball match.

He was surprised at how little guilt he felt when he saw his wife face to face. For some strange reason, he couldn't quite equate what he'd done with Connie as unfaithfulness. Had he slept with a stranger he'd probably have been riddled with guilt.

Aimee had given him a quick peck on the cheek and informed him she was going to have a shower, unable to hide her relief when he told her that he hadn't been able to get a reservation in the Saddle Room and had tried several other popular restaurants with the same result. 'Hardly surprising,' he'd told her, 'you didn't give me much notice.'

'We'll do it another time. Stick the beef bourguignon and the chive mash from the Butler's Pantry into the microwave and we'll open a bottle of wine here,' she'd suggested, taking out her phone to call one of her staff to remind them that the new Louise Kennedy crystal was not to be used at any event other than the O'Leary wedding. If her clients were paying a million and more smackers for this wedding they deserved brand-new crystal, Barry could hear her say in her sharp, no-nonsense manner. Personally, he felt that spending a massive amount of money on a high-society wedding, such as many of Aimee's blue-chip clients were doing, made it more like a corporate occasion than an intimate ceremony where a man and woman made the most important commitment of their lives. The more lavish the affair, the less personal it became, and he was pleased that Debbie and Bryan had not gone down *that* route.

Aimee had turned up her nose when she'd heard about the barbecue proposal, and he knew she was expecting charred ribs and burnt sausages. He was somewhat concerned himself about what to expect and was quite relieved that none of his golf companions were coming to the wedding – they might think he was a cheapskate – but he had a sneaking regard for Debbie and Bryan that at least they'd stuck to their guns and not been influenced by the blatant consumerism that drove the wedding industry.

Debbie had been at her most prickly when she'd told him they were having a barbecue, and he hadn't enquired about the menu in case she got even more bristly. Aimee had raised her eyebrows when he'd told her that they'd refused her offer of help and were planning a barbecue. 'Hope they get the weather for it,' she remarked tartly, clearly unimpressed.

He'd gone for a game of golf that evening, since they weren't dining out, and had been relieved when she had fallen asleep as soon as her head had hit the pillow that night. He was too resentful to make love, but she didn't even seem to notice, and it had been almost a week before she'd turned to him in bed one night and begun to kiss and caress him in the dark. It had been over quickly, and that too had made him feel hard done by. She was probably ovulating and feeling horny was his first thought but, perhaps not, he'd decided the next morning. She'd said they didn't need to use a condom. It must have been PMT horniness; it wasn't because she had any great desire for *him*, he thought resentfully. She might as well have said, 'Service me,' because that's what he felt he was doing. He'd made love to her mechanically and, when she'd fallen asleep immediately afterwards, he'd lain beside her feeling aggrieved and full of self-pity.

It was all about her these days, and he was getting fed up with it. No wonder he'd turned to his ex-wife. Why *should* he feel guilty? Aimee was excluding him from her life and, even worse, Melissa was seeing very little of her. He'd gradually become the primary care-giver and his wife didn't even seem to notice.

She'd bought Melissa make-up and exclusive jeans from Milan which had sent their daughter into a state of ecstasy, but she'd hardly seen her for the next week. She'd had to fly to Galway to oversee an awards gala and that had entailed an overnight stay. Then she'd had to travel to Kildare for another big society wedding. It was an extremely busy time of the year for her, and she was too exhausted to do much more than flop on the sofa when she got home, any time between nine and ten at night.

They'd even had to cancel a planned trip to Paris for Melissa's mid-term break because of Aimee's busy schedule. Once Debbie's wedding and the O'Leary one that was taking up so much of her time were over, he was going to have a serious talk with his wife and let her know *exactly* how he was feeling.

The sun sparkled on the Liffey as Aimee slowed to throw her coins into the toll basket on the East Link. The traffic was light, thankfully, and she drove through without having to queue. She'd often spent an hour queuing to get through the toll bridge in rush hour. It really was a glorious morning, and she lowered her window to let the breeze drift into the car. Debbie would be pleased. It was a perfect day for a wedding after all the rain they'd endured. It would be over by tomorrow and hopefully Barry would relax and stop being so moody because, by heavens, he was moody these days, she thought ruefully.

He didn't even seem to be appreciative of the fact that she'd changed her mind and told him she'd go to the wedding with him. She'd felt she should be at his side, seeing as he seemed to think it was so important that she and Melissa should be there. Melissa was all excited about going now, especially since Debbie's visit. Aimee couldn't quite figure out what had caused Debbie's change of heart, especially where Melissa was concerned, but it made her daughter happy, and that was all that mattered. Then she'd been informed that Barry intended driving Debbie and Connie to the church. Had she realized that she wouldn't have bothered going to the wedding, she thought crossly as she swung up Alfie Byrne Road and headed for Clontarf.

Could Debbie not have hired a wedding car like most normal brides? She wouldn't let Barry walk her up the aisle – what was she doing letting him drive her to the church? Using him, that's what she was doing, and Aimee's fool of a husband couldn't see it.

Once this wedding was over he'd be dropped like a hot potato and then he'd be crying on her shoulder about it. Step-families were such a drag. She'd Googled a website for second wives one day while she'd been waiting on the phone to get through to an insurance company and had identified with a lot of the women who found the demands of the wives and children of the first marriage impossible to put up with. Some of them couldn't take the strain imposed by the first family and the second marriage also cracked.

She supposed she had been luckier than most. She'd never had to make a huge effort to get to know Debbie like some of her acquaintances had had to with their step-children. Aimee had got away lightly until the wedding. And it was only the lead-up to it that had caused her irritation.

In fairness to Connie, apart from the wedding, her financial demands had not been unreasonable and, once Debbie had started working, Barry had ceased to pay maintenance. Connie had never looked for spousal maintenance – at least she'd had the self-respect to support herself and not leech off her ex-husband. Some ex-wives had no qualms or conscience and bled their long-suffering ex-spouses dry. Of course, she knew, too, that there were lone wives with children who barely scraped a living because of their husband's meanness. If she and Barry ever split up, she'd at least have the satisfaction of knowing that she could depend on herself for all her financial requirements. She would never, ever be dependent on a man to support her.

A flash of bitterness darkened her face. Her father might not have rated her very highly compared to her brothers, but she'd shown him and proved herself more capable than any of them. Even to this day she could still remember overhearing his dismissive words to a colleague who had asked what she intended to do when she left school.

'Well, she won't be keeping me in my old age, she's a bit of a dunce, you know, failed physics and science, barely passed maths. The best she can expect is to do some secretarial course and go and find a husband to keep her.'

His flippant, unkind words had wounded her to her core. He'd always put great emphasis on being good at maths and had insisted she study physics and science in secondary school despite the fact that she'd shown no aptitude for them whatsoever.

Ken Davenport was a heart consultant and had wanted his children to follow in his footsteps in the medical field. Her two older brothers had resisted fiercely, wanting to follow their own paths, and so he had invested all his hopes in her, but she had failed the science subjects badly and had had to repeat her Leaving Cert to get the necessary points to do a catering course in a third-level college.

Her father thought it a frivolous, lightweight career option and usually had some smart comment to make whenever they got together. He wasn't impressed either when she'd got married to a divorced man with whom she had had a child out of wedlock. Her mother, Juliet, quiet and reserved in contrast to her husband's bombast, encouraged Aimee to live her own life and not allow herself to be browbeaten.

Watching how Juliet had had to put her needs and desires aside to devote herself to her husband and his career, Aimee had been determined never ever to be dependent on any man. Ken Davenport had me me me down to a fine art and Juliet came a very poor second. It drove Aimee mad watching her mother subjugate all her needs so that her husband could be the centre of attention.

Aimee had only agreed to marry Barry when she'd felt she was his financial equal, and the way she was progressing in her career it was quite on the cards that she would pass him out in terms of salary in the long term. She'd earned more than he had the previous year. If he couldn't cope with that, she wasn't going to lose any sleep over it. Why couldn't men be pleased for women when they did well? Why did they feel threatened or that it was a slight against their masculinity? When she'd first started dating Barry he'd been hugely impressed by her drive and ambition and had encouraged her enormously. But lately he was complaining about how much time she spent at the office or on her BlackBerry, almost as if he begrudged her her career success. Were all men the same? she wondered crossly as she drove past St Anne's Park and observed the early morning walkers out with their dogs. It was a nice area, she noted approvingly as she sped towards Howth.

Her mobile rang and the Bluetooth connected. 'Aimee, there's been a disaster – the idiot who delivered the cake tripped, and the whole thing is a complete mess. A write-off!' The frantic tones of her assistant echoed around the car.

'For crying out loud, Mandy, shove his mush in it and tell the cretin he or his company will be paying for it. I'll pull in and make a few phone calls. Say nothing to the clients for the moment until I see if I can sort something. I'll be there in ten minutes.' Aimee pulled into a lay-by and, completely focused, began to make the necessary phone calls.

'I'm sending my PA over in a taxi, she'll be there at one thirty. Give her the black Mark Jacobs dress, the little black and gold Pierre Cardin clutch bag and the Jimmy Choo black slingbacks. The bag and the shoes are laid out beside my dressing table; the dress is hanging in my wardrobe. And take the cerise silk embroidered wrap out of the drawer where I keep them, fold it in tissue paper and give her that as well, OK?'

'OK,' Melissa agreed dutifully.

'Then get a taxi to the Shelbourne and meet me there at two thirty and we'll walk over to the church together. Right?'

'OK, Mom, no problem. See you.'

'And go easy on the make-up,' Aimee warned.

'Sure. See ya, Mom.' Melissa couldn't wait to hang up and tell

Sarah the great news. What a stroke of luck that her mom wasn't going to make it in time to pick them up in Dun Laoghaire and then get back into town. And if she wasn't here, she couldn't dictate what she should wear to the wedding. Melissa did a little twirl around the lounge before hurrying out to the balcony, where Sarah was lying on a lounger sipping a Bacardi Breezer, listening to the Kaiser Chiefs.

'Great news – Mom's not coming back to pick us up. We've to get a taxi. We can wear what we liiikkkeeee!' she yelled.

'Random!' Sarah shot up from her lounger. 'So are you going to wear your jeans and the green Paris Hilton top?'

'You bet,' grinned Melissa.

'Your mom will freak.'

'I know, but she won't be able to do anything about it and it will be worth getting grounded not having to wear that . . . that scabby dress she wants me to wear.'

Aimee had bought her an expensive dress in Miss BT with a zigzag pattern that she assured Melissa was very fashionable. Melissa had seen Kate Moss wear a dress like it and it had looked cool but, somehow, it made *her* look like a demented green and black zebra. They'd had a huge row and Aimee had accused her of being a selfish, ungrateful brat. *That* had hurt. She'd gone into a sulk and had barely spoken to her mother for a week afterwards. Aimee had somewhat made up for things by buying her a fabulous pair of Rock & Republic jeans when she'd been in Milan, as well as all the MAC cosmetics she'd asked for. To make up for not bringing her to Paris for her mid-term, she'd said. Lots of the girls in her class had gone abroad that week, to Marbella or Tuscany to their parents' villas and apartments, and she'd felt fed up having to stay at home, hanging around Dun Laoghaire, but the Rock & Republic jeans were a very welcome substitute for her Paris trip.

She'd known better than to suggest wearing them to the wedding. Aimee would have said no outright. But Aimee wasn't here and wouldn't be able to do anything about it.

'Quick – let's get over to yours and get your white jeans and nick your sister's studded cami. I'll wear my stilettos, the Lindsay Lohan ones,' Melissa suggested excitedly.

'Cool, cool, let's go. Here – finish this with me.' Sarah handed her friend the drink and she took a swig of it. They'd treated themselves to two Bacardi Breezers each to calm their nerves and give themselves a nice buzz before the wedding, seeing as they were alone in the penthouse. Barry had gone to get the car washed and valeted and was going directly to Greystones when he was finished.

'We need to get a move on. Come on – and pinch your sister's GHD as well so you can do your hair the same time as I'm doing mine,' Melissa urged, on an absolute high of excitement.

Giggling, they hurried into the lounge, grabbed their bags and keys and raced out to the lift to go and get Sarah's change of costume before the PA arrived.

An hour and a half later they stared at their reflections in the mirror on the back of Melissa's wardrobe door. Melissa did a pirouette so the beaded halter jersey top swung with her to reveal the distinctive Rock & Republic logo on the back pockets of her jeans. They were a size fourteen and she was poured into them. She'd had to lie on the floor and, with Sarah's help, pull the zip up with a shoelace. It had been a struggle, but she'd got them closed. Fortunately, the halter-top covered the bulge of fat that oozed out over the waistband.

'You're so skinny,' she exclaimed enviously as she looked at her friend, a vision in skin-tight white jeans, a gorgeous black studded cami with spaghetti straps, and white peeptoe stilettos that made her look even taller and skinnier than she was.

'You've lovely boobs,' Sarah pointed out. 'I've got fried eggs.'

'I hope these Lifttits stay in place, or I'll be drooping all over the place,' Melissa said worriedly, giving a little tug at her boob aids.

'Leave them alone and stop fiddling. Are you sure my hair's OK?'

'It's fine,' Melissa assured her, running her fingers through her own dead straight black tresses, the result of frantic hair-straightening that had threatened to go awry. She stared down at her zebra-print stilettos. She'd seen Lindsay Lohan wear a

274

pair almost exactly the same style, had fallen in love with them and had been on the look-out for yonks for a pair. She'd seen them one day when she'd been shopping with her mother.

'Darling, they look cheap even though they're not,' Aimee said dismissively when she'd pointed them out, and she'd known better than to pursue it, but she'd gone back into town on her own two days later and bought them. She'd nicked fifty euro out of one of her mother's handbags and another twenty out of her dad's wallet when he'd been on the phone, and had made up the rest with her pocket money. She thought they were fabulous, and Amanda O'Connell, the girl she most disliked at school, had been pea-green with envy when she'd worn them to Wesley one Friday night with a pair of black leggings and a smock top.

Her feet had ached for a week afterwards but she didn't care. She'd looked cool and been envied by one of the 'in' crowd. Needless to say, her mother and father had been at a function and hadn't actually seen her outfit, as she'd stayed over at Sarah's and Mrs Wilson wasn't as particular as Aimee about what the girls wore to their Friday-night disco.

'I don't think we should meet Mom in the Shelbourne,' Melissa said thoughtfully, eyeing their reflections. They looked completely cool, but she knew that Aimee might not see it that way, and she wouldn't put it past her mother to send them home to change.

'Where will we meet her?' Sarah stuck her hand on her hip and struck a pose.

'At the church. I'll tell her we were running late.'

'OK,' Sarah agreed, studying a very annoying zit on the side of her nose that no amount of concealer would hide.

'Stop squeezing it,' Melissa chided as her friend's hand went to the forbidden zone. 'Come on, let's grab a cab. Let's go find ourselves a man.'

'Have you got the camera? You know . . . for the evidence.' Sarah giggled.

'You bet.' Melissa plucked her neat silver digital out of her bag and waved it in the air.

'And breath freshener in case we get off with a bloke?'

'Got that too.' Melissa had all angles covered.

'And I've got mints, so no one will cop that we were drinking.' Sarah handed her friend a Polo.

'Let's go then.' Melissa beamed, feeling thoroughly sophisticated.

Arm in arm they clip-clopped out to the lift in their stilettos, giddy with anticipation.

The car looked good and smelled good, Barry thought with satisfaction as he indicated left and came off the N11 on to the Greystones slip road. It was hard to believe that Debbie was getting married today, he mused as he slowed down behind a combine that was crawling along. He remembered vividly the day Connie had found out she was pregnant and the leaden lump in his stomach when he'd realized that he was trapped.

He remembered the myriad emotions he'd felt when he'd held his daughter for the first time. Her big blue eyes staring up at him, as though sizing him up. Those big blue eyes had looked reproachfully at him many times, he reflected with a pang, remembering the hurt and pain in them when he'd leave after one of his visits to her. At least now they were on speaking terms and he was sharing her day. It was a start, and for that he was grateful.

He was looking forward to seeing Connie again. She had made excuses not to see him since their little episode, and he wondered was it because she was afraid she might be tempted again, no matter how coolly she seemed determined to play it. He certainly hoped that was the case.

He was pissed off with Aimee big time. She couldn't even give him the day of his daughter's wedding without haring off to work. Any normal woman would have been heading off to the hairdresser's and the beauty salon, but not his wife. She hadn't even waited to have breakfast with him or Melissa.

If he got a chance to have sex with Connie again he was going to take it, he decided. Why not have something special on the side with her? If she was interested and it made her happy he was definitely going to go for it. Now that Debbie was no longer living with her it would be good to come and visit so that she wouldn't be lonely and Debbie wouldn't be wondering why he was calling.

And why wouldn't his ex-wife be interested? he reflected, smiling as he remembered how she'd enjoyed their lovemaking. She'd been manless long enough. Some TLC would bring a glow to her cheeks and make her feel special and wanted again. He'd be doing her a favour, Barry decided, feeling surprisingly cheerful as he put the boot down and sped past the big machine, anxious to get to his ex-wife's house without further delay.

CHAPTER TWENTY-FIVE

'I wasn't expecting you so early.' Connie opened the door to let Barry in. She was in her robe, but her hair had been styled, cut and highlighted earlier that morning. It was a fashionable, shorter look than she usually wore and it suited her.

'Nice hairstyle.' He smiled at her, leaning over to kiss her cheek. He inhaled her perfume, a light floral scent utterly different from the heavy, cloying scents Aimee often favoured.

'Thanks,' she said, waving him towards the kitchen in a distracted manner. 'The make-up girl is upstairs with Jenna and Debbie, and I'm next. Will you go and make yourself a cup of tea? There's cold meats and salads in the fridge if you want something to eat. There's Stafford's sliced bread if you'd fancy a sandwich. It's lovely bread.'

'I might do that,' he said agreeably. 'It will be a while before we eat, so there's no point sitting through the wedding with a rumbling stomach. Do you want anything? Will I make something for the girls?'

'Umm . . . I suppose you could make a few sandwiches now that you're here, we might as well make use of you.' She grinned at him, looking tanned and healthy, her eyes bright and sparkling as the excitement of the day began to kick in.

'Hard to believe, isn't it?' he said as he shrugged off his jacket and she took it from him to hang on the hallstand.

'I know. It went in the blink of an eye.'

278

'Warp speed!' He grimaced, and she noticed how much more grey was flecked through his hair and how his features had become less firm and more puffy. He was heavier, too, than the skinnymalinks she'd married. But his ageing gave him an air of mature gravitas, not the manifestation of weight gain, wrinkles, memory loss and twinges that seemed to be her experience of the ageing process, she thought sourly. What other argument could there be that the Divine was not a woman?

'I remember the day she was born.' Barry interrupted her musings.

'Me too,' she said dryly. 'It was a long, hard labour.'

'You made a great job of her,' Barry said quietly.

'I did my best. I don't know if it was enough, but there you go.'

'Don't *ever* have a doubt about that,' Barry exclaimed, a wave of guilt washing over him. 'I'm sorry the way things turned out. I have regrets too, you know. Not a day goes by that I don't have regrets.' He touched her cheek.

'This isn't the day for regrets, Barry.' She turned away to go back up the stairs, breaking the moment he was trying to create.

He wished that he could prolong that brief interlude of intimacy, familiarity and shared experiences that were exclusive to them. He wanted to hear her say that he *had* been a good father and done his best by them. He wanted his ex-wife to acknowledge and affirm his good points so that he could try and escape the terrible guilt trip he had been on ever since Debbie had bluntly put it to him what a mark his leaving, his rejection of their family unit, had made on her. He felt riven with guilt for the childhood traumas his departure had inflicted on her. For the first time he'd had to confront the fact that he had behaved selfishly and self-centredly. And he was having trouble dealing with it.

There was no one he could really talk to without portraying himself in a bad light, and he was particularly unwilling to go down that route with Aimee. He appreciated why she wouldn't be particularly anxious to hear his confessions of culpability. It wouldn't be a good reflection on her judgement if she started to think that she'd married an irresponsible fly-by-night and not the successful, sophisticated businessman that she knew him as. It was ironic that Connie was the one who would be the most understanding of his turmoil . . . and the most forgiving.

'I've got my suit in the car – I'll get dressed here if you don't mind.' He changed the subject, not wanting to push her where she obviously didn't want to go.

'No problem at all,' she said easily. 'Can I have some mustard on my sandwich?'

'You always were a hot thing,' he joked, heading out to the kitchen, pleased at least to be with them on the day.

'Your dad's here,' he heard Connie call to Debbie, who murmured something indistinct from the confines of her bedroom. Barry sighed, making himself at home, exploring presses, finding cutlery and plates before opening the fridge to take out the cold cuts of meat that Connie had cooked the day before. He buttered the bread, listening to the laughs and chat wafting down the stairs. He felt a moment of happiness and hominess that caught him off guard.

How nice it was to be with his ex-wife and daughter and not to be made to feel like a visitor, an unwanted guest, as he'd so often felt in the past when he'd called to visit Debbie. He stared out the kitchen window at the riotous mass of flowering shrubs and pots with their trailing, scented blossoms and thought what a relaxing haven Connie had created. There was a serene tranquillity about the house and garden that appealed to him, and he wondered if he was feeling his age.

He liked his penthouse, but style triumphed over comfort there and his current family equation was far from tranquil at the moment, with he and Aimee passing each other like ships in the night. When he'd told Connie a few moments ago that he had regrets, he hadn't been lying. The events leading up to Debbie's wedding had him questioning his life, the decisions he'd taken, and even his second marriage.

Was he having a mid-life crisis? Was it observing Debbie's rite of passage and wishing he had been, and was, more involved with his first family? Was it Aimee and her career? If he were honest, would he admit that he sometimes felt inadequate when he measured her increasing success against his own line of business which, though successful, had levelled out and was going nowhere fast. He didn't know. All he knew was that he felt very restless and dissatisfied lately, and here, right now, in this small, comfy cottage, he felt very much at home.

'What was I going to do next?' Connie stood perplexed in the middle of her bedroom, trying to remember what she had come upstairs to do. Her memory was gone to the dogs. 'Friggin' peri-menopause,' she muttered, gazing around to try and remember. Her bag, that was it, she needed to sort it out. She slung it on the bed and opened it with trepidation. It needed a good clean-out but today wasn't the day for it. Connie gazed at the contents of her trusty, well-worn leather handbag trying to decide what she needed to bring to the wedding and what could go to the hotel in her small overnighter.

The small cream clutch would carry only a fraction of what she lugged around with her on a daily basis. A sucky clove sweet stuck to its plastic packaging caught her eye, and she absentmindedly pulled it out and popped it in her mouth. She could hear Barry clattering around downstairs opening doors and drawers. He'd been all ready for an emotional moment if she'd indulged him, but she'd nipped that smartly in the bud. Today wasn't about him or her or their regrets; it was about making sure Debbie's day went as smoothly and as happily as it possibly could. That was her priority. Barry needed to make it his.

It wasn't all about him. When she looked back on their relationship, it always *had* been about him, *his* needs, emotional and otherwise. It was liberating not to feel she had to indulge him any more. Still, she was glad for Debbie's sake that he was here and that they would be going to the church as a family group. She was particularly glad that Melissa was coming to the wedding. Blood was thicker than water, and Melissa and Debbie had an opportunity now to become close, despite all that had happened in the past. She very much hoped that they took it, and she would keep an eye on their progress and urge Debbie to be proactive in nurturing the relationship. The day might come when she'd need a loving sister.

A sister was a blessing. Connie would have loved one of her own. She had Karen, though. Her sister-in-law had stuck with her through thick and thin over the years, and Connie was looking forward immensely to their week in Spain when all the madness was over. It would be a time just to chill after the hassles of the last few months.

'Mum, your turn.' Debbie strolled into the bedroom wrapped in a terry-towelling robe.

'Hon, she did a *fabulous* job!' Connie gazed at her daughter with pride. Debbie looked radiant with a natural-looking make-up that highlighted her beautiful blue eyes and high cheekbones. Her copper hair was piled loosely on her head with just a few silky tendrils framing her face.

'I want to kiss you, but I'm afraid I'll smudge your make-up.' Connie hugged her but avoided touching her face. 'I'm proud of you, darling, I hope you'll be really happy,' she said with a lump in her throat.

'Don't, Mum,' Debbie warned as her own eyes began to glitter.

'Right, OK. I'm off to get the crevices filled in – hope she has plenty of Polyfilla!' Connie pulled herself together. They had both agreed there would be no tears but it was hard to keep composed. There was so much she wanted to say to her precious daughter. They had been such a tight little unit for so long. Having her in the house the previous night had been a treat. She'd slept like a log too. She always slept better when Debbie stayed the night.

Adjusting to living on her own had taken a while. It was the all-encompassing silence that pervaded the house that had taken such getting used to when Debbie had moved out to live with Bryan. She truly was letting go of her daughter today, and there was a sense of loss that was unexpected. Maybe if she and Barry were still together, it wouldn't be such a jolt. They'd be able to talk about all that had gone on during the wedding and do the post-mortem late in the night, cuddled together, the way married couples did after momentous events. That was the thing she'd missed most from her marriage, the bedtime intimacy and the sharing of the 'Wait until I tell you what's happened' moments. She brushed the thoughts aside irritably. She didn't need to be reminded of her loneliness right this moment.

Maybe she just had PMT and was extra emotional, Connie thought, knowing that Debbie wouldn't welcome any soppy discourses right now.

'You better say hello to your dad, he's downstairs making sandwiches,' she suggested as she drew away and made for the door.

'Oh great, I'm starving,' Debbie exclaimed, and Connie burst out laughing. 'You go, girl,' she grinned, astonished by her daughter's lack of nerves.

'Well, it's ages since brekkie, I've spent the morning being beautified and it will be a long time till we sit down to the barbie,' Debbie said to justify her hunger.

'Don't worry, I'm in full agreement. Tell your dad to make a sanger for Jenna as well,' Connie called over her shoulder as she wandered into Debbie's bedroom, where the make-up miracle was to take place.

'Barry's making tea and sandwiches for us, girls,' she announced.

'Thanks, Connie, I wouldn't mind a cuppa and a bite to eat to keep me going. You sit here.' Her niece jumped up, waving her hands around and gesturing for Connie to sit down.

'You look smashing, Jenna. Wait until Karen sees you.'

'She won't recognize me. Ma's more used to seeing me in jeans, with my hair tied back with a bobbin.' Jenna laughed, twirling around to admire her sophisticated reflection. 'Have I become a lady after all?'

'That might be pushing it,' teased her aunt, who knew what a tomboy Jenna was at heart.

'I think you're right. A day of this kind of stuff' – she blew on her nails – 'will do me for a year. As soon as these are dry I'm off to get my tea. I'll make a fresh pot for you when you come down.'

'Thanks, hon.' Connie smiled as the bright-eyed, sunny young woman waltzed out the door in her finery with not a care in the world. Connie felt a stab of envy as she watched her go. She'd been young and carefree and athletic once. Just like her niece and daughter. She'd had a firm, supple, slender body. Optimism and eagerness for new experiences had been her motivator. Nothing daunted her.

Middle age, with all its cares and hormonal and body changes, hadn't even been a minuscule cloud on her bright horizons. She'd taken it all so much for granted, never dreaming there would be such changes, emotional, physical and spiritual, wrought in her. Youth truly was wasted on the young, she thought regretfully, knowing that some hard work and discipline was going to be called for to keep herself in reasonable shape once this wedding was over if she was not to slip even further down the road of saggy flab.

'Do your best with the crow's feet and give me cheek bones,' she instructed, smiling at Laura, the make-up girl, as she settled into her chair and prepared to be transformed.

'Hi Dad. Mum said for you to make a sandwich for Jenna as well, she's just letting her nails dry,' Debbie instructed her father as she watched him expertly carve slices of pink ham and place them in a pile on a plate.

He turned to look at her and his eyes widened. 'God, you look so grown-up! You look *beautiful*.' He couldn't hide his sentiment.

'Thanks,' she murmured, surprised by his reaction. It was rare for him to compliment her.

'Bryan's a very lucky young man. I hope he knows that,' he said, feeling a surge of emotion as he beheld his daughter.

'He does, and I'm lucky too,' Debbie assured him as she leaned over and pinched a slice of ham.

Barry cleared his throat. 'I'm glad to be part of your day. I'm glad you were able to forgive and forget and let bygones be bygones, it really means a lot to me,' he said awkwardly. He reached out and took her hand.

'I'm glad too, Dad. It's made Mum happy,' she rejoined, feeling a multitude of emotions at this extraordinary moment of familiarity. Not only was she getting married today, she was having a day of father–daughter moments which she'd longed for all her life. Now that they were happening, she wasn't quite sure how to handle them.

'And *you*, what does it mean to *you*?' he asked her earnestly, wishing that she'd say that it made her happy, longing for her to tell him that he could walk her up the aisle. He was her father: it was his right, his duty. What would people think when she went up the aisle on her mother's arm? Did women have any idea how they could emasculate men? he wondered as he willed his daughter to respond more effusively.

'You're right, it's good to let go of the past, it was a heavy burden to carry,' she hedged, perching on the edge of the table as she wolfed the piece of ham.

'I would have let it go long ago if you'd wanted,' he reminded her, unable to resist an opportunity to let her know that it was her stubborn stance that had caused a lot of their problems.

'Easier said than done. You didn't have to deal with what I had to deal with,' she riposted, unwilling to shoulder all the blame. If he thought this one day was going to make up for years of emotional neglect he could think again. He wasn't getting off the hook that easy.

'True.' He conceded defeat. 'Are you all set for today?' He changed the subject, disappointed that she wouldn't give him the affirmation he was looking for on this most special of days and aware of the slight hostility that had crept into her tone.

'Yeah, I've been on to the hotel; everything's OK their end. Our rooms are confirmed. A friend of mine has done the flowers. The violinist rang to check about the music so, unless Bryan doesn't show up, everything's on track. How's Melissa?' Debbie welcomed the return of predictability to the conversation. She had no intention of getting into any emotional stuff with her father today. It was hard enough keeping her mother from turning into a puddle, without ending up in floods herself.

'She's moaning about the dress Aimee got for her, says it makes her look like a spaced-out zebra. I stay out of these things.' Barry made a face, and she laughed and began to relax. 'Herself and Sarah think they're going to get off with some of Bryan's friends, they think they're thirty not thirteen.' Her father raised his eyes to heaven.

'Thirteen's a horrible age,' Debbie said sympathetically, remembering what it was like to be a spotty, unsure, overweight teenager.

'I can't remember that far back – Melissa claims I'm pre-historic and I feel it sometimes.' He smiled at her, and this time her smile was genuine. It seemed almost surreal to be having a normal light-hearted conversation with her father. It *was* a pity it had taken so long to get to this level in their relationship and he was right, she had to take her share of the blame for that. At least their reconciliation had happened before the most im-portant day of her life. For all her previous opposition to his role in her wedding she was surprised at how good it felt to have him with her right now. It could have been more like this when she was growing up if she hadn't let her bitterness and anger dictate her behaviour. She still had a long way to go, she thought regretfully, remembering how she wouldn't give Barry any leeway a few moments ago. Many children came from broken marriages and had good relationships with both parents; she should have got over herself long ago and stopped acting like a ninny. Sometimes she could be her own worst enemy. Still, she'd held out the olive branch and this was the outcome, and it couldn't be more welcome, she comforted herself, not having enjoyed her moments of self-reflection. Examining her behavioural flaws was not what she'd imagined she'd be doing on her wedding day.

'When you said "rooms", is Connie staying at the hotel, or is she coming back here?' Barry asked casually as he poured two mugs of tea as if he'd been presiding over their kitchen for ever and a day.

'God no! How awful and lonely would it be if she had to get

a taxi back here? She's booked a room so she'll be able to have a few drinks and not worry about getting home and feeling too lonely when the day is over.'

'That's good. Excellent thinking!' Barry approved, handing Debbie a plate of neatly cut triangle sandwiches.

'Just as well I came a bit early,' he remarked as Karen, who had come around the back of the house, let herself into the kitchen in time to snaffle one.

'Just what I need,' she exclaimed. 'Well done, brother.'

'Glad to be of service.' He poured her a mug of tea, which was gratefully accepted.

'Well, niece, are you all set to go? You look beautiful, and very relaxed for a bride,' Karen approved as she sat down at the table and took a gulp of tea.

'More or less ready now. Mum's getting her make-up done, Jenna's drying her nails and then all we've to do is to put our dresses on.' Debbie sat down beside her at the table and held out her cup for a refill.

'Well, this is nice.' Karen sat back in her chair and smiled. 'I thought there'd be pandemonium.'

'I'm here, feeding and watering the women – all they have to do is concentrate on looking stunning which, as you can see, is exactly what's happening, so there's no panic whatsoever,' Barry boasted.

'Oh yikes! I forgot to remind Bryan to bring his passport; I'd better go and send him a text. Oh God, where did I put the booking email for our tickets?' Debbie shot up out of her chair and raced from the kitchen.

'As you can see . . . no panic,' Barry reiterated, chuckling as he filled the kettle to make another pot of tea for Jenna, who had barely avoided being careered into by her cousin on her way out the door. Twenty minutes later all was calm; texts had been exchanged, ticket email had been located and Connie and Laura, the make-up girl, had marched into the kitchen demanding to be fed. Barry's eyes widened when he saw his ex-wife, looking the most glamorous he'd ever seen her.

He gave a low whistle. 'You look terrific! Your eyes are

amazing. You look ... you look great.' He was clearly impressed.

'Let's hope it lasts until I get Madam up to the altar. I'm afraid it will all get washed away if I start bawling,' Connie joked as she took the mug of tea he handed her.

'No crying! You promised!' Debbie warned.

'Easier said than done, Miss. Wait until it's *your* daughter walking up the aisle,' her mother declared, taking a welcome sip of hot, sweet tea, trying to ignore the look of surprise and appreciation in her ex-husband's admiring gaze. He'd never looked at her like that before, even when they were married. She couldn't deny it was a rather satisfying response.

Karen, noting everything that was going on, smirked and gave her a wink, and Connie had to restrain herself not to start laughing. Karen was a brat; she knew *exactly* what she was thinking.

Now that the day was upon them Connie felt almost laidback. So far, things were going to plan. What was the point of worrying and getting emotional? She might as well just sit back and enjoy herself.

'I hope we won't be sitting with that smug upstart Barry.' Stella Dillon clattered the cups and saucers into the sink.

'Don't say that,' her husband remonstrated, struggling with the last clue in the Crosaire.

'I *will* say it. He shouldn't be coming to this wedding, if you ask me,' his wife retorted. She wasn't looking forward to her granddaughter's wedding one bit. 'And neither should that Aimee one. Has she no idea how to behave? Has she no manners?'

'Stella, it's none of our business, and you mind *your* manners today, for Connie's sake. If we *are* sitting beside them, or if they come and talk to us, we'll be polite. Do you hear me now?' Jim Dillon said firmly, lowering his paper to give her a stern gaze over the top of his bifocals.

Stella's lips tightened. It was rare for Jim to put his foot down, and when he did he meant it. Men just didn't understand these things. Barry Adams had walked out on their daughter, no matter what way Connie liked to dress it up. He was going to be at this wedding with his hussy and their child. Just what society was coming to when first and second families mingled casually as though everything were normal she could not for the life of her understand. The carry-on of today's generation left a lot to be desired; it was extremely unsettling the rate at which society was changing. Divorce, separation, children born out of wedlock raised not an eyebrow. Drug-taking for recreation was the norm. Children drank when they were barely in their teens. This was the world her granddaughter was living in and it troubled Stella enormously.

She often felt she was on a different planet when she compared how it was now to when she was growing up. Marriage was treated with respect, having children was honoured; rearing a family within a marriage was seen as a good thing, a fine achievement. Now it meant nothing. Kids reared themselves while their parents worked all hours to buy their SUVs and their massive TVs and their holiday homes and the like. It was all about keeping up with the Joneses and impressing their peers, and child-rearing was left to crèches and schools, whose responsibility it certainly was not. Parents were responsible for their children. That was Stella's firm conviction, and the way children turned out had a lot to do with their upbringing. How Debbie had turned out as well as she had was a great reflection on Connie. And what had her daughter ended up as? Stella thought bitterly . . . a lonely, not very well-off divorcée, whether she liked it or not, thanks to that good-for-nothing husband of hers.

Barry Adams was Connie's husband no matter what he thought. And that Aimee one had no business calling herself 'Mrs Adams', no matter what *she* might like to think. Using her maiden name didn't fool Stella. And if Jim thought for one second that she was going to sit meek and mild and be polite to that . . . that Judas and his . . . his Jezebel he had another think coming. Mister Barry Adams might think that all was forgiven and forgotten, but she'd be letting him know in no uncertain terms that, as far as she was concerned, she'd *never* forgive him for walking away from his legitimate marriage to their daughter. Or for walking out on Debbie.

'Do you hear me, Stella?' Jim persisted when she didn't respond.

'I hear you,' she said flatly, whipping the milk jug and sugar bowl off the table and leaving him under no illusion that she was not best pleased.

Aimee glanced at her watch and groaned. She was leaving it very tight to get back to the office to change into her wedding outfit. She was almost tempted to go to the wedding in her work suit. It was smart and elegant, if a little severe. Why she'd changed her mind about going to this damned wedding she could not fathom. It wasn't even as if she and Barry were going to the church together. She should have stuck to her guns and stayed away. A thought struck her. Surely her husband would be sitting with her in the church? Or would he feel he had to sit with Connie up at the front?

She certainly hoped he felt his place was with her and Melissa. She was his *wife*, she thought crossly, wondering why on earth she was even bothered by such a thing. She was Aimee Davenport, who had never needed a man to affirm her or her place in society. But these last few months she'd been hearing more and more about Connie and what a good mother she was and how she had made such a fantastic job of raising Debbie. Almost as though Barry was comparing her and his ex and their mothering skills.

She didn't think Connie had made that good a job of raising her daughter. Debbie was a spoilt, immature brat who only thought of herself, in her view, Aimee thought bitchily, remembering their last unfriendly encounter at lunch in Roly's when her step-daughter's behaviour had been less than mature and gracious. *And* when her husband had most certainly not stood up for her, she remembered in disgust.

Well, he'd better be by her side today where he belonged, Aimee scowled as she whipped her BlackBerry out of her bag, thoroughly disgruntled by these most uncharacteristic feelings of resentment and, even worse, possessiveness and jealousy. Every single silly female trait that she despised was rearing its ugly head and making her feel the way she hadn't felt in a long, long time. Edgy, rattled and less than in control. And Aimee didn't like it one little bit.

Chapter Twenty-six

'It was nice having your father here, even though it wasn't planned, wasn't it?' Connie said as she eased Debbie's wedding dress over her head. They were on their own for a moment. Jenna had gone downstairs to put her overnight case in Karen's car, and Laura was in the loo.

'He really made himself at home. He was very relaxed, wasn't he? I think he knows he made a mistake leaving us, Mum,' Debbie said earnestly. 'I think he misses you. He kept looking at you.'

'For goodness' sake, stop that nonsense, Debbie. I didn't see him looking at me. You're imagining things. And trust me on this one, I'm happy the way I am, thank you very much. I don't want *any* complications in my life,' Connie said very firmly, lying through her teeth as she slid the A-line satin skirt down over her daughter's hips.

Of course she'd been aware of Barry's admiring gaze, very much aware, and she couldn't deny that it gave her a certain amount of satisfaction to see how the tables had turned in their relationship. He was the one who had walked out on her and made her feel less than a woman. He was the one who had left her questioning every aspect of her femininity and her personality. He was the one who had met and married a beautiful, successful younger woman, and he was the one now, unless she was very much mistaken, sending out strong signals that he'd like to resume some sort of a relationship with her, which might lead to God only knew what in the future.

But Debbie wasn't to know that, and Connie certainly wouldn't be telling her, despite the fact that their daughter had copped that Barry was behaving quite differently towards her. If Debbie realized that she'd already slept with him she'd be gobsmacked and possibly horrified, Connie thought with a stab of guilt, unable to look at her daughter as she pretended to pick a piece of thread off the hem.

'But aren't you lonely, Mum?' Debbie interrupted her ruminations as she wriggled around until the skirt fell in the right folds.

'Not *that* lonely,' Connie said emphatically, giving a little tweak at the ivory lacy top until it sat perfectly.

'He really likes being here. He fits in here actually,' Debbie said slowly. 'It felt like a "proper" home down in the kitchen this morning, didn't it?' There was a touch of wistfulness in her tone that caught at Connie's heartstrings.

'I suppose it did. I'm sorry it wasn't like that for you growing up,' she said sadly.

'Aw, Mum, I wasn't saying that to hurt you . . . I . . . I just thought it felt nice,' Debbie said hastily, looking at her feet. 'It felt like a "real" family.'

'We are a "real" family, when all's said and done, Debbie,' Connie said defensively. 'Barry was always there for you and would have played a much bigger part in your life if you'd wanted him to.' She wasn't going to let Debbie off the hook on that one, she thought crossly, annoyed that her daughter had made her feel defensive. 'Would you like your father to give you away? I wouldn't have any objections.' She studied her daughter intently.

'You reared me, you give me away,' Debbie insisted firmly.

'Well, in a "real" family the father gives the daughter away,' Connie said tartly.

'Ah, don't get into a huff, Mum,' Debbie implored, realizing she'd been a tad insensitive.

'I'm not. Let's forget it.' Connie gazed admiringly at her

daughter. 'It's a beautiful dress. It's so understated and classy. You look fabulous.'

'Thanks, Mum. I feel fabulous,' she exclaimed, relieved that a tiff had been averted. She beamed, radiant with happiness, and Connie couldn't help but smile back.

Let her always be happy, she prayed, wishing that she could protect her beloved daughter from life and its hard knocks.

'Wow!' Jenna stood at the door, smiling at her cousin. 'Drop-dead gorgeous!'

'You look pretty knock-out yourself.' Debbie grinned. Her bridesmaid was wearing a silk aquamarine, figure-hugging dress that showed off her tanned, slender body perfectly.

A far cry from the meringues for brides and bridesmaids that had been so prevalent when she'd been getting married, Connie reflected as she helped her niece arrange Debbie's veil over her upswept hair. She stood back to look at the result and felt a lump as big as a golfball in her throat seeing the bridal vision in front of her. This was her little girl, the most important person in her life, and today she was going to have to let her go. Pride, joy, loss, sadness – a cocktail of emotions – left her hardly able to speak.

'Come on, let's go show your father.' She swallowed hard.

'OK, but first I want to thank you for being the best mother a girl could have,' Debbie said, softly leaning over to kiss her. They held each other tightly, silently. Tears shimmered in Debbie's eyes and her lip wobbled. 'I love you, Mum,' she whispered.

'And I love you, Debbie,' Connie said huskily, feeling tears slide down her cheeks.

'OK, you two, break it up,' Jenna commanded, taking control. 'Otherwise there's going to be a Niagara of tears and your make-up will be ruined and I'll have failed dismally in my duty and Ma will give me hell,' she added plaintively.

Connie and Debbie laughed in spite of themselves and it was a smiling trio that made their way down the stairs to the lounge, where Barry was fastening his cufflinks, having changed into his suit.

His jaw dropped and he chewed his lip as emotion threatened to overwhelm him. 'Debbie . . .' he said shakily, holding his hand out to her. Connie could see that his eyes were suspiciously bright.

'Do you like it, Dad?' She smiled at him, taking his hand and raising her face for his kiss.

'Oh yes, my darling girl. I love it and I love you,' he said with heartfelt pride and love as he tenderly kissed her forehead.

'I better get out of here or I'll bawl. It will only take me five minutes to slip into my dress,' Connie muttered, petrified she was going to lose it again. And this time she wouldn't be able to contain it. She hurried from the room, struggling to keep control of her emotions.

'Do you need some tissues?' Debbie called after her teasingly, and Connie gave a tearful smile as she ran up the stairs. Her daughter knew her so well.

'Stop now,' she ordered herself sternly as she slid out of her robe and took her dress down off the hook on the back of the bedroom door. That moment with Barry and Debbie had nearly been the undoing of her. It was one she'd always hoped for and never thought would happen. Momentous events had certainly taken place within their family in the past few months, but this had surpassed everything. 'My darling girl', he'd called their daughter, and Debbie hadn't rebuffed him. She'd been delighted. Someone was working miracles for them this day, Connie thought gratefully as she unwrapped the tissue paper and let it fall on the floor, revealing the dress she was wearing to the wedding.

She skimmed it down over her head and let it settle around her, the material soft, yielding, as it snaked down over her hips. She settled the straps, straightened the seams, stepped into her shoes and slipped on the cream bolero jacket that finished off the outfit.

Connie stood back and looked at her reflection in the mirror and felt a moment of pride. She *did* look good, and she wasn't going to be modest about it, she thought with a grin. Slender and supple – no, definitely not, she thought ruefully, but the half-stone she'd lost was noticeable and she looked sensual and womanly, she decided approvingly as she studied the curve of her waist to her hip.

Her dress, a purple hammered satin with a slight cowl neck and narrow lace straps, had an asymmetrical seam across the body which drew the eye down to the bubble hem, which fell just to the knees. It was simple and unfussy and the bias cut was extremely flattering. The neckline showed a hint of tanned cleavage and she wore an amethyst on a gold chain that emphasized her colour and nestled provocatively between her breasts. The jacket was a smart contrast and gave the outfit its final touch.

'Certainly not mother-of-the-bridey,' she muttered with satisfaction as she twisted and turned, admiring herself. Aimee could arrive in the most expensive haute couture – which she probably would, Connie thought snootily – but it wouldn't cost her a thought. This outfit would take her anywhere and Debbie could be proud of her.

'Right. Chin up, let's get going,' she said to Hope, who was rubbing herself against her leg looking for a cuddle.

She bent down, lifted her little black cat and gave her a kiss. 'See you tomorrow, darling. I'll have *loads* to tell you,' she murmured against her silky ear, as Hope meowed companionably before marching downstairs ahead of her mistress with her tail held high.

'*Mum, it's gorgeous. So sexy!*'

'*My God, Connie! You look . . . stunning!*'

'*I don't think I'm going to get a look-in with any of the men at this wedding, Auntie!*'

Connie laughed at the reaction of the trio in the lounge who were awaiting her arrival, sipping the pink champagne that Barry had brought.

'Mum, that dress is fabulous on you, and the colour is perfect. It's really sophisticated. I've never seen you look so well. I don't know what I was expecting . . . a . . . a two-piece with a hat!' Debbie confessed, her eyes sparkling with delight as she made Connie do a twirl.

'Gee, thanks.' Connie made a face at her.

'Well, it's a real change of image for you – maybe I was exaggerating about the hat,' Debbie teased, thrilled with her mother's new look.

'Ma said it was very glamorous, and she was right. You look the biz, Connie. You and me should go on the prowl.' Jenna grinned, raising her glass to her.

'Definitely,' laughed Connie, having this mad vision of herself and Jenna trawling the nightclubs.

'A glass of bubbly?' Barry held a slender flute out to her, his eyes moving up and down as he took in every bit of her.

'Thanks,' she said gaily, more than pleased at their reactions. She hadn't shown Debbie the dress she'd bought, wanting to surprise her, and she'd certainly done that, judging by her daughter's response. Only Karen, who had been with her when she bought it, had seen it. And, if it hadn't been for her sister-in-law, she'd never have considered such a chic, expensive outfit. Karen had pooh-poohed her fears that it was too young and too girlish for her mature years.

'Absolutely not! It takes ten years off you. You're not going to this wedding looking like a frump. It's about time you changed your image and spent a bit of money on yourself. It's not at all girly, trust me. Classy, sexy, yes – girly, no! Would I let you out in something that wasn't right for you?' she demanded. 'Would I let you out looking like mutton dressed as lamb? Especially with Aimee coming to the wedding.'

'No,' Connie admitted, still unsure. Mind, it did camouflage her tummy wobble very well, and the slight ruching under the neckline was very flattering to her boobs.

'Buy it, and don't show it to anyone until the day of the wedding,' Karen had instructed, and Connie was glad she'd done as she was told, and even more pleased that she'd lost the few pounds since buying it, making it hang even better on her.

Barry's fingers lingered on hers as she took the glass from him. 'You look amazing,' he said softly, his eyes full of admiration. Connie felt another frisson of satisfaction as she took a sip of the pink liquid. The tables *had* turned nicely in their relationship and she was human enough to enjoy it. It was an added and unexpected bonus to this – up until now – dreaded wedding. And it was a surprise to her that she felt this way.

Her self-confidence was soaring again after the interactions between her and Barry. He'd made it obvious that he was interested again. If it was in her, she could lead him up the garden path and drop him as callously as he had dropped her. Would she be that bitchy? Getting your own back was a most satisfying thing to do, but surely she was mature enough to have got over *that* particular itch! Sometimes she surprised herself, Connie thought wryly, as she held out her glass for the top-up he was offering her.

'This is nice champagne.' She smiled.

'Only the best for the day that's in it,' her ex-husband declared, topping up the girls' drinks before coming to stand beside her again. 'That's a terrific colour on you,' he said appreciatively. 'I've never seen you look so dressed up.'

'You look pretty nifty yourself,' she praised, and his eyes lit up. His dark, expensively tailored suit looked extremely well on him. He looked every inch the successful, affluent businessman that he was.

'Here.' She picked up a white carnation that was lying beside Debbie's bouquet of sweet pea, pink roses, freesias and jasmine. She tucked it into his buttonhole, tweaking it until it sat just right. What a wifely thing to be doing, she thought. He was wearing an aftershave that was very perfumed. No doubt a gift from Aimee. She always did go for the strong scent.

'Thanks,' he murmured. His arms tightened around her, and before she knew it he had given her a kiss on the lips. She caught Debbie's astonished *I told you so* look and almost laughed.

Today was a day for game-playing, Connie thought in amusement, and she would play them. Her life would be boring enough when all the excitement had died down. 'Right, drink up everyone, we've got a wedding to go to,' she ordered crisply, pushing away from Barry. If it had just been the two of them in the room, would she have kissed him back?

That was twice in less than a month that she'd felt his lips on hers and enjoyed it. She needed a man, that was her problem. Pity Bryan's friends were so young. She didn't think a toy boy would be her style but, then, who was to know? Once Debbie was married, she had no real commitments any more. The only person she had to think about was herself. *How liberating*, she thought with a sudden sense of giddy recklessness.

If a man was what she wanted, it was time to go and find one!

Chapter Twenty-seven

Judith opened the boot of her car and stowed her overnight case neatly into its immaculate interior. She was so looking forward to this day. She was meeting her friend, Jillian, in a hotel on a picturesque lake, just at the edge of Virginia in Cavan, and they were going to indulge themselves in all manner of beauty treatments in the hotel's luxury spa. She'd booked a facial, manicure and pedicure and a body wrap and massage. The thought of it had kept her going for ages, especially during the last week in the office, when all the talk had been about Debbie Adams' forthcoming wedding.

She'd found it irritating, to say the least, and a skittish atmosphere had pervaded her section, which had led to much chit-chat, gossiping and sloppy work. As a consequence, she'd had to put her foot down and was made to feel like a real party-pooper. She wasn't paid a good salary for being popular, Judith acknowledged, but it annoyed the hell out of her that some of her staff acted like sixteen-year-olds, when they should know better.

Three of the girls were going to the wedding, and two of them had arrived back to work an hour and a half late after lunch earlier in the week with the excuse that they were buying the wedding present from the collection that had been taken up in the office. Judith had been hopping mad and let them know in no uncertain terms that buying wedding presents was something to be undertaken on their own time, whether it was a staff collection or not. She'd received a few filthy looks after that particular edict. She knew she was being a little heavy-handed but she didn't care. She was in such foul humour in the weeks following her bust-up with Tom that she wasn't interested in being popular at work.

She found herself irrationally resenting her co-workers' thoughtless, carefree joie de vivre. Judith felt as though life was rubbing her nose in it, reminding her of what she could have had if she'd stood her ground and left home when her father had died.

Most of the girls had gone out that night for a booze-up with Madam Adams, and a few of them had arrived into the office the following morning hungover and unable to concentrate on their work. The wages and salaries section couldn't afford to make mistakes and, if mistakes *were* made, it was Judith who got the flack for it. She'd had to be extra vigilant the past week and she resented it enormously. Those girls were getting paid well for doing a job that had to be double-checked by her because she couldn't depend on them. She knew she was beginning to think like a cantankerous old biddy – even worse, she was turning into a cantankerous old biddy, she'd thought glumly as she locked up that night at the end of a fraught day.

She'd gone home like an antichrist, and Lily had told her if her job was too much for her she should consider changing it, which had put her in an even worse humour. Her mother hadn't a clue about responsibilities; she couldn't even take responsibility for looking after herself. Judith had felt like telling her to shut up and mind her own business and had restrained herself with great difficulty. She'd been very tempted to go on a bender, but memories of the last one and the self-loathing she'd felt after it were still relatively fresh so she went for a walk in the park instead. That hadn't helped much either. All she had seen were couples walking hand in hand, and that had made her feel even more depressed and alone.

Thank God all the wedding nonsense would be over after today, Judith thought, looking at the clear blue sky and thinking what a perfect day it was to be getting married. Typical of Debbie Adams' luck. It had pissed rain for the past three days, sheets of it lashing down on the country, causing floods and traffic chaos. The unseasonable, appalling weather had dominated the news and discussions on global warming criss-crossed the airwaves. Judith had been rather pleased that it was raining so hard, having heard that Debbie, who always had to be different, was having a barbecue. She knew she was being mean-spirited, wishing disaster on the younger girl's day, and that made her feel even worse about herself, if that was possible.

It seemed, despite her sour bad vibes, that her colleague's wedding feast wouldn't be a wash-out after all. Judith felt envy smother her, its tentacles squeezing her insides. How was it that some people seemed to have everything in life so easy and others, like her, had to struggle? she asked herself yet again.

She was a good person – she'd taken care of her father, and she was still making huge sacrifices for her mother – could she not have been gifted with a kind man and the security of marriage? Was she so unworthy? she wondered in a sudden deluge of self-pity.

Debbie Adams no doubt would be knocking on her office door soon enough to tell her that she was pregnant and looking to book her maternity leave and, then, she'd be like the rest of the mothers who worked for the firm, expecting as their due special conditions to go for medical check-ups and, then, when they eventually did swan back to work after the birth, time off to collect their brat from the crèche, or to bring it to the doctor or for any other of the host of excuses that she was presented with daily.

Yesterday, she'd overheard Jacinta Cleary's frantic attempts to get someone to collect her daughter from school because her childminder had taken ill, and she obviously hadn't been successful, because she'd come and *informed* Judith that she was taking a half-day's leave, ten minutes later. Everyone else had to give notice that they were taking annual leave; the mothers in the firm just *took* it, without a thought as to whether it impacted on the work the rest of them had to do.

You really were penalized for being childless and single, at work and at home, she thought grimly. Well, she wouldn't be giving Debbie Adams one bit of leeway, because she didn't deserve it. She wasn't even a good employee in her single state; it was far from likely that marriage would make any improvement in her work ethic. Getting married and having children was *her* problem and not her employers'. Judith frowned, the enjoyment going out of her day as she had a vision of Debbie floating up the aisle, blissful, radiant, and taking it all as her due.

She felt a sudden vicious, irrational loathing of her young fellow worker as she slammed the boot shut and went into the house to ring her sister to see what was keeping her. Cecily was taking Lily for the weekend but, as usual, had not arrived as planned, and was sure to have some outlandish excuse for her tardiness.

She was heartily sick of her family, sick of them pulling out on her, treating her as though she was there solely for their convenience, thinking that she had no life of her own. *Well, you don't have a life of your own apart from work,* she thought moodily, wondering why she was going into destruct mode and ruining the day she'd been looking forward to so much with her negativity.

Sometimes she was her own worst enemy. What was her problem? Was she afraid of life? Was it this fear that had kept her from taking a risk that might have allowed *her* to walk up the aisle? Was she more like her mother in that regard than she cared to admit? Afraid of change, afraid of new experiences and the challenges life threw up? Afraid of standing on her own two feet? 'Oh for God's sake, give it a rest,' she muttered, stalking into the house like a demon.

Lily watched her daughter's face redden with temper as she spoke to her sister on the phone. Her heart sank. Cecily was obviously going to be late and Judith was getting into one of her humours. They were getting worse lately, and Lily was at her wits' end. Ever since she'd come home from the hospital

303

several weeks ago, Judith had been in increasingly bad form. Lily had demanded to know what was wrong with her but had got a surly 'Nothing' in reply.

'Well, don't be taking your bad temper out on me,' Lily had retorted, but she was concerned nevertheless and knew something was up. Her daughter had come home from work in foul humour every day last week. Lily had suggested that if she wasn't up to the job she should change it for one with less responsibility. Needless to say, Judith had gone through her for a short cut and told her 'not to be talking ridiculous nonsense!'

It had to be more than the change of life, Lily fretted as she'd retired to her sitting room to lick her wounds. She envied her neighbour across the road, who was going out to the cinema with her two daughters, who were most solicitous of her and obviously loved her dearly. Salty tears had slid down her cheeks and she'd never felt as lonely. Neither of her daughters loved her. She was a burden to them, Lily knew that. But, of her three children, she loved Judith, the only one who hadn't abandoned her. She worried about her and she felt guilty because she'd held her back.

All the delight she'd felt that her eye operation was a success and that she could read again with ease was tempered with anxiety. Did her daughter have no idea how nerve-racking it was to be considered such a burden? Had she no idea of the fears that tormented Lily? What would happen if she became frail and dependent? Would Judith dump her in a nursing home, fed up at having to make continuous sacrifices?

Lily felt a flutter of fear, that familiar black, soulless companion that had accompanied her all her life. She'd seen the reports on the news about nursing homes closing because of bad conditions. She'd read about the elderly being left abandoned in these places by their families, with no one to come and visit. Growing old was frightening. Nothing was assured. She felt no sense of security at all. The way Judith was behaving these days was enough to keep even a buddha on edge, Lily reflected. She'd been relieved when her daughter had told her that she was going for a walk after her rude retort. The palpable air of tension had eased as Judith closed the front door behind her and, for the first time since Ted had died, Lily wondered would she be better off living by herself. At least she wouldn't have to be worrying about whether anyone else was in a good humour or not. Her nerves wouldn't be jangling every evening listening to the key in the door and wondering what sort of mood Judith was in.

Lily sighed as she remembered that recent uncharacteristic contemplation. She'd been tempted to tell Cecily that she was going to stay on her own when Judith had her night away with Jillian. But, as usual, she'd chickened out. Now she was sorry, she decided, as she heard the kitchen door slam and Judith snap.

'Well, I'm going now. I can't wait for you. You were supposed to be here half an hour ago. It's typical of you, Cecily, you don't give a damn about anyone else.' Judith marched into Lily's sitting room, grim-faced. 'Ma, Cecily's running late, and if I don't go I won't get there in time and I'll miss some of the treatments I've booked.'

'Just go, for goodness' sake, and leave me in peace. I know I'm nothing but a burden to the lot of you,' Lily retorted defensively, cross at yet again being made to feel like a nuisance. 'The sooner I'm dead the better.'

'Ah, stop that!' Judith snapped. 'I've enough on my plate without you talking that kind of nonsense.'

'I don't talk nonsense,' Lily flared, stung at having had that accusation thrown at her twice in as many weeks. 'It's how I feel and someday, when you're my age, you'll know what it's like.'

'And what about how I feel?' Judith shrieked, her eyes blazing with a sudden ferocious anger. 'How do you think I feel when a young one half my age is waltzing up the aisle today and I could have been like her and done the same thing if you hadn't got your claws into me because you were too selfish and self-centred to think about anyone except yourself when Daddy died? How do you think I feel, Mother? Thanks to you, I'm seen as a bitter old spinster at work and – guess what?' She thrust her face up close to Lily's. 'That's what I am. A bitter, twisted – I won't call myself an old maid because at least I had a few shags in my life – but bitter and twisted, with no hope of anything better, is what I am, so don't *you* be telling *me* how *you* feel today. Sometimes, Mother, believe it or not, life's not all about you!' Her lips were drawn in a thin line; she looked almost feral.

Lily was so shocked at this vicious and unexpected onslaught she couldn't move or speak. Her heart flip-flopped into palpitations and she could hardly breathe. But Judith was oblivious to her distress, she was so angry.

'I'm going, and when that other selfish cow comes you can tell her to get some milk because we're almost out and I don't have time.' She didn't even wait for Lily to respond but stalked out of the sitting room. The front door slammed and a tomb-like silence descended on the house so that all Lily could hear was the thudding of her heartbeat, which was hammering against her chest. She heard the rev of the car's engine and the car roar off down the street, the noise fading as Judith drove further away.

Lily made her way to her chair, slowly, and sat down, utterly dazed. It was out in the open now. All that simmering fury and resentment that had fuelled Judith all these years and which, up until now, she had managed to contain in surly restraint. There could be no going back from this day. There was no façade to hide behind. The truth was out, ugly, hurtful and insurmountable. How could they recover from this and live together in any kind of harmony? The vile things her daughter had said to her about being selfish and getting her claws stuck into her shocked Lily to her core. And calling herself bitter and twisted. *And* revealing that she'd had sex. If she were behaving normally Judith would never have divulged such private information. She must be very stressed indeed to have blurted that lot out, Lily thought anxiously. She was behaving like someone on the edge of a breakdown. The idea frightened Lily. A breakdown was hard to claw back from; she wouldn't want her daughter to go through that vale of tears. Lily knew she should be dismayed at Judith's revelation but she wasn't, no matter what the church said about having sex outside of marriage. The church didn't put its arms around you at night and make you feel loved.

She was glad for Judith that she'd had some intimacy with a man. She hoped it had been comforting and satisfying and not just a shag, as she'd called it. Lily had loved that side of life with her husband; she'd always felt safe and secure in his arms and she'd missed their closeness so much when it was gone. Sleeping alone in her bed had been the loneliest, hardest thing to get used to.

What was she going to do? How should she deal with this? Her hand trembled as she raised it to wipe the tears from her eyes. It had to end. For both their sakes. Lily sat up straight as her breathing began to return to normal and her heart rate started to slow down. Let her ungracious daughter go, and let the other selfish one come and make her excuses, and then she'd tell her to get out of her sight. She wasn't going to be made to feel like a nuisance again this day. She was sick of them all. Not one of them had a decent bone in their body. She should have stood on her own two feet a long time ago and, if she had, she wouldn't be in the mess she was in now. Dependent on them for peace of mind. She could get a home help for herself. That lady, Mrs Meadows, whom she'd shared a room with in the hospital, had a home help who did her hoovering, cleaning and some light shopping.

Lily's needs were few anyway. It would be lonely sleeping in the house on her own, she thought sorrowfully, but thousands of people had to live alone and they managed it. Judith hated her, and rightly so, she'd ruined her life. Lily started to cry again. She was angry with her daughter but she understood why Judith had exploded as she had. It must be hard watching the young girls in the office getting married and knowing that her own chances of finding a husband were slipping away. Who married fifty-year-old women with elderly mothers tied to them? Lily cried bitter tears for her daughter as much as herself.

First thing on Monday morning, when Judith was gone to work, she was going to ring the bank manager and make an appointment to go and see him. Anything had to be better than this purgatory, she decided as she wiped her eyes and went out to the kitchen to make herself a cup of tea.

CHAPTER TWENTY-EIGHT

'Hell, look at the time.' Bryan glanced at his watch and saw with dismay that he was running quite late. He'd gone for a manicure and decided to treat himself to a facial as well, which had taken longer than he'd expected but had been most relaxing and enjoyable. His best man, Kenny, was at the house when he got home and they'd sat at the kitchen table drinking coffee and eating his mother's homemade tea brack while she and one of his sisters titivated themselves upstairs.

'Better get my suit on and leg it. If I'm late, Connie will be giving me the evil eye.' He made a face.

'Mothers-in-law – don't talk to me,' groaned his friend. 'Mine thinks motorbikes are dangerous and is always giving me grief about it.'

'Tell her to frigg off. Come on, let's get into our gear.' Bryan drained his coffee and left his cup and plate on the table for his mother or one of his sisters to clear away.

'Handsome dude,' he said twenty minutes later, admiring his reflection in the mirror. Kenny had changed in ten minutes, but he had taken his time. His light-grey Armani suit and red silk shirt looked the biz. It had cost an arm and a leg, but he was determined he wasn't getting married in a monkey suit and, besides, he'd get a lot of wear out of it, so he viewed it as an investment piece. His friends would be impressed and, if you couldn't impress people on your wedding day, when could you do it? he reasoned.

'Are you ready, darlin'? Let me see you.' His mother knocked and poked her head around the bedroom door. She was wearing a black feathery creation on her head and a red jacket over a black and red patterned skirt which had a swirling fishtail effect. It looked very dressy on her, he thought proudly as he struck a pose for her. 'I just need to gel my hair and I'm ready. What do you think?'

'I think you look like a Hollywood star. You look *magnificent*. Debbie's a very lucky girl. I hope she knows that.' His mother gazed at him approvingly.

'I think she does,' he assured her confidently as he rubbed some gel on his fingers and ran it through his black hair, which fell boyishly over his left eye. He looked a little like a young Bryan Ferry, he decided as he styled his long fringe. Arty. Intelligent. It was a look he cultivated. His image was important to him.

'Right, Ma, I'd better go, I'm running late. See you there, and make sure you and Vera bring my cases to the hotel,' he instructed as he hurried downstairs.

'Don't you worry about a thing, son, everything will be looked after. Now go and enjoy your wedding,' his mother said, trying not to cry as she followed him down the stairs. 'You won't forget us now, sure you won't? There'll always be a bed here and a dinner on the table if you ever need it,' she told him as he took the helmet Kenny handed him.

'I know that, Ma,' he said, bending down to kiss her cheek. She enveloped him in a bear hug. 'Mind my suit, Ma,' he said anxiously, not wanting it to get creased.

'Sorry, pet.' She pulled back and patted him down. 'Ah, son, I miss you something terrible,' she said sadly. 'The house isn't the same since you left. I can't believe how long it's been.'

'That's life, Ma,' he said cheerfully, used to her sentimental ways. 'I'd better go. If I'm late I might be coming back to live with you full time if Debbie gets mad at me,' he teased, placing the helmet carefully over his hair. 'Come on, you and Vera need 'to get going too.' He ushered her out the door, where his sister was sitting in her car. The neighbours were waiting for him to wish him well, and he enjoyed their banter and good wishes before finally managing to bundle his mother into the car, laughing as Vera roared off down the drive, putting Alonso to shame.

'Kenny, let's get the show on the road,' he ordered his best man, looking forward enormously to his big day now that it was finally here.

'Where are you? I'm waiting in the Shelbourne.' Aimee tried to hide her exasperation as the phone reception crackled.

'Sorry, Mom, there was a traffic tailback due to an accident in Blackrock so we decided to get out of the taxi and get the Dart. We'll get a taxi from Tara Street directly to the church, and we'll only be a few minutes,' Melissa explained airily as the train whooshed past the Merrion Gates.

'For goodness' sake, Melissa, you should have given your-selves plenty of time. I told your father we wouldn't be late. Get there as quick as you can.'

'Sure, Mom, no sweat. See you there. Byeee.' Melissa hung up and threw her eyes up to heaven. 'Mom's panicking. But she's meeting us at the church, so things are going to plan. If we leave it to the last minute to go in she won't be able to fly off the handle in public, so we should get away with it OK.'

'I think she'll still be pretty annoyed; your mum is much stricter than mine,' Sarah remarked as she took out her compact and checked her make-up for the umpteenth time.

'Tell me about it.' Melissa grimaced. She knew her mother would be far from pleased with her change of outfit, but she still felt it was worth the hassle. She looked cool in her new jeans and low-cut top. That dress her mother had bought her was totally *un*cool. Every guy at the wedding would have run a mile if she'd worn it. Sometimes her mom had no clue about fashion – she was so into her work suits and her cocktail dresses and clothes for *women* that she completely forgot what it was like to be a teenager. She wanted Melissa to wear the type of clothes *she* wore.

Aimee would never dream of wearing jeans to a formal occasion. She wouldn't allow Melissa to wear very short minis or belly tops. Sarah was right. Her mother *was* quite strict really, Melissa reflected. Just as well she had to travel a lot and Melissa could get away with wearing cool gear when she was going out. It was hard enough trying to be the same as the rest of the class without having to wear clothes that were totally awful. If she'd worn that dress she'd never have been able to show the photos around at school without some of the horrible, bitchy bullies sneering and jeering at her. Melissa sighed. Some of her classmates were tarty skangers. They picked on the quieter ones and made their lives a misery.

The best thing to do at school was to fit in as much as possible and keep your head down. If the bullies thought you were different they'd come after you and she so didn't need that. She'd seen the way Amanda O'Connell and her little gang undermined people's confidence with their whispering campaigns. She'd seen them turn best friends against each other, pretending one had said something about the other. Shelly Anderson had had to leave the school because of bullying, and she'd been so upset by the harassment she'd taken tablets and had to have her stomach pumped.

Melissa and Sarah had admitted to each other that they were ashamed they hadn't stood up for Shelly and tried to help, but they hadn't wanted to draw attention to themselves and have Amanda and co. turn on them. They swaggered around so full of confidence and seemed to be able to do whatever they liked. Their parents had loads of money, especially Amanda's. She'd caught her mother snorting coke at a party she was throwing and had boasted about it in class the next day. She thought it was a really savage thing to do. She planned to do it herself, and soon, she assured her classmates. She'd already smoked pot and had taken a few E tabs.

If Melissa caught her mother snorting coke she'd be totally upset, she pondered as the train slowed to a halt at Tara Street. A heaving mass of shoppers surged through the doors and, dizzy with excitement, Melissa and Sarah tottered along the platform in their high heels, eager for the opportunities that awaited them at Debbie's wedding.

'Aimee, good to see you. You're looking extremely well. Are you going somewhere nice, all dressed up?' A stocky, balding, fair-haired man held out his hand to Aimee as she strode through the elegant foyer of the newly refurbished Shelbourne.

'Roger, how are you? Great to see you.' She took his hand and gave him a firm handshake, very pleased that she was looking her best. Roger O'Leary was the multimillionaire property developer whose daughter's wedding her firm was catering for. He was their biggest private client and she kept that in mind always, although she disliked him and his attitude that his money could get him whatever he wanted.

'Have you time for a drink? Let me buy you one?' he offered, eyeing her appreciatively. 'Just flew back from Cork in the chopper, to have lunch with one of my local TDs. He got a junior ministry after the election. Good to keep in with these guys and keep them on their toes. Half the cabinet will be at the wedding,' he bragged, waving at a young female journalist heading into the Horseshoe Bar.

Oh for God's sake! Aimee thought in exasperation. He was such a vain, pompous ass. Roger was nothing to look at, but he was a well-known lady's man. His long-suffering wife had given up on him long ago, and the rumour was that she had sought solace in the arms of another long-suffering wife who moved in their elite circle. Roger's greatest attraction was his wallet, Aimee thought grimly as she managed to evade his grasp. He had precious little else going for him except his hard neck.

'I'd love a drink with you, Roger, but I'm on my way to my step-daughter's wedding and I'm running a little late,' she apologized, glad she had a legitimate excuse not to take him up on his offer.

'Oh! Where?' he eyed her cleavage and then slid his gaze lasciviously down her tanned legs. Her dress, a black washed-silk radzimir off-the-shoulder with a chunky gold zip on the back, came to her mid-thigh. It was sexy and elegant, from the latest collection of one of her favourite designers, Marc Jacobs. Roger certainly seemed to think so, as he couldn't take his eyes off her.

'University Church,' she said crisply. 'And I really must hurry.'

'I'm heading in that direction myself, I'll walk with you,' he suggested, and her heart sank. Just what she didn't need. A fat, dirty-minded little oompa-loompa trotting along beside her when she was in a hurry.

'A good opportunity to bring you up to speed on what's happening with your own wedding,' she said smoothly, hoping to deflect any enquiries as to where Debbie was having her reception. She took off at speed out the door and down the hotel steps, walking as swiftly as her Jimmy Choos would allow.

She was telling him about the bone china she'd sourced when she spotted a woman with two children beaming at her as they walked towards her. It was Gwen and her kids. Aimee's heart sank further. Gwen was looking less than smart in a pair of jeans and a black vest top and a creased linen jacket, her hair escaping from the clasp that was doing a poor job of holding it up. The kids were arguing, and she could hear her friend telling them to behave. How mortifying, she thought in dismay. She didn't want Roger to get the wrong impression about whom she mixed with. Gwen would understand if she didn't stop to talk, she thought uneasily as the gap between them closed.

'Hey, this is a surprise, great to see you, you look—' her friend started to say before Aimee cut in coolly.

'Gwen, how are you? Making the most of the good weather? I'll give you a call some time,' just slowing her pace to make her greeting. She barely had time to detect the startled look on her friend's face before she passed her without looking back. 'My dentist's secretary – I must make an appointment for a check-up,' she fibbed, and then launched into a description of the flowers and handmade Rathbornes candles she'd ordered for the tables.

She hoped Gwen wouldn't be mad with her, she was sure

she'd understand that she couldn't stop to chat when she was with a punter. Aimee brushed away her disquiet as she did what she did best – schmoozed her client.

Gwen Larkin turned to look back at Aimee and stood rooted to the spot, shocked. She knew *exactly* what had happened: Aimee had just blanked her. Mortified, hurt, angry, she stared after her erstwhile friend, noting how stylish and affluent she looked in her designer clothes.

OK, so she wasn't wearing any designer labels and she wasn't dressed to kill, Gwen thought angrily, but she wasn't exactly a bag lady. Aimee hadn't wanted to introduce her to whomever she was with, that was exceedingly obvious. A client, no doubt, but even so, Gwen couldn't believe that her so-called friend had actually spoken to her the way she had, as though she were a mere acquaintance not worthy of a minute of her time. She had even tried to avoid making eye contact. Gwen was so wounded she had to struggle not to cry.

All the times she'd sat listening to Aimee moaning on the phone or boasting about this swanky lunch she'd been to or about her latest acquisition, or a holiday that she'd booked or a business trip to Milan or Paris. In fact, the only time Aimee rang her was when she had something to brag about, Gwen realized as she resumed walking, remembering how she'd phoned a while back to tell her she was getting an expensive new kitchen installed.

She felt disgusted with herself for not seeing what was going on. She'd actually stood up for Aimee to their friends when they'd said she was getting above herself. She'd made excuses for her behaviour, saying that she was very busy. Gwen hadn't wanted to believe what the girls were saying, that Aimee wasn't interested in friendship with them any more, that she'd moved on and left them trailing in her wake.

They were right, Gwen acknowledged, remembering the unreturned phone calls, the unanswered texts and emails. Aimee wasn't interested in them and she was a fool for trying to hang on to what was obviously no longer a friendship. She was a fool and an idiot and a doormat. Tears prickled her eyes as she walked with her head down, afraid people would notice that she was crying. She felt gutted. The others wouldn't be surprised, but she'd still believed that she and Aimee had a friendship and that, when the other woman wasn't so busy, she would have had time to go for lunch, or a drink, or even a coffee to catch up with what was going on in their lives.

It certainly was now more than obvious that Aimee didn't give a hoot and that Gwen was the needy one in the relationship. If she was needy, then there was no equality in the friendship. Aimee had seen that and spun her up and down like a yo-yo when it suited her. And she had let her do it, Gwen thought with dismay. Why had she struggled so long to keep up the friendship? What was the point in trying to keep something going when it had clearly faded away? Their friendship, if it could ever really have been called a friendship, was long past its sell-by date. Aimee put no value on it and never had, Gwen realized, suddenly feeling extremely foolish over the years she'd spent investing so much into a non-relationship. She *had* good friends. She didn't need to be with someone who cared less about her.

No one had ever looked down their nose at Gwen before or made her feel small. And she had just allowed someone to do that to her. How *dare* Aimee Davenport belittle her? Who did she think she was, the jumped-up little snob? She had some nerve. Gwen came to a sudden halt. She wasn't going to let that bitch get away with that. She wasn't going to let that snooty wagon walk all over her and treat her like dirt. She wasn't going to be a doormat for Aimee Davenport to wipe her posh shoes on ever again. And she wasn't going to take any more of her rudeness, because it *was* rude and dismissive not returning calls, texts or emails. It *was* rude making arrangements and then breaking them because some 'business thing' had come up. It was downright bad-mannered ignorance, she fumed. Good manners cost nothing. Her dismissive little stunt five minutes ago was the last such stunt she'd *ever* pull on her, Gwen vowed, her jaw jutting aggressively.

'Kids, come back. I just need to have a word with someone, it won't take long, and I don't want *any* arguments,' she said in a tone that brooked no dissent. Her two girls looked at her and at each other, startled by her uncharacteristically determined tone, and followed meekly behind as Gwen turned on her heel and hurried back the way they'd come, her eyes pinned firmly on Aimee's black-clad form in the distance.

'You girls OK in the back?' Barry glanced in his rear-view mirror at his daughter and niece and smiled.

'Fine, thanks,' said Debbie happily.

'Nice car,' approved Jenna.

Barry turned to look at Connie, seated beside him. 'You OK, Connie?'

'Great,' she assured him, thinking that Barry and Aimee had a very nice lifestyle as she touched the soft cream leather of her extremely comfortable seat and felt the refreshing cool whisper of the air conditioning against her cheek. Would Barry and she have been so affluent if he'd stayed with her? Who knew? Her mobile rang and she saw with surprise that it was the agency. What did they want? she thought in dismay. They knew she'd taken a few days off for the wedding. 'Yes?' she said, un-impressed that they were ringing her on her day off.

'Don't worry, Connie.' She could sense the smile in the office manager's voice. 'I know it's Debbie's wedding day, but some-thing's come up that might be long-term and might suit you. It's part-time, job-sharing with another nurse, and it's near Greystones, so I thought of you.'

'Right, sounds interesting. Tell me more,' Connie said perkily, relieved that there was no emergency that would eat into her few days' leave.

'An elderly lady in her early seventies who lives on her own, has mild Parkinsons and oodles of money, so she employs round-the-clock nurses. You wouldn't have to do nights. Just mornings or afternoons. I know you wanted to cut down your hours and I thought this would be right up your alley. The nurse you'd be replacing is going on maternity leave and isn't sure if she's going to come back. Want to give it a try?'

'Sure,' Connie agreed. This sounded exactly what she was looking for.

'The only thing is, you've to go and meet Mrs Mansfield so she can interview you, and one of her little foibles is that she doesn't like nurses wearing trousers and likes them to wear a cap and look like "proper" nurses.'

'Hmm – is she difficult?'

'No, not at all. She just likes nurses to look like nurses, so she told us.'

'I could live with that if the money and conditions are right and if Mrs Mansfield and I click.'

'I couldn't imagine anyone not clicking with you, Connie,' her manager said warmly.

'Oh, trust me, there's one or two.' Connie laughed.

'I'll text you the address and phone number and you can make contact with her in the next few days. I hope it suits you.'

'Thanks a million for thinking of me, I'll let you know,' Connie assured her.

'Enjoy the wedding.'

'Will do, bye,' Connie said gaily, delighted with this turn of events. How timely for this to occur just when she'd been considering working fewer hours and taking time out to enjoy her life. Maybe it was a good omen.

'Good news?' Barry asked as they came off the slip road on to the N11.

She told them the gist of it.

'Just what you were looking for, Mum, go for it,' Debbie urged. 'You shouldn't have to keep working full-time. You can take the Dart into town and we can do lunch, or meet up for a drink after work and go shopping, and spend time together on your days off.'

'That would be nice, Debbs. I'd enjoy that.'

'Mam and I could meet up with you and we could have a girly night every so often,' Jenna interjected.

'Now *that* would be fun,' grinned Connie.

'You wouldn't have to commute,' Barry commented, as he put

his foot down and they cruised smoothly along the fast lane.

'I know, that would be a real bonus and it would save me a bob or two. It sounds like the perfect job for me.'

'Well, I hope it works out for you, you deserve it.' He gave her hand a quick squeeze and she squeezed back, with a burst of happiness, delighted that they were driving their daughter to her wedding and that all was well between them.

She glanced at her watch and wondered had Bryan left for the church yet. Debbie had assured him that she wouldn't be late. It wouldn't do him any harm to be left twiddling his thumbs for a while and wonder if she hadn't changed her mind, Connie thought caustically, and then gave herself a silent telling-off for being nasty about her prospective son-in-law.

The traffic was flowing freely and it seemed like no time before they were driving around Stephen's Green with Debbie on the phone to a friend of theirs who was holding a parking space for them outside the church, which faced directly on to the street.

'We're just coming now, Martin, we can see you. Has Bryan arrived? Tsk! Typical. OK, see you in a sec,' she said, sighing.

'Martin's pulling out so you can pull in, Dad – see the red car there? – and Bryan's not here yet,' Connie heard Debbie say as Barry indicated to pull into the space that had been held for him. A small group of their friends stood chatting at the church entrance, waving at her as they manoeuvred into the parking space.

Connie bit her lip. She could smack Bryan. How mean of him not to be at the church. Debbie had promised him she wouldn't be late and he didn't even have the decency to make sure he was here before her. A little flicker of doubt ignited. Just say he left her daughter standing at the altar! Debbie would be devastated but, if Connie were honest with herself, she'd be just as happy. Debbie would get over him and meet someone more worthy of her. She turned around and saw the tense anxiety in her daughter's face. *I'll kill the bastard*, she thought.

'Look, here he is, keep your head down so he doesn't see you. It's bad luck.' Jenna held her bouquet up over her cousin's face as a motorbike roared to a stop just ahead of them, Bryan astride it, behind Kenny, grinning from ear to ear as he took off his helmet and handed it to his best man.

His brother-in-law Kevin hurried over and took the keys from Kenny. 'I'll park the bike – you go on up to the altar,' he suggested helpfully.

'Is Ma here?' Bryan asked, in no hurry.

'Yes, she's in the church and Vera's parking. Get your ass up the aisle pronto, you're keeping your bride waiting,' Connie could hear him saying. At least he had some cop on, she thought crossly as Bryan disappeared into the church porch.

'No rush, Debbie,' she murmured. 'We better give them a minute or two to compose themselves. Let's turn our phones off before we go into the church,' she suggested.

'OK, Mum. At least he's here now,' Debbie said, relieved, as she and Jenna switched off their phones. Martin tapped on the window with a pay-and-display docket for Barry. 'Got one for you when I was getting my own,' he said kindly.

'Thanks very much indeed,' Barry said appreciatively, taking it from him and sticking it on the dash. 'How much do I owe you?'

'A pint some time,' Martin laughed, winking at Debbie before moving off to join the throng of guests and usher them into the church so he could start taking the wedding photos.

'That was helpful. Nice chap,' Barry remarked. 'Are you nervous?' he asked, turning around to look at his daughter.

'No, I feel quite calm now that we're here,' she told him. 'I think I'll get out and straighten myself up, now that Bryan's gone in.'

'Let me open the door for you,' her father offered. 'So this is it,' he smiled, as he helped her to step out on to the pavement.

'Yeah, Dad, I guess it is. Thanks for driving me in.'

'It was a pleasure. I loved being with you and your mother this morning, and thanks for including me.' He looked so earnest that her heart melted and she felt affection for him. It was such a good feeling after all the years of bitterness and anger she'd directed towards him. On impulse she took his hand. 'Do you want to walk up the aisle with Mum and me?'

'Debbie!' he exclaimed, his eyes lighting up. 'Are you sure?'

'Yes, Dad.' She leaned over and kissed him.

'Maybe you should ask your mother. I wouldn't want to muscle in. She's the one who reared you, after all. She's entitled to give you away,' he said hesitantly, not wanting to cause any resentful feelings in his ex-wife.

'She'd be happy about it, honestly. She asked me would I like you to give me away. She said she didn't mind,' Debbie told him. 'Open her door and I'll say it to her and you'll see,' she said confidently.

'I asked Dad if he'd like to walk up with us – is that OK with you, Mum?' she asked lightly, knowing what her mother's response would be.

'That's fine with me, darling. I'm delighted. I think it's the right way to do it.' Connie smiled broadly as she got out of the car. 'This is the way it should be.'

'Thanks, Connie, you're the best,' Barry said huskily, delighted. Connie felt emotion overwhelm her and her lip started to wobble.

'Stop, Mum, you promised,' Debbie warned, swallowing.

'Right, you guys, smarten up. Tears are not allowed.' Jenna came around the back of the car and wagged her finger at the three of them.

'Debbie, your bouquet's crooked. Connie, your label is sticking up, let me fix it. Barry, straighten your tie. You can cry all you like after Martin's taken your photo,' she instructed bossily, and they laughed as the moment was broken. Martin busied himself taking the photos, but he was experienced, and he snapped quickly, knowing that spontaneity went out the window if the photo wasn't taken in the first few moments. He took a dozen in various poses before telling them he was going up to the altar to position himself for Debbie's arrival.

They were just arranging themselves to make the walk up the aisle when Barry looked to his right and saw Aimee heading briskly in their direction.

'Oh! Here's Aimee, we should let her go in first, I suppose. She must be running late,' he murmured. 'Who's that behind her? I know that woman.' He squinted in the bright sunlight. 'Oh, it's her friend Gwen. Don't know what she's doing here.' Connie, Jenna and Debbie turned to look as Barry's glamorous wife hurried towards them.

'Come on, Aimee, don't keep us waiting,' Barry called, thinking his wife looked a total knockout in her wedding outfit. He hadn't seen that dress on her before. It was classy, he had to admit, feeling a moment of pride as she came up to him.

'Sorry I'm late. Are the girls here?' she asked breathlessly.

'I don't know. I didn't see them. They're probably inside. Didn't they come with you?' he asked, perplexed.

'No, I got delayed. They came in themselves. Debbie, you look lovely,' Aimee said distractedly, just as she heard her name being called.

'Aimee, a word, please.' A grim-faced woman marched up to them and her tone was decidedly unfriendly.

CHAPTER TWENTY-NINE

Aimee looked horrified as she saw Gwen bear down on her with a face on her that would curdle milk. *Oh no, this can't be happening!* She almost groaned in dismay. 'Gwen, I'm delaying the wedding, I need to be in the church. I can't stop to talk – I'll call you tomorrow,' she said lightly, her tone disguising her panic.

'This won't take long, believe me,' her friend said cuttingly. 'Just who do you think you are, pulling a stunt like that, you toffee-nosed bitch?'

Connie, Debbie and Jenna couldn't believe their ears as they turned, stunned at Gwen's aggressive remarks. They watched agog as Aimee blushed crimson, mortified beyond belief that her friend was creating such a scene in front of them.

'Now just a minute, Gwen,' exclaimed Barry. 'You can't talk to my wife like that.'

'Yes I can, Barry. I won't let *anyone* treat me like dirt.' Gwen turned on him in fury, her eyes like flints.

'I'm sure you're mistaken. There's no need to be like this, Gwen, calm down,' he insisted, perplexed.

'I don't know what you're talking about, Gwen.' Aimee tried to regain control of the situation. 'I know I didn't have time to stop and chat back there. I was with a client and I was running late for the wedding. Honestly, that's all there was to it,' she placated. 'I'll phone you tomorrow and we'll have a good natter.'

'You needn't bother your skinny ass, Aimee Davenport,' Gwen exploded, furious that Aimee was talking down to her as if she were a six-year-old. 'You didn't want to introduce me to that flashy guy you were with. You pretended you hardly knew me. You were ashamed to stop and talk to me because you think *you're* someone and the other girls and me are nobodies now that you've gone up in the world. We're OK to phone when you've something to boast about like your "fabulous new state-of-the-art kitchen" or your "to-die-for" landscaped deck.' She imitated Aimee's D4 accent. 'Well, let me tell you something, you sad wannabe, some day you're going to need your friends and you won't have any. And how *dare* you look down your bumpy nose at me—'

'For God's sake, Gwen,' Aimee interjected hotly. 'This isn't the time or the place. You're embarrassing me. Please, not now, let's have this discussion another time,' she urged, humiliated that this was taking place in public and in full view of Barry's first family. She couldn't believe that Gwen had flown off the handle like this. It was *totally* out of character. Her friend was usually so easygoing.

'I couldn't give a fiddler's if you're embarrassed. Have a taste of your own medicine and see what it's like.' Gwen was as white as a sheet, her voice shaking. 'I'm finished with you, Aimee, not that it will make any difference. You're probably just as glad. You don't know what it means to be, or to have, a friend, and I feel sorry for you because you're the loser, believe it or not. Go live your flashy life with your flashy friends, and I hope they'll be there for you when you need them.'

'Ladies – and I use the term lightly,' Connie's tone left them in no doubt as to her feelings, 'this is way out of line. Can you both go and sort out your differences elsewhere?'

Gwen turned to face them. 'Girls, I'm so sorry for this, but you can blame Aimee here, she's starting to believe her own publicity. I'm sorry for you, Barry, you're a nice guy – too nice for the likes of her – and I don't care if you're annoyed with me for saying it. Sometimes you have to have your say. I apologize for delaying your wedding.' She turned on her heel and strode off, leaving a stunned silent group standing on the pavement.

'I'm sorry about that, it was a misunderstanding,' Aimee murmured, crushed, her hand shaking as she placed it on her husband's arm for support. 'We should go in and not keep Debbie waiting any longer,' she suggested.

'Actually, I'm walking up the aisle with Debbie,' Barry said curtly, wondering what in the hell had happened. He couldn't believe the spat that had just occurred with his usually poised and sophisticated wife and one of her friends.

'Oh!'

Aimee's exclamation hung in the air like a firecracker about to fizz as she digested this piece of information, and another awkward silence descended on the group. 'I should go in then,' she said coldly, feeling like a pariah as a taxi pulled up alongside Barry's car and Melissa and Sarah tumbled out, all legs and high heels and giggles.

Barry and Aimee stared at them, horrified. 'I thought she was wearing a dress? For heaven's sake, Aimee, could you not have kept an eye on them! Look at the state of them, they look like they're going to a bloody disco,' Barry fumed as he caught a glimpse of his daughter's generous cleavage.

'Oh, don't annoy me. Why didn't *you* keep an eye on them? I was working to help pay for this damned wedding don't forget,' flamed Aimee, saying the first thing that came into her head.

'Excuse *me*, that's totally uncalled for!' exclaimed Connie, not sure if she'd heard right. 'We don't need your money, Aimee. Or your attitude.'

'For crying out loud, Aimee, what a thing to say. That's the height of bad manners.' Barry was aghast.

'Deal with it,' retorted his wife before stalking into the church alone, incandescent that he had chastised her in front of Connie and Debbie.

Connie stared at Barry, furious. 'She's stepping way over the line, Barry,' she said tightly. 'I don't want her money. How dare she say a thing like that? We need to talk about this later—'

'Take no notice, please, Connie,' pleaded Barry, thinking all his worst nightmares had come together. '*I'm* paying for the wedding out of *my* salary. I—'

'Hi, are we late? Sorryyeee,' Melissa trilled, having paid the taxi driver. She deliberately avoided her father's eye. 'Debbie, you look wicked.' She gazed at her half-sister in awe. 'I love the top – it's just like you described it.'

Her praise was genuine and Debbie, who had been standing, horrified at Aimee's parting remark, managed a smile.

'Thanks, Melissa. I'm glad you like it.' She gave her a little wink. 'Love your gear,' she whispered as she leaned over and gave her a kiss.

Melissa blushed with pleasure. She knew her parents were mad with her but Debbie understood, and it was her wedding, after all.

'Girls, go in and get a seat, we need to get moving,' Connie suggested, trying to act normal. She was hopping mad with Aimee. Just what did she think – that she and Debbie were paupers?

'Hiya, Connie,' Melissa smiled, oblivious. 'Sorry for being late.'

'No problem, I'll talk to you later.' Connie smiled at her, amused, in spite of herself, at the thirteen-year-old's attempts to walk in her high heels. 'Go on in,' she repeated, shooing them in with her hands.

Barry was furious, his face mottled red. He was hugely embarrassed. 'Sorry about all that,' he muttered. 'Take no notice.'

'It's a bit much, Dad,' Debbie protested heatedly. 'I don't want to feel under a compliment to Aimee.'

'You're not,' he insisted. 'I'm telling you now, I'm paying for your wedding out of my salary, it has nothing to do with Aimee.'

'Well, why did she say that?' Connie demanded, affronted. She wanted to smack the other woman hard across her Botoxed face. She'd succeeded in ruining her day with her smart, insulting comment.

'Look, I don't know why. I think the . . . the misunderstanding with Gwen upset her and she just lashed out at me . . .' He trailed off miserably. 'I suppose you don't want me to walk up with you now,' he said to Debbie. 'And I don't blame you. This has been a horrible start to your wedding and I'm terribly sorry.'

'It wasn't your fault,' Debbie said flatly, her high well and truly evaporated.

'Forget it, Barry, these things happen. It's over. Let's concentrate on the matter in hand.' Connie took control, feeling sorry for her ex. He looked deflated and dejected, and she knew he was humiliated by his wife's uncalled for and unnecessary barb. What a bitch she was for belittling him in front of them. 'You OK and ready to go, Debbs?'

'Yep,' Debbie said stoutly. She couldn't believe what had happened. That woman had really laid into Aimee and let her know what she thought of her. Good enough for the stuck-up bitch, she thought privately but she felt sorry for her dad, who looked very put out. It was mean of Aimee to make a show of him in public and she felt almost protective of him, which surprised her. She could be as much of a bitch as Aimee and tell Barry she'd walk up the aisle with her mother, but she didn't want to. She wanted him with her. How amazing was that, she thought, pleasantly surprised by her reaction. Maybe Aimee had done her a favour with her spiteful taunt. Right now she felt closer to Barry than she had ever felt in all her adult life. 'Come on, Dad. It will be practice for when you're walking Melissa up the aisle,' she said kindly, taking his arm.

'Sorry about all of this, Debbie. I don't know what it's all about,' he said sombrely.

'It doesn't matter. All that matters right now is that you and Mum are going to walk me up that aisle to Bryan, and then we're going to have the greatest hooly ever,' she encouraged, squeezing his arm.

He smiled down at her. 'You're right,' he said firmly. 'This is *your* day and nothing's going to spoil it.'

'Exactly,' agreed Connie, smiling at him as she took her daughter's other arm and, with Jenna bringing up the rear, the trio walked slowly up the aisle of University Church, accompanied by a haunting violin solo of the Wedding March, to where Bryan was waiting for his bride at the altar.

Aimee stood, back rigid, as the bride and her parents made their way up the aisle. Melissa and Sarah were at the other side of the church, well away from her wrath. Melissa might think she'd got away with this little exploit, but she was sadly mistaken. When she got her on her own she was going to go through her for a short cut and tear strips off her.

Aimee was so angry she was ready to detonate. How dare Barry make a show of her in front of those three by chastising her about Melissa's clothes? True she'd got her own back by sending her cheap shot across his bow – and it *was* a cheap shot, she conceded, but he damn well deserved it. It was bad enough that Gwen had decided to throw a hissy fit in front of an audience because her ego was bruised, without her own husband adding to her abject mortification.

How could he betray her? Because that's what it was, a betrayal. Turning on her in front of his first wife and daughter. Had he no loyalty? The trio glided past looking like they'd been friends for ever and playing the happy-family card to the hilt, even though Debbie and he had been at each other's throats for years. As soon as Barry came down to sit beside her she would tell him she was going home. She was damned if she was going to take part in the rest of this sickeningly hypocritical charade.

It could have been one of his proudest moments; instead, Barry felt inadequate and a wimp. He'd finally made his peace with his eldest daughter and had been looking forward to his role as father of the bride, and Aimee had pulled the rug from under him and disgraced him in front of his ex-wife and daughter. What a thing to say, he reflected, as he walked past his wife at the edge of a pew, her face averted from them, staring straight ahead like an ice queen.

What a disaster the day had turned into. They could have brushed the spat with Gwen under the carpet, he supposed.

And maybe he shouldn't have confronted his wife about Melissa's unsuitable clothing, causing her to fling her slighting remark. He knew where she was coming from when she'd said it, but it was the fact that she'd belittled him in front of Connie and Debbie that was so upsetting. Had she no loyalty towards him? he wondered as he noted his ex-mother-in-law giving him a polar stare.

Get over it, busybody, he thought dismissively, smiling sweetly at her.

You slept with Connie – where were your loyalties? a little voice said.

That was different, he argued with himself. *Aimee didn't know about it. You didn't humiliate her in front of her family.*

You betrayed her all the same. Barry gave his head a little shake. Such thoughts to be having while walking his daughter up the aisle. Connie was right: he should concentrate on the matter in hand, if he was to get through the rest of the day.

She wasn't going to let Aimee get away with it, Connie decided as she caught a glimpse of the other woman standing alone at the edge of a seat near the back of the church. Who did she think she was, causing scenes and bad feeling at Debbie's wedding? She had some nerve. Her hand tightened around Debbie's, and she felt her daughter squeeze back.

Everything had been going too well. It had been such a lovely, almost relaxed morning in the house with Barry. And then the good-humoured trip into town and the possibility of a new nursing post had been the icing on the cake. She'd felt the day was going swimmingly until Aimee and her enraged friend had had their unedifying brawl on the steps of the church.

And then, to cap that, the complete and utter arrogance and insensitivity of her to claim that she was working to pay for Debbie's wedding. That had been lower than low. She wouldn't cause a scene today but she would let Aimee Davenport know that her behaviour was totally unacceptable, Connie vowed, smiling at Karen, who was looking at the progression of the three of them with surprised delight.

*

Bryan felt a frisson of excitement as the notes of the Wedding March wafted through the church and the congregation turned to watch Debbie's advance up the aisle. He saw with a start that Barry was on one side, and Connie on the other. What an unbelievable sight, he thought, proud of his fiancée that she'd overcome her almost lifelong antipathy towards her father to allow him to walk her up the aisle.

Connie looked very well, he thought magnanimously, watching his mother-in-law-to-be smile to someone in the congregation. But it was Debbie who stole the scene. Glowing, radiant in her ivory wedding dress, joy shone from her eyes, and he began to realize that her happiness was now very much his responsibility. Up until now they had had escape routes if neither of them were happy with the way their relationship was going. It would be difficult to flee from now on, should things take a bad turn. *Don't think like that on your wedding day*, Bryan chastised himself, wishing that the thought hadn't pricked its way into his consciousness just as he was about to wed.

Bryan looked a dish in his new suit, Debbie thought and her face split into a massive grin as he turned to look at her. Suddenly all the hassles of the last few minutes and the stresses and strains of the past few months faded into oblivion as Barry placed her hand in her future husband's and his hand closed over hers in a comforting clasp.

'Look after her,' her father instructed the younger man, kissing her on the cheek.

'I will indeed,' Bryan said, still amazed that Barry had been included in the walk up the aisle. 'Well done. You look gorgeous,' he whispered as he drew Debbie to him and kissed her.

'Be happy, the both of you,' Connie said as she relinquished her daughter to his care.

'We will, Mum, and thanks for everything,' Debbie assured her. Connie kissed her tenderly and they shared a look of mutual love before she stepped away, tears brimming in her eyes.

'Don't cry, Connie,' Barry comforted as she made for her seat, overcome. She hoped with all her might that Bryan was the right husband for her daughter and, at that moment, she felt more alone than she'd ever felt in her life.

Barry's heart went out to his ex-wife. He could imagine how hard it was for her as he led her to her seat. A sudden dilemma presented itself. Should he leave her sitting alone and go down and join Aimee? He'd noted that she, too, was on her own, the girls having scarpered to the other side of the church, no doubt not wishing to have her fury inflicted on them.

The memory of her spiteful remark came back to him and, on the spur of the moment, he followed Connie into the seat and knelt down beside her. She looked startled. It had obviously just dawned on her that he'd chosen to kneel beside her for their daughter's wedding rather than leave her alone and go and sit with Aimee.

'Thanks,' she murmured gratefully. 'I appreciate it.'

'No problem. I wouldn't leave you on your own on a day like this,' he whispered back as the priest began the ceremony to join Debbie and Bryan in holy matrimony.

Aimee could not believe her eyes. Barry had joined Connie in the front seat and left her to sit alone in the church in a wedding she did not want to be at and had only attended because he wished it. He was deliberately snubbing her. Her own husband was making her feel as unworthy, and as second rate, as her father ever had.

Well, no one snubbed Aimee Davenport these days, and *no one* ever put her in second place.

As everyone knelt to hear the priest begin the ceremony, Aimee stood up and stalked out of the church. This was one wedding she had no intention of wasting her precious time on and, when Barry and Melissa got home, she would be making her feelings felt in a manner that would leave them in no doubt as to just how angry she was. If Barry Adams was so concerned about his first wife, maybe it was time he went back to her, Aimee thought viciously as the doors of the church closed behind her and she emerged blinking into the sunlight.

Where was her mother going? Melissa wondered as she heard the staccato tap-tap of her shoes fade away. Maybe she'd got a call from work; there was always some sort of emergency these days. She hadn't really wanted to come to the wedding anyway, so she wouldn't be too disappointed, Melissa thought, feeling quite relieved that something had called Aimee away. She wouldn't have to face her temper imminently, and with any luck she'd be asleep by the time they got home tonight because she was never able to keep her eyes open these nights, she worked so hard. Things were working out very well, Melissa smiled happily as she scanned the seats in front of her and saw a very satisfying amount of dishy fine things.

Stella's lips thinned as she noted her detested son-in-law kneel shoulder to shoulder with Connie, just ahead of her in the front seat. What a hypocrite he was. And she'd seen that wife of his with her dress halfway up her legs as though she was a teenager. As tarty as they come, no modesty and no class at all, thought Stella as the sound of high heels clattering along the aisle made her turn around. Where was that one going making such a racket? she wondered, seeing Aimee disappear through the doors. And why was Barry kneeling beside Connie as if they were still man and wife?

Her eyes lit up. Maybe the fool had come to his senses and realized who his *real* wife was. Maybe this wedding was a blessing in disguise and at long last things could be the way they were always meant to be.

'I do,' said Debbie, and her heart was overflowing with happiness as Bryan slid the ring on her finger, where it rested as though it had been there for ever.

'I do,' said Bryan a few moments later and felt the slightest bit trapped as his wife slid the round gold band along his finger.

'Let's hope they live happy ever after,' Barry said as he clasped Connie's hand in his and they watched their daughter kiss her new husband with enthusiasm.

'Is there such a thing?' Connie arched an eyebrow at him.

'Yes, I think there is. And I think there's such a thing as a second chance,' he said slowly, as family and friends burst into a round of applause around them.

CHAPTER THIRTY

Judith heaved a sigh of relief as she came off the M50 at the Blanchardstown roundabout and took the N3 to Cavan. The traffic had crawled along due to a traffic accident and she was running late. It was good to be able to put her foot down on the accelerator and finally feel the miles fly by. A dull headache throbbed at her temples and her neck and shoulders felt stiff and tense. She drove with grim determination, cursing as she got slowed down again in Dunboyne with more heavy traffic dawdling at a snail's pace. By the time she got to the hotel, she'd be so tense all the massaging in the world wouldn't be able to help her, she thought irritably as she eventually got through the village and the traffic opened out again.

The day she'd been so looking forward to had been thoroughly spoilt, and all because she'd let her temper get the better of her. She'd completely lost it with her mother – and over something relatively trivial, which shouldn't have led to such a blow-up. Judith bit her lip as she overtook a black Audi at speed. She'd lost control, no doubt about it, and although it felt good at the time, she was beginning to feel very ashamed.

She shouldn't have said those things to Lily, even though, at one level, they were true. That outburst had been stored up inside for years. Silently bubbling and simmering, never far from the surface and, today, the flash point had been reached. Her mother's long-suffering-martyr act had finally been too much to endure and it didn't help that Judith had been teetering on the brink of erupting all week, thanks to a combination of irritation with the Debbie Adams carry-on and crucifying PMT.

Why couldn't her sister have made an effort for once in her life? she thought in frustration. If Cecily had only turned up on time none of this would have happened. Judith would have been halfway to the hotel now, and the anticipation of a day of pampering and a night of leisurely eating, drinking and chatting with her friend would have lifted her spirits the further she got away from Dublin. The interlude would have refreshed her, kept her going for another while. But that chance of rest and relaxation had evaporated. Now all she'd be thinking about was the look of shock and dismay on her mother's face when Judith had lost her head and ranted and raved at her like a madwoman.

'Oh Ma, I'm sorry, I shouldn't have said what I said,' she muttered as tears welled up in her eyes and guilt smote her. She blinked hard, the misting tears blurring her vision. Great sobs shook her body as pent-up grief, frustration and misery erupted out of her and she cried with abandon, not caring who saw her.

She was driving around a narrow bend when she heard a sharp bang and the steering wheel juddered in her hand, pulling to the left as a blow-out in a rear tyre caused the car to shake violently. She saw she was heading for a tree in the ditch and for a split second she knew she could wrench the wheel to the right and avoid it.

What's the point? I'd be better off dead, she thought in utter desolation as the car hit the solid, unyielding trunk.

'Dad,' Judith called out as the car crumpled around her and darkness enveloped her.

'I'm so sorry I'm late, Ma, Gerard got delayed at the tennis club. They didn't get a court when they'd booked one, so he wasn't home in time to collect Billy from Scouts and I had to do it. Are you ready to go?' Cecily asked breathlessly when Lily opened the door to her, two hours later than the agreed pick-up time. 'If we can leave now it would be good. I'm in a bit of a rush, I've to pick up a pair of trousers I left into the dressmaker to be altered. I'm going to a garden party tomorrow afternoon after I've dropped you home.'

Her younger daughter stood jangling her keys impatiently. Her hair was styled and, from the heavy sweet scent wafting in her direction, Lily surmised that she'd just come from the hairdresser's and *that* was the reason she was late, no matter what nonsense she was spouting. Cecily was always the same when she called, forever in a hurry; anxious to spend as little time as possible in the house she grew up in.

'I'm not going with you. If you can't have the good manners to come and collect me when you say you will, and then you can't wait to drop me home so you can go to a garden party, why on earth would I want to?' Lily snapped.

Cecily's head jerked up. 'What?' she said, not sure if she was hearing right.

'I don't want to come with you, miss. I'm fed up being made to feel I'm a nuisance by my family. None of you have any feelings for me. Judith's gone off after giving me a right mouthful of cheek because you were late. Could you not have been in time for once in your life? Could you not put yourself out? It wouldn't have killed you to be here when you said you would. Judith doesn't ask you to do much. She was meeting her friend for a day out. It wasn't much for her to ask, you selfish little biddy.' Lily's hurt and anger had a target and she wasn't going to hold back.

'Excuse me, Mother, that's not fair,' exclaimed her younger daughter. 'I've a family, kids, routines, I can't just drop everything when Judith expects me to.'

'You never drop *anything*, *that's* the problem. You've left it all to Judith to deal with. No wonder she gets irritable, I feel sorry for her because you and that other lazy lump never give her a thought . . . or me, for that matter.' Lily's eyes glittered, and her cheeks were stained a dull purple. She was almost wringing her hands with agitation.

'You're in a fine humour, Mother, and you're being *totally* unreasonable,' Cecily retorted, stunned at this unexpected and, in her view, undeserved onslaught.

'You might think that, and why wouldn't you? You always were a selfish little madam and I let you get away with it. You scuttled off as far as you could when your father died and I had my nervous breakdown. You left it all to Judith to deal with and now she can't take it any more. She went out of here this morning having said terrible things to me and all because you couldn't make it your business to be here on time. So you can go back the way you came on your own because I'm staying here and sleeping in my own bed and I'm not going to put you or Gerard out ever again. He can play tennis until the cows come home, and you can go to garden parties. I don't give a fig about the pair of you,' Lily spat, enjoying the feeling of not having to restrain herself and being able to say *exactly* what she felt like saying without worrying about the consequences. She was never ever going to be under a compliment to any of them again. It felt extremely liberating to be saying these things. What a fool she was not to have said them years ago. She could have saved herself untold misery, Lily thought with a flash of regret.

'Mother, that's horrible,' protested her daughter. 'We do worry about you. It's not a question of putting us out. You're being very mean.'

'Am I? Well, it's time for me to stand up for myself and not be pushed around by you lot any more. I've had enough of being a burden. I'm thinking of selling the house and going into a nursing home,' she fibbed, enjoying the look of absolute horror that crossed her daughter's sharp little face.

'You can't do *that*.'

'Why not?' demanded Lily, almost relishing her daughter's consternation.

'Well ... because ... because you don't need to go into a nursing home.'

'I'll be the judge of that, miss,' declared her mother.

'Have you discussed this with Tom?' Cecily demanded, shaken by what she was hearing.

'What would I be discussing my business with him for?' Lily

scoffed. 'He had the cheek to ask me had I made my will when I went into hospital. He didn't care about my health, he was only worried about getting his whack.' Her nostrils flared in disgust.

'I'm sure he wasn't. I'm sure he was only making sure that your business was in order. It's very *important* to have a will made when you have property,' Cecily informed her patronizingly. Lily wanted to smack her. Did she think she was a fool?

'Well, I won't have property if I sell it, will I?' she said slyly. 'So I'll just have to make another one and you can all go and take a running jump. I'm going to leave whatever's left to charity,' she retorted, knowing that Cecily would go running to Tom and they'd have a pow-wow and wonder how they were going to handle this crisis.

Lily had no intention of reneging on her promise to Judith to leave her the house, but it was good to keep the other pair on their toes, she thought with a rare feeling of satisfaction. Not having to keep all her emotions suppressed for fear of them abandoning her was most refreshing. She felt in control of the situation. That was a first. Judith was going to leave her, she was sure, and the others didn't want her, so the thing she'd feared most had come to pass but, amazingly, now that she had to face it, it wasn't as frightening as she'd thought. The fear of it had been worse than the actuality of it, Lily realized, and her heart soared on eagle's wings. *I'm free,* she thought. *I can do what I like and I'm not afraid ... well, only a little bit,* she admitted. She couldn't wait for Cecily to leave so she could practise 'freedom'.

Her daughter pursed her lips in annoyance, not at all happy with the way the conversation was going. 'Mother, are you coming with me or not? I don't want to be standing here arguing,' she snapped irritably, opening the front door wider. A squad car pulled up behind her SUV. 'Who's that for, I wonder?' Lily frowned, peering out through the front door to watch the officers get out of the car. A house down the road was let. Maybe the tenants were drug suppliers. An apartment not too far away had been the scene of an arrest recently. It had been shown on the evening news. It was a posh apartment in lovely grounds, not one of those eggboxes that were springing up all over the place. You just never knew what was going on in your neighbourhood. Lily tutted as the guards put on their caps and walked towards them.

'They're coming in here,' she gasped, her hand going to her throat. The police coming to your door could only mean bad news.

'Why do you think they're calling here?' Cecily asked. 'Hello, officer, is there a problem?' She greeted the young policewoman who stood on the step. Lily couldn't speak. Something awful had happened, she just knew it.

'Is this the home of Judith Baxter?' the policewoman asked politely.

'Yes, yes, what's wrong? What's wrong with Judith? I'm her mother,' Lily demanded, finding her voice.

'Perhaps we should go inside where you could sit down,' the policewoman suggested kindly. Lily felt a bleak feeling of dread rise up from the pit of her stomach and permeate every fibre of her being, smothering her with fear.

'Tell me what's wrong with Judith? She's had an accident, hasn't she? That's why you're here, isn't it?' She tried to keep the hysteria out of her voice.

'I'm afraid she has, Mrs Baxter,' Lily heard the policewoman say, and then the hall faded in and out, wavering before her eyes, before she fainted away into oblivion.

'I was glad Barry sat with you in the church; it was sort of . . . fitting. Where's Aimee, did she not come?' Karen murmured as she and Connie stood outside the church while the photographer tried to gather everyone for the group photo. Connie could see Barry on his mobile phone, and he wasn't looking too happy.

'I've loads to tell you – there was a bit of a barney outside the church with a friend of hers and then she and Barry had a tiff, and I think she must have gone home because she's not here now. We'll try and get a few minutes together at the hotel,' she whispered as Barry made his way in their direction, putting his phone back into his pocket.

'Aw, hell, I'll never last,' Karen moaned. 'I'm dying to hear all about it. Look at the get-up of Melissa. That top's very low and those jeans just about fit her. I'm surprised Aimee let her come in jeans. She usually has the poor kid in designer stuff at the few family dos we've had.'

'Sshhh, that's part of what the tiff was about.' Connie shushed her sister-in-law as her ex-husband joined them, looking grim-faced. 'Hi, Barry, everything OK? Is Aimee still here? I don't see her around,' she asked delicately.

'No, she's gone home in a snit. Sorry about that,' he apologized grumpily. 'I suppose Connie told you about the carry-on?' He turned to his sister.

'What?' Karen feigned complete innocence, widening her eyes at him.

'It's nothing – forget it, Barry. Look, we should get this group photo done so the guests can carry on to the hotel for the champagne reception while Debbie and Bryan are having their photos taken in the Green.' Connie changed the subject, feeling a little sorry for Barry. All the enjoyment had gone out of the day for him and that was a pity. Aimee had a lot to answer for, she thought crossly. A daughter's wedding day was very special for any parent. It was no day to go around causing scenes and upsetting people. Had it been Melissa's wedding, how would she have felt if Connie had carried on in a similar way? She'd behaved disgracefully as well as disrespecting both Connie's and Debbie's feelings. It just wasn't on, she decided grimly and she was going to let Madam Davenport know that. Connie intended making her feelings known before this day was out.

Debbie had never felt so loved in her entire life, and it was wonderful. *I'm married. I'm Mrs Kinsella, Bryan's my husband and I'm his wife*, she thought joyfully as she emerged from yet another hug, grinning from ear to ear. She caught sight of her new husband surrounded by his mother and sisters, and their eyes met and he winked at her and she felt a glow of pure happiness.

What a wonderful day she was having – apart from the

incident with Aimee, but she certainly wasn't going to let that interfere with her pleasure. When she'd turned to kiss her mother in the ceremony at the sign of peace and seen Barry sitting beside her in the front row she'd been delighted for Connie. Delighted that she wasn't sitting on her own, delighted that, for once, Barry had put Connie first over Aimee. She wondered briefly how the other woman felt about Barry staying up the front with his first wife. Sore, Debbie hoped, with a little smile, remembering Aimee's condescension towards her and her mother over the years. But then she forgot all about her as one of the girls from the office came over and enveloped her in an affectionate embrace. From the corner of her eye she could see Melissa and Sarah smiling at her. Melissa had obviously not worn what Aimee had expected her to wear and Debbie applauded her little act of defiance. The more she got to know the younger girl, the more she liked her. 'Excuse me a sec,' she murmured to her friend. 'I just need to get a photo with my sister.'

'Melissa,' she called. 'Come on, let's get a photo taken together.'

'Cool,' agreed the teenager, a little abashed as she teetered over in her heels to stand beside her.

'Hope you enjoy the rest of the day now,' Debbie said as they slipped their arms around each other's waists.

'You bet. Thanks for asking us, Debbie,' Melissa said with heartfelt gratitude.

'Look, I know I wasn't very friendly before this, I had a few issues to deal with and I'm sorry. They had nothing to do with you. I really want us to be friends as well as sisters. Deal?' She looked into her sister's bright blue eyes, which were overly and inexpertly made up. Debbie smiled, thinking that, in spite of all the make-up and the sophisticated clothes, Melissa couldn't hide the fact that she wasn't much more than a kid.

'Legend. I'd really like that too, thanks, Debbie,' Melissa said earnestly as the photographer, with an eye for a good photo, snapped away, catching the moment when they smiled at each other in an unposed photo that each of them would cherish in years to come.

Aimee flung her clutch bag on the sofa, kicked off her sky-scraper heels and poured herself a glass of chilled orange juice before sinking down on the sofa. What a bummer of a day. She lay back against the cushions and sighed deeply. It was stressful enough having a five-tier christening cake being ruined two hours before the event and having to find a replacement, but then having Gwen make a show of her outside the church in front of the Adams women was too much. She supposed she should at least be thankful that Gwen hadn't staged her performance in front of Roger O'Leary. She'd never have lived that down. Professional suicide. She nearly broke out in a cold sweat thinking about it.

Aimee scowled. Gwen had caused her a lot of grief with her utterly childish behaviour. What she'd done was unforgivable. She'd been like a kid throwing a tantrum. You *will* notice me! Aimee sat up straight. She needed to vent. Why the hell should Gwen get away with making her look like a complete tosser? Because that was what she'd done. How dare she? Aimee found her BlackBerry and dialled Gwen's number.

'Yes, Aimee?' Gwen answered frostily.

Don't give me that attitude, thought Aimee, narkily launching into an offensive. 'Gwen, where do you get off making me look like a—'

'Fuck off, Aimee, and don't ring me *ever* again,' came the cutting retort before the other woman hung up, leaving Aimee staring at the phone, stunned. Quiet, malleable, impressionable Gwen had just cursed at her before hanging up on her. Well, that was that then! She would never have anything to do with her again. Gwen would have a snowball's chance in hell of getting back in her good books, Aimee fumed.

She stood up and went to her bedroom, anxious to change out of her dress. Now that she didn't have to attend Debbie's reception she had some unexpected time to herself. She'd go down to the gym and have a good work-out to try and get her head straight again. Try and feel some sense of control. She had some prepared meals from Donnybrook Fair in the fridge if she was hungry later, but right now she had no appetite for food she was so pissed off. Her mobile rang and she saw that it was Barry.

'Where are you?' he said tersely.

'Home.' Her response was equally terse.

'Well, thanks for all your help in making the day run smoothly. Thanks for all the support,' he said sarcastically.

'Any time,' she said abruptly before hanging up on him. She had no intention of defending her behaviour to her husband. There was no denying she *had* behaved badly, and she certainly wasn't proud of herself. Barry had been wounded to the core by her comment about her working to pay for the wedding. She should never have said it. She'd lost her cool and it had come out in the heat of the moment as her resentment overflowed. But she had said it, and it couldn't be taken back, so her best course of action was to weather the storm as quickly as she could.

He had every right to be annoyed with her, she thought glumly as she sat on the edge of the bed. But she had just as much right to be annoyed with him: he'd left her sitting on her own in the church. He'd made a choice between her and Connie in a very *public* arena and Connie had won. What did that say about the current state of their marriage and his loyalty to her?

She sighed. Was she completely overreacting? This was all so unlike her, Aimee thought despondently, flicking through the latest copy of *Vanity Fair*, which she'd picked up off the chaise longue at the end of the bed. It was pleasant just to sit and do nothing; maybe she wouldn't bother going to the gym, maybe she'd just sit out on the deck, the 'to-die-for' landscaped deck. She gave a wry smile, remembering Gwen's mocking imitation of her. It was only jealousy on her ex-friend's part, she comforted herself.

She slipped out of her dress, wrapped a sarong around her and opened the French doors. It was hot outside and the faint breeze that drifted in off the sea was a welcome relief. She was about to lie down on one of the loungers when she saw the alcopop bottles lying on the deck.

I'll kill the pair of them, she thought in utter dismay, her heart sinking like lead. Her first instinct was to phone Barry and tell him that their daughter and her friend had been drinking secretly but, with all that had gone on earlier, she knew that would be the last straw for him. Another scene at Debbie's wedding would be one scene too many.

She was furious with Melissa. Her daughter had really taken advantage today. Wearing those jeans and that top to the wedding had shown a total disregard for both her parents. And now this. Drinking behind their backs was a step too far. A day of reckoning was coming with Melissa, one that she wouldn't forget in a hurry, Aimee vowed as she picked up the bottles and brought them into the kitchen to have on display as evidence for when her daughter came home.

'I know Dad wouldn't mind us having a glass – remember, he allowed us to have one the day Debbie called,' Melissa said confidently as she and Sarah edged towards the tall, slender champagne flutes full of bubbly gold liquid that was practically begging to be drunk. 'And, anyway, I have to celebrate something really important.'

'What's that?' Sarah asked.

'Debbie and me – my sister and me. She wants us to be friends as well as sisters,' Melissa said giddily, delighted with her earlier encounter with Debbie. '*That's* real important. That's something to celebrate with champagne. It's just brilliant, you know. I used to think she was a real snobby bitch, and she probably thought I was the same, and she's not like that at all. She apologized to me. Can you believe that?'

'Wow, that's pretty impressive.'

'You bet it is – my dad's going to be over the moon about it. It's what he's always wanted. He'd *want* us to have a glass of champers if he was here.'

'You're absolutely right,' her friend agreed, eyeing the very handsome young foreign waiter, who winked at her. She blushed and went beetroot as he offered her a glass. 'And one for my friend, please,' she said, trying to appear sophisticated.

'Of course,' he agreed, winking again, handing her a glass for Melissa. Sarah had a brainwave as they moved away.

'Do you think he'd have his photo taken with us? We could ask him to take his tie off, and then he'd look like a guest,' she suggested to Melissa, who had taken too hearty a gulp of her bubbly and was trying not to choke.

'Wicked idea. No one would know he was a waiter. Sarah, you're a genius. You ask him.'

'No, you ask.'

'It was your idea.'

'It's your sister's wedding.'

'Oh! Oh, OK then,' Melissa agreed. She cleared her throat and moved back to the table where the waiter was loading champagne flutes on a tray to circulate among the guests.

'Um . . . we were just wondering if we could have a photo with you,' she ventured.

'A photo, here?' He stared at her in surprise.

'If you wouldn't mind. We're doing a photo journal, we want to have a record of every . . . er . . . phase of the wedding,' she fibbed. That sounded plausible, she thought, pleased with the word 'phase'. Sarah gave a thumbs-up behind his back.

'Why not?' agreed the hunk, eyes twinkling.

'Um . . . er . . . could you take your tie off?' she requested, feeling a blush begin.

'Oh! Why no tie?' He had the sexiest foreign accent; she wouldn't mind getting to know him outside of work, Melissa thought wistfully, longing to have a boyfriend. A boyfriend would make her life almost perfect.

'Less formal.' She smiled.

'I understand,' he said gravely, comprehension beginning to dawn. 'But I can't delay too long,' he explained. 'I'm working, and my boss wouldn't be too happy seeing me getting a photo taken with a beautiful girl.'

'Right. It won't take a minute. You can tell him it's for a photo journal if there's any problem,' Melissa said hastily, hardly able to believe her ears that he'd called her 'beautiful'. If she'd been wearing that awful dress he wouldn't have said that. Changing her outfit was well worth any hassle she was going to get from her parents if this was the outcome. 'Here's the camera, Sarah. Will you take the first one and then I'll take one?'

'Sure.' Sarah put her glass down and positioned the viewfinder.

'Smile,' she instructed as Melissa edged closer to the hunk. He took off his tie and slipped an arm around her. 'Hold your champagne glass,' Sarah advised. 'And you hold one too,' she suggested to the waiter.

'I can't drink on the job,' he demurred.

'Just for a second – quick,' Melissa urged, grabbing Sarah's glass and handing it to him, thinking how clever her friend was. Holding champagne glasses would make them look *soooo* sophisticated. She couldn't wait to show the photos around the class when they went back to school in the autumn.

Sarah took two photos for good measure. And then she changed places with Melissa to have hers taken. 'Thanks so much, er . . .'

'Micah. And you're welcome. Enjoy the wedding.' He laughed, putting his tie back on. 'I should get back to work – have another glass of champagne.'

'Don't mind if we do,' giggled Melissa, taking a glass. This wedding was turning out so much better than she'd initially expected. And to think she'd once dreaded it. She studied a crowd of Debbie and Bryan's glamorous friends quaffing champagne and nibbling canapés.

'Let's go and do a couple of lines,' she heard one blonde lollipop head say to her friend, who was wearing a black fedora trimmed with a magenta ribbon that matched exactly the silk blouse she wore with black palazzo pants. The blouse, slashed to the waist, revealed a generous amount of tanned flesh.

Imagine having the confidence to wear an outfit like that, Melissa marvelled as the two young women strolled off nonchalantly to do drugs.

'Are you drinking alcohol, Melissa?' She turned to find her grandmother looking at her in disapproval.

Oh butt out, Gran, she thought irritably, hoping no one had heard.

'Dad allows me to have champagne on special occasions.' She kissed her grandmother's soft cheek. 'You look lovely, Gran,' she complimented, hoping to deflect any more discussion of what she was drinking.

'And where *is* my son?' Her grandmother raised her eyebrows at this information.

'Getting his photo taken with Debbie and Bryan.'

'And where's your mother? Did she come?'

'Well, she was in the church earlier, but I don't see her now. I'm not sure if she's coming to the reception. She might have to go back to work, there was a crisis earlier at some job she was working on,' Melissa explained. She'd had a quick look around for Aimee when the photos were being taken outside the church and not seen her, but she wasn't too anxious to go looking. Lots of the guests had strolled off to the hotel once the group photo was taken. She and Sarah had been among the first to go, in an effort to avoid her parents. She knew a mega ticking-off was in store. And she didn't want that happening at this very cool occasion.

'I see. Well, don't drink any more of that on an empty stomach,' her grandmother warned. 'You might get me a cup of tea like a good girl. I'll be sitting on a sofa in the foyer.'

'OK, Gran,' she agreed, trying to hide her irritation. Even though she loved her Granny Adams she was damned if she was going to dance attendance on her for the rest of the evening. She procured the desired cup of tea and brought it out to her grandmother, who was chatting to Karen. She edged away discreetly. 'Thank God for free seating,' she whispered to Sarah as they skirted a group of Bryan's workmates and their girlfriends.

'Yeah, let's decide who we're going to honour with our presence,' Sarah grinned, taking another two glasses from *their* special waiter and enjoying herself massively.

Connie took a deep breath. She wanted this over and done with so she could enjoy the rest of the day. She was standing watching Martin photograph Debbie and Bryan in Stephen's Green.

She and Barry had just had their photos taken with the bridal pair, and Barry had gone back over to the church to get the car to drive them all to the hotel. For the first time that day she was on her own. She scrolled down her contacts list, selected the name she wanted and pressed the dial button. The number rang for a few moments and then a woman's voice answered. Cool, clipped. Not very friendly.

'Aimee, it's Connie,' she announced crisply. She heard a sharp intake of breath.

'Yes, Connie,' the other woman said snootily. She didn't even sound abashed, Connie thought crossly. She was damned if she was going to go easy on her now, with *that* attitude.

'This won't take long, Aimee. I thought I'd be able to say it face to face but you obviously felt you couldn't stay—'

'Under the circumstances I thought it would be best if I didn't,' Aimee interrupted coldly, not allowing her to finish.

'Understandable,' agreed Connie, equally frosty. 'Brawling in public is rather draining, I'm sure. However, that's not why I phoned you. Strictly between us, Aimee, I just want you to be very clear about one thing: Debbie and I don't want one red cent of your money. We never have and we never will. And I object strongly to your totally unnecessary and uncalled for remark to Barry when you were going into the church. Whatever Barry chooses to contribute to the wedding is *entirely* up to him. We don't need it, but he's Debbie's father and he wants to. That's *his* business. And I respect his wishes. But if you ever make a statement again, like you did today, I won't be as restrained as your friend was earlier, Aimee,' Connie said icily.

'Point taken,' Aimee clipped.

'*Excellent*. Let's hope we never have to have a conversation like this again. Bye,' Connie said briskly and hung up, not giving Aimee a chance to answer.

'Well done,' she muttered, relieved, proud of herself that she'd made her feelings known and glad that that ordeal was over. Aimee Davenport would think twice about trying to make her and Debbie feel under a compliment. And there'd be no more smart cracks at any function the two families might ever have to attend in the future. Borders had been set. Sometimes a woman had to draw her boundaries and stand up for herself. She'd handled it well, she decided, feeling satisfyingly empowered as she saw Barry's car pull up on the other side of the railings.

It hadn't surprised her that the other woman had gone home. Only someone with a very hard neck would have stayed and brazened it out. Aimee probably wasn't too impressed either that Barry had stayed up the front of the church with her. He'd been between a rock and a hard place there, she conceded, feeling sorry for the difficult position her ex-husband was in. Nevertheless, it was Debbie's wedding day and she'd welcomed his place at her side. It had made the ceremony less lonely for her. And it wasn't as if she'd been making demands on Barry for the duration of his second relationship. She'd scrupulously avoided doing that and Aimee, although she might not think it, was very lucky in that regard. Not having Barry at her side for a lousy couple of hours for one day in her life wasn't going to kill her.

She'd think twice about looking down her superior nose at her again, Connie thought with satisfaction. That superiority had been hard to stomach over the years, but today she'd certainly had the last word and made her feelings crystal-clear. Aimee had been noticeably taken aback, especially when Connie had implied that she'd resort to violence in the event of a repeat performance. Connie grinned. It might take some of the starch out of Aimee's sails if she got a good puck in her posh mush. Another episode like the one earlier and that was *exactly* what she would get.

'Bitch, bitch, *bitch!*' seethed Aimee. The incorrigible cheek of Connie Adams. The absolute, incredible nerve of her to ring their home phone and speak to her the way she just had. Aimee wasn't too sure if she'd dreamt the conversation. No one had ever told her off like that before. In fact, no one had ever spoken to her like that in her entire life. She'd been hauled over the coals twice in the one day, and Connie's had been the far more effective and humiliating rebuke, she acknowledged wrathfully.

From this day forward there would be no quarter given between her and Barry's ex. Up until now, Aimee had tolerated Connie. She'd always felt a cut above her husband's middle-aged, frumpy first wife. Today she'd seen her in a far different light. Connie had looked decidedly unfrumpy in her wedding outfit, in fact she'd looked smart and chic. *And* she'd been very much in control of the whole situation that had developed, leaving Aimee feeling decidedly wrong-footed, a feeling that was rare for her these days.

From the start of this damn wedding, Aimee had felt as though the sands were constantly shifting under her feet. She supposed it was the only time in their association that she'd had a long-drawn-out awareness of the 'first family'. She'd been lulled into a false sense of security. Bad mistake.

She'd underestimated Connie, but not any more. The other woman had become a formidable enemy. This day a line was drawn and Connie Adams would never step over it again.

CHAPTER THIRTY-ONE

You can't fall apart, Judith needs you, Lily said silently, willing herself not to have hysterics as she sat by her daughter's hospital bed, holding her hand. Cecily was out in the corridor on her mobile phone to Tom, who was coming in to do the night shift.

Judith looked so pale and vulnerable as she lay unconscious surrounded by machines and monitors and tubes, her face bruised, her arm in plaster. She was in a coma.

Lily had known the minute she'd seen the guards coming to the door it was something bad about Judith. True to form, she'd gone into a swoon. Her heart had been pounding so fast and her knees had just turned to jelly. She was angry at her weakness, angry that she'd felt faint again a few hours ago walking down the long hospital corridor to get to her daughter's bedside. This was no time to be weak. If she gave into herself this time there'd be no going back. She remembered how she'd taken to the bed for months after Ted had died. But then she'd had Judith to take care of her. Now it was her turn to take care of Judith.

Cecily had told her that she'd have to come and stay with her while Judith was in hospital because she wouldn't be able to stay in Drumcondra. She wasn't having that, Lily decided. She'd been prepared to stay on her own for the night that Judith was away and she was still going to try it. She wanted to stay in her own home. She always felt like an awkward guest in Cecily's. At least she could do as she pleased at home. There was a bus to the hospital that she could get on the main road; she could go to see Judith without depending on anyone else for a lift. When her daughter was fit and well again they could talk about her future and what she wanted to do and where she wanted to live. Lily shook her head in disbelief. Who would have thought when she woke up this beautiful, sunny morning that the day would turn out to be so horrendous?

She stroked her daughter's hand, wishing that there was some response from her. If Judith died, what would she do without her? How could she live with any peace of mind knowing that they'd parted on bad terms? Tears prickled her eyelids and she brushed them away. Judith had enough to deal with without her bawling. The nurses had told her to talk to her. Lily cleared her throat. What would she say? She looked at her daughter lying waxen against the pillows, her forehead drawn in a little frown as if she were going through some intensely private struggle that demanded all her concentration. She looked like a corpse already, Lily thought in dismay.

'Come on, Judith. Come on, pet. Don't go like this. Don't go after cross words between us. Don't do that to me. At least let me tell you to your face how grateful I am to you for taking such good care of me,' Lily whispered. 'Wake up for me so that we can make our peace.'

'Well, she won't come home with me and I can't stay with her. Can you take her tonight?' Cecily whispered, standing at the end of a corridor talking to her brother.

'No. We have Glenda's sister and her husband staying, the guest room's taken. She'll have to stay with you,' Tom insisted.

'Well, she won't, and there's nothing I can do about it.'

'Just tell her she has to come with you for a few days until we sort something,' Tom said, exasperated.

'I'm telling you she's staying put,' Cecily snapped.

'Ma's not going to live by herself! You know what she's like.'

'Well, she told me earlier on, before we knew about Judith having the crash, that they'd had a row before she left. Ma said she's had enough of the lot of us and she says she's going to sell the house and go and live in a nursing home.'

'You're not *serious*!' He couldn't believe his ears.

'I am. That's what she said.'

'For fuck's sake, there'll be nothing left. Those nursing homes cost a fortune and she's still relatively young,' Tom exploded.

'Tom! That's an awful thing to say. You should be ashamed. Judith could die. Doesn't that bother you?' Cecily started to cry.

'Yeah, it does. Of course it does. We had a row, too, so we weren't speaking either, so that doesn't make me feel very good,' he muttered.

'What did you have the row about?' Cecily sniffled.

'Ma's will. Judith thinks she's getting that house.'

'Yeah, well, that might not be an issue now and we'll be left to deal with Ma, and Tom . . .'

'Yes?'

'I'm not doing it on my own,' his sister warned. 'Because if I'm left with her, she *can* sell the house and go into a home, as far as I'm concerned. I wouldn't be able to cope with her like Judith did.'

'I hear ya,' her brother snapped. 'I'll be in later.'

He was something else. Judith was lying in a coma and could die, and all he was worried about was his inheritance. Even she wasn't that callous, Cecily thought as she walked reluctantly back along the corridor to join her mother at her sister's bedside. Her stomach rumbled; it was teatime and she hadn't eaten since her breakfast. Lily would be in the same boat. She didn't want her fainting in a heap on her again. That had been scary. She should go and get her to eat something. Cecily sighed. She felt burdened. And guilty. Whether she liked it or not, she was going to have to take some responsibility for her mother. Now she was going to get a taste of what her sister had had to cope with for so long. In the space of a couple of hours Cecily's world had been cast into upheaval and she felt utterly daunted.

'I just couldn't imagine Aimee in a slanging match.' Karen grinned as she and Connie managed to grab a moment together to catch up as they drank a very welcome cup of coffee.

'Well, Aimee wasn't *saying* that much. She was trying to cool the other one down, but she wasn't having it. Aimee was mortified. Then Melissa arrived, looking like she was going to a nightclub, and both she and Barry were horrified so they had a go at each other, and that's when she stomped off into the church saying that she'd been working to help pay for the wedding and Barry should have been there to keep an eye on what Melissa was wearing. She was sorry she'd said it, though, by the time I was finished with her. I'd say she was fairly shocked when I rang her. I was the last person she expected at the other end of the phone.' Connie grinned.

'No wonder she scuttled off.' Karen pursed her lips. 'I heard her clattering down the aisle. I'd say Barry deciding to sit beside you in church didn't go down too well either.'

'I was surprised about that myself, to be honest. I wasn't expecting him to. But I was glad for Debbie, she was pleased about it,' Connie said lightly. 'It was no big deal as far as I'm concerned and, if that's the reason Aimee took off, she has little to worry about.'

'Well, it certainly isn't a boring wedding.' Karen laughed, enjoying the gossip.

'It's a bloody warm wedding though.' Connie blew some air up her face.

'Oh dear, feeling hot, are we?' teased Karen.

'Yes, and it's global warming that's the cause of it, so don't even mention any of your crackpot theories, or the M word,' Connie warned. 'Oh cripes, there's Mam and Barry having a little chat, that's enough to make anyone feel hot and bothered. I bet she'll have a go at him. Oh no,' she groaned. 'I don't need that on top of everything else.'

'So what? Let them at it. It's not your problem,' advised Karen. 'The wedding's going great, it's relaxed and fun despite the behind-the-scenes shenanigans. Here, get this into you.' She grabbed a glass of champagne from the good-looking waiter Sarah and Melissa had been ogling and handed it to her sister-in-law.

'He's rather dishy, isn't he?' Connie murmured appreciatively. 'I've decided I need a man for a bit of diversion.'

'I've been telling you that for years,' laughed Karen. 'You go, girl, it's all about *you* now.'

'You look well,' his ex-mother-in-law said brusquely as Barry came by the table to enquire if everyone had a drink.

'Thank you, Stella. Are you enjoying the day?' he said smoothly, determined not to be irked by her. She was one person he hadn't missed when he and Connie had separated.

'It's very nice and er . . . informal.' She managed to make it sound like an insult.

'That's what Debbie and Bryan wanted, and it's their day,' he said briskly.

'I hope they'll be very happy.' The unspoken implication, *Not like you and Connie*, hovered.

'I hope so too.'

'And is your . . . er . . . other family here?' Stella sniffed.

'Debbie's sister, is here, yes.' He nodded.

'Ah, would that be the plump young girl in the jeans?'

Crabby old crone, Barry thought, wondering how Connie and her mother could be so different.

'I must introduce you.' It was hard to stay polite.

'Do that, I'd like to meet her,' his ex-father-in-law said, holding out his hand in greeting and shooting his wife a stern look. 'Very nice wedding, Barry. Well done to you and Connie.'

'Thanks, Jim. I hope you enjoy the rest of the evening,' he said warmly. He'd always liked his father-in-law, a quiet man who had never interfered. Unlike his wife.

'It was nice to see you sitting beside Connie in the church. It brought back memories of the day Debbie was christened, when you were still man and wife, although I suppose the church would still consider you man and wife even now,' Stella observed, saccharine-sweet. Connie and Barry had not sought a church annulment seeing as Aimee hadn't wanted to have a religious ceremony.

'I don't have much time for the church, to be frank.' Barry had

354

had enough. The gloves were off; he wasn't going to kowtow to Stella any longer. He'd tried to behave politely, but she wasn't playing the game.

'Ummm,' sneered Stella. 'Well, I suppose that's fairly apparent.' Her beady eyes gleamed triumphantly at her withering put-down. Barry kept his temper with difficulty. He wanted to tell her to get lost and have some manners, but he wouldn't upset Connie by giving her mother a tongue-lashing.

'How could you take a religion seriously when its titular head goes around wearing a pointed hat, very expensive red designer shoes and chunky gold jewellery? And tells other churches that they're not "proper" churches. Grow up, I say. Get over yourselves. Thanks but no thanks, Stella; you can keep *your* church. Poor Jesus must be disgusted. Isn't all this nonsense supposed to be said in His name?' he retorted.

'The Pope is infallible,' Stella pointed out, aghast at his scorn.

'Bully for him! Aah, look, here's the food. Tuck in and enjoy,' he said, relieved at the interruption, as a huge platter of steaming food was placed on the table.

'Good enough for you and the chap is right. Now whist up and stop trying to cause trouble, Stella.' Jim chuckled, leaning over to help himself to a succulent Peking duck roll.

That told you, Stella. Barry grinned as he moved away to join his mother and aunt at their table.

He scanned the menu. Nice grub, he approved as he read it.

Selection of Appetizers
Thai fishcakes with lemongrass and coriander and
a sweet chilli dipping sauce
Crispy vegetable and noodle spring roll with a cucumber
and red onion relish
Soy-glazed Peking duck rolls with hoi sin sauce
Prawn crackers

Buffet-style Main Course
Barbecued chicken breasts South-East Asian-style with
a nuoc nam dipping sauce

Sizzling swordfish in banana leaves
BBQ fillet steaks marinated in balsamic and rosemary
with honey-mustard pan jus

Baby baked potatoes with olive oil and coarse sea salt
Chargrilled vegetables with slow-roasted tomatoes and melted red
peppers tossed in garlic and thyme
Mesclun leaf salad with fresh herbs and a lemon vinaigrette

Dessert
Passion fruit tart with vanilla cream and fresh berries
Handmade chocolate bags filled with blackberry fool

Tea/coffee/green tea/peppermint tea
Homemade truffles

Not a burger in sight! He could have brought any of his golfing buddies to the wedding and not been embarrassed. Well done, Debbie and Bryan, he silently saluted them. The smell wafting from the barbecue in the courtyard was mouth-watering, and he realized he was starving as a waiter placed a platter of appetizers on the table.

'Help yourselves and eat up, everyone,' Barry urged. 'I'm going to enjoy this, and the great thing is, I don't have to make a speech afterwards.'

'Well, we'll be thankful for small mercies,' his mother said dryly, biting into a mouthful of fishcake. 'Where's Melissa and her friend?'

'Keeping well away from me,' he said acidly. 'She pulled a fast one and didn't wear the dress Aimee bought her, and she knows we're not too happy about it so she's avoiding me like the plague.'

'Ah, she's young,' pacified his mother. 'What child likes the clothes their mother chooses for them?'

'She likes them well enough when they're expensive jeans and tops, but you don't wear them to a wedding. She looks like she's going to a disco,' he grumbled.

'Well, I'm sure there will be one later. Don't give out to her too much.'

'Softie.' He smiled, glancing over to where Melissa and Sarah were laughing their heads off at something Debbie was saying as she took a photo of them with Bryan and the best man.

'Nice sight, isn't it?' Connie smiled as she followed his gaze. She'd just stopped at the table to make sure her in-laws had been served their starter.

'It's a great sight, one I thought I'd never see. We did well.' Barry got up to stand beside her.

'We did very well, considering everything, Barry. And thanks for all the support with the wedding. I think it's going better than I'd expected, to be honest. Because I just wasn't sure what it was going to be like.'

'I know. It's very laid-back but everything's just right. So let's relax and enjoy ourselves. We've done our duty,' he suggested, loosening his tie.

'Try the fishcakes, Hilda, they're scrumptious,' Connie urged her ex-mother-in-law. 'Joan, don't be shy, eat up.' She smiled at his aunt.

'Had one, going to attack the spring rolls now,' laughed Barry's mother.

'Me too,' echoed her sister.

'Enjoy it. Try everything. See you later.' Connie smiled warmly at the two elderly ladies before moving off to complete the rest of her rounds.

'I'm very, very fond of her and I always admired her for the way she didn't let your break-up stop me from seeing Debbie. She's a dote,' Hilda declared.

'Yes she is, the best in the world. Connie's a very classy lady.' Barry watched his ex-wife stop at another table to talk to Bryan's mother.

'Pity you left her,' his Aunt Joan murmured *sotto voce*. She didn't like Aimee at all and could never understand why Barry had done a runner on Connie.

'What?' Barry turned to face her, not having heard what she'd said.

'I was simply agreeing with you.' She smiled innocently. 'It's a wonder she hasn't been snapped up. Now that Debbie's reared and flown the nest she'll have the freedom to live her own life.'

'I suppose she will.' *And I hope I'm a big part of it*, he thought as he took a very welcome draught of ice-cold beer.

CHAPTER THIRTY-TWO

'Are you happy?' Bryan asked as he swept Debbie around the floor for their first dance as man and wife, to the sound of 'I Can't Help Falling In Love With You'.

'Deliriously. Are you?' She snuggled into him.

'Yeah. It's been a fantastic day, better than I hoped it would be. Everyone's enjoying themselves. And they're all saying how different it is. I'm glad we didn't go the "boring" route.'

'Me too, everything went so well. The food was fantastic; the violinist played beautifully; no speeches, no formality. We pulled it off and the parents were great. They let us have it the way we wanted and they rowed in behind us,' Debbie said gratefully.

'Your dad's been sound, and those two kids are having a grand time.' Bryan laughed, glancing over at Melissa and Sarah, who were flirting with one of his mates and giggling hysterically.

'Ohmigod, you're soooo funny,' Melissa was chirruping.

'They're a bit pissed. Dad's really taken his eye off the ball there.' Debbie nibbled his ear.

'He's too busy following your mother around,' Bryan observed. 'I think he wants to get back with her. They're getting on very well.'

'Do you think?' She pulled away a little and looked at him in surprise. 'I think *exactly* the same thing. Wouldn't that be perfect, if our wedding brought them back together?'

'It might cause complications,' he pointed out, pulling her back to him. 'Don't forget there's Melissa to think of.'

'Pity. I'd like to see my mother happy,' Debbie said regretfully.

'She's happy. Now let me make you happy,' he grinned, giving her a long lingering kiss as their guests cheered before joining them on the dance floor.

Connie laughed heartily as her partner, one of Bryan's friends, swung her around enthusiastically as they danced an Irish reel to the toe-tapping sound of a bodhran, fiddle and banjo.

'This is great fun,' she gasped. 'A fantastic way to end the night.'

'The night's only starting, woman,' Steve scoffed as he spun her into his arms.

'It's been a good wedding, hasn't it?'

'One of the best I've ever been to, thanks very much to yourself and Debbie's dad. You were great to let them have the wedding they wanted. A lot of parents impose their own ideas on a wedding. My mother and sister had terrible rows.'

'That's a shame. We felt it was important that they should do their own thing. It wasn't worth the hassle to argue, to be honest,' Connie said, hardly able to talk she was so breathless.

'I've been to three weddings in the last year. Dull, long-drawn-out ordeals. Getting a wedding invite is like getting a summons these days, and my heart sank when I got the invite to this one, but I've had a ball. A barbecue was a terrific idea. Now, come on, Missus, let's show these kids how to Riverdance.' Steve smirked, giving a good imitation of Michael Flatley as he tried to tap dance. Connie hooted with laughter. She hadn't had as much fun in ages. It was great to let her hair down, and the candle-lit courtyard was buzzing as a buttery full moon hung suspended in the sky, adding to the atmosphere.

Aimee, you're missing a fun night, she thought, as she kicked up her heels and joined her dance partner in a riotous jig.

Barry scowled as he watched Connie dance uninhibitedly with a chap young enough to be her son. She was tipsy and she didn't care. He'd had one dance with her, a waltz, and then she'd been off dancing with every young buck who asked her. She ought to act her age, he thought crossly.

Melissa and Sarah were in the middle of the throng in their bare feet, having abandoned their high heels to join in the Irish dancing. Their eyes were suspiciously bright, their cheeks roaring red, and he figured they'd been imbibing a little too heartily, even though he'd bought them several rounds of soft drinks. He felt guilty. He'd been so busy trying to impress Connie he hadn't given them much thought. If he brought the pair of them home in this state he'd lose the high ground that he inhabited over the money issue. Aimee would never let him forget that he'd allowed their daughter and her friend to have too much to drink. He'd had a few drinks himself as the night wore on, and he certainly wouldn't be driving home but, hell, he was at his daughter's wedding. If he couldn't relax and enjoy himself at that, when could he?

He could always book the girls into a room, he supposed. That would be the icing on the cake for them, he thought fondly, glad to see his youngest daughter so giddy and happy-go-lucky, even if she was a little the worse for wear. He made his way to reception and was lucky enough to secure a twin room for them, as there were still vacancies. He gave his credit card details and a thought struck him. He didn't particularly want to go home tonight either. All he had to look forward to there was an arctic welcome and sleeping on his own side of the bed with no crossing over the dividing line. He'd be as well off staying, and that way he'd be able to escort Connie to her room. Who knew what might happen? he thought, feeling suddenly horny as he remembered their last night of passion. 'Would you have another double room for myself?' he asked the young man behind the desk.

'Yes sir. We have doubles and suites free, whichever you prefer.'

'A double's fine,' Barry said, flipping open his mobile. '*Girls and I staying at hotel,*' he texted Aimee, and wasn't surprised not to get a reply.

*

Aimee read Barry's text and felt a surge of self-pity. They must be having a good time if they were staying at the hotel. He obviously didn't mind leaving her on her own while they partied the night away. And to think Melissa had once moaned so much about having to go to the wedding. What an irony.

It had been the pits of a day, Aimee thought dejectedly. She still couldn't get over Gwen turning on her the way she had. No doubt she'd been on the tom-toms to Jill, Sally and the rest of them. Let them gossip – what did she care? She rarely saw them these days anyway. They'd miss her more than she'd miss them, she thought irritably, getting into bed.

She turned over on her side and pulled the soft Egyptian cotton sheet over her shoulder. Barry's text had been short and sweet. He was obviously still mad about her behaviour. Maybe it was just as well he was staying the night at the hotel. There was nothing worse than lying in bed in tense, glacial silence. She was feeling a little off colour anyway. Probably exhaustion, she thought tiredly. It had been a rough couple of weeks work-wise. She needed to be on top form for the O'Leary wedding next week. It was key to the advancement of her career. And advance she would, Aimee vowed as her eyes closed and she fell into a fitful doze.

'I'm telling you, she barely let on she recognized me.' Gwen took a slug of wine and tried to ignore the anger she felt after Aimee's snub. 'She was walking out of the Shelbourne with some burly, florid bloke in a pinstriped suit—'

'I bet that was Roger O'Leary, that property guy she's doing the wedding for,' Jill reflected, savouring her melt-in-the-mouth lemon sole. 'Nice restaurant, I haven't been here before. Good choice, Gwen,' she complimented her friend.

'Well, I guessed we wouldn't get a table next door in the Troc at such short notice but I thought we might be lucky here for a late supper. I love their tapas.' She, Jill and Sally had met in Salamanca on Andrews Street to hear, face to face, about the ending of Gwen's friendship with Aimee.

'Girls, I'm telling you, I was so mad I turned around and went right after her and I know it wasn't a very nice thing to do and that it had nothing to do with them, but I had it out with her in front of Barry and his daughter and first wife on the steps of University Church. The daughter was getting married and Aimee was going to the wedding. And wait until I tell you what I said.' Gwen took another sip of wine before regaling them with the whole sorry saga.

'Good for you, the snobby cow,' Sally said stoutly. 'She thinks her shite is Christmas pudding.'

'Sally, don't be so vulgar,' reprimanded Jill, laughing. 'Well, the signs were always there that we were gradually being dropped, but that was downright rude, Gwen. And you of all people didn't deserve it – you were always very kind to her. And you always stood up for her.'

Gwen's face crumpled and she burst into tears. 'I can't believe Aimee did that to me,' she wept. 'It really hurt.'

'Don't cry, Gwen; she's not worth it. Friendship is wasted on her. You still have us,' Sally comforted, putting an arm around her shoulder.

'I know and, thanks, I really appreciate it, but it hurt all the same.' Gwen pushed away her Spanish omelette, her appetite gone.

'Gwen, she's the loser, big time. And the time *will* come when she needs a friend and there'll be no one there for her, and she'll only have herself to blame.' Jill spoke authoritatively. She'd seen it all before, ambitious women becoming absorbed in their careers and losing sight of what was really important in life. A good friend was priceless and, after her own recent traumatic break-up, she knew that better than anyone.

'Melissa, I want a word with you.' Melissa's heart sank as her father called her from the dance floor. She was feeling pleasantly woozy and on a complete high. This was the best night of her life. She'd bopped her ass off and had loads of photos taken with totally hot guys, and she and Sarah were going to have the best time ever boasting about this night of nights.

Her dad was probably calling her to tell her it was time to go home. He hadn't said anything about her clothes. That would probably happen when they were on their own, as he wouldn't embarrass her in front of Sarah. He was good like that. She sighed as she made her way to where he was standing.

'Yes, Dad?' she said warily.

'I don't know if you deserve it, but I've booked a room for you and Sarah tonight. Now, I think you've had enough to drink and I won't be letting on to your mother that you've been imbibing, because it's not on, you know. This is strictly a one-off,' he said sternly.

'Oh Dad, you're the best dad in the whole wide world.' Her eyes lit up and she flung her arms around him.

'Go on.' He laughed. 'You have me wrapped around your little finger.'

'That's what dads are for,' Melissa informed him, hugging him tightly.

'Your mother's not best pleased—'

'Dad, please can we talk about that tomorrow? This is one of the most seriously cool nights of my life,' she begged.

'Well, enjoy it then.' He softened and she gave him a kiss before heading back to the dance floor.

'Yessss!' she exclaimed. Staying overnight with Sarah in a lovely hotel – what a treat. And he hadn't said much about her clothes or how much she'd drunk. She might very well get away with it by the skin of her teeth. Aimee might have calmed down by tomorrow. 'Sarah.' She tugged at her friend's top to get her attention. 'We're staying in the hotel tonight. Dad's booked us a room.'

'Hey, legend! That's savage. Thanks so much for asking me to come, Meliss, I've never had so much fun in my life.'

'Me either, let's go dance.' Melissa twirled out on to the floor and bumped into the blonde lollipop head. 'Sorry,' she apologized.

'Hey, mind where you're going,' slurred the other girl, her eyes glazed.

'Sure, sorry.' Melissa edged away. Lollipop head was out of her tree for sure.

'Who is that little fat tart?' she heard her say to Fedora Head, as Sarah had christened her.

'Dunno,' said Fedora Head, who looked equally spaced out, her hat jammed down over her ears to keep it on, one boob perilously close to falling out of her blouse. 'She keeps asking the fellas to have her photo taken with them. How sad is that?'

'Don't mind her,' Sarah said, seeing Melissa's crestfallen look. 'She's out of it. It's all the coke she's been doing. Look at her hat, she looks like Charlie Chaplin.'

'I suppose,' agreed Melissa resentfully. Hearing herself called a little fat tart had pricked her feel-good bubble, and she couldn't quite get it back, even when she and Sarah had finally gone to their room and opened two Bacardi Breezers that a friend of Bryan's had bought for them on the QT.

As she lay woozily in her bed, feeling sick, sorry that she'd drunk that last alcopop and listening to Sarah snoring, Melissa vowed that she was going on a strict diet and no one would ever call her fat again.

'I suppose there's no point in me staying,' Tom said to the nurse as she checked one of Judith's monitors and straightened one of her IV lines.

'We can call you if there's any deterioration, and her vital signs are strong, so that's a plus,' she said kindly before gliding silently out of the curtained cubicle.

Tom chewed his lip. He was tired, he had a long drive ahead of him, but if he left Judith now and she died on her own, how would he feel? His mother would never forgive him. But she more than anyone should understand, surely? He hated hospitals. They frightened him. He was afraid Judith was going to die while he was there. He'd never seen anyone dying. Would she choke or gasp for breath?

He felt panicked. He hadn't been able to stay with his father when he was dying. Judith had done that. Judith had done a lot of brave things, he thought, looking at his pale, eerily motionless sister. She looked small, shrunken in the bed. Tears sprouted from his eyes. He had to get out of here. 'See you,

Judith,' he muttered, slipping out of the cubicle and making his way out of the HDU and down the long, deserted corridor to the lifts and exit.

Lily lay wide-eyed in her bed, tossing and turning. It was just like when Ted had died. She'd lain there waiting for the phone to ring, knowing that if it did ring, it would be with the worst of all news.

Tom had phoned earlier to say he was going home, that there was no point in him staying any later. Lily hated the idea of Judith being alone with none of her family beside her. She would go in as early as she could tomorrow. The sister had told her she could visit whenever she wished. That sister was very kind. All the nurses were. Judith was being well taken care of. The only other comfort she had was that the sister had told her that Judith's vital signs were strong. Everything depended on the swelling of the brain and how that went. Lily could only hand it up and trust in God.

Still, she could be at Cecily's, feeling fluttery and agitated, she consoled herself. At least she was in her own bed, in her own house and that in itself was a comfort. With a deep sigh, Lily took her rosary beads from under her pillow and began to say her prayers for her stricken daughter.

'Come on and have a last drink with me,' Barry urged as they stepped into the lift to go to their rooms on the third floor. He pressed the button and they glided smoothly upwards. Their family members were gone, and only a few of Debbie and Bryan's friends remained in the residents' bar. The bridal couple had staggered off to bed a quarter of an hour previously, having said their goodbyes. They were up at the crack of dawn in the morning to go to the airport. Debbie had given her father and Melissa the warmest of hugs, and that had made the day perfect for Connie.

Bryan too had hugged her tightly and thanked her, and she decided she'd give him the benefit of the doubt. She'd never seen Debbie look so happy and that was what counted.

'A little one, we deserve it. We put in a long day,' Barry coaxed.

'I'm not drinking any more, I've enough drink taken.' Connie gave a tipsy giggle.

'Ah, just one, for old time's sake,' Barry insisted as the doors opened and they walked out into the corridor.

'Well, a spritzer then,' Connie agreed good-humouredly. 'What room number are you?'

He checked his key. '322.'

'Right, we're nearest yours then, it's just across the hall there.' She pointed out his room, pleased that she wasn't completely squiffy.

'OK.' He swiped them in and turned on more lights.

Connie flung herself down on the bed, lying back against the pillows, and yawned as Barry rooted in the mini bar for white wine and a mixer. 'That was a great night,' she said, wriggling her toes as she kicked off her high heels.

'Well, you seemed to enjoy it.' He handed her a drink.

'I did. Once I'd done my duty and made sure everyone was fed and watered, I said to hell with it, and I enjoyed myself enormously. It's a long time since I've danced like that.'

Barry sat down on the bed beside her and took a slug of his beer. 'You weren't short of partners,' he said off-handedly.

'I know, it was great . . . and at my age too.' She grinned, looking up at the ceiling, thinking it was a mistake to relax on the bed. She was beginning to feel sleepy.

'There's nothing wrong with your age, you're a fabulous woman,' her ex-husband said huskily, putting his glass on the bedside locker and leaning over to kiss her.

Taken by surprise, she involuntarily kissed back but, as the kiss deepened and he began to caress her breast, she struggled up and pushed him away. 'Stop, Barry, we're not doing this again.'

'Why not? You enjoyed it and so did I. We're good together,' he cajoled, trying to push her back against the pillows again.

'*Stop*, Barry!' This time there was no mistaking her tone and he pulled away, disgruntled. 'But I thought you wanted to?'

he protested. 'I thought when you lay down on the bed—'

'Oh, for God's sake! You thought wrong, Barry. Once was one time too many as far as I'm concerned. Now I'm going to my room and we'll forget it ever happened.' She swung her legs over the side of the bed.

'Why? Is that Steve fella waiting for you?' he said nastily, stung at being rebuffed. 'I don't like you flirting with young men, like you were this evening. You're not Mrs Robinson.'

Connie stood up, picked up her shoes and stared at him, her eyes flinty.

'Even if Steve *is* in my room that's my business and not yours. And if I want to flirt, I damn well will flirt. I'll live my life the way *I* want to. I'm a single woman and I can see and be with whomsoever I want, and don't you ever forget that. And don't you dare ever question me like that again,' she snapped.

'Sorry,' he muttered. 'I'd just be worried about you.'

'You don't have to worry about me, Barry. I'm not your responsibility. I ceased to be that a long time ago. I'm glad today went well. I'm delighted you and Debbie patched things up but, for me, that's as far as it goes. I have my own life to lead now and I intend to live it to the full. Sleep well, I'll see you in the morning,' she said coolly and walked out of the room, leaving him staring after her in disbelief.

Connie padded barefoot down the corridor, shaking her head. Where did Barry get off telling her how to conduct her personal life? What a nerve. What did he think she was, his concubine?

Just as well she'd nipped that in the bud, she thought, yawning her head off as she let herself into the room. She should never have had sex with him in the first place. It was her own fault. She was hot and sweaty after all the dancing and the bed looked so clean and crisp and welcoming. Connie knew she'd feel much better if she had a quick shower. Twenty minutes later, clean and smelling of L'Air du Temps body lotion she slipped between the sheets. She stretched before turning on her tummy, drawing one leg up to her chest. She felt strangely liberated. It definitely was the end of one chapter in her life and the start of another, she thought drowsily, and she was looking forward to it. A new job on the horizon, hopefully, and who knew after that? Maybe she might meet someone but, even if she didn't, she'd made sure Barry was in no doubt as to where she stood with him. She yawned again and was asleep in seconds, downright relieved that the wedding had gone off without any major hiccups.

'You read that all wrong, mate,' Barry scowled as he undressed for bed and switched out the lamp. He lay, tossing and turning, annoyed for making such an ass of himself in front of Connie. She'd given him a fine piece of her mind too and pulled no punches. She was so much more assertive now than when she was married to him. He liked it. He liked that she knew her own mind and wasn't afraid to speak it. In the old days she would have bent over backwards to accommodate him and keep him happy.

The good old days, he sighed. They were long gone. What a rollercoaster of a day today had been. First Aimee turning on him, and now Connie. Debbie was the only one who was on speaking terms with him, apart from Melissa. Given all that had gone on between them previously it was an irony indeed.

CHAPTER THIRTY-THREE

'Take deep breaths, Lily,' Lily instructed herself as she stood waiting for a bus to take her to the hospital. It was 8 a.m. and she was alone at the stop. Every so often a car would drive by, but the road was quiet compared to the usual mayhem and traffic congestion of a weekday morning. Sunday was a good day for her first venture alone on a bus in a long time. Ted was looking after her, she was sure of it.

She'd slept fitfully and woken at quarter to six to find sunlight slanting through a gap in the curtains. She'd lain in that half-waking state for a moment or two until she remembered, and an icy apprehension gripped her. Judith was very ill. Her heart began to race, but she made herself breathe deeply and sit up. The hospital hadn't phoned, so that was good, she calmed herself as she made her way downstairs and filled the kettle.

Lily busied herself in the kitchen, but she couldn't settle. She needed to be with Judith. Cecily had told her that she'd collect her and bring her to the hospital in the afternoon, but she couldn't wait that long. Cecily wasn't even going to her garden party. Lily was pleased about that. At least her younger daughter had some sense of decency.

Grimly determined, Lily washed and dressed and put on her pale blue summer jacket. If Judith opened her eyes today, she would find her mother sitting by her bedside holding her hand.

As she stood nervously peering along the Drumcondra Road

in search of a bus on the horizon, she was nearly tempted to hurry back home, but she thought of Mrs Meadows, who'd shared a ward with her a few weeks back. She'd been so vibrant and independent, and she was older than Lily. And had more complaints. Lily was still healthy, despite her nerves.

'Stop giving in to yourself,' she said crossly, spotting a green double-decker at the traffic lights at Fagan's. Her grip tightened on her handbag. 'Come on now; think of Judith,' she told herself sternly, bravely putting out her hand for it to stop.

'Does this bus go to Beaumont Hospital?' she quavered, as the doors whooshed open.

'Yes it does.' The driver smiled at her.

'That's where I want to go,' she said, stepping aboard.

A minute later she was sitting in the almost empty bus, exhilarated. She'd done it. Lily smiled. It was a small step, but it was a step towards freedom, hers and Judith's.

'Judith, you'd be proud of me,' she told her daughter twenty-five minutes later as she sat holding her hand. 'I got the bus in to see you. And I stayed the night on my own. Sent Cecily home with a flea in her ear for not coming on time yesterday. Did you sleep well? It's time to wake up now like a good girl.' She peered anxiously at her, wondering if she'd heard a word she'd said.

'Did she come to at all?' she asked the nurse who'd come in to change her drip.

'No, Mrs Baxter, I'm afraid she didn't. The doctors will be here later on their rounds and you can have a word with them. But just keep talking to her and hold her hand. That's the best thing that you can do for her.'

'I'll do that, don't you worry,' Lily assured her. 'She minded me very well, you know, especially when my poor husband died. Now it's my turn to mind her.'

'Good morning, Mrs Kinsella.'

Debbie woke to find her new husband smiling down at her.

'Morning,' she mumbled, sleepy-eyed. 'What time is it?'

'Time you were up. We got us a plane to catch to the good ol' USA.'

'Uuuugg,' she groaned. 'Do we have to get up? Couldn't we just stay in bed and make love and go asleep again?' she entreated.

'Are you mad? Make love first thing in the morning! We're an old married couple now,' he teased.

'Aaww,' she giggled, sliding her hand down over the curve of his hip.

'We could have a quickie in the shower,' he suggested, leaning down to kiss her.

'Better than nothing,' she grumbled, yawning widely as he hauled her out of bed.

'We should have given ourselves a day to get over the wedding,' she reflected as they walked arm in arm into the bathroom.

'We can sleep on the plane. C'mere, I'll wake you up,' Bryan promised, drawing her into the shower and turning on the spray.

'Babes, we need to get a move on,' he declared twenty minutes later as she sat in a towelling robe drying her hair. He was shaved and dressed, and he flicked the channels on the slim, widescreen TV, waiting for her to finish.

'Look at the state of that car,' he remarked as the TV3 news flashed up a shot of a wrecked blue Bora embedded in a tree as they did a piece on weekend road deaths being up compared to the same period of the previous year.

'Judith Baxter has a car that colour,' Debbie mused. 'Thank God I won't be seeing her for another three weeks. She does my head in.'

'If you don't hurry up, we won't have time for breakfast,' her husband complained, flicking to Sky sports.

'Nag nag nag, is this what it's going to be like?' Debbie ribbed, but she put her skates on, ravenous after their early morning love-making. Now that she was up and showered, she was looking forward to her honeymoon in New York with huge anticipation.

It wasn't so bad being married, Bryan reflected as he gazed at the gold ring on his finger. He was on a complete high. The wedding had been a great success and now they were going to New York on their honeymoon. He was sitting at an internet screen in a small area of the lobby, trying to book tickets for a show on Broadway. He keyed in one of their joint credit card details, yet again, and the same message flashed up. Card declined. This was disturbing. Debbie wouldn't be too happy if she knew. They'd have to transfer much-needed funds from their current account. He opened his wallet and pulled out another card. His new wife didn't know he had another credit card; in fact, there were a few things Debbie didn't know about him. Primarily, that he had a second bank account and a second credit card.

There was nothing wrong with keeping separate accounts. A chap at work had advised him on the matter. He was married with three kids, but his relationship with his wife had always been a bit jaggy. He had been stashing a few quid away every week for years in case everything went belly up. 'Don't see why women should get everything when they haul you through the divorce courts, especially when they're earning their own money,' he'd told Bryan in a drunken discussion one night. It was a strategy that made sense to Bryan, and he sighed with relief that while that joint credit account might be maxed out, his own personal and private account was quite healthy. Whistling, Bryan paid for the tickets just as his spouse emerged from the lift, looking around for him in the deserted foyer.

'Here, babes, just checking a few emails.' He waved. 'I've ordered a taxi for us, now let's eat – we don't want to hit New York on an empty stomach. *Never mind an empty credit card*, he thought, feeling just a tad guilty that he was not being completely upfront with his wife.

'Girls, have whatever you want for breakfast. I'm having mine in my room and I'll meet you in the foyer,' Barry instructed down the phone a couple of hours later as he lay in bed watching golf on the TV.

He had dithered over phoning Connie's room to ask did she

want to join him and the girls for breakfast, but he decided to leave it. It would be too awkward and he didn't want Melissa copping on that there was discomposure between him and Connie. She might mention it to Aimee and he certainly didn't need a grilling from *her*.

Anyway, Connie might not want to have breakfast with him after last night, and he'd feel twice as bad if she refused outright. Much as he loved his younger daughter, listening to two twittering teenagers was not ideal when coping with a hangover.

He wasn't looking forward to going home either, he thought glumly as Harrington sank a putt. Aimee would be aloof and then she'd have to have one of her 'talks' with him to get it all out in the air, and he just didn't need that right now. It was a pity he couldn't stay here all day and let the rest of the world go to pot. Barry scowled as he picked up the phone to order room service.

Aimee had spent a very satisfying morning at her computer answering and firing off emails. She'd been up since seven. The penthouse was unusually peaceful and Zen-like. A perfect atmosphere for working in. She glanced at her watch. Barry and Melissa were probably having breakfast. She hadn't heard from either her husband or her daughter since the previous day.

Attack would have to be the best defence, she decided as she shut down her computer and strolled out to the balcony to get some fresh air. There was a regatta in the harbour and yachts at anchor bobbed up and down on the waves while others streaked across the bay as an easterly breeze caught their billowing sails.

She was feeling a lot better this morning. What had happened with Gwen had happened and there was no going back. She had a punishment planned for Melissa that would ensure that she never stepped over the line again. Barry and she were going to have to have a talk and get things sorted. She had no time for 'atmospheres' and, besides, she needed no distractions this coming week. Her whole focus would be work. Months and months of planning were coming to fruition. This wedding event would be her stepping pad to bigger and better things, and Aimee had no intention of allowing anyone – family or friends – to scupper that.

'What are you having?' Sarah enquired as she tonged a croissant and a Danish on to her plate.

'Might just go for some fruit and muesli,' Melissa said glumly. She'd had a terrible job getting her jeans on after yesterday's feast. And the button was in danger of popping.

'Oh, Melissa, you can have that at home. Look at all this gorgeous food – I'm having a fry-up too,' Sarah protested.

'Nope,' Melissa said resolutely, spotting Lollipop and Fedora Head drinking coffee and smoking at one of the tables outside. They had no food in front of them. 'Anyway, I don't feel very hungry. I've got to face my mother, don't forget, and I know she must be mad as hell because she hasn't even sent me one text since she saw me yesterday.'

'Oooo, right. How totally grim. I'd forgotten. I better not come home with you. Your dad can drop me off first,' Sarah said sympathetically as she helped herself to a muffin.

Aimee heard the front door open and composed her features in a cold, stern mask.

'Hi Mom,' Melissa said with false bravado as she walked into the lounge, followed by her father. Barry merely nodded and went to go out on to the balcony with his Sunday papers.

'Before you go, Barry, would both of you come into the kitchen please,' Aimee said coldly. Father and daughter looked at each other, perplexed, but followed Aimee.

'What are these?' She pointed to the four empty Bacardi Breezer bottles on the kitchen counter.

Melissa groaned inwardly. She and Sarah had been so excited about going to the wedding on their own they'd forgotten to hide the evidence.

'Well?' Aimee said icily.

'We were thirsty,' Melissa muttered.

'And what's wrong with Coke or Seven-Up? How dare you go drinking behind our backs?' she rebuked.

'Well, Dad let me have champagne,' she said sulkily, and then caught her father's warning glare.

'That's different. He offered it to you. You know full well you are not allowed to drink alcohol. It looks like we can't trust you on your own here. You certainly can't be trusted to wear suitable clothes to a function. In fact, I don't know if we can trust you at all. And I'm very surprised at Sarah. I thought she was a well-brought-up type of girl. Her mother would be horrified if she knew the carry-on here. Now go to your room and stay there, and do not go on the computer until I give you permission. Is that clear?'

'But Mom—'

'Enough, and I want those jeans when you've taken them off.'

'Why?' Melissa demanded.

'You'll see. Now get out of my sight.' Melissa knew there was no point in arguing when her mother was in one of her vicious moods.

'So, thirteen and drinking alcohol?' Aimee turned her attention to Barry. 'What are you going to do about it?'

'I think you've dealt with it without any help from me,' he retorted coldly and walked out on to the balcony to read his papers in peace as Melissa scurried off to her bedroom.

What the hell did her mother want with her jeans? she worried, flinging herself on her bed and cuddling her rag-eared teddy-bear. What a vile stroke of luck her finding the empties. Now she had two strikes against her. It didn't give her much leeway for a third. She took her phone out of her bag and began to text Sarah to warn her that she'd be getting a less than friendly reception from Aimee the next time she met her.

The traffic was heavy along the N11 as Connie took the turn-off for Greystones. Everyone was probably on their way to Brittas to make the most of the good weather after all the torrential rain.

She yawned. She was tired. Yesterday had been hectic but most enjoyable. She grinned, thinking of her efforts at Irish dancing. Well, apart from the odd hiccup, she conceded, as she slowed down behind a car towing a caravan. Aimee's mêlée and Barry's jealous outburst had been unexpected, to say the least.

She'd seen her ex-husband briefly as she'd come into the hotel having had a stroll around Grafton Street that morning. He was paying his bill and Melissa and Sarah were sitting on a sofa waiting for him.

'Morning, girls. Did you sleep well?' she greeted them cheerfully. Melissa was looking somewhat despondent. Still had to face Mama, Connie guessed.

'Fine, thanks,' they assured her, Sarah with more gusto than her friend.

'Good. Morning, Barry,' she said evenly as he joined them.

'Connie.' He was equally polite. 'Were you out and about?'

'Yeah, I went for a walk along Grafton Street seeing as I was in this neck of the woods. I'm not usually in town on a Sunday morning. But I better settle up myself and get home. Have a few chores to do,' she'd said breezily. He looked hungover and in bad form.

'Right. See you around, I suppose.' He met her gaze.

'I guess so.'

'Good luck with the new job, I hope it all goes well for you. Let me know if you get it.' He managed a smile.

'Sure,' she said, taking pity on him. She leaned across and gave him a peck on the cheek. 'See you. Bye, girls, have a good summer. Melissa, if you ever want to see Hope, let me know, your dad has my number. You're welcome to come too, Sarah.'

'And am I welcome?' her ex-husband asked dryly.

'Of course you are, Barry,' she said briskly, before walking over to the lift to collect her belongings from the room.

Connie enjoyed the drive home, mulling over the events of the morning. Men were as bad as children, she reflected as she parked the car in her drive and opened the door. Hope shot out from under the lilac tree to welcome her home, purring like a tractor.

'Hello, Miss Hope.' She smiled, bending down to pat her

before putting her key in the door. She'd thought that she'd be very lonely coming home after the wedding but, surprisingly, she didn't feel at all lonely. She was going to have a lazy afternoon on her sun lounger with all the worries of the wedding behind her. A new job and lifestyle beckoned. No more commuting, if she was lucky, fewer working hours, and more time for herself.

'I'm optimistic, Hope, that's what I am. Very optimistic,' Connie informed her cat gaily as she shook out some cat food for her little companion.

Epilogue

Barry rubbed his eyes blearily and yawned.

'Sorry, did I wake you up?' Aimee apologized, her back to him as she inserted gold earrings into her ears and sprayed Chanel No 5 liberally around her.

'It's OK,' he grunted, yawning again. She looked groomed, alert. She was ready for anything, the epitome of the successful businesswoman, he thought sourly, remembering that today was the day she'd been working towards for months like a Trojan.

'What time will you be home?' he queried, stretching.

'God knows,' she said coolly. 'Take Melissa out for dinner somewhere or get a Chinese. I never got a chance to get any shopping in. Or perhaps you could do a shop later, we're running low on the basics.'

'I was hoping to fit in a game of golf. I did the shopping the last two times.' He knew it was childish tit for tatting, but she wasn't the only one with a career.

'Whatever,' she snapped. 'Eat in, eat out, it's entirely up to you. I won't be here.'

'What's new?' he retorted sulkily.

'Barry!' she eyeballed him. 'I haven't time for this right now; we'll discuss it next week. Just give me a break and stop trying to make me feel guilty, because it's not going to happen, so deal with it.' She stalked out of the bedroom, grim faced. He heard her have a brief conversation with Melissa and then she was gone. Silence floated around him and he felt his body relax as if he'd just exhaled a large breath.

He sighed. Since the wedding, there had been so much tension when she was at home. Staccato conversations. Point scoring. It certainly wasn't a high point in their marriage, he thought glumly, turning over on his side and pulling the sheet around him. The roles were slowly but subtly being reversed. It should be him off out to work at the crack of dawn while she did the shopping and took care of Melissa. He had two chances of that happening. Slim and none, and it bugged him. He was obviously going to have to get used to it because as far as he could see, Aimee was going full-steam ahead with her career and he and Melissa could like it or lump it.

Melissa could not believe what her mother was saying to her at that hour of the morning. She'd gone to the loo at half past six, bleary-eyed, and when she came out Aimee was in the hall putting her keys into her handbag. Then she'd dropped her hand grenade. 'Morning, Melissa.' Not too friendly. Not too cool. The way she'd been all week since the wedding. 'I'm just off to work but, before I forget, I want you to iron those jeans today, I'm giving them away to a charity shop,' she said calmly as she took one last look at herself in the mirror and flicked a piece of fluff off the shoulder of her black trouser suit.

'You're giving my Rock & Republic jeans to a *charity* shop?' Melissa's jaw dropped in shock.

'Yes, Melissa, I am. I'm filling that yellow bag and they're going in it. I'll be dropping it into the shop later this week. It might make you think twice about going behind my back again. I was very disappointed in you.'

'Please, Mom, don't do *that*; ground me for a week even. I'm the only girl in my class with those jeans,' she pleaded.

'Sorry, Melissa. I've made up my mind. Now, if you want to get back in my good books you can clean out your wardrobe and throw those magazines into the green bin, your bedroom is like a tip. I won't be home until late tonight so don't stay up.'

'Why would I want to get into your good books ever again, Mom? You're like totally mean.' Melissa turned and stomped into her bedroom and burst into tears. She heard the front door close as she got back into bed. Her mother was a cow, she thought bitterly, crying into her pillow. It was a week since Debbie's wedding and the atmosphere in the house was toxic. Her father was very grumpy and hardly talking to Aimee when she was at home, which was actually very little of the time, because she was completely absorbed with the big society wedding that was happening today. Sarah was on edge about meeting Aimee because she was afraid she was going to get the cold shoulder; they hadn't actually met since the discovery of the empties.

It was all very stressful and not even the deeply satisfying selection of wedding photos she'd downloaded from her camera was giving her much comfort. Her stomach rumbled. She was hungry, but she'd lost four pounds since the wedding and she was going to lose a whole lot more. It was extremely rewarding to stand on the scales and see the needle showing a loss. Let her mother take the jeans – soon they wouldn't fit her anyway, Melissa thought defiantly. The day stretched out ahead of her. She was bored. Her dad would be playing golf in the afternoon. She took her phone off her bedside locker and texted furiously. It was too early to send. She'd wait until around nine, she decided, saving it to her outbox.

Melissa lay in bed fantasizing about the clothes she'd wear when she'd lost a few stone and how her sexy waiter would seek her out and become her first lover, waiting for her at the school gates. She would be the envy of every girl in her class, she thought drowsily as she fell back asleep.

You had to be cruel to be kind, Aimee thought grimly as she drove through the massive wrought-iron gates of Chesterton House and saw the gleaming white roof of the massive marquee that had been turned into a blue and white palace. Melissa would learn the hard way that sneaky, underhand behaviour was not acceptable. She banished thoughts of her errant daughter and selfish, ungracious husband and hurried up the steps to the main house. She was scheduled to have a fifteen-minute conference with the wedding planner at seven thirty. She could see the delivery vans arriving with their fresh produce for the wedding feast. She had sourced every ingredient from organic producers, and the menu would put a Michelin-star restaurant to shame. Oysters, lobster, salmon, fillet steak, lamb, watercress for the soup, and herbs for flavouring, the best of Irish produce. The strawberries, raspberries and blackberries for the roulade had been specially grown for the occasion. It was a triumph for her to have stuck to the letter of her brief, and she was very pleased with her organizational skills, which had been tested to the limit. She felt a huge sense of achievement. Her company would receive a whacking great fee for this and she would be on the up. Time to negotiate a new wage increase, she thought with satisfaction.

'Thank God you're here, Aimee,' Belinda, the fraught wedding planner, declared as she phoned her to find out her whereabouts. 'I'm over in the marquee – can you meet me there instead? The seating has to be completely rearranged because some of the guests have cancelled and two of them have fallen out with each other and will have to be placed miles apart, and I'm sick of the whole shaggin' lot of them. The more money they have, the more badly behaved they are.'

'Stay calm, we'll sort it,' Aimee said reassuringly, her mind racing ahead as she got into work mode.

Hours later she was beginning to wilt. The bride, a big girl, squashed into a most unflattering designer bodice which had been bought in the US, had had hysterics at the thought of a couple of hundred of her father's high-profile guests looking at her and had to be calmed down with a mild sedative.

Seeing Jasmine in her unflattering gown, which had cost an arm and a leg, Aimee marvelled that no one – the mother, the bridesmaid or, indeed, the designer himself – had stepped in and said big girls with flabby arms and plump shoulders did not look good in strapless bodices. Debbie's gown, with its plain skirt and tailored, beaded top, had looked far more elegant and chic. The bodice look was not flattering to many brides who wore it, and Jasmine O'Leary was one of them.

Still, that wasn't her side of things, Aimee thought with relief. And, so far, the marquee, with its crystal chandeliers and subtle, tasteful table décor, was getting a lot of praise. The newly-weds and the guests were seated, a course of Galway Bay oysters or fish chowder was being served and there was a hum of laughter and conversation. Roger O'Leary walked over to her and put an arm around her waist.

'Fantastic job, Aimee. You've done us proud. I'll recommend you to everyone here – they've been asking about you,' he said exuberantly.

'Thank you, Roger. Now you should go and take your seat, the guests at your table are waiting on you before they eat,' she pointed out.

'Right. But we'll talk later,' he assured her, his face even more florid in his dress suit. He looked like a little penguin as he made his way back to the table. But at least he'd had the courtesy to come over and praise her for the job she'd done.

A waiter carrying a salver of oysters walked past her, and the look of them and the smell of them made her feel suddenly nauseous. Aimee broke out in a cold sweat. She needed to get to a loo, and quickly. Swallowing hard, trying to quell her nausea, she made her way to the toilets and was discreetly and quietly sick.

She wiped her mouth and took a few deep breaths. What the hell was wrong with her? This past week she'd been feeling tired and vaguely nauseous and sometimes even light-headed. She'd been like that once before, she thought with a growing, fearful sense of dread.

It was unthinkable, she couldn't be. She couldn't possibly be pregnant . . . or could she? She remembered the last night she'd had sex with Barry. It was when they were half asleep, and she'd done a quick calculation in her head and decided she was OK not to have used a condom, her periods were imminent, she was sure, and that was why she'd felt so horny. But they hadn't come, and she'd been so stressed she'd forgotten about them. Surely she hadn't miscalculated!

'Oh God Almighty, don't let me be pregnant, please. Not now, not when things are really taking off for me,' she muttered as her phone rang, and Belinda started to say that two of the chefs were having a row and could she deal with it. If they weren't careful she'd barf all over them, she thought viciously, hoping against hope that it was just a tummy bug she'd caught.

A baby was the last thing she and Barry needed. He didn't have to know she was pregnant, if that was what was wrong with her, she thought wildly as she made her way to the kitchens. She had options. This was something she should deal with herself.

Squaring her shoulders, Aimee strode into the kitchen, grim-faced. Two squabbling prima donna chefs didn't stand a chance the way she was feeling.

'Ohmigod! Bryan, I've just got an email from Carina at work. Judith Baxter's in a coma in hospital. She had a car accident the day of our wedding. It was her car we saw on the news last Sunday morning,' Debbie exclaimed, shocked as she read it out to him. He was at a computer next to her. They were in an internet café off Battery Park, checking and sending emails before heading off to their favourite deli for breakfast.

'That car was a write-off – if she survives it she'll be lucky,' Bryan declared as his fingers flew over the keys on his computer.

'Mam's going for her job interview today, she says. I really hope she gets it. She deserves it.' Debbie read out her mother's email.

'Umm,' her husband murmured, not really interested. One of his mates had sent him an email asking him if he was going to the Galway Races in August, as usual, now that he was tied to the sink.

'*Of course*,' he wrote. '*Count me in.*' He wasn't going to forgo his annual trip to the races with the lads. He wouldn't mention it to Debbie just at the moment. She was having anxiety attacks about the amounts of money they were spending. They'd had to pay the interest on their credit card at the bank at the airport and after a week in the Big Apple they were almost maxed out again. 'We'll worry about it when we get home, we're on our honeymoon,' he soothed over and over, wishing she'd stop harping on about money.

'*Just don't say anything about it until nearer the time,*' he typed. It was best to be prudent at all costs. 'Come on, wife, let's go have breakfast, I'm starving,' he ordered, logging out.

'Just let me finish this email to Mum,' she murmured, typing furiously. '*Just going to have breakfast and heading off on the ferry to Staten Island and the Statue of Liberty. Having a wonderful time. Miss you, see you soon, lots of love, Debbie xx,*' she wrote before logging off. It was amazing how much she missed her mother, she thought in surprise. She was longing to see her to tell her all about the terrific time she was having in New York. They had visited galleries and museums, gone to the theatre, shows and films and shopped like there was no tomorrow. The only thing marring her pleasure was the ever-increasing credit card bill.

It was all right for Bryan to say they were on their honeymoon, but it was all going to be facing them when they got back to Ireland. Reality was going to sink in and they were going to be pretty smashed. It would definitely be time to pull their horns in, she reflected as Bryan paid their bill. If any overtime came up she was definitely going to take it, she decided, and then remembered Carina's email.

Would Judith survive the car crash, and would she come out of her coma unscathed? Debbie certainly didn't wish her boss anything bad, but wouldn't it be a great relief if she weren't able to come back to work? Imagine never having to face Batty Baxter again? That certainly would be one less worry to have to deal with, Debbie thought as she tucked her arm into her husband's and they went off to indulge in waffles drenched in maple syrup, and good strong coffee.

*

'I'm afraid my daughter's in hospital, she's in a coma and she won't be reading for a while, so I've brought back her library books,' Lily told the young man at the desk in the library.

'I'm sorry to hear that,' he said, taking them from her. 'What happened?'

'A car accident,' Lily said sadly. 'It's terrible to see her lying there.'

'I couldn't imagine it,' he said compassionately.

'I go in every day to see her. And I talk to her. I don't know if she hears me or not, but it's all I can do for her.'

'God is good,' he said kindly. 'Hope for the best.'

'I will,' she said, touched by his kindness.

'And do you read yourself?' he asked as he ran a little pen over the label in one of the books.

'I used to. I must get back into it, but my time is taken up now with the visiting,' she explained.

'Have a look around some time. Don't be a stranger,' he said as she was leaving.

What a nice young man, and imagine him saying 'God is good' at his age, when most young people didn't even know there was a god, she reflected as she hurried down Millmount Avenue to get her bus.

'I was at the library this morning, Judith, I left in your books and I spoke to an extremely nice young man. When you're better I must take up reading again. Sure, I can go by myself now to pick my books,' she said to her sleeping daughter as she sat in the now-familiar cubicle stroking her hand. This was their world, white curtain rippling gently as nurses slipped in and out to attend to monitors and drips, sometimes stopping to talk, sometimes not, depending on how busy they were. They were kindness itself. They minded her as well as minding Judith and she would be forever in their debt. Did they even know, Lily wondered, what a difference they made? Turning a nightmare into something bearable. It comforted her greatly when she left Judith in the evening to know that her daughter was so lovingly minded.

'You'd be proud of me, all I'm doing.' She settled back in her chair for the chat. 'I even go shopping in the Spar across the road. And I went for a little walk in the park one day. Cecily and Tom are amazed. I know they are. They thought I'd fall to pieces. But I couldn't do that this time. You need me and I have to be strong for you.' Lily studied her daughter carefully to see if there was any flicker of recognition. She looked very peaceful today, she thought, acutely aware of any little change, imperceptible to most, but not to her, who had sat by her bedside for a week, day in day out.

'I was thinking,' she said as she leaned down to take her knitting out of her bag, 'that I could get a book for you and read it to you. We could start with poetry, if you like, and then I could read you some of those Roman books you and your father liked. I can read with no bother now,' she continued as she took the ball of wool off the needles and unwound it a little.

'That would be nice, Mother,' Judith said weakly.

'I think it's a good—' Lily stared at the bed in shock as comprehension dawned. Judith had just spoken to her. She was looking at her, a small smile playing around her lips.

'You're awake!' Lily gasped.

'Where am I?' her daughter asked, her eyes flickering to the monitors and drips.

'You're in hospital. You had a car crash, don't you remember?' Lily stood up and leaned down to her. Judith shook her head and winced.

'Hurts,' she murmured, licking her lips.

'I'll get the nurse, don't move.' Lily shot out of the cubicle. 'She's awake, she's awake, oh thank God, thank God.' She burst into tears as the sister and a nurse hurried in to attend to Judith.

Another young nurse came up to her and put her arm around her. 'You come with me, now, and I'll get you a nice cup of tea. They'll have to do tests on Judith for the moment but we have to mind you too.'

'It's a miracle,' whispered Lily, overcome with relief.

'Miracles do happen, we see them every day,' the nurse smilingly replied.

'Can I just say one thing to her before I go?'

'Of course, come in with me.' She opened the curtains. The sister was asking Judith her name and where she worked and her date of birth.

'Mrs Baxter just wants to have a word with Judith and then she's going to have some tea,' the young nurse explained.

Lily took Judith's hand. Everything else faded into oblivion. 'I just wanted to say I love you, Judith. And we'll sort something,' she said earnestly, never taking her eyes off her daughter.

'Thanks, Ma,' Judith croaked, squeezing her hand feebly. Lily squeezed back gently.

'You get well now; there's a good girl. I'll be back in a little while. I've a lot to tell you. You'll be surprised at what I was up to while you were asleep.' She smiled at her daughter and joy filled her heart as Judith smiled back. Lily leaned over and kissed her on the forehead. They had made their peace, and Judith was going to be all right, Lily just knew it. Everything else could be sorted. God, indeed, was good.

Judith lay quietly as the nurses did what they had to do, shining lights in her eyes, asking her questions. She could not remember the car crash, nor did she want to. She felt very peaceful. Her mother had told her she loved her. Judith was sure that she had heard her saying that she'd been to the library and the Spar supermarket. This was unbelievable. Her mother seemed sprightly and in control, far from the nervous, anxious Lily she knew.

How long had she been like this? Her arm was in plaster. Was her car all right? Who was running her section at work? For a brief moment she felt agitated, and then she let it go. There was nothing she could do about anything right now. She was too tired to think about anything. She felt an unaccustomed sense of calm that was very soothing. Lily had said she'd be back. She could get all the answers to her questions then. But if Lily's new-found confidence was as a result of her accident, then it was a mixed blessing indeed, Judith thought as she closed her eyes, content to let all her worries drift away.

*

'Oh, what a lovely cat,' Connie exclaimed as a little black and white moggie jumped up on her lap.

'Oh good, you like cats,' Mrs Mansfield approved as she sat in a chair by the window, studying Connie carefully.

'I love them, I have a little black one myself called Miss Hope.'

'What a nice name.' Mrs Mansfield smiled.

'She came from a litter called Faith, Hope and Charity,' Connie explained. 'She was the runt and I took her out of pity. She's a great little companion.'

'And tell me, do you like horses?' queried her prospective employer.

'I love them,' Connie exclaimed. 'I used to ride a little, but that was a long time ago.'

'We used to breed horses, you know? Before my husband died. He died and left me with a young family to rear.'

'That was tough,' Connie sympathized.

'It helped that we were very wealthy, of course,' the old woman said matter-of-factly. 'I had nannies to assist me. I sold the stables and kept a couple of my favourite horses. My granddaughters love riding, so I have two mares for them. I can't ride of course, unfortunately, but I go to see our horses and talk to them. It would be part of your duties to bring me.'

'That would be no problem, Mrs Mansfield,' Connie said calmly, smiling at the elderly, white-haired lady sitting in the chair opposite her. She was thin, angular, with a fine-boned face that gave a hint of the beauty she'd once been. Bright blue eyes stared out over high cheekbones. Her creamy skin was soft and unlined. And a long straight nose emphasized the aristocratic air she exuded.

'I like you. I think you'll do. I'm very straight – if I have something on my mind I say it, and I expect you to do likewise. I'm very glad to see you wearing a proper uniform. It shows you take a pride in your job, very important that. I don't like trousers on nurses. Too casual for my liking. You've made a good impression, my dear,' Mrs Mansfield said briskly. 'Enjoy your holiday, and I'll see you when Martha goes in a few weeks' time.

Now go and tell Rita to give you a cup of tea before you leave, and she can tell you all about me.' The old lady's eyes twinkled, and Connie laughed.

She liked her. Prickly, yes, a little, but she had a sense of humour and was alert and lively. This could be a very interesting position.

'Go down the hall to the left and you'll find the kitchen at the very end,' Mrs Mansfield instructed and, although Connie didn't really want tea, she felt she better do as she was bid. She followed the directions and pushed open the old-fashioned wooden door into a big bright airy kitchen that had a farmhouse feel to it. A man was seated at the table drinking from a big green mug. When he saw her he uncoiled himself from the chair and stood up.

'Hello,' he said politely. 'Were you sent down to have a cup of tea?'

'I was,' she said, wondering who he was. He seemed very at home in the kitchen. She wondered was he one of Mrs Mansfield's sons.

'You better have one so,' he said, pouring her a mug. 'Rita's gone out to the greenhouse to get some vegetables.'

'Right,' Connie said, taking the mug from him. 'Thanks.'

'Drew Sullivan,' he said, holding out his hand. 'You must be the new nurse.' He eyed her up and down.

'That's me.' Connie for some ridiculous reason felt a blush rise to her cheeks under his blue-eyed stare. He was tall, six foot at least, lean and rangy with a craggy, weather-beaten face and intense eyes. His grey hair was cut tight to his scalp and he was dressed casually in jeans, riding boots and a navy short-sleeved polo shirt that showed off his tanned, muscular arms.

'I look after her ladyship's horses. I have a stables and livery business a mile down the road. Mrs M insists I come, personally, to be paid every week. But I'm fond of her. She's an interesting old lady and she has a good heart. You could do worse,' he informed her, still studying her as he drank his tea.

'I see,' she said. 'I'm Connie Adams. Nice to meet you,

Drew.' She held out her hand and it was taken in a firm clasp.

'Likewise,' he said, draining his tea and rinsing his mug under the tap. 'Well, I must be off, time's passing. See you around, Connie. Good luck with the job.' He raised a hand in salute and then he was gone, loping across the yard to a muddy black jeep.

'Aw, is Drew gone? He's always rushing somewhere or other. Hi ya, I'm Rita, I'm chief cook and bottle-washer.' A young woman with her hair tied up in a ponytail and an infectious grin held out her hand when she came in carrying a basket of vegetables a few moments later.

'Hi Rita, I'm Connie Adams,' Connie introduced herself.

'Isn't he a fine thing? I keep telling my husband I'm going to run away with him.' Rita laughed, looking out the window and waving at Drew as he turned the jeep in the courtyard and drove past the kitchen. He grinned, showing even white teeth, and raised his hand in a wave.

'Is he married?' Connie asked.

'Divorced and not looking, according to himself. Are you married?'

'Divorced and not looking either.' Connie laughed.

'Are you going to take the job if Mrs M offers it to you? She's nice to work for.'

'So I hear, and she's offered it to me already.'

'Ah, great stuff. So you'll be starting in a couple of weeks?'

'Yep. Looks like it.'

'I think you'll enjoy it.' Rita busied herself popping broad beans out of their pods.

'I hope so,' Connie said, feeling quite at home already.

Half an hour later, she let herself into the cottage. 'I'm back,' she called.

'How did your interview go?' Melissa emerged from the sitting room with a purring Hope snuggled up under her chin.

'Got the job.' Connie grinned. 'I'm so sorry I had to go out.'

'I didn't mind. Thanks for letting me come over and meeting

me off the Dart. I was like so bored. My dad said he'd come and collect me when I texted him to say I'd come to visit.'

'Did he? I can put you on the Dart and save him the trouble,' Connie said lightly, not particularly wanting a visit from Barry.

'Whatever suits,' Melissa said airily. 'Can I have a look at more photo albums of Debbie and Dad when they were young?'

'Sure, go and sit out on the lounger and I'll bring them to you and then I'll get out of this uniform and we'll have a cup of tea.'

'Will I make it for you?'

'That would be nice, love. I'll run up and change and ring your dad,' Connie replied, enjoying the girl's company.

'OK,' agreed Melissa.

'Barry, Connie here,' she said a few minutes later as she sat on the side of the bed. 'Hope I'm not disturbing the game.'

'Hi, Connie. No, I'm finished. I'm in the clubhouse. I was just going to have a coffee and then I'll drive down and collect Melissa.'

'Please don't put yourself out,' she said firmly. 'I'll put her on the Dart, and it will mean you won't be stuck in the traffic. It's much easier, believe me. And it would suit me better. I'm going out later,' she fibbed.

'Oh! Where?'

'With friends,' she said off-handedly. She was delighted that Melissa had asked to come and visit, but she didn't want Barry using it as an excuse to come and visit too, and she wanted him to know it.

'That's a shame. I'd like to have seen you.'

'Another time,' she said. 'Now I must go and get out of this uniform. I'm baked.'

'How did the interview go?'

'Got it.' She smiled.

'Well done, Connie, well done,' he said, pleased for her.

'Thanks. I'm delighted. See you,' she said before hanging up. She wasn't going to give her ex-husband any more chances to make a move on her. That chapter of her life was over. She was moving on.

*

Barry took a gulp of coffee and stared unseeingly out the window. Connie was definitely giving him the cold shoulder. Collecting Melissa would have been a very reasonable excuse to go and see her. She sounded very perky and lively. He wished he felt the same, he thought disconsolately. His wife was working her butt off and wouldn't be home until late. His daughter hadn't even wanted to have their usual doughnut and coffee treat this morning; his ex-wife was going out with friends and didn't want to see him. So much for family, he thought crossly.

Who were Connie's friends? Were they male or female? he wondered. She'd certainly dropped him like a hot potato once the wedding was over, he thought self-pityingly as he drank his coffee. Maybe if he sent flowers to congratulate her for getting the job she might soften her attitude. He only wanted to be friends, for heaven's sake, he assured himself. What was the problem with that?

He flipped open his phone and dialled 11811 and got the florist he always used. 'Two dozen yellow roses,' he ordered, giving his credit card details and Connie's address. He'd woo her, he decided. Women loved to be wooed. It might take a while but he'd keep at it until he got the results he wanted. Once Barry Adams set his mind to something, he got it, he reminded himself, feeling more optimistic by the second. He liked nothing better than a challenge. And although Connie had never challenged him in their marriage, things had most certainly changed in that regard, and *that* was what made it all the more interesting.

'Bye, love, come again soon,' Connie said, giving Melissa a hug before she boarded the Dart for home.

'I will and thanks, Connie. I had a great time. I just love Hope.'

'And she just loves you,' Connie said kindly. 'Text me when you're home.'

'I will,' she promised as the doors closed behind her.

Connie watched the Dart pull away from the station and

decided on the spur of the moment to go for a walk on the beach. It was a lovely evening and the sun was beginning to sink. She drove back to the beach at the end of her road and strolled across the stony pebbles to the edge of the shore. She stepped out of her sandals and walked along, letting the water wash over her feet. She was wearing cut-offs so she was in no danger of getting her trousers wet.

Today had been a good day, she reflected. A fresh start with her new job. A feeling of well-being enveloped her. This was *her* time, she mused, inhaling the bracing sea air. Ahead of her, a man threw a stick to a golden Labrador, who galloped into the sea after it. He was tall and grey-haired. A bit like the man she'd met at Mrs Mansfield's.

Drew Sullivan. A nice name, she thought, remembering the way his blue eyes had studied her intently. Why was he divorced? she wondered. Did he have children? What was his history? No doubt she'd find it all out from Rita once she started working there.

Yes, life certainly promised to be interesting. Connie laughed as the golden Labrador came galloping in her direction and showered her with sea spray.

Drew Sullivan sat on his veranda looking at the sun sinking behind the gentle rolling hills, setting fire to the sky in the west.

He took a draught of chilled beer and stretched out his long legs. He was tired. It had been a busy day; he was going to have an early night, he decided. His thoughts meandered here and there and he remembered his visit to Mrs Mansfield's. That new nurse, Connie, was a good-looking woman, he acknowledged, with curves in all the right places. He'd seen the way she blushed when he'd looked at her. He did that on purpose. Get women to blush first and then they wouldn't see that he was shy behind his bold façade.

She had a good twinkle in her eye, she'd have a bit of fun in her, he reckoned. Not that it made any difference to him. Women were a disaster, and he steered well clear of them. Best to stick to horses. She'd nice eyes, though, very nice eyes that looked at you straight and unflinching, Drew thought, before he fell asleep with the cool evening breeze whispering against his temples like a woman's caress.

To be continued.

Acknowledgements

Cast your cares upon the Lord for He cares about you.
                                                    – I Peter 5:7

Dear Lord, thank you for taking my cares and for supporting me in very hard times. My thanks also to Our Lady, St Joseph, Mother Meera, St Michael, St Anthony, the Holy Spirit, White Eagle and all my Angels, Saints and Guides who guide, protect and inspire.

To my dear and precious family and extended family, who are my greatest blessings.

Friends are God's way of minding you and He has minded me well. To all my kind and loving friends who give me such love and support and are always there for me and were, especially so, this year. A special mention and huge and heartfelt thanks to Alil O'Shaughnessy and Pam and Simon Young, whose constant, unstinting kindness helped more than they'll ever know.

To Francesca Liversidge. Dearest friend as well as editor.

To Sarah, Felicity, Susannah and Jane, my wonderful agents at Lutyens & Rubinstein, who are always there working away on my behalf. I really appreciate what you all do and know how lucky I am to have you.

To all at Transworld who are so supportive and enthusiastic about my books even after all this time. I wish I could name you all, but I would like to say a special thanks to Jo, who is always so reassuring and sorts out all my problems. And to Vivien, Rebecca, Deborah and Sarah Day, who put manners on the manuscript in the nicest possible way.

To Gill, Simon, Geoff, Eamonn, Fergus and Ian of Gill Hess Ltd, who put up with a lot of wingeing and never make me feel bad!

To Declan Heeney, the bane of my life (or am I the bane of his?) but I love him. And to Helen Gleed O'Connor, who makes publicity fun.

To Eoin McHugh, my new colleague ... Here's to New Beginnings!

To all my colleagues in New Island. You're a great team and I'm so proud to work with you on *Open Door*.

To Frank Furlong, AIB Finglas and Eileen Redmond and Ciara Doggett, Anglo Irish Bank, for sound advice and lots of laughs!

I'd like to take this opportunity to thank with deepest gratitude all the staff in the A&E, Special Care Unit and ICU of the Mater Hospital and all who were involved in the Memorial Service in November. We greatly appreciate all you did for my mother and for us. Your loving kindness made our loss more bearable. There aren't enough words to tell you how grateful we are.

And to Keith Massey and staff, and Father Brendan Quinlan, I express the same sentiments.

And to the family of my late cousin, Fergus Halligan, we will never forget his kindness.

A most warm and special thanks to all my dear readers. All the letters and kind comments mean so much. I hope you enjoy this book and that all good things, and Blessings come to you.